The Redemption

David Billingsley

This book is a tale of fiction. Any similarity of characters or events to true life is completely coincidental.

ISBN-13: 978-1492312154

FOR
MOM and DAD

Prologue
Treasure Valley Regional Medical Center, Boise, Idaho
December 1981

On a still December night in Boise, Idaho, while the town slept, Frank Lorda made a decision to have a healthy newborn daughter— someone else's daughter. He wasn't there to steal a child. It was just a simple trade.

Outside the entrance to the emergency room, he leaned against a concrete pole and puffed on a Lucky Strike. The night air was hard, and snow crystals drifted under the streetlamps. Only his three-year-old Chevy pickup and a white sedan occupied the hospital parking lot.

In the distance, an eighteen-wheeler chugged away toward Interstate 84. Given the time of morning, the driver was likely heading out to start another job. Frank's own cab, a ten-year-old Freightliner, was sitting idle in a friend's dirt lot four blocks south of his house in the North End.

He tugged back his sheepskin jacket sleeve to see the dial on the black Timex. 5:52 A.M. Only hours ago, he'd been crammed in the maternity waiting room with sweaty Irish and Basque relatives, watching them wrestle for the phone to call even more relatives to proclaim success.

Penny Anne Lorda. Born 1:37 A.M.

The time of birth was like the start to some ominous countdown. Frank had been through this before, first with Jesse, then Samuel, both now in the care of the Lord Almighty. His wife Annie, detached from the birth proceedings courtesy of what the doctor had called epidural anesthesia, had joked with him minutes before Penny arrived. "Third time's a charm," she had said.

Frank wasn't so sure then. Now he was certain the old saying was a downright lie. God had no intention of proving him wrong.

The delivery had been smooth, another C-section. In the recovery room, Annie had fallen asleep after a minute or two of caressing Penny's soft face. A male nurse then left with the baby in tow in a rolling bassinet, moving through the hospital like a mouse in a maze. Uninvited, Frank followed at a distance until he was lost. After a few frantic moments on the wrong floor, he found the nursery just in time to view a scene he would never forget.

Under a blaze of nursery lights, a round, short man in green scrubs and a dark-haired, slender woman in a nurse's outfit stood over Frank and Annie's child. The man was Dr. Soloman, the physician who had delivered Penny. Frank had yet to see the good doctor without a smile accompanied by a laugh and a pat on the back. This time the medical man pursed his lips over and over and settled into a frown that appeared to hurt his face. He kept glancing at a clipboard and then back at Penny, bundled in the bassinet. The young woman, a nurse Frank would meet up close in a few hours, shook her head, and then leaned down and stroked Penny's blanket. Next, as if on cue, they both stared through the viewing window directly at Frank. Recessed into the shadows, he was sure they couldn't detect his presence.

The image of their faces would carry Frank for the next three decades, easing his pain in future moments of doubt. He would commit an inconceivable act. But it was the ultimate act of love. He couldn't let Annie down one more time. No more dead children. No more false hopes. Within weeks he would be vindicated. His natural child would pass away, and the rest of the world would be ignorant of it all.

The snow abated. Frank stared through the sliding glass doors that led back inside. Dry snow grains blew like dust in a small circle below his feet. He glanced at his watch again. 5:55 A.M. Time to go. He tossed the butt of his cigarette into the miniature whirlwind and stepped it out with the toe of his cowboy boot. He would do this for Annie.

Frank reached into the crib and fingered the plastic wristband. As it should be, it was snug. The name, his surname, stared back from a pink index card attached to the head of the bassinet.

He moved to a nearby crib occupied by one of a set of twins, the only other residents of the nursery. This child was similar to Penny. Both had tufts of dark hair sticking out of their beanies and pinkish newborn faces. From a casual glance, dimensions and weight appeared to be close.

A blanket was tucked tightly around twin number one like a tiny mummy. With some effort, Frank loosened the blanket, found the wristband, and wiggled it. Surprisingly, it slipped off. He stuck the wristband in his pocket. The infant's eyes seemed to trace his every move. Her saggy cheeks were marked by a bruise, perhaps a result of the delivery. There was a subtle cleft in her chin Frank had not noticed until now.

He focused his attention back on his daughter. She had a little mark by her ear absent on twin number one. From his pocket, Frank removed a red Swiss Army Knife. His hands shook as he started to pry open one of the smaller blades. Great care was important here. An errant nick of the skin and it would be all over—

"Would you like to hold your child?"

He froze. The knife tumbled into the crib and bounced to rest inches from Penny's bundled body.

It was the young nurse. With a tired voice and puffy eyes, she looked to be on the tail end of a long night shift. She slid her hands under the bundle and brought Penny to her chest. Frank glanced at the knife, then the nurse. Maybe she'd seen it. Maybe she'd been watching him.

An older nurse, who could have been the evil librarian Mrs. Barstow from Frank's grade school days, appeared at the station in the back of the nursery. He had not seen her before. She crossed her arms as he caught her attention. The young nurse cradled Penny, glaring in the direction of her elder peer. The older nurse did an about-face and disappeared.

A well-dressed man, carrying an air of importance, passed under the spotlight in the exterior hallway. He glanced at Frank and disappeared into the void.

Suddenly the place seemed to be crawling with people. Don't think, Frank said to himself. Just stand on the ledge and jump.

"Thank you, Ms. Vasquez," he said, noting the red nametag attached to the woman's uniform as she transferred the bundle into his arms.

The nurse nodded. "It's Miss and it's Christine."

"Quiet night?" he asked, drifting away from the bassinet, carrying the nurse's attention with him.

"Penny and the Post twins," she said. "Sounds like a bubble gum group." They both laughed softly.

If Christine Vasquez had seen anything, she was good at hiding it. Maybe the police were on their way. Frank could leave, but then what? He took a deep breath, as if he were taking another drag on a Lucky Strike. Not a bad idea at the moment.

"Your little girl is in big company tonight." The nurse nodded at the other occupied bassinets. "That's Donita and Katlin Post. You know, of the Post Sporting Goods fame?"

The mention of the Post name was a surprise. Frank had noticed the big black letters on the pink cards, but he'd not made the connection that the twins belonged to *the* Posts. He certainly knew the name. Andrew and Sonya Post were the new Idaho elite. Post Sporting Goods was a regional powerhouse and expanding rapidly. And the patriarch, Andrew Post, had barely entered the third decade of his life.

"I'm sure *they* are healthy," Frank said.

"They go home today. It's their first, or I guess their first and second. Is this your first?"

"This is our third. My first two children passed away."

The nurse opened her mouth to respond but seemed unable to.

"It's okay." Frank lowered his eyes to his daughter. She instantly drew him in. He quickly looked away. "Our first child never saw the light of day."

"Miscarriage?"

"No, Jesse lived two hours. Then Samuel came along a couple of years ago. He made it two months."

"I'm so sorry."

The nurse moved toward Penny's bassinet. Frank stepped into her path. "Dr. Soloman seemed a bit concerned about Penny," he said.

As if she wished to be rescued, the woman gazed back toward the nurse's station and out into the hallway. "Dr. Maxwell, your pediatrician," she said, nodding rapidly and queuing Frank to nod along with her, "will be here soon. Let him check your daughter over before you get too concerned."

Frank glanced out into the hallway. The bundle in his arms moved just enough to let him know she was there.

Maybe he should wait for this Dr. Maxwell. Supposed to be the best around. Surely if he did, the opportunity would pass. Some life-sucking issue would be documented on Penny's chart. The Post twins would be given a clean bill of health. Penny would be tested, poked, and prodded. The Post twins would go home. This couldn't happen again. Not to Annie.

The nurse looked at the clock on the wall. "Listen, my shift is about over. Would you like me to stay?"

"No. You go on home."

"I can stay."

"It's not necessary."

"You can hold her for as long as you want. I need to brief Nurse Phillips, and then I'm sure she'll be back to interrupt you as soon as I'm gone. She doesn't like anyone in her nursery, not even the parents. Don't let her push you around." The young woman winked, touched Frank on the shoulder, and headed back toward the nurse's station.

This was it. Time to jump.

The nurses were changing shifts. Christine Vasquez was leaving. The old nurse, this Nurse Phillips, had not examined any of the three nursery patients yet. Annie, his beloved, had seen Penny for the briefest of moments. What about the Posts? Were they as self-absorbed as powerful people were thought to be? So self-absorbed that they wouldn't notice? Frank could only hope. He would tell the old nurse his daughter never had a wristband. Then there were the charts. What had these medical people scribbled on the clipboards? Even if he had the chance to read the information, he wouldn't understand a word.

His heart began to race. This was not right. Yet not doing this was not right either.

He placed Penny back into her crib, stared into his daughter's eyes, and whispered as he picked up his knife and started to cut the wristband. "Do you think people *think* just before they jump? You know, the people on the ledge. The people that don't jump are there for attention. But the ones that do, I don't think they think much about it. They just jump."

The wristband popped off. He stuck it in his pocket and slipped twin number one's wristband onto Penny. The last name "Post" stared back at him.

With one final glance around the room and into the hallway, he confirmed the Lord Almighty was his only judge. He picked up Penny, wrapped her into a tight bundle, and placed her in the bassinet alongside twin number one. He lifted twin number one and placed her in Penny's bassinet.

He couldn't help but look back toward his daughter. This was goodbye.

Chapter 1
Annie Lorda's Residence, North End, Boise, Idaho
33 Years Later

Annie Lorda sat in a rocker and stared at the letter on the bedside table as if it would tell her what to do. She needed Frank's thoughts. He'd left the letter for her and only her. His last words in a battle with lung cancer had not been about their life together, their love for one another, or any other intimate thought. They had been about the letter.

He'd said he was desperately sorry about something. That she'd never forgive him.

After the funeral, Annie had placed the letter on the bedside table with every intention of destroying it. She had no desire to confront Frank's demons. Now, one year to the date of his passing, it still sat in its place—an arm's reach from where she slept.

Day by day, the mystery of its contents had tormented her. She had conjured up a number of scenarios—most involving "the other woman." Who would she turn out to be? Some lonely, middle-aged divorcee down a remote stretch of highway? Maybe a young floozy who traveled the roads with truckers or an elegant woman he'd met in a club in Portland or Seattle. Maybe someone right under her nose, though it was tough to imagine who that might be.

She closed her eyes. Darkness accentuated every sound—the wind outside stirring leaves on cottonwood trees, the creaks of the hardwood under her rocking chair, the pavement noise of a sedan passing down 14th Street, the toot of a horn in the distance—all punctuated by the Benson's dog yelping for its dinner.

She opened her eyes to find Frank, bone-thin, expression hollow, resting on the edge of the bed. A worn quilt dropped from her lap. Tears fell from her eyes. She knew it was an apparition—an incomplete picture of Frank she'd stored from his last days in the hospital.

She wiped her cheeks and stood. The vision vanished, the letter remained. She moved toward the bed, her feet cool to the touch of the hardwood. Her fingers traced the worn edges of the bedside table. She picked up the envelope and pulled it to her chest.

Get this over with.

She closed her eyes again. "What is this, Frank?" she whispered. "You're in God's hands. I believe in you. Can't it just end this way?"

She thought of all they had been through together.

They had married young. Frank immediately went to work driving a small delivery truck between Boise and Portland. Though he tired of the same route, the money was good. Carefree and in love, they soon decided to try for kids. Their first two children died prematurely. The combined events were devastating for Annie. Frank dealt with it by not dealing with it. Spiraling toward a divorce, Annie decided they should try one more time.

The result, a bundle of energy named Penny, saved their marriage. Penny was a challenge from day one, but she was alive, and Annie could deal with a few bumps in the road. By secondary school, Penny grew into a handful. There was the junior high bout with darkness, Goth clothes and all. Then her affinity for the high school drug and alcohol scene. After graduation Penny drifted around with a bad crowd, unable to hold any one job for more than a few months. Then she married and divorced a smokejumper. Annie had at least gained a terrific grandchild out of the mess.

About the time Penny started grade school, Annie went to work as a business manager at the Wick's Pharmacy in Hyde Park. Frank's situation improved considerably after he purchased an eighteen-wheeler and became a long-haul independent trucker. Together they made enough money to be comfortable. Life was much better.

Then it wasn't. Frank had always been a fidgety person, and he'd smoked his entire life. Like all the other smokers, he said it calmed his nerves. After Penny was born, Annie banned him from lighting up in the house, hoping he might finally quit. He never did.

With time he began to complain of shortness of breath. His breathing problems turned into a smoker's cough, and the smoker's cough turned into a hack. Annie started to notice blood in his spit. She forced him to go to the doctor, only the second time he had been near a physician since Penny's birth. Within weeks he was being treated for lung cancer. Doctor Hamilton said his chances of surviving a year or more were slim. He was right.

The following ten months were a hellish adventure of chemotherapy, radiation, weight loss, specialists, and hospital wards—all to postpone the inevitable. Bills piled up. Bills Annie could never pay. If it had been her, she would have just stayed home. Let God decide her fate. But this was Frank. She couldn't let go, and she thanked the Lord for every extra minute he survived on this earth.

Now all that was left was the letter. Annie ripped it open and pulled out a single sheet of folded yellow paper.

One year ago, she had said goodbye. Today, of all days, she would listen to Frank one last time.

She returned to the rocker, put her bifocals on, and unfolded the letter. Frank's poor handwriting covered the page. Her hands shook so much she had a hard time reading. The letter contained both relief and a shock so surreal it didn't seem to make sense.

The chime of the doorbell coincided with the sound of the lock disengaging in the front of the house.

"Hey. *Andale!*" It was the restless voice of Penny Lorda.

On Annie's lap, the letter stared back. She'd spent the last few hours battling her conscience and her deceased husband. She'd read once there were over six hundred thousand words in the English language. None of those words, or any combination thereof, could describe how she felt.

Frank had always been a brutally honest man. There was no doubt the person they had raised for thirty-three years was not their own flesh and blood. Frank had switched their child with another. *That* was a certainty.

Images flooded her mind: changing diapers, school plays, arguments, Penny's two attempts at running away, the failed marriage, and the grandchild she cherished.

And the pain of Frank's secret. Compared to this, his cancer must've seemed like a mild cold or even a godsend. The emptiness returned, as if she had just lost him all over again. Yet there was anger too. She wanted to slap him. He'd transferred this terrible secret, and now what?

"Ma?"

Penny's outline flashed through the light at the end of the hall, headed for the kitchen.

On an ordinary Monday night, Annie would have been sorting coupons at the kitchen table and making sure the grocery list was in order. Rain, snow, or shine, Penny would be there to take her to the store. On a nice day, they would walk. Penny would hijack a cart and push it back to Annie's house, groceries and all, returning it "whenever."

"This place looks like an advertisement for some home magazine." Penny's voice carried from the kitchen. For the first time, Annie wondered about the curious traits and habits of her daughter. Frank would sit in the garage and discuss politics, sports, bird hunting, and mechanical stuff with no one in particular. He fell asleep before his head hit the pillow. He was a mess at the kitchen table. Penny was just like him.

Annie drifted back to the night Penny joined the world. What could she remember? The delivery had not been too difficult. Frank had decided to forego the delivery room. He must've been out smoking up a storm and finding ways to steer clear of the family. Dr. Soloman had held the baby up for her to see. The next memory was the recovery room. Annie had the shakes from the drugs, and Frank had sat with her, holding her hand. A nurse had placed the baby on her chest at some point. *She had held her baby. Once.*

"My God," she whispered. The tears flowed uncontrollably.

"What the hell?" Penny stood at the bedroom door. "You opened it! Dad's letter."

"We can skip the store tonight," Annie said, managing her best to recover.

"Screw the store. Let me see it." Penny stepped into the room and reached for the folded paper on Annie's lap.

Annie snatched the letter up to her chest. "No! This is between your dad and me." She hopped up, brushed past Penny, and moved briskly toward the front of the house.

"It was bad," Penny said, a half-step behind. "You never cry. That has to be some bad shit."

"Thirty-three years old and you won't clean up your mouth." Annie walked to the sink and grabbed a dish towel. Trying to steady herself, she pressed her palms against the edge of the countertop.

Penny placed her hand on one of the almond tiled counters and rubbed the surface. She traced her finger along the top of the refrigerator. "Absolutely sterile. Bitchin'." She spoke as if she were alone. "I could manage too if I didn't do the nine-to-five plus a kid."

Annie started to wipe the kitchenette.

"Geez," Penny said. "That's like dry humping. This place is like a freaking clean room."

The words ripped through Annie like a gunshot. She whipped around to face her daughter. The Goth was long gone, but the deep mascara and black dreadlocks streaked with dark red were all too familiar.

"Why do you talk like that? Your father didn't put you up to it! I certainly didn't! Who the hell are you?"

Penny's dark complexion drained to the color of milk. Her lips parted, though they formed no sound.

Annie threw the towel to the ground and shook her head. The tears were gone. She spoke in the direction of the bedroom. "Why did you do this?"

Penny stared down the hall toward the invisible target of her mother's voice. She plucked her phone from her pocket. "Hey, it's Ma. Come now. No, just get your ass over here!" She hung up and held the phone tightly in her hand. "I'm no good at this."

No reply seemed adequate. Annie stared into the front room of the house. No doubt Penny had called Matt, and he would come in a heartbeat. The front room was full of antique furniture: red cherry wingback chairs from the twenties, one of those slightly curved Victorian loveseats circa 1910, an oak lamp table of unknown origin, and a porcelain urn lamp from France *à la* 1890. Frank had found every piece on his journeys. He'd no knowledge of antiques, but he had managed well enough. Except for a worn quilt rack, the pieces looked like they'd rarely been used. And they had all been acquired after Penny had come into their life.

Annie walked over to her daughter, who stood frozen in place. "Please go home."

"Look. I respected you and Dad. You just let that letter sit there on your table. I so wanted to rip it open and see what Dad was hiding. If you weren't going to share, why'd you even tell me about it?" Penny tapped her foot rapidly. "It was another woman, wasn't it? No. Impossible. Not Dad."

"Your father was faithful until the day he died," Annie said softly. "Now go. And call Matt and tell him to turn around and go home."

"What about the store? We always go on Monday."

"Not this Monday."

Penny reached out. Her hand fell short of her mother's shoulder. Then she headed for the door, speaking with her back to Annie. "I love you, Ma."

The door opened and closed and Annie was alone.

Chapter 2
Post Outfitters Superstore #49, Meridian, Idaho
Thursday Midnight

The woman zigzagged through the crowd as if she wanted to be seen. Minutes earlier, at the stroke of midnight, Andrew Post had emerged from the store entrance to witness a sea of camouflage and brightly colored sportswear belonging to hunters, fishermen, joggers, cyclists, and weekend warriors seeking freebies and opening day bargains. These were his fans, his customers. They were all necessary, but none seemed interesting until *this* woman.

The photographer motioned for Andrew to move back a tad. He frowned and stepped a bit closer to the seven foot tall letter "P" that guarded the massive entrance to the new Post Outfitters Superstore. The photographer snapped a dozen or more pictures, enough so that Andrew was certain a suitable one could be found to mark the opening of his forty-ninth store.

White spots from the photographer's blitz of activity gave way to a multitude of small flashes from hundreds of smartphones and pocket cameras, courtesy of the gathering crowd. Andrew craned his head to see past the curiosity seekers. She was still there, pressing forward through the human maze.

The meeting earlier in the day with his security team replayed in his mind. After the crazy man with the pistol in Spokane, they were taking no chances. He'd received a death threat in the mail a few months ago along with a white powder that turned out to be baking soda. The letter had warned of "the real thing" or something much worse. And just this week a persistent woman had been calling and visiting the Post Corporation headquarters, insisting she connect in person with Andrew Post. She had refused to disclose her reason for requesting such a meeting. His staff had kept recordings of her phone calls and copies of her emails. She had simply stated her desire to meet with him in private—nothing else. Her last name was Lord or something like that. She was now on the always up-to-date list of threats.

To some degree Andrew cared little if someone stuck a revolver against his head and pulled the trigger. It would be a kind of atonement for his sins—his penance for the many misdeeds of his personal life. Professionally, he was done. It was time to pass off the reigns of Post Inc. to his daughter, Donny.

The financial media had spread rumors of his imminent retirement, and some of his own had suggested the same. What then? Sit on a porch and watch the traffic fly by? Not likely. Live up on the Payette, miles from the nearest paved road, away from the insanity? Maybe.

An army of photographers was escorted to Andrew's position by Post Inc. public affairs. The media followed his every move, occasionally unleashing a virtual lightning storm that made it impossible to see anything. Questions jumped through the air from behind the bank of flashes and bright video camera lights.

"Mr. Post?" It was a female voice, likely some up-and-coming blonde reporter using the store opening as an excuse to waylay him. "Mr. Post, is it true you are stepping down?"

He simply smiled at the cameras and nodded his head toward whatever waving onlookers he could see.

"Any comment on the Denver problems?"

He bit down on his lip and shielded his eyes in an attempt to locate the source of the questions.

"Denver problems?" Just as the words escaped, he knew it was a rare mistake. Spin the media to his advantage, his people would remind him.

"One of your staff, a Mr. Fenton Cooper, was heard saying, and I quote, 'Post Outfitters will crush the locals in Colorado as we've done everywhere else.' Said local competitors would be packing their bags before the end of the year. Care to comment on that?"

Andrew ignored the question. He scanned past the lights for the zigzagging woman. He put his hand above his eyes, but it was of little use.

The voice continued, "The Blendale City Council has discussed reneging on your permits."

God, he hated the media. He made a mental note to find out what station employed this woman. She would be put in her place. He walked over to the massive store entrance and faced the following media army. He held his arms out like a circus ringmaster and smiled. "This is what I'm here to talk about."

The scene behind Andrew was an event. Store employees and the Post corporate entourage, decked out in the yellow and forest green colors of wildland firefighting crews, were shaking hands, passing out discount coupons, and giving away surprise packages filled with items the company could coerce its suppliers to give away for free or for a cut-rate price. Guarding the entrance, bronze life-size replicas of elk, cougars, bears, mule deer, and other prized wildlife of the Northwest stood above the crowd on pedestals. Chiseled out of stone, sockeye salmon, cutthroat trout, northern pike, sturgeon, and other notable fish of the region lined the front entryway.

The extravagant midnight openings were the brainchild of his daughter, and the concept had been a huge success. Instead of the usual multiday grand opening affair, Donny had sold Andrew on the idea of giving away a hundred thousand dollars in merchandise in a single hour commencing at midnight on the date of the store opening. Of course, it would be one hundred thousand dollars at retail price, still a pretty sum even at or below cost.

Andrew knew the public were suckers for "free." Give it away for half the price and nobody shows. But give it away for free and even a staunch Marxist will line up.

The faces in the crowd appeared friendly. They favored his stores. Yet they read the papers. The scandals. The rumors. The big bad corporation. His brilliant PR group countered with the positive impact of the Post presence. It was a perpetual battle not unlike running a political campaign.

On cue, several of the new store employees lined up to shake his hand. He smiled and exchanged pleasantries while the cameras buzzed away, and perfectly planted questions echoed from behind the lights.

He answered them all, sometimes laughing, and at other times delivering a tone of concern that seemed to mesmerize the crowd. When he spoke, they listened. When he moved, they followed. It was not every day an Idahoan could catch a glimpse of Andrew Post, much less shake his hand.

"Mr. Post?"

The voice stopped him in his tracks. His smile vanished. It was not the familiar tone of the polished media or one of his plants in the crowd. It was a desperate voice.

He scanned the crowd and spotted her mixed in the gaggle of reporters. They locked eyes. Her face displayed a yearning. She had to speak to him.

For some reason, Lacy Talbert's face popped into his head. She had a look of despair moments before she died. Like this woman, Lacy had desperately wanted to speak to Andrew, he'd said nothing, and he had regretted his indecisiveness to this day.

The woman stepped forward and half-waved in his direction. She was handsome and thin with gray shoulder length hair, slightly taller than Andrew and roughly the same age, but her face held the scars of stress, as if she'd been plucked out of a photo of the struggling souls stranded on the Great Plains during the depression.

Andrew glanced left and right. He could tell by their heightened demeanor that his bodyguards were onto the threat. They would avoid a scene if at all possible.

Oblivious to the development, one of the Post public relations officers, a young man with dark hair and an unnaturally smooth face, pushed Andrew toward a waiting reporter with one of the affiliates out of Seattle. These interviews were irritating. Fortunately, they were interchangeable no matter the town or the store. The questions, usually emanating from some slick punk or blonde bimbo not yet savvy enough to make the anchor desk, were easy to answer. Andrew knew his lines by heart. *We were pursued by the city. We are good citizens and pay our taxes, produce an abundance of new jobs, and try to help the local shops prosper.*

This time it was the slick punk, though he primped like a girl. Andrew grinned. He would commence with the interview, hoping his security company had the situation in hand. The kid reporter launched into a series of disconnected questions and accusations. Andrew answered each one with ease. The kid stumbled on a question about negotiated tax incentives. Andrew chuckled, then stopped abruptly.

The woman had pushed her way to within a few feet of his location. They locked eyes again. She stuck her hand into a knitted, homemade handbag.

His time had come. His bodyguards had failed him. The woman's hand would come out of her bag, a shiny pistol would emerge, she would squeeze the trigger with a look of satisfaction, and a bullet would end up lodged in his head—just like Lacy Talbert.

He swallowed over and over. His throat ran dry. A circle of security men engulfed him. There was no gunshot, only shouting and frantic radio chatter. A claustrophobic human shield funneled Andrew toward his limo like a leaf caught in a swift stream. In the wake, a distressed voice carried through the air. "Mr. Post!"

Seconds later he was inside the limo, watching one of his bodyguards place his imposing presence in front of the car door. Armor plating and protective glass shielded Andrew from the outside world. He could see the commotion. The reporter he'd skipped out on, the rest of the media, and some Internet paparazzi were in the thick of it. A forest of arms reached up from the trailing crowd, taking video and images from every conceivable brand of mobile phone and pocket camera. He'd have another public relations issue after this was all said and done. His driver, a Korean named Choi, glanced over his shoulder for instructions.

Andrew cracked the window and watched as the police, only a

dozen yards away, cuffed the woman. She craned her neck back toward his limo. Her expression was not one of fright or hysterics, but of failure. They hustled her away with the media circus trailing a short distance behind.

A few straggling photographers and future customers snapped pictures of the limo. The bodyguard stepped in their way and leaned down to the window. Through the crack, he slipped Andrew a sealed envelope.

"What's this?"

His bodyguard shrugged. "Said she was trying to hand this to you."

Andrew couldn't get the woman's expression out of his mind. He could stop and give her an audience. Then he'd spend the rest of the night explaining such a mistake to his daughter, his public affairs group, and his security team.

He closed the window, gave his okay to move out, opened the envelope, and started to read the note. Fortunately, it held no powdery substance. He looked up in time to catch a final glimpse of the woman. Her head was down. The police were asking questions.

Chapter 3
Post Corporation Headquarters, Boise, Idaho
Thursday, 1:00 P.M.

"Who's responsible for this?" Andrew's voice was firm, not elevated.

He looked around the crafted mahogany boardroom conference table, daring all who sat within his sight to make eye contact. The room was full of accountants, lawyers, and MBAs, most of whom he moderately trusted.

Fenton Cooper and Donny Post sat at the far end of the table, flanked on both sides by the rest of the corporate staff. Andrew and his right hand man, Rafi Thuban, sat at the opposite end, separated from the others by several empty chairs.

"Cooper, you're the lead on this store," Andrew said.

Fenton Cooper rose up in his chair, glanced over at Donny, and started to speak. "We've had a bit of an incident—"

"I don't give a damn about incidents!" Andrew paused to settle himself. "You are paid to get this store open. This is our first venture into Colorado, and we are months behind."

Only Rafi Thuban dared to meet Andrew's scowl. Thuban, a half-breed, the product of a Pashtun father and an English mother, spoke in more of a manner associated with the King's English than the Pashto of his Afghan upbringing. It wasn't clear to the rest of the Post Corporation exactly what job Rafi did, and Andrew liked that.

"Tell Mr. Post what incident you speak of," Rafi said, holding his hand out toward Andrew as if it would bring some semblance of calm to the room.

Cooper leaned back in his chair and raised his arms up in a surrendering gesture. "The city reneged on our permit."

Andrew hit his open palm on the table. He measured the group carefully. Still no one looked his way. The accountants were busy pouring over reams of paper documents. The CIO—the chief information officer—and his nerdy assistant, who spoke in some language only the CIO understood, were fingering their smartphone screens and playing with tablet computers. He never liked the computer guys. They were like fiber. They were necessary to keep things flowing, but you'd have something else if given the choice. The top corporate lawyers, Gavin and Sam, sat patiently. They were paid enormous sums of money for keeping his company out of trouble. They were worth every penny, but they *were* lawyers.

Then there was the operations group represented by Donny, Fenton Cooper, and some nervous frizzy redhead junior assistant. The redhead constantly played with the leather lining on her chair. Andrew tried his best not to smile.

He kept his focus on Fenton Cooper. It was past time to have it out with this Ivy League bum. Cooper had completed a successful expansion campaign in Arizona, but like a number of these high-strung execs, he'd let his ego get the best of him. The Colorado expansion should've been no different than Arizona. Play the bedroom suburbs against each other and obtain the right mix of subsidized costs, tax relief, prime location, and demographics favorable for the next supercenter.

"I thought this one was in the bag," Andrew said. "I have a board meeting next week, an annual shareholder's meeting in July, and this is what I'm going to report? What's going on with this, Gavin?"

The lawyer loosened his tie. Sweat beads formed on the man's forehead. "One of the local shops had some tie-ins with the home town politicos. Think there was some kind of family deal going on. They put the kibosh on us."

"We didn't know about this?" Andrew surveyed the room. There was no response. "And when were any of you going to bring me this news? I can keep up with asinine statements to the press by our illustrious Mr. Cooper, but you people need to keep me up to date on any issue that might set back our progress. We've spent"—he snapped at the accountants for information—"how much trying to open this store?"

Both accountants started to thumb through various printouts.

"For the permits, the property, plans, and anything else all of you have wasted my money on so far?"

"Just a minute now." The chief financial officer, the CFO, cheeks approaching the color of a fine blush wine, was leafing through more printouts. "We'll have that. Just a minute."

"Forget it. I'm beside myself." Andrew paused for effect. "You guys said we'd break ground in February. Here we are in June, and we've got nothing to show. How do you expect to maintain twenty percent growth if we can't open new stores?"

Andrew stood and leaned out over the table. "This situation is pathetic. Mr. Cooper, you opened your mouth in Denver and cost me your salary for the next decade. And the rest of you didn't have the guts to mention that the locals have dug in their heels."

He snapped his fingers, and Rafi handed him a folder. He snatched out a piece of paper and held it high in the air. "Last month's report, Thursday staff meeting, May 14th. Summary: Several small issues continue to delay the Denver store. Curtis working close with Blendale City Council to resolve a few straggling local concerns. Not deemed significant. Expect progress to resume shortly with groundbreaking by June 1st. Fenton Cooper."

He paused again and scanned the table slowly. "Nowhere in here does it say, 'Mr. Fenton Cooper personally trashed our already delayed schedule by being an ass.' No, I had to read that in the papers."

Fenton Cooper leaned back again, blinking his eyes excessively. Andrew had won. The actors in the room could have been in a wax museum. No motion. No sounds of breathing. No life.

Andrew turned his back on the table and approached the window. The view of the City of Trees was inviting. The Boise River and nearby downtown reminded him of a better time, a challenging time, roaming the streets as a young man, wondering if he could make it until his next paycheck. A day in those shoes would be the perfect prescription for his mood.

"I'll expect this to be back on track by the end of the month." He returned to his chair, scanned the table, and paused, savoring the silence. Then he spoke directly at Cooper. "Screw this up again and you can let your ass hang on the line somewhere else."

The Post senior executive team departed quietly. Rafi and Andrew remained as Haddy Benson, Andrew's executive secretary of twenty years, joined them at the table, eyeing the departing employees as they filed out. Haddy, a painfully thin woman, barely five feet tall, was the same age as Andrew. She occasionally let him know she was his senior by a mere three days. Rafi said she had a permanent look of disapproval.

"What's my schedule?" Andrew asked.

Haddy looked down her nose at her planner through a pair of black-rimmed bifocals. "A conference call at five to speak to the California regional office about sales quotas for the third quarter. Gavin would prefer some time with you before six to discuss a lawsuit that he thinks will be dismissed in Medford."

"That's the little company that says we stole designs from their website," Rafi said. "I will handle this."

Andrew rubbed his forehead and closed his eyes. "Anything else?"

Haddy said no and left Andrew and Rafi behind closed doors.

Andrew nodded. "Denver?"

"We're rectifying the issue. The lease costs on"—Rafi looked down at his notes—"the GoCo Outdoor Center will be increasing significantly. Lucky for us their lease contract is up for renewal shortly. They will have little choice but to relocate."

Andrew had no idea why he'd become so obsessed with the Blendale Supercenter. Colorado had been a land mine from day one almost five years ago. Trying to find the right deal and location, they'd struck out twice. Donny eventually shifted their sights into Phoenix and Tucson, knowing they'd be back. He needed to do something. Fill a void. The Blendale store was the only option at the moment.

"The GoCo Outdoor Center?" Andrew laughed. "Where do these people come up with these names?"

"Actually, they are quite a little success."

"How are we—"

Rafi held up one hand and continued, "We will use the lease negotiations to our advantage. We may even gain the appearance of supporting the competition in a fight against the big bad strip mall operator. We help them find a new location, which helps us and them. Trust me, my friend."

"The permits and the city? I don't want a prolonged legal battle. Whoever this GoCo imbecile knows will be fuming if his friend is put in a bind."

"Do not worry. GoCo is a small operation. The issue is not competition, but politics. GoCo is forced to move. Post Inc. steps in to help. We become the good guys. A year from now, nineteen out of twenty peasants within twenty miles of our new store will belong to us. The formula always works. As for the politics, if the council does not see the light, we will go to plan B."

"Plan B?"

"The root cause of our problem is a councilman by the name of Heber. He has other issues. Since this is an election year, he won't want his affair with a seventeen-year-old publicized." Rafi sat back in the chair, clasping his hands behind his head, reminding Andrew of an Afghan version of Pu-Tai, the friendly Buddha, though with a more protected smile and not quite the paunch.

Andrew raised his eyebrows. "We have evidence of an affair?"

"A few photos."

"And the bad press?"

"Ah, Mr. Cooper's mess. It will pass. Trust me. We are bloody well off with this one. You will take care of the board?"

"They're fine as long as they get paid."

"Millions of dollars for sitting in this room four days a year."

"It's a necessary evil. We have the right people." Andrew nodded, indicating it was time for the next subject.

"Twenty percent growth?"

Andrew stared out the window, watching people walking, trotting, and riding along the Boise River Greenbelt. "Ten percent same-store sales. Twenty percent top line. Stretch goals."

"The target is fifteen percent, bottom line, for all stores. We are scaling quickly. The high growth days are behind us. You can only push these people and these numbers so far."

"Next subject."

Rafi never flinched. "Mr. Fenton Cooper?"

"Let's let Mr. Cooper soak in the marinade a bit before we put him on the grill."

"He is going a bit too far, yes?"

"I expect nothing less than perfection, especially from people I don't like," Andrew said. "If Mr. Cooper can't come through for us, there are a number of others who will."

"I don't believe it is Mr. Cooper's business performance that irritates you."

Andrew said nothing.

"Fenton Cooper sleeps with your daughter," Rafi said. "And he sleeps with Cinderella."

"Who?"

"Cinderella Marshant. Cooper's new personal assistant."

Andrew frowned.

"The redhead," Rafi said. "Miss Donita is not too interested in Cooper. He is like the mouse. She plays with him."

"And that disturbs you more than me."

"It should disturb us both."

"She's a grown woman."

"Excuses."

Rafi was more right than wrong. Andrew didn't like Cooper playing around behind the curtains with his daughter. But the real irritation was Cooper's increasingly brash behavior. His Operations VP had been screwing up to embarrass the Post Corporation. Most likely Cooper believed the scuttlebutt about Andrew's imminent retirement and thought Donny would soon be the CEO, leaving Cooper in a position to be her right hand man. *The new Rafi.* It wasn't the first time someone had tried to play Donny. No doubt Cooper was stirring the pot to show the board that Andrew was slipping, hoping the board and the major stockholders would apply pressure on him to retire. Not today.

"And the hallway rumors?" Rafi said.

"Cooper and teenage girls? You buying that?" Andrew smirked. "Unless, of course, you started the rumors."

Rafi frowned. "If I knew such a thing to be true, I would—"

The speaker phone on the table buzzed. "Mr. Post, this is Cassy down at the front desk. I'm sorry to bother you."

Andrew pressed the button to speak. "What is it?"

"There's a woman down here trying to gain access through security. She says it is urgent, and she must speak with you now. Normally, I'd turn her away, but—"

"But what?"

There was a brief moment of silence, and then the speaker came to life again. "She's very insistent, and I think you might know her."

Rafi leaned toward the speaker. "What does she want?"

"She won't say. But she did give security her ID. Her name is Angela Lorda."

"Thank you, Cassy. We'll take care of it," Andrew said.

Rafi raised his eyebrows. "Does this Angela Lorda ring a bell to you?"

Knowing Rafi knew the answer, Andrew saw no need to respond.

Rafi walked over to a podium at the other end of the room and tapped on the menu screen of a small communications device. Behind him a fifty-two inch monitor came to life. A few mouse clicks and keystrokes later, the screen displayed multiple security camera images. He clicked on the one in the lower right. It displayed a shadowed view of an empty front lobby save a security officer at a semicircular desk and a solitary figure sitting in a lobby chair, staring at her feet.

"I will have her removed," Rafi said.

Andrew held his hand up and walked to the screen. Even from a distance, the woman still had the same wanting look on her face. She was plain. Had the same gray ponytail of scores of Idahoan women who had descended from miners, farmers, ranchers, and lumberjacks. She wore a cheap fleece jacket, no doubt bought from one of the big-box discount stores.

"Just tell her I'm not available," Andrew said.

Rafi bowed his head and tapped a few buttons on the speaker phone.

A voice with a military tone answered. "Yes sir?"

"Have the woman in the lobby removed. Immediately. Tell her Mr. Post is not available. Tell her we will take legal action if this harassment continues."

Andrew placed his hand gently on Rafi's shoulder and leaned over the phone. "Just tell her I'm not available."

The voice replied, "Yes sir."

Andrew returned to his desk, scribbled a note, and punched a button on the phone. He glanced at Rafi and then carefully folded the note in two. "Haddy, please deliver a medium-sized women's Poneral fleece jacket to Ms. Angela Lorda, compliments of the Post Corporation. Believe she lives in the North End. And come in here and ensure this note is given to her before she leaves the premises. She's at the front desk."

He clasped his hands behind his back and walked to the window. The view, backlit by a spotless blue sky and fierce sunshine, was stunning.

Rafi remained at the conference table. "You either need a rest, my friend, or there is something you are not telling me. I do know of this woman."

Andrew turned to measure Rafi's expression. Had his confidant made the connection between Angela Lorda and the Post family? Did he know Angela Lorda's daughter was born on the same night as Donny and Katlin? Rafi was a master at saying just enough and nothing more. Determining what he knew was usually a guessing game. Andrew guessed—hoped—Rafi had not made the connection between the two families.

"She is the woman from our security briefing yesterday," Rafi said. "The one arrested early this morning. All over the morning news. The police never released her name and never charged her. Why would that be?"

"Now you worry me. She did nothing wrong. You suggesting I tried to cover something up?"

"I have no need to suggest something I am quite sure of," Rafi said proudly. "Someone identified her in a picture in the paper this morning. They are—what do they call it—tweeting about her. Everyone knows her identity."

Andrew patted Rafi on the back. "This is not an issue for you to be concerned with."

"My man says she gave you a note. The police know nothing of it."

Andrew nodded without a response.

"We have dealt with many like her before, though I see no clear motive. She wants your money, like the others?"

Andrew looked away. "Sometimes I wish I could walk down the street and work a few shifts at the State Street store. Sonya and me.

Like old times."

Rafi placed his palms flat on the table as if to steady himself. The mere mention of Andrew's marriage problems was one of the few subjects that appeared to upset his long-time associate.

"Only you stand in the way of reconciliation with Mrs. Post," Rafi said. "She waits for you to do so. You are not the first one to be cheated on. She is not the first one to disown her child. Keeping her as a prisoner will not bring you back together. Retribution for her past sins is *your* solution."

"Do I look like I want to talk about this?" Andrew said. "God knows you won't except for your insistence that I clean up my marriage."

Rafi's stance was difficult to comprehend. Andrew had been reprehensible so long ago, but so had his wife, Sonya. Rafi believed Andrew kept Sonya trapped in her own home, aided by fear, drugs, alcohol, and money. To Andrew, this was patently false. He cared for Sonya. He had no control over her fears and vices.

"Maybe we should talk about your marriage or marriages," Andrew said. "Problem is, I don't know anything about your wife or wives, except she or they live across an ocean and a continent and don't need your presence anymore."

Rafi remained calm. "What is done is done."

"Exactly," Andrew said. "What is done is done!" The statement referred not to Rafi's private life nor Andrew's failed marriage but to an expressly forbidden topic—the birth of the twins and the night Katlin was pronounced dead. *What is done is done.* It was the last thing Rafi had said at the conclusion of a prolonged and heated argument they'd had so long ago. Shorthand for a terrible time in Andrew's life that he could not wash out of his memory.

Andrew glanced at the monitor just in time to see Angela Lorda leaving the lobby. She kept looking back toward the camera as though she knew he was there. As she stepped out the door, Haddy appeared on the screen, racing to catch her.

"I had the perfect life, the perfect wife, the perfect everything," Andrew said quietly.

"I do not know what this woman is to you."

"She's nothing. I give her a little gift. Maybe she stays out of our hair. You stick to the Post Corporation business. I will tend to my own affairs."

Rafi held his arms outward. "Your affairs. The Post Corporation affairs. They are the same."

Chapter 4
Post Corporation Headquarters, Donny Post's Office, Boise
Thursday Evening

"Fire the bastard if he can't get it done!"

Everyone on the sixth floor should've heard Donny Post screaming into the phone behind her office door.

Andrew did as he rounded the corner. Donny's secretary forced a smile as he passed. He ignored the effort, stepped inside his daughter's office, and shut the door. Donny hit a button on the speaker phone and stood with her hands on her hips, glaring at her father.

"I appreciate you keeping your cool in the boardroom." Andrew spoke in the soothing tone reserved to unnerve the weak. It was quite reassuring no one knew whether his next action would be praise, a full assault, or rejection. It was a necessary tactic to maintain control, though it had little effect on his daughter.

A steady thump, the sound of Donny's foot tapping the carpet in a rapid-fire motion, reminded Andrew of the pent-up energy she possessed. She'd busted her tail bringing the company from what she termed "white-trash-hunter caterers" to a premier corporation pandering to the new well-to-do adventure crowd. She had taken it from Post Sporting Goods to the Post Corporation and renamed the stores to Post Outfitters. Growth of Post Inc., a nickname to the company faithful, had accelerated since she had been given free rein over operations at the unprecedented age of twenty-eight. Now, five years later, twenty-seven small stores and one concept superstore in the Pacific Northwest had morphed into thirty-five outlets and fourteen elite superstores covering the territory of almost every western state. Sales had soared to nearly three billion dollars last fiscal year. And it wasn't enough. Not for Donny.

"Dirt and sagebrush," she said as she approached her office window.

"That's what you see. I see the City of Trees."

"When you're gone, we go to Portland. A view of Mount Hood. I'm packing up the whole place."

Andrew smiled. A temper tantrum of a two-year-old. "Yes, that would be more suitable to your tastes. Expensive, but you."

"You're a product of Oregon. *Eastern Oregon*. More dirt and sagebrush. You hide under your refined disguise. You carry yourself like some British nobility, but you can't hide your roots." Donny turned to face her father. She was striking. Raised by men, she had somehow turned into a woman. The tabloids called her "the body" of the Post Corporation.

Perfection. That's what Rafi called her. He was nearly right. Donny had one physical trait Andrew had teased her about in her youth—a narrow scar running from the cleft of the chin to the right edge of the bottom lip, the result of a ski racing accident. The white scar, in contrast to her soft cinnamon-tinted skin, was usually covered on her chin by makeup. The tear in her lower lip was more difficult to hide. Rafi said she looked as though she were forever biting down on it.

"I want to live with real people, not these backwoods talk radio hicks," she continued. "I want to live near the ocean. Ski the Cascades—Mt. Hood, Bachelor—not this place."

"Winston sent you a test pair of his newest performance skis. They're at the house. Best on the market. Twenty-two hundred bucks a pop if they perform reasonably well. When the snow flies, he wants your thoughts."

"I don't understand why you are being so stubborn about this!"

"I'll assume we are back to talking about business. We've discussed my strategy *ad infinitum*. It has not changed. I let you lead, but there is a leash."

Donny crossed her arms. "Did I buy that for you?" She licked her lower lip, touching the scar with the tip of her tongue.

"Good catch." Andrew peered down at the charcoal suit that seemed to defy any signs of wear. "It's an L'Tepo. Hand-finished. Quite comfortable."

"Post Outfitters *America*. That's where we're headed once you move on."

"Oh, back to business," he said, a slight smile on his face. "You've not done poorly with me. I'd like to take a small amount of credit for our little empire."

"We pay dividends for God's sake. Growth companies don't pay dividends. They reinvest or buy back stock. Reinvest in things like new stores. Capital investments! You say twenty percent growth—it's really fifteen—and then you pay dividends."

"We've been through this before." He picked up a sketch of the new store he had helped to open eighteen hours ago. The architecture was an art form in itself, every detail vetted by his daughter. "You better be right about the Meridian store," he said.

"When have I failed you?"

"There's always a first time."

"You'd be pissed if I made just one mistake."

He lifted his head up long enough to make eye contact and then returned to examine the drawing. "No, *you'd* be pissed."

She put her hand up to her face, closed her eyes, and clenched her teeth. "Faster. We need to move faster. I can make twenty percent if you get out of the way."

"Thought you said it was really fifteen?"

The tapping foot revved. Donny's whole body started to shake in rhythm. "Go for the kill. Isn't that what you taught me?"

"Yes, but I'm a patient hunter. You'd shoot anything in your sights."

"But I'd at least fire the gun! It's not my fault that idiot Cooper mouthed off in Denver. Go ahead. Blame me for it. I know that's why you're here. Stick a fork in me."

"Don't flatter yourself. Your employee screwed up. And I could blame you, but that would be pointless. The blame flows uphill. Ultimately it falls on me. You may think you run this place, but I'm still the CEO and majority shareholder."

"Why don't you just fire me now? You've done a lot worse things than fire your own flesh and blood."

Andrew patted one of the binders in the bookshelf and headed toward the office door. He stopped in the doorway. "I keep you here to torture you. I suggest you review your paycheck. You'll still find my corporation's name at the bottom, not yours."

Donny spoke softly, "It's all electronic now."

Andrew laughed. "Of course it is. Come to the house some night. Have dinner with me."

"I don't come to the house. Not as long as *she's* there."

"She's still your mother. It might help if you came by."

"She's not my mother. We've been through this."

"They say time heals all wounds."

"*They* are wrong."

"You are something to gaze at." Fenton Cooper had been waiting for Donny's father to leave.

"Stuff it, Cooper. He's not stepping down any time soon." Donny closed her office door and slid her back up against it.

Cooper pressed his wiry body into Donny's, trapping her to the doorframe. "Why don't you cut your hair short again? I like the bitchy look."

A passerby in the hallway would have seen Cooper shoved backwards several feet. But given the hour, most of Post Inc. had escaped to their homes.

"*Donita, tenemos el lugar para nosotros.*"

"I'm a bit tired of that, Cooper. I'm not in the mood."

"So why did your parents give you a Spanish name? Maybe you aren't a Post after all."

"Screw you, you little preppie pretender." Donny left her place by the door, walked up to Cooper, grabbed his tie, and yanked him toward her. A wanting pair of fingers slipped around her waist. It was a good thing he was tall. She'd tired of looking down on men. The tie felt good in her hands. She tended to measure up the men in her life by their ties or lack thereof. Her father told her to notice the kind of shoes a man wears. That it would say much about his values and his attention to detail. But in her opinion the ties held a better correlation. First, no synthetic cheap stuff. They had to be silk, and she favored hand-woven material like the fabric she was now grasping. The pattern didn't matter as long as it didn't contain large fish or numerous repetitions of someone's favorite sporting goods—ties they actually sold in the Post stores.

Donny spoke quietly. "If my father or Rafi returns, they'll run you out of town."

Cooper tilted his head slightly and raised his lips. "We might have to make sure he doesn't return, now or in the future."

"He knows about us. I told you we needed to be more discreet."

"How do you know he's on to us?"

"He knows," she said with a wink. "And with your boneheaded move in Denver, he'll have his excuse to have you for lunch. I've seen this before. Won't matter what you do. You're history."

"You're quite happy about this, aren't you?"

"Yes, because not only does he have you where he wants you, so do I." She stood on her tiptoes, kissed Cooper on the forehead, and then pushed him away.

"If I were you, I wouldn't be so full of myself." Cooper pulled a small metallic device from his pocket and waved it in the air.

"You little bastard. You gonna blackmail me?"

Cooper danced over to Donny's desk, set his smartphone on the desktop, and plugged the device into the phone. After a few swipes on the screen, an audio file started to play. The voices of Rafi and Donny's father echoed from the small speaker.

Donny leaned forward onto the desk. "What is this?"

"Just a little staff meeting surveillance. This gem is encrypted. Even if they found it, they'd never tie it back to me."

"I wouldn't be so sure." She paused. "You think you have something here?"

"I do." His hands slid under her skirt and returned to her hips.

"He's coming after you at some point," she said, brushing his hands aside.

"His threats have been heard."

Donny listened to the rest of the recording while Cooper sat on the edge of the desk, waiting for a reaction.

The recording ended. She said nothing.

Cooper started to walk around the room, imitating Andrew's purposeful stride, hand gestures, and tone of voice. "Your father is wilting. Or maybe he likes this woman. Thuban will do something to quiet this lady if she doesn't disappear soon. You know he will. Or even better. Maybe your father goes for this woman. There's opportunity here. I smell it."

"Okay, I'm not following you. I thought you were talking about the poor schmuck who's having an affair with some jailbait in Denver."

"That's interesting." Cooper moved over to the office door and checked the hallway through the window. "But that's just more Post Inc. funny business. People expect it. Now Andrew Post putting the heavy on a poor woman in Boise who lost her husband last year?"

"How do you know that?"

"I did a little of my own investigating."

Donny smirked. "My father was right. You are an imbecile."

"Yes, but an imbecile who might get you closer to a chance to expand this foot-dragging corporation and rid ourselves of the tyrant."

"An affair?" She laughed at the ceiling. "He sent her a jacket. This is my father you are talking about. He hasn't been with a woman in years."

"About time then. You'd do anything to move him out of that chair and take over this place. Besides, he's not exactly enamored with you."

"Right. He hates me. That's why I'm...in charge...of you."

"You're too beautiful to belong to your father." Cooper closed the distance again and fused their bodies together. "You know Thuban will do something to quiet this woman down. Affair or not. She must think she has something on your father. Thuban won't let this go. And I have a feeling about this budding romance. This will be interesting. Don't want to miss a chance, do we?"

"I'm not playing your game."

"Right. You'll play. I know you too well."

"You ever noticed Father and I have the same opinion of you?"

"Are you in?"

She made a circle out of her lips and gave him a sad little girl look. "I won't let you hurt my father."

"No intention of hurting the man. He just needs to step down. You said he's close to making a decision. When the story hits the press, convince him it is time. Or convince the board to convince him."

"What story?"

"Don't know yet, but there will be one. I guarantee it."

"You better be careful you aren't part of the story."

Donny sat up on the edge of the desk and pulled Cooper toward her. She leaned back on the cool surface as he pressed down onto her body.

Cooper grinned. "You can help me pull this off, because I know...you...are a bad girl."

Chapter 5
Post Corporation Headquarters, Andrew's Office, Boise
Late Thursday Evening

In the shadows of his office suite, a small banker's lamp the lone source of light, Andrew sat. The halls and floors of Post Inc. were as deserted as the hospital had been on that night so long ago. He placed the letter on his desk and read it again.

Mr. Post,

I know you don't know me, but hear me out. Attached is a copy of a letter my husband gave me at the time of his passing last year. I have the original, and no one else has seen it. You will no doubt be surprised by its contents. I can tell you my husband was an absolutely honest man, so there is <u>no</u> question that the words he relayed are the truth. I ask that you speak with me very soon. I am not here to cause you problems, but I believe it is in our best interests to discuss this issue. I'm sure this matter would best be dealt with in private.

Angela Lorda

Just as he finished the attached letter for the second time, a voice startled him.

"My friend, it is after nine o'clock." Rafi stood at the door, worn leather briefcase in hand.

"Thought you'd gone home already," Andrew said.

Rafi set down his briefcase and entered the office. Andrew noticed his friend's uninterrupted concentration on the letter on the desk. "I was"—Rafi paused and smiled—"monitoring Mr. Cooper. He has been with your daughter for the last several hours. The security cameras caught him sneaking back into the conference room to retrieve some device under the table. We can only suspect he was a little too interested in our conversation."

"Interesting. I'll assume you will get the device," directed Andrew.

Rafi nodded. "I suggest we no longer use that room for discussions."

Andrew rose and roamed the gray shadows painting the rest of the room. The lights of Boise gave off enough illumination to show concern on Rafi's face.

"You must deal with Cooper," Andrew said.

"It will be done, my friend. He has gone too far."

"He served us well, at least in the beginning, but he's poison for my daughter and the company. Donita comes first. Get rid of him."

Rafi bowed his head slightly but remained silent. A small flame briefly lit his face, followed by the ghost of bright orange ashes. Cigar smoke drifted through slits of light entering from the outside windows.

"I need one other favor," Andrew said, moving toward the window and away from the smoke. "This woman—she is my business and only my business."

The room remained still for some time. Andrew watched the cars flowing through the downtown streets. Somewhere in that mass of humanity, his daughter was likely having a bourbon and Coke with Fenton Cooper. Or maybe they were locked in sweat one floor below.

He'd considered showing Rafi the letter. The stakes were too high. If the letter turned out to be false, Rafi would destroy the Lorda woman with a full-scale assault on her reputation. Rafi would not worry about whether the poor woman might be in a position where she believed the letter, but its contents were false. Andrew's gut told him this was probably the case—that this woman believed an untruth. Rafi would do anything to avoid having the media, private investigators, lawyers, or the law digging up information on the birth of the twins and Katlin's death. *What is done is done.* They'd agreed and Rafi wouldn't let Angela Lorda change that.

Given the wild chance the story was true, Rafi would pressure the woman to keep silent. Either way, this poor woman didn't deserve such attention. Besides, Andrew had broken the agreement. *What is done* had been partly undone. It was best Rafi remained ignorant of his betrayal.

Angela Lorda was trouble and a mystery at the same time. There was something more to her than Andrew could easily describe. Her story was farfetched. Was there any harm in helping her? What would it hurt if she believed the letter? She didn't appear to be the kind of woman who would want to be in the public eye. The ones who had come before her had always been accompanied by cheap lawyers or unruly relatives. She seemed to be alone in her quest. It was out of bounds to trust someone like her or anyone on the outside. It was out of bounds for Andrew to take such a matter into his own hands.

He would go see her. Measure up her story and decide on subsequent actions.

Footsteps of Rafi leaving brought Andrew back. "Angela Lorda?"

"As you wish," Rafi said.

Andrew wasn't convinced.

Chapter 6
Broad Street Coffee Bar, Near Downtown Boise
Friday Afternoon

"This is a bit of a strange request," said Preston Sanduski, president of the First State Bank.

The afternoon was breezy and raw, and a light rain fell from a flat layer of gray clouds. Andrew and Sanduski sat at a small round table in the back of the Broad Street Coffee Bar, a little venture Andrew had helped fund a decade ago for an old high school friend. Even with intense competition, the shop survived and made a decent profit. He often cited the place as an example of how the little guy can thrive despite pressure from big corporations like his own.

Sanduski wore a cheap blue suit and a pair of comfortable black shoes. He looked more like a mortician than a banker.

Mr. Johnson, Andrew's lone bodyguard for the outing, stood near the front door. Other patrons came and went, getting their fix and paying little attention to the celebrity they had likely overlooked in their rush to become caffeinated.

"Just make this happen," Andrew said.

"Can I ask why you'd want to pay this off?" Sanduski's voice cracked a bit as he said it.

Andrew noticed a middle-aged woman at the counter staring in his direction. He nodded toward her. She picked up her coffee drink and headed for the exit.

"No, you may not. It cannot be tied back to me. There can be no trail. You won't speak of this to anyone."

"You can be assured of our cooperation."

"Yes, I suppose I can. Make sure this is done and send me documentation showing the loan paid. There can be no connection to me. I need this today."

Andrew stood, patted Sanduski on the shoulder, placed his hat on his head, pulled on his overcoat, and left the banker behind.

Chapter 7
Penny Lorda's House, North End, Boise
Friday Dinner Time

Penny Lorda placed her house key on the counter, threw her purse on the floor, and raced to switch on the furnace. Summer was a week away, but today felt like the damp cold of March.

Earlier in the day, in between selling smokes and restacking the shelves, she had watched the lowering clouds from the window of Smokes and More, a downtown smoke shop where she worked four days a week. If it had been a few months earlier, snow would've eventually reached the valley floor. Instead, the sky had only produced a cold rain.

"Serena? Get the mail."

Penny walked back and forth through the small three bedroom structure on 14th street, one of many houses built before World War I, just blocks off the stately Harrison Boulevard. She dreamed of owning one of the larger houses on Harrison or even on Warm Springs, sitting on the porch, watching her friends fly by toward the ski area or waiting for the hordes of kids at Halloween. Sort of a normal life—a place where families were important, and kids still roamed the streets with little fear of the monsters that stalked the big cities. Yes, there were some problems in Boise, and she'd seen some of them firsthand. A few potheads and meth freaks, some of whom also happened to be friends of hers. Some gang-wannabes. And stupid criminals who seemed to want to rob banks in the middle of the day.

"Serena? Where are you, *gurl?*"

She caught a glimpse of her ten-year-old peering out the backdoor at the rain.

"Is it gonna snow?" Serena asked.

"Not likely. No Bubba the snowman this close to summer."

Penny patted Serena on the head and turned toward the front door, ready to scurry to the mailbox and return to her warm retreat, where she would soon curl up on the couch and wait on her mother for dinner.

Yet the nicotine was calling. She'd step out on the porch and light up first. Serena would nag her like a second mother. She knew she should stop.

As she approached the door, smacking the bottom of a pack of Camel Lights, her eyes focused past the window toward the front yard.

The cigarettes dropped to the floor.

Her breathing quickened, yet she kept eye contact. A man in a long black overcoat, hands in his pockets, stood on the sidewalk about halfway up to the porch, watching her. He wore a felt Fedora—at least that's what she thought it was called—and carried a small black umbrella. His shoes and pants, sticking out the bottom of the overcoat, portrayed a man who dressed expensively. Shadows from his hat obscured the details of his face. He appeared to be old.

Serena ran up behind Penny and hugged her. Like a human shield, Penny kept her body between the man's line of sight and her child.

"What's wrong, momma?"

Penny looked over her shoulder at Serena. "You stay right there! Don't freaking move!"

"Momma, who is it?"

She glanced back at the front window. The sidewalk was empty.

She contemplated walking outside. Surely she was overreacting. Maybe the man was at the wrong house. But something about him said otherwise. She would call Matt. Let the Boise PD handle this. That's what Matt would say. He'd told her more than a few times that Boise was a safe place, but all towns had their kooks.

It was the right man. The suspect, on foot and on the opposite side of the street, was in no hurry. No doubt his path led back to 14th street.

Matt Downing was surprised the man didn't take notice of his official police presence as he drove by. He was usually in an unmarked sedan, but tonight he was driving the standard squad car, pulling another extra patrol shift. He preferred the overtime to the safer security jobs a number of his peers favored. It was a required part of a cop's life if he wanted to make a decent living.

He pulled into a driveway, turned around, and caught up to the man as he was stepping into a cross street.

The suspect, dressed as Penny had described, glanced at the squad car and continued on his way.

Matt parked at a corner house a short distance ahead, exited the car, and moved onto the sidewalk directly in the path of the man. "Kind of a damp night for a walk," he said.

The man tipped his hat. "Officer Downing." The tone was not friendly.

"What brings you out here?"

"Out for a walk."

Matt did his best to match the stone face staring him down. The two men had a mutual disdain for one another. The man's daughter, Donny, Matt had been told, was way too sophisticated for a Boise cop. And Matt had watched the man slip past the law one too many times. The only thing worse than the bad guy getting away was the bad guy slipping through the system in broad daylight. The man on the sidewalk was a master of the latter.

"Got a call from a woman down the street. Says a man fitting your description was watching her."

Andrew Post did not reply.

"I'd be careful out here, Mr. Post. Never know who might see you."

Post nodded once, stepped around Matt, and continued his trek down the street.

Matt called out, "Have a nice evening." He returned to the squad car.

This was certainly an interesting development. First, Annie's arrest early Thursday morning. No explanation for her stalking Andrew Post. Then she was mysteriously released by the Meridian PD. Matt's contacts in the nearby bedroom community could only state that the order to release Annie had come from the Meridian chief of police. Her picture had appeared in the *Boise Tribune*, an unfriendly foe to the Posts, while the local television stations, often standing atop the Post bandwagon, had buried the story deep in their newscasts. Social media and local blogs were buzzing about the incident. In the usual Post fashion, all official evidence had been cleansed away. Then there was Annie's letter. Penny had said her mother had finally opened it, and whatever was inside was enough to bring Annie to tears, something Matt had only witnessed once back when Frank Lorda passed away. And so far, Annie had been silent through it all.

And now this.

Matt pulled out a notebook filled with personal scribbles detailing evidence related to open investigations. He had an entire section on the Post Corporation. Opening it to the next blank page in the special Post section, he started to write. He noted dates and the sequence of events over the past week involving Annie, Penny, and the Post family. He abruptly stopped writing, put the pen away, closed the book, and tossed it on the passenger seat. Details would come later.

Chapter 8
Penny Lorda's House, North End, Boise
Late Friday Evening

"What the hell is this?" Penny handed the paper to Matt.

"Not a nice word!" The grade school voice of Serena echoed through the house, anchored in one of the back bedrooms.

Penny lifted her head up toward the ceiling and smiled. "Mind your own business." She pushed her sleeves up and fell into a worn, wingback chair.

In his all black uniform, Matt remained standing near the front door, examining the piece of paper. "What happened to Friday night dinner at your mom's?"

"She's acting all weird. Says 'not tonight.' Who am I to disobey?"

"You're kidding, right?" He held the paper in the air. "Where did this come from?"

"Stuffed in my mailbox. In this."

She was holding a plain white cardboard document holder with no writing or postage on it. Her sleeves fell enough to partially cover the snow leopard tattoo on her forearm.

Matt returned his attention to the document in his hands. "Why don't you get those things removed?"

"Screw you. What are you, my mother?"

"More bad words!" said the little voice in the back of the house.

Matt recalled Penny's story about the snow leopard, her initiation into a modest set of personal tattoos and piercings she now possessed. She'd told him she had no memory of the night she walked into the Victory Tattoo Studio a decade ago and demanded a large rendering of a cat on her butt cheeks just below her beltline. They refused her. She called it "some bullshit liability excuse." Apparently, she had no idea stoned and drunk was not a good condition for being inked. Soon after, she returned to the studio clean and sober, and demanded the snow leopard instead of the cat.

"Okay, the tattoos I guess I can handle, but your hair? Jet black fits you. Black dreadlocks with red tips?" Matt threw his hands toward the floor and jumped around the room, puffing out a reggae beat.

"You are such a white boy. My boss likes it. I think he's still hot for Bo Derek." Penny started to laugh at her own joke and a snort escaped.

"Classy," Matt said, unable to control his own laughter.

Penny tossed the small pillow she was cuddling in Matt's direction. He leaned and the object bounced harmlessly off the front door.

"Like little Donita." She put her head down, stuck her lips out, bit her lower lip, and mocked an overdone frown.

"God, you have a mean streak."

"Let's smoke a joint."

"Ain't gonna happen. And you aren't going to, either." Matt tapped the document with his finger. "I don't understand this."

"Can't you read? Says my house is paid up. And just in time since my wacked-out boss cut my hours again."

"Has to be a mistake. What'd the bank say?"

"I just got the fucking thing." They both glanced toward the back of the house, expecting more verbal punishment. There was no response. "I'm kind of liking the feeling. Maybe I won't call the bank. Seems that stranger might be looking out for me."

"I've got to get back to work. Maybe your mother had something to do with this."

Penny's shoulders started to shake coincident with her silent laugh. "Are you kidding me? Ma doesn't have enough to pay her own bills. Besides, I think my own ma would tell me."

"Maybe it has something to do with your dad's letter."

"I don't think so. Why would Ma be freaked out if Dad left her a big wad of cash? Wouldn't she just come over and tell me I don't have to fork over seven hundred and ninety-six dollars every month?"

Matt shrugged, still staring at the document.

Penny jumped up in one swift motion and peered out the front window. "What about this sidewalk dude? You've done everything you can to avoid the reason I called the *po-leece*."

"Got to be a mistake."

"The man?"

Matt looked over his shoulder out the front window. "So this guy was peeping into your house?"

"No."

"Threatened you?"

"No! He was standing on the sidewalk, nearly on my porch, staring into my window—the one by the door."

"Why were you looking outside?"

"Am I being interrogated here?" She held her arms outward. "Cuff me and do what you want with me."

"Can you give me a description?"

"Yep. He's a sexy-looking young man. Not quite the smooth talker he was in high school. Could use a shave to get the black scruff off his face, but he should've kept the longer black hair we all wanted to run our hands through."

"Real funny. The man on the sidewalk?"

"I don't like the paramilitary look. Let your hair grow out again."

"Think I'll be going, *Ms. Landon.*"

"Foul! We agreed that bastard ex-husband of mine was off limits."

The tiny voice of Serena cleared the corner and landed in the front living room once again. "Not nice!"

"Find something to do!" Penny yelled back.

"Like Donny Post is off-limits?" Matt took a few steps toward Penny. She pulled her legs up to her chest.

"Do you want me to do anything?" he said.

Penny's expression turned serious. She whispered, "I didn't like that creep staring at me. Suppose he's some kind of pervert."

"Tell me what he looked like again."

Rubbing her forehead with the back of her hand, she continued in a low voice, "Was in a long coat. Black coat. Average height. Gray hair mixed with some black. Two dark dots for eyes. And nice dress pants with shiny, pricey shoes. Had one of those businessman hats on. That's a Fedora right?"

"A businessman pervert who came by to pay off your house?"

"You are such an asshole tonight!"

Matt held his hands up and waited. Why did she toy with him so much? Despite her problems, Penny was the best thing in his life. He loved Serena like his own child. If given the chance, they could make a go of it. Every time he came close to broaching the subject, Penny retreated. Said they were too different. Said he was a cop and might disappear one night. Said she couldn't handle that. It was an obvious cover. This was Boise. He was pretty safe as far as cops go.

He recalled the difficult night six years ago that changed both of their lives. He'd been a street cop for three years. About two in the morning, he received a call from Jody Felkins on the North End. His buddy had spotted Penny staggering around at a house one street off Bogus Basin Road where a pretty good party was winding down. Felkins was ready to call-in a couple of units to break it up and was expecting an arrest or two. He thought it best for Matt to get Penny out first.

Matt arrived, walked straight through the sickly sweet aroma of cannabis in the front living room, found Penny passed out, carried her out to the squad car, and drove her home.

Finding her wasted at a party was a bit of a surprise. She'd cleaned herself up pretty well after Serena was born and, to his knowledge, had been faithful to the cause.

At her house, Penny's husband of five years, Austin, was nowhere to be found. His absence wasn't unusual since he worked as a smokejumper and sometimes spent entire summers away from home. But Serena, four years old at the time, was missing as well. Matt discovered her whereabouts later that night by calling the most likely babysitters—her Grandma Annie and Grandpa Frank.

It was about noon the next day before Penny pulled herself out of bed. Still in her underwear, she sat in the tub and let cold water pour down on her body from the shower head. Matt sat next to her in silence. Then she told him. Austin had left. No explanation. No cheating girlfriend. No issues with money. No mention of her lifestyle. Just left her a simple note with one statement. *I don't want to be married to you anymore.* She was crushed.

From that day on, Penny and Matt had been inseparable. Somewhere lost in a confusing mix of a brother-sister boyfriend-girlfriend relationship. Together nevertheless.

Matt took the rest of the description of the man on the sidewalk.

"I noticed you didn't write a lot," Penny said as he headed toward the front door. "You usually take ridiculous notes."

He didn't respond. He already knew who was staring into Penny's house. The issue was why? What was Post up to? He certainly had the funds to pay off her mortgage and to keep such an act a secret. Why Post would want to do that or why he would deliver the message personally in broad daylight was puzzling.

Matt was convinced Annie was the center of all things related to this mystery. Through chatting with her friends online, Penny already knew about her mother and the situation at the new Post store. Matt had told Penny everything he knew about the event, fueling further Penny's displeasure with her mother and Andrew Post. Coming clean about tonight's incident would likely lead to some kind of confrontation involving Penny, Post's security company, and the Boise PD. Or she might insist they head right over to the Post Estate for some questioning. For now, it was best to keep quiet.

The good news was that he was on the trail of Andrew Post.

Again.

Chapter 9
North End, Boise
Sunday

Like two strangers sharing a busy downtown sidewalk, Penny and her mother, Annie, traveled side-by-side in silence toward the church. The morning air was crisp, but intense sunshine and lack of wind made their skin feel warm, hints of summer officially only days away.

Serena outpaced the women by a house or two. "Not so far ahead," Penny said.

She couldn't shake the image of the man on her sidewalk. It didn't help that her mother was still acting strange, and even Matt was a bit off. The whole town was abuzz about her mother's bizarre behavior at the Post store last week. Her ma hadn't spoken a word about it or about the letter.

"Where's Mr. Matt?" Serena said, skipping back to Penny.

"He worked late last night. You know that. Every other week."

Serena frowned and then skipped back down the sidewalk. Penny felt a hand on her shoulder as she was about to shout. "She's fine," Annie said. "Let her go."

"Yep, where's Mr. Matt," Penny mumbled. There. A chance for her mother to chat up her favorite subject—Matt. Tell her she should marry the guy. They were made for each other. And on and on. Instead, the comment was ignored.

Penny owed her mother and Matt more than she could ever repay. If it hadn't been for the two of them, Serena would be somewhere else. Her ex would have won the custody battle. Matt had stepped into the role of father, something he had a knack for, and her ma had become the backstop, the safety cushion.

"That thing with my house," Penny said, "the bank won't say a word. They act like it's a mystery. Said they're trying to trace the payment. I showed them my statements. Don't they have to come clean on this?"

There was no reply. Her mother's attention remained focused on the distant crowd gathering near the west entrance of the sanctuary.

Penny couldn't identify anything unusual. "What's the matter?"

Annie lowered her head toward the sidewalk and picked up the pace. It was all Penny could do to keep up.

By the time they had reached the sanctuary steps, Annie had overtaken Serena and, to Penny's surprise, passed right by her grandchild. Penny grabbed Serena by the hand and ushered her inside.

In the back of the sanctuary, she found her mother, motionless, standing like a bride waiting for the music to cue up. Annie appeared to be looking for someone and seemed unaware of the crowd moving around her and into the pews.

Penny grabbed her arm and pulled her along. Turning heads and muffled conversations accompanied their movement until they were seated in their usual spot—aisle seats, halfway to the front.

Penny was used to the attention. Every week they stared at her like she was some kind of homeless person. For once the prying eyes were on someone else.

The congregation standing, Reverend Lowell in the back of the sanctuary, his hands stretched out toward the sky, was delivering the benediction. Penny was so deep in thought about Matt, the stranger, and the house payments, she somehow missed the entire service.

The spot on the end of the pew was empty. She whispered to Serena, "What happened to Grandma Annie?"

"She left."

"Was she sick?"

"Dunno."

"Did she tell you where she was going?"

"Unh uh."

The prayer ended and the worshipers started to file out. Several people in Penny's area stopped to shake hands. She absentmindedly said something to each one while looking toward the exit.

She scanned the daylight through the back double doors and shuddered. It was difficult to make sense of what she was seeing. It was her mother talking to a man—*the stranger*. They were engaged in a lively discussion.

"Let's go!" She yanked Serena's arm and maneuvered her way through the milling crowd. A jam-up near the preacher at the back door kept her progress to a crawl. Reverend Lowell made eye contact and seemed destined to shake hands. Penny moved to the right into the last pew and raced toward the corner exit doors.

Out on the steps and into the sun, she could barely see. Her mother was approaching, every eye following her movements, every mouth covered by a hand in hushed conversation.

On the curb, a stretch limousine was sitting behind a van loading senior citizens. The stranger stood by the back door of the limo, waiting on an oriental man with a driver's cap to open the door. The man and the driver disappeared into the limo and it pulled away.

Penny was shaking. "What were you doing talking to that man?"

Annie looked around nervously. "Who?"

"The man in the limo. The child molester!"

"What?"

"He's the one on my sidewalk!"

"I don't think so. That was Andrew Post."

"Post?"

Annie opened her purse and shuffled the contents, darting her eyes back to Penny and Serena, then back to her purse. "I need to go home."

Penny jumped around her mother, blocking her attempt to leave. "Ma, what the hell is this? You were talking to him."

"I was talking to several people. He came up and shook my hand." She stepped around Penny and started down the walk. "That's all."

"You seemed to be having quite the conversation," Penny said, her voice escalating as she followed a step behind. "Why would you do that? They said you tried to get to him at his store last week. You hate the Posts. Matt hates the Posts. Dad hated the Posts."

Departing parishioners remained attentive and continued to mumble to each other. Her mother's pace quickened. She waved her hand dismissively in the air. "He was apologizing for the other night. Now can we please go home?"

Penny trailed closely behind, dragging Serena like a rag doll. It was the first time her mother had even acknowledged "the other night." "Matt talked to a Meridian cop who was at the store that night. He said you were yelling out Andrew Post's name."

Annie shook her head and accelerated her pace.

Penny halted. "He was on my sidewalk. I don't understand."

Penny could hear Matt locking his mountain bike on the front porch followed by a brief knock on the door. She managed to run by the front room, half-dressed, covering herself with a pair of sweats as he entered the house.

"Come on in," she said as she passed by. "Freaking Peeping Tom yourself."

"You want my help or not?"

"Depends on the kind of help you're offering," she yelled from her bedroom. She returned to the living room, wearing the sweats she used to hide herself.

Matt pitched himself into an armchair. "It's warm enough for shorts."

"I didn't shave my legs."

He grinned. "Well, let's go do it. Don't want to waste a nice afternoon like this."

"If I took you up on that, you'd go screaming out the front door."

"That I might. Not sure I'm up for such a big job."

She picked up a little sunflower pillow and faked a toss in his direction. He didn't budge.

"So you think your mother has a thing going with Andrew Post?"

"That's not what I said."

"Come on. Take a walk with me. Serena?"

"She's with her grandma. They belong together."

Matt jumped up and held his hands outward, blocking the doorway. "We've got the place to ourselves."

Penny shoved him backwards. "Not with me, you don't."

To the unaware, Matt and Penny, despite their differences, could have been husband and wife traveling down the North End side streets. They occasionally held hands or walked arm-in-arm, nodding to the throngs of late spring gardeners, cyclists, dog walkers, or those content to enjoy the nice day from their porches. The two were a common sight. The neighbors knew they were friends, though one got the feeling they were all rooting for more.

At the very least, maybe the good cop could turn the street kid. Maybe get her to fix her hair, loosen up on the eyeliner, and encourage her to buy some clothes that didn't look as though they'd been thrown out by some thrift shop.

They turned onto Harrison Boulevard, an expansive tree-covered thoroughfare lined with an eclectic mix of architecture from the turn of the twentieth century. Penny passed her favorite house, a mission-style two-story with rising white columns, a large porch guarded by stone vases, and a beautifully manicured yard. She wondered what people did to make enough money for a house like that. Andrew Post could probably buy them all.

"So you've been quiet about Post," she said. "You afraid I'll bring up Donita?" She accented the name heavily.

Matt nodded to an elderly woman talking on a phone in her yard and proceeded to survey the street in both directions. Then he spoke as if he were lecturing a suspect, "You're not a nice person when you're stressed. And the Posts are not a family you want to deal with."

They stopped at a cross street and waited for a little hatchback with a rat tail to sputter by. When they reached the other side of the street, she threw a friendly punch into his ribs. "And?"

"And that's it."

"You're a cop, right?" She reached over and tugged his chin to force his head up and down. "Right? Right. Well, put the facts together, *dee-tective*. Ma reads a letter from Dad. She gets arrested for stalking Andrew Post. They let her out free of charge. A photo in the paper but no name mentioned. Little TV news coverage, but everybody knows it happened. Post peeps into my house after delivering my paid-off mortgage. Ma has a conversation with the man in front of the church. What does all this mean to your detective mind?"

"Not much."

"Not much? Fuckin' A. The man…and I mean…*the man*…paid off my mortgage. Why? Cause Ma has something big on him, and it's in that letter. He probably wanted me to see him on the sidewalk. Scare me or something. Or maybe scare Ma."

Matt faced ahead and said nothing.

Penny pulled on his arm. "Come on. We ought to go over to his house and kick his ass. I'm not afraid of him or his goons."

"That's what I was afraid of. Your mother is not exactly the bribing type, and you said their conversation today looked civil."

"Yeah, but she's acting nuts."

"You going to read the letter?"

"Ma doesn't want me to. Besides, now that she opened it, it's disappeared." Penny stopped and pulled Matt to a halt. "You're too quiet. You're hiding something."

"Okay. The other night, I knew it was Andrew Post on the sidewalk. I saw him."

"You saw him! Freaking cop." She jabbed him in the ribs again, hard this time.

"Okay. Okay. I thought you might do something stupid like go over to his place."

They walked past another couple of houses, dodging a lady pushing a yellow jogging stroller.

"And that's it. You think I'd go nuts. Maybe you needed to investigate first. Maybe get Donita's take on the case."

Matt shook his head but kept staring forward down the street. "Jesus," was all he said.

Penny could tell by his demeanor she should stop. She couldn't help it. One thing about Matt—when his voice softened like that, she'd hurt him. She grabbed his arm and held on a little more firmly.

Chapter 10
The Post Estate, Boise Foothills
Sunday Night

Andrew Post never wanted to be conspicuous. He owned a modest home hidden in the foothills close to Boise, away from all but the most curious. His neighbors were well-to-do, they left each other alone, and that was just fine.

Until the Spokane incident, he had never seen the need for much security. He had the typical home alarm system and a gated yard. Now high tech cameras monitored his estate, and at least one security guard remained on the property at all times. These were extreme measures for Boise. Sonya, his wife of four decades, hated the intrusive lifestyle, despite efforts to privatize her side of the house. A few years ago, she would have escaped to Sun Valley or McCall for at least half the year. Lately she hid in her own little enclave, soused from the late morning until well after midnight. She had her visitors, but Andrew wasn't interested in who they were or what they were doing. She was living her life. He was living his life.

He was rarely home early. Sunday evenings were special. If he wasn't working—and he usually was—he'd leave for the weekend. But he had always returned for his time to relax. He'd just taken dinner when the front door clicked and Rafi Thuban entered. Besides family and security, Rafi was the only person with authorization to enter Andrew's part of the grounds unescorted.

"Sorry to bring you over," Andrew said, sipping a glass of Bouchard Lalande, vintage 2004. "Would you like some?"

Rafi smiled. "Yes. Yes. Some cheap wine."

Andrew snapped his fingers, and one of the servants brought a wine glass and the bottle. "Leave it here. Thank you. That'll be all tonight, Manny."

Rafi nodded. "Very good cheap wine."

The intercom buzzed. "Mr. Post, Mr. Scott is here at the gate."

"Let him in."

Devlon Scott entered the house and everyone knew it. He was everything Andrew hated in a man. Loud. Cheap suits. Profane language. He smelled like cigarette smoke and looked like a cross between a retired NFL linebacker and a true blood Irish cop.

"Will you have some wine?" Andrew said, knowing the answer.

"Not much on vino. Got some news for you, Mr. Post." Scott pulled out a cigarette and wisely placed it back in the pack.

"Let's hear it," Andrew said.

"The IT guys found several suspect audio files on Cooper's office laptop. They were encrypted, but the idiot uses the same password for everything. Just as you thought. Creep's been recording private conversations around the company, including some between you and Mr. Thuban."

"All of these files must be destroyed, including any backups you can find," said Rafi, "and please check Mr. Cooper's apartment as well. Be discrete."

Scott walked over to the wet bar and reached into the cabinet for a shot glass. "My boys are on it. The guy probably has other copies on the Web, on a stick, maybe his phone." Scott produced an airline size bottle of whiskey from his jacket and poured it into the glass. He threw the contents into his mouth in a swift and familiar motion.

"Clean up what you can. Leave it to me to deal with anything else Mr. Cooper is hoarding," Rafi said.

Andrew took another sip of wine, leaned back in his chair, and shut his eyes. He lifted his chin and spoke upward, "Help yourself to some good whiskey." He heard the clinking of bottles behind him. No doubt Scott knew where the good stuff was stored. "And then leave."

"Yes sir."

Heavy footsteps headed for the front door. "May I?"

Andrew didn't have to open his eyes. The man was on his way out with the whole bottle. Andrew waved his hand in dismissive approval and listened for the door to open and shut. The sound never materialized.

Rafi rose out of his chair as if some head of state had entered the room. Andrew turned to see Sonya standing in the doorway of the hall that separated their two sides of the house. She wore black workout tights covered by an extra-large grey T-shirt. Her hair was cut short, similar to the way Donny used to wear her hair. In fact, she was Donny, tall and slender, but decades older and worn by alcohol. Andrew looked back over at Scott, who appeared to be stuck at the front door, his eyes also locked on the woman in the doorway.

Within minutes Sonya and Rafi disappeared into her part of the house. Scott left without a word. Andrew could hear the muffled conversation followed by periods of quiet. Rafi was likely telling her to clean up her life, give her marriage a chance, or some such nonsense. Sonya was probably shaking her head, saying she would leave soon.

In reality, Andrew had no idea what they were saying.

"He is a swine. Why do you not let me terminate him?"

Andrew opened his eyes to see Rafi examining him from the other chair. At some point, he had dozed. According to the clock, it had been about forty-five minutes.

"I thought you told me that in your country being a good host is traditional, even to your enemy."

Rafi frowned. "This is not Kabul, my friend. Besides, if I were home, I would offer Mr. Scott some drink, feed him, and then kill him for this. He sleeps with your wife. Right under your nose."

"She needs someone."

"Incredible! You punish her."

"She is free to go."

Rafi laughed. "Free? She says she will leave, but she is frightened of you."

"She is only afraid of being alone."

"As you are?"

"Now you give me a chance to laugh. You're about the last person on earth that thinks Sonya and I have a future together."

"You are my friend, and that is why I tell you these things. This is not right. For you or her. And"—Rafi lifted his glass to examine the contents—"we are all alone."

Andrew reached for the remote and turned to a classic movie channel. Some black-and-white gangster flick was playing. He kept the sound muted.

"And why do you do that? You could at least turn on the captioning, so I don't have to suffer with you here," Rafi said.

"Who's suffering? I'm relaxing."

"You don't know how."

"I'm enjoying the movie and listening to nothing. What do they call those?"

"Tommy Guns. That's Cagney. White Heat. If you turn it up, we could listen."

Andrew shook his head. How did this half-breed Afghani-Englishman know so much about American movies? He seemed to be an expert on everything American.

Rafi lopped his feet up on the coffee table. "You brought him here to irritate me."

"Enough about Scott. He's sneaking around to the other side of the house anyway. Having him report to us first keeps me in control."

"He is a swine. If you don't rid us of him, I will."

"Easy my friend. If anyone gets rid of Scott, it will be me."

"I have done some investigating on this Angela Lorda," Rafi said.

"She has no money to speak of. Owes a six-figure sum for past medical expenses. She barely has the capacity to pay her current bills. She is delinquent on one credit card but only by one month. And her daughter is barely better off. *She* works at a North End smoke shop, the place near Julio's Restaurant. They have a decent collection of cigars. Her hours were cut a week ago because of your overspending friends in Congress. Behind two months on her house payments until her mortgage note was mysteriously paid off a few days ago. In full."

Andrew punched the remote and tossed the device onto the coffee table. Cagney disappeared off the screen. He stood up and headed toward a row of floor-to-ceiling windows framing a wide view of houses dotting the foothills.

"I have upset you, yes?" Rafi said.

"What do *you* think she wants?"

"I think you know. But you tell me nothing. Nothing about the note."

"You're one to talk about saying nothing. The note doesn't concern you. Humor me. What do you think she wants?"

"She has something on you, true? We offer her money, she goes away. Or, we provide incentives for her cooperation. This is what I suggest. She and her daughter have no money. Her child has drugs in her past and probably in her present. She cannot care for the poor little grandchild, and family services should do something about that. Of course, the daughter's friend, the policeman you like so much, could be a minor irritant as well. We have dealt with him before."

"I *have* spoken to her," Andrew said, "and I intend to do so again."

Rafi showed no indication of surprise. "Your driver has told me this. You have made a serious error, my friend. You paid her price?"

"I'll forget you said that. Nevertheless, I want you to forget everything you know about her. This is a direct order and a request, in that order. You stay away from her, her daughter, and her granddaughter. No more investigation. No more following Angela Lorda around. Understood?"

"As you wish." Rafi held up his wine glass in a toasting gesture. "And Mr. Cooper?"

"Mr. Cooper should seek employment elsewhere. We should give him an incentive to relocate."

Chapter 11
Annie Lorda's Residence, North End, Boise
Monday Evening

The house was familiar. He'd grown up in one just like it—a small wooden box, a few bedrooms, an efficient kitchen, and a living room adequate for a sparse selection of antiques. The place was clean, and this woman obviously cared for what she could afford. Most of the flat areas—the top of an upright piano, the surface of two end tables bracketing a Victorian style couch, the mantle above a small brick fireplace, and the walls in the front hallway—were covered with family pictures. It was evident Angela Lorda came from a large family but had managed only one child herself.

The memories of Andrew's existence in Ontario, a small dust-ridden town along the Oregon-Idaho border, flashed in his head like an old movie. Struggling to find enough money to keep Andrew and his two brothers in coats, shoes, and clothes, his mother had always looked as though she would pass away from exhaustion. Lawrence Post, more of a stranger than a father, had been a field hand and a part-time mechanic who'd fled and never returned. Later in life, James, Andrew's younger brother, had told Andrew their mother cheated on their father, and that's why their father left. To this day, Andrew denied the story. His mother had been the one to hold the family together.

She had passed away thirty-five years ago just as Andrew was achieving his inaugural business success. He'd made a promise to pay her back someday, a promise her death had prematurely erased. This place, Angela Lorda's house, could have been his childhood home. The woman moving across the living room with the tray could have been his mother from those days so long ago.

"I hope hot tea is okay."

Andrew nodded.

"You frightened me at the door. You were the last person I expected to see." She offered him a cup. Her hands shook ever so slightly.

"I told you I would contact you, Mrs. Lorda."

"Make this easier and call me Annie."

"And call me Andrew, if you wish."

"I'm sorry for the mess. I might've cleaned a bit if I'd known..." Her voice trailed off as she straightened the tray on the table and sat on the couch across from Andrew. A mix of determination and sadness in her eyes spoke to him as they had at the store opening.

"There is nothing to clean," he said, scanning the room. "I feel like I'm trespassing just sitting on this fine furniture."

"My daughter says I'm the enemy of dust bunnies. Well, she has a more colorful name for them."

"Now the note—" He stopped and contemplated what to say. Words usually came easy. He was here for discovery—to find out what this woman wanted. Nothing more.

"I might've dressed nicer too. I had no idea you meant you would come to my house." She touched the collar of her bathrobe, peered into her tea cup, and then glanced out the window.

"I'm here alone," Andrew said. "Why the commotion? Why come to the store opening?"

"Right," the woman replied with a nervous smile. "I called your headquarters. Visited your building. Emailed you. Spoke to customer service, public affairs, and investor relations. Even found your house. Guess I was stupid, thinking I could walk up to you and have a conversation."

"It would have been a very public conversation."

"My plan was to hand you the note. That's all."

"You could have mailed it to me or handed it to one of my people."

"I didn't want to chance anything. I ended up passing it to one of your goons after all."

"They're my security detail, bodyguards if you will."

"Sorry. That's what Penny calls people like that."

"Well, your persistence paid off. I'm here."

She nodded. "Yes, I can see that."

"You believe your husband." It was more of a statement than a question.

"I believe my husband."

"And if you believe, then the person you have raised is not your true daughter. My flesh and blood as you would have it."

Annie Lorda put her cup on a Disneyland coaster on the coffee table. There was no shake in her hands this time. "Mr. Post. I've had a few days to digest all of this. I may not be the smartest person, but Penny is my daughter. I've raised her and I love her."

"I understand. But if you are correct, if your husband was telling the truth, your natural daughter passed away years ago."

"I can't change that."

"So you want money?"

"You put it so bluntly. I don't *want* anything. My daughter is a single mother, and she is related to the wealthiest man in the Northwest. She barely gets by. I barely get by. She's your flesh and blood. At the simplest level, I thought you would want to know the truth."

"Actually, I'm fourth."

"Sorry?"

"Fourth wealthiest," he said, "in the Northwest."

"Sorry, I don't have the scorecard."

"Touché."

They both paused. Neither spoke. Andrew was an expert negotiator. He would not play his hand yet. But he wanted to say something. Seconds passed like minutes. Was this woman feeling the same yearning to speak? Was she waiting *him* out?

"My people would say this sounds like blackmail." As the words left his lips, Andrew knew he may as well have thrown his cup of tea at the woman.

She reacted instantly. "I know what you're thinking. You're more worried about this going public, even if it isn't true. You don't want to be seen discrediting a poor widow. Maybe I force the issue and insist you are tested. Even if Frank was wrong—and he's not—I'd assume the whole affair would be a public relations fiasco for someone like you."

Tested. Andrew pursed his lips.

The exchange brought out a side of this woman he had not expected. She was tougher and more intelligent than her demeanor or background would suggest. Maybe even a threat. And she was pressing. Most likely she was acting out of character, trying her best to appear to be the one holding the upper hand. Or maybe it was a case of the mother being backed into an economic corner. "Desperate" was the word that kept creeping back into Andrew's mind. Desperate people did desperate things. That might work to his advantage. What she didn't know was that he held an ace up his sleeve. She wouldn't like the truth.

"Let's assume I don't care," he said. "Go public. Even if your husband actually pulled off such a stunt, what difference would it make?"

She scoffed. "Right." Their eyes met and then she looked away. "You have an incredibly successful daughter who is the heir to your business. I suspect that is of great importance to you. At least according to what I've read, it took you some time to recover from the issues with your marriage and such. Doubt you want anybody digging into your affairs again."

"My affairs are none—"

"Yes, I know, you've done nothing wrong. My husband is the bad guy here."

"Well—"

"Let me finish." She held her hand up in front of Andrew's face.

He sat back in the chair.

"Silence would benefit me, you, and our daughters," she said. "To speak out would serve no purpose. The intriguing part here is that people usually root for the little guys—in this case Penny and me."

She was correct. Andrew would not allow such an accusation to go public but for reasons this Angela Lorda could not understand.

He waited.

She paused as well, seeming to gather her thoughts. She continued. "I believe there is something else on your agenda."

"You have the floor."

She didn't hesitate. "You were almost able to hide my interaction with you at the store the other night. One of the policemen told me you had intervened. Had me released with no charges whatsoever. But you had to know you couldn't completely bury the story. That's impossible in this day and age. Then you show up at my daughter's house in broad daylight and at my church to have a conversation with me in front of the entire congregation. You *want* people to know something."

"And that would be what?"

She shrugged. "Maybe you're building up a defense already. You're helping the poor little woman and her daughter. And the mere fact you're here tells me something."

Lifting his teacup in a toasting manner, Andrew bowed his head. "You should work for me. Your logic is impeccable."

"Don't worry." Resignation filled her voice. "I don't plan on saying a word. I'd rather Penny not know. She has had a rough time, but now she's relatively happy. I suspect your Donny is happy too. I'd like to keep it like that. I just felt an obligation to let you know. Give you a chance to weigh in on the situation. Maybe give her what she deserves."

Angela Lorda's vow of silence was the key. Andrew had completed enough of his discovery. Clearly, she believed her husband. The story was hard to fathom. Maybe it was true, or maybe her husband had made up the story. Andrew knew little of her past. It was impossible to measure up motives regarding such an outlandish claim, especially her husband's motives. If she wasn't going public, what difference did it make? Let her believe what she wants to believe.

Had she forced the issue publicly, Andrew would have had two choices. Try and discredit her or pay her off. He would have chosen the latter. It would've marked the first time he'd been successfully blackmailed. If that didn't work, he might have to act like the man everyone thought he was. No matter, he could not risk people digging into the birth of his daughters.

With that out of the way, he was unsure of how to proceed. He always had a plan that included every contingency, but not this time. His gut told him to build her trust. Slowly.

"I'm at a loss. How would I 'give her what she deserves' without her knowledge of it?" he asked.

"You're kidding. Andrew Post can make a lot of things happen. Anybody from around here knows that. You don't have to flood her with money. Just make sure she's taken care of. Protected."

"With all due respect, your daughter will be on to us. As you stated, I'm sure she and a few others suspect something already."

"The shelf life of gossip is incredibly short."

"So your daughter will allow this to fade away? Even as I support her financially?"

"Absolutely not. She'll hound me until I either tell her or die, and I won't be the one to tell her. I meant the rest of the world would lose interest." She reached down and turned one of the empty coasters in line with the edge of the table. "Listen, I don't have a plan. I thought you should know about Penny. What's next is up to you. You want to get up and leave, that's your choice. You won't hear from me again. If you want to tell her the truth, then we need to talk about this some more because I'm not real comfortable with that."

"I certainly could," Andrew said, trying to feign disinterest, "walk away, that is." He paused to measure her reaction. Her face said, Don't leave.

"There is another option. A relationship between you and me." The spur of the moment idea spilled out of his mouth.

Angela Lorda's face looked like someone trying to interpret a foreign language.

He continued. "You said yourself my marriage is a farce. After the appropriate period, we break up. The press would favor us. A relationship with someone such as you would be great for the evening news and selling papers."

"Someone such as me? You mean some kind of low-life trailer-trash?"

Andrew shook his head. He'd blasted out some ridiculous proposal, and the woman's reaction was predictable.

He pressed on. "That would take care of everyone else, but not your daughter. She would want to know why you approached me in the first place." He snapped his fingers and leaned forward in the chair. "We could tell her that you and I had met before that night, and I had invited you to the opening. The arrest was simply a mix-up with security. I freed you as soon as I could. We could probably manufacture an alternate letter from your husband that makes some sense. It could work."

"It would be nice if you were serious and didn't mock my entire existence. Seriously, me and you. Someone such as me? It's the stuff of Hollywood, not real life. Some of those tabloid people might buy it. Penny would think I went off the deep end, though she thinks that already."

Andrew knew he had made a series of mistakes. In business, it rarely happened. In relationships, Rafi was right. He was a mess. He suddenly felt a need to backpedal. Angela Lorda was correct. He'd been dealing with her in plain view of the entire world, not because he had some grand plan, but due to simple carelessness. He would help the woman, but that would be the end of it.

"Mrs. Lorda—"

"You really expect me—"

"It's my turn." This time it was Andrew who put his hand out to halt the other half of the conversation. He stood, put his hands behind his back, and slowly walked the room as he spoke. "About four or five times a year someone threatens to sue me or my corporation for personal reasons. They claim I have ruined their company, their marriage, their neighborhood, even their soul. One woman claimed she bore my illegitimate child. An elderly man said my store employees in Redding, California, stole his pets, stuffed them, and put Barney and Ollie on display in the store. You see, when you have wealth, everyone wants a claim to what is yours. But even more important, when you have power, they want to strip it from you. They'll do anything to succeed. In the end, they always lose and I always win."

"You must be very proud," she said. "I may not have much, but I'm not an imbecile. I know who they say you are. A formidable and arrogant businessman. Maybe even—"

"A killer? Ah, the story always returns to Lacy Talbert. I suppose you believe I killed her too?"

"Well, that's not where I was going, but most everyone thought so."

"That's what the media implied. I can honestly tell you I've never killed anyone." He reached for his tea cup and took a sip. "I admit my mistake. I admit the affair."

"It cost you your marriage."

"Not so. Sonya and I have been together for forty years. We've lived together in the same house for the last thirty-two."

"Right. Lived together? Seriously?"

The conversation ceased. Angela Lorda returned to sipping tea and straightening items on the table. Andrew sat, leaned back, pretended to relax, and watched her intently. What was it about this woman? She was nondescript, totally opposite from both his elegant spouse and daughter. On the other hand, her personality was spirited, and she was surprisingly articulate. She was either absolutely honest or working some masterful scheme.

"I'm no killer, Mrs. Lorda." Andrew felt like he needed to say it again.

She looked at the ceiling and laughed. "Now that's a good quality to have. Whatever your sins, I'm not the one to judge you."

"You believe money will bring happiness to your child? Your family? Closure to your life?"

"I never mentioned money, but it wouldn't hurt. Let me ask you something, Mr. Post. Do you only provide money for your daughter? What about love and support? Spirituality, morals, and guidance? A place to go? Some safe haven if things get bad? It's what parents do."

"But you said you don't want your daughter to know me. I'm not the good guy in your eyes. What else could I give but money?"

"I don't know! Maybe she can know you. I don't have all the answers. Protect her. Support her. I only have so much to give." She paused, then continued with a soft laugh, "Look at me. You mock me with your affair suggestion. I even considered it, for a split second. Not an affair, just a friendship of some kind. But I know you're playing with me—some kind of game that I don't understand. You come in here all nice and then try to turn the tide by acting like I'm blackmailing you. Listen closely to my every word and then threaten me in some subtle way. Probably the same kind of game you play in your everyday world. The least you can do is love her as if she did know the truth."

"You don't believe I can do that, do you?"

"I don't believe *you* believe you can do that."

Andrew placed the tea cup on the tray and gathered his overcoat and hat. This woman had the upper hand. "I must admit, you are either the most honest person I have ever met, or you have a great act. If it's the latter, it will turn out to be a serious mistake."

She sat unperturbed. "You're running away."

He started for the front door. Now he was the one who couldn't look into *her* eyes.

"If you had doubts about my story, why the payoff?" she asked. "It would have made sense to have more information before shuffling money our way."

Andrew stopped and started to speak.

She cut him off. "Why did you pay off my daughter's house?"

He placed the hat on his head. "There is no evidence I was involved in such an act. If I were to do such a thing, it would be a gesture of goodwill."

Her expression narrowed and her words came very fast. "In case I was going to blackmail you. In case I was going to spill the truth. Some kind of insurance policy or down payment. Is this how your game is played? Or maybe you really did want to do it. Or maybe you just want to confuse the hell out of me. Well, mission accomplished!"

"Oh, please," Andrew said, "have me tested! First, it will take every dollar you have to hire enough lawyers to force the issue. You won't win, and you'd have to go public. Second, you won't get the results you want. In fact, we can skip the lawsuits."

He took a step toward the woman, tilted his hat upwards, and stared into her mounting scowl. "I'll be glad to do it, and I'll even foot the bill."

She said nothing. Her face said it all.

He softened as he turned for the door. "Consider the money a gift. You owe me nothing. I owe you nothing. We're even." He tipped his hat and opened the front door. "Thank you for the tea and for being such a gracious hostess."

Chapter 12
Donny Post's Apartment, Downtown Boise
Monday Evening

The security guard waved the key in front of the elevator card reader. "Hope you've had your shots, Detective." The guard snuck out just as the door closed.

The elevator raced upward nonstop to the 18th floor. The car came to rest, and Matt exited into a small antiseptic lobby containing a cushioned bench that resembled a church pew, a table with a house phone, a fresh floral arrangement, and a single door with the words "Penthouse Suite" engraved in script on a gold name plate.

He started to turn back toward the elevator. He heard a metallic tap, and the door to the suite opened. Donny Post stood before him, eye to eye, slicked-up in a pinstriped women's business suit, barefoot, her pure black hair curved across her cheekbones in the medium shag she had been sporting recently.

"Little late for work," he said, trying to break the ice.

"We work 24/7." She stuck her forefinger in her mouth, examined Matt from head to toe, and pushed the door open just enough for him to enter.

The instinct to flee was mounting. Matt had questioned many a person in Boise and never ran across someone he couldn't handle. But none of those people were Donny Post. None walked or smelled like Donny. She was like a drug, the crack cocaine of sexuality.

His phone started to vibrate. He glanced at the screen. It read "Penny." It may as well have read "guilty." He didn't answer.

"You coming?" She pushed the door open wider, let it go, and started toward the interior of the flat. He caught the door before it shut and crossed the threshold.

A backlit waterfall against an obsidian wall stood in his path just inside the door. To the left was a living room that deserved its own name. Black leather chairs and a wraparound white couch sat in front of a spectacular glass table that seemed to generate its own light. Two enormous flat-screen televisions hung on the wall on either side of a see-through fireplace bricked by decorative granite blocks. An aquarium filled with exotic fish lined the back of the longest segment of the couch. A floor-to-ceiling view of downtown Boise extended around half the room.

"You can do what you want in here. You can see out, but they can't see in." The breath of her words stirred the hairs on his neck. Somehow she'd managed to sneak up behind him. Some cop, he thought.

Donny moved in front of him, threw her jacket toward one of the chairs, pulled her shirt out from her skirt, and wiggled slightly. "How do you like the place? Unzip me."

"I think you can manage. It's a bit more than a cop can afford."

"The zipper or the place? Only been in for three months. I love it already."

This was a bad idea. He should have met Donny at work, but being seen in public with her usually led to problems. For him, not her. She had no qualms about generating trouble between him and Penny.

"You're no fun." She reached back and let the skirt fall to the floor. The scene was like a flash in a music video. He wasn't certain whether he saw bare skin under the skirt or some small fragment of lace. Her shirt fell fast to her thighs, hiding the answer to this question he shouldn't be pondering at the moment.

His pulse pumped as if he had passed the tenth or eleventh mile marker on his bicycle, traversing the steep Bogus Basin Road. Despite a chilling temperature in the room, a trickle of sweat dripped down the middle of his back.

Donny picked up her skirt and started around the corner to the right of the waterfall. He thought it best to stay put.

He yelled in the direction of her exit. "Why would your father be interested in Penny?"

A muffled voice replied, "Why are you asking me?"

"It's not healthy to question your father."

There was no answer. The intent was to gain as much as possible from Donny without telling her too much. Nothing came without a price. She would want something for each piece of information she gave away.

A minute or two later she appeared dressed in athletic sweats. Matt was relieved but also disappointed.

"Come in the kitchen. I can have Orlando conjure up something exquisite for a late dinner. You hungry?"

Matt looked around. He'd not heard any servants or any other noise other than the hum of the fish tank. "I ate with the peasants a few hours ago."

"Nice," she replied with a mock smile, licking the small scar on her lip. "Over there." Donny pointed to a floor-to-ceiling wine rack in the back of a kitchen that was the size of a small condo. "Pour me a glass of Riesling. The unmarked bottle on the second shelf."

"Your own brand?"

"A present from a friend in the business."

She tossed him a corkscrew, and he went to work. "Thought you'd have a machine or a servant to open the wine."

"I do have one." She squinted and smiled, as if she held deep, dark secrets.

"This Orlando—"

"He's my chef on demand. Probably over at Father's tonight."

"And the people that keep this place so spotless?"

"Why," she said in her best Scarlet O'Hara imitation, "I assure you, Matthew, we are alone."

"I like to know who might be listening."

She opened one of four stainless steel built-in refrigerator doors and pulled out yogurt and a tangerine.

"That's dinner?" he asked.

"I can eat more if you think you might need more to hold onto." She pulled back the edge of the tangerine peel with her teeth and instantly unclothed the fruit from its cover.

Donny had not lost her skill at luring the opposite sex into her lair. Matt had known her since elementary school, though she'd rarely attended anything remotely related to public education. They'd met at Bogus Basin in a ski racing event. Even at twelve years old, she could disable any young boy's common sense. She was the first girl he'd kissed, and the first he'd made love to, though there was about a five year separation between the two events. Both days he'd never forget.

"Your little friend. She has nicer love handles." Donny pulled up her shirt, revealing a toned mid-section, and pulled her sweats down on her hip. "Not much to hold onto here. Why don't you fetch me some cheesecake, and I'll see what I can do."

"Donny—"

"Suit yourself." She jumped up backwards onto the kitchen island and started on the yogurt. "What can I help you with? You know I'd do anything for you." The tone was instantly businesslike.

Matt handed her the glass of wine and leaned over the island at the other end. He paused to consider what he should reveal. "I saw your father the other night. He was out in the rain. He'd been at Penny's house."

She shook her head and said nothing. She pushed a spoon of yogurt into her mouth, savoring each bite.

"He walked up the sidewalk, looked into her front door, and left."

"You followed him?"

"No, but it was him. Trust me."

"Sure," she said, working the bottom of the yogurt cup.

"And?"

Donny tossed the cup toward the sink. It hit on two sides and almost bounced out but fell back in. "Two points. My shoulders are aching. Could you rub them a bit while we talk about this?" She pulled her top off, revealing a thin, white tank top.

Within seconds she was leaning back against Matt with her head tilted down.

The room was quiet save the remote hum of traffic on the street below and bubbling noises coming from the fish tank. A pleasant chime pinged ten times somewhere in the room with the giant televisions.

"Okay," she said, "I'll talk. You rub. Deal?"

Matt placed his hands on her shoulders. She started to make quiet noises that could have come out of the triple X joint he'd raided on the outskirts of town.

She reached up and placed her forefingers under the straps. "If it would make this easier, this can come off."

He pushed her hands back down. "No need. I can reach everything I need to already."

"What do you know about Annie Lorda and Father?" she asked. Donny was a master. She would give away just enough to keep him interested. She'd made a career out of this behavior, not just to Matt and not just for sex, but for everything she wanted.

He stopped the massage. "Let me ask the questions."

"Surely you know she was arrested for stalking my father?"

The massage continued. "Keep talking."

"You know Angela Lorda was arrested last week at the opening of our new Meridian superstore, which I pretty much designed by the way." She leaned her head back into Matt's chest.

He took his fingers away. She leaned up again and tilted her head downward. He continued the massage.

"You are serious, Officer Downing. Maybe you should cuff me. Keep me under control."

He pushed her away and started toward the front door. This was going nowhere, and the guilt was bubbling up in his throat like he'd just left a truck stop diner. He'd reached the entryway when he heard her call out, "Okay. Okay."

She'd not come running, yet this was about as much compromise as he'd expect from Donny.

They both made their way into the living room. She plopped

sideways on one of the two leather chairs, and he sat at the end of the couch a few feet away. She'd put her sweatshirt back on. A hint of disappointment tugged at Matt. Her body was a work of art, and even with the constant barrage of sexual innuendo, he still liked to look at it. Though he'd never tell her, he loved to touch it as well.

Donny spoke first, returning to her businesslike tone. "You've been after my father for years. Is it for me or you?"

"What?"

"Father doesn't want me associating with you—the simple cop." She smiled, her teeth as white as ivory. "You've been trying to bring him down since you started this cop thing. I'm sure you're a bit frustrated in more ways than one."

"I think we've been over this before. Your father thinks he's above the law. Can you keep to the subject?"

"This *is* the subject. You're obsessed with my father and you know it. Why not add me to your obsession? I'm game, even if Father is not."

Matt shook his head. Silence ensued.

Finally Donny spoke up. "As you wish. Father has been acting a bit strange, I'll admit. I'm sure he has his reasons for toying with this woman." The tone when she said "woman" was pure disdain. "But she also might have something on him, and he is personally working the issue. A little out of the ordinary. Is this official police business?"

"Huh?"

"Is this off the record?"

The question caught Matt by surprise. "Sure, off the record."

"They've been passing notes."

"Again?"

"Notes. Wednesday night, that woman gave Father a note. Actually, she convinced Big J, one of Father's bodyguards, to hand-deliver it. They thought she was pulling a gun, and it all ended in one big fucking circus. What a PR nightmare!"

"Might've been nice to let the police have a look at the note."

"Why not ask her about it yourself? She's like your mother, right?"

"Can we keep this professional?"

"I can." Donny winked and touched the scar on her lip with the tip of her tongue. Matt wanted to look away but found himself staring.

She continued. "Okay, after every schmo in town figured out who Angela Lorda was, after the *Tribune* printed that picture, we told the press she was released due to pressure from Post Corporation lawyers. The *Tribune* actually printed it. It made your police buddies over in

Meridian look bad. Brilliant move on our part. Actually, I had no idea why she was released, but the trail led back to Father."

"It was a bit more than that. I checked with Meridian PD. Someone made certain that any official record of what happened that night disappeared. Never happened. No police report, nothing. I had a friend of mine at the paper ask for a copy of any reports related to the incident. Just to double-check. Sure enough the Meridian PD said it had been misplaced." Matt's phone buzzed on his hip. He ignored it. "You said traded notes?"

"She came to the office the next day. Sat in the lobby for a while. Father wouldn't see her. He sent her a new jacket and a note of his own."

Matt considered this new piece of information. Anyone who knew Andrew Post knew he was unapproachable and was careful with anyone who might be dealing threats. The man and his corporation lived on the margins of the law, and his success seemed to hinge on his personal un-involvement.

"Don't suppose you know anything about the content of either note?" he asked.

"Nope. She might have something on him. Or maybe he's scheming. Neither Father nor Rafi are talking about it, and I don't ask. Has nothing to do with me. One more thing. Off the record?"

"Yep."

"He visited her house earlier tonight. Might still be there."

"How do you know this?"

"His driver has a thing for me. Called me earlier to chat and told me he dropped Father off. Now it's your turn."

Worry mixed with a surge of excitement. Matt was hoping some clean explanation could push all these events aside and put some distance between Annie and Penny, and Andrew Post. Yet it was clear the Lorda family had drawn the interest of Post. He needed to find out why.

"Your turn," she repeated.

"For what?"

"I told you something, you tell me something." Her tone was terse, as if she had suddenly transformed the conversation into a business deal. "Lay it on the table."

Matt stood and paced, wondering what else he could give up. "Okay. Someone paid off Penny's mortgage. I thought it was a mistake. Went over to First State this morning, and Cecil Benson, one of the VPs, wouldn't tell me anything. Acted like it was a big mystery.

Said he'd check into it, but I get the feeling nobody at First State will be knocking at my door with information."

"Maybe you got the wrong bank," Donny said, sipping the wine and suddenly seeming disinterested.

"She has the paperwork and four years of monthly statements. Your father could pull off something like that. In fact, I think he delivered the documentation to Penny's house after the note was paid."

"In person!"

"Yes."

"No shit! She must have something big. He usually brushes the riffraff aside and lets Rafi deal with it. Hopefully, your little friend and her mother know who they're playing with."

Matt stopped his pacing and stood over Donny. "Now it's your turn."

"Nothing else." She leaned her neck over the arm of the couch and arched her back. "Just me and my starved body left."

He started toward the door. "Thanks."

"You don't have to go. I'm behaving." She smiled, her bare feet hanging off the couch, kicking like a bored child. "Stay and have dinner. We can sit on the couch and watch the lights...the fish...whatever. Reminisce about old times. We could have an encore. You pooped out on my sixteenth birthday."

"Pooped out? I had a lifetime of liquor and sex in one night. And I've paid for it for way too long."

"You missed me?" She mocked a seductive smile that made him recall that night.

The event was Donny's sixteenth birthday bash on Payette Lake in McCall, a party every kid in Boise had wanted to attend. He'd ridden up with Duane Yaeger on a Friday night with every intention of returning on Saturday morning so he could catch Penny's birthday party in Boise. Somehow he ended up in New Meadows in another cabin alone with Donny and with what seemed like an entire liquor store. The memories of that night, his first, were like a book with pages missing. It wasn't the young boy and girl experimenting. It was a drunken boy and a woman who wouldn't quit. There were things he did that night that he was sure would never be repeated in his life. It was shameful and intoxicating—like Donny.

By the time he'd sobered up, it was Saturday evening and Duane Yaeger had left him behind. He'd missed Penny's party in Boise. To make matters worse, he was one of only ten kids who had been invited. Others told him Penny had seemed unexcited and distant, always looking for him to show. That next week, he and Penny spoke. She never mentioned the party. He tried to apologize, but she quickly changed the subject. To this day, she does not speak of that birthday party or Donny's. And to this day, he has been hands-off to Donny and, in his own confusion, to Penny too.

"Stay," Donny said, patting the leather on the couch.

Matt looked at the ceiling. "You and Penny were born a day apart." This simple fact he'd known all his life suddenly became interesting.

"Same hospital, Sherlock. Hard to believe they'd put me in the same room with your girl."

This fact he had not known. "You never mentioned you were in the same hospital."

"Never asked. Kind of irrelevant, don't you think?"

"What time were you born?"

Donny laughed. "Father said I can wait out the competition in negotiations because I was born five minutes before midnight." Then the smile disappeared. "My sister was officially born the next day. I would've liked to have had a sister."

Matt barely heard the response. His mind was racing with a new infusion of information. The Posts and the Lordas were somehow intertwined. Related in some way. And now the two women in his life, past and present, had been born in the same hospital on the same night.

He reached the front entryway. Donny was still in the chair, sipping her wine. "Hey," he said softly. She didn't respond. Her face was pointed away toward the windows and the lights of the outside world.

A vibration from his phone indicated a new message. The screen displayed text from Muholland, the Desk Sergeant on the evening shift. Said to meet deputies from Boise County up at Lucky Peak Reservoir concerning an abduction.

He reached for the door handle, stopped, and turned around. She was what all men dreamed about late at night, but in real life, they had best keep their distance.

Right now her solitary figure on the couch reminded him of how lonely she appeared at times. That's what kept drawing him back. She needed him.

Chapter 13
Near Lucky Peak Reservoir, Boise County
Midnight Tuesday

The nine-year-old Ford Ranger coughed as it topped the small hill on Highway 21 near Lucky Peak Dam. Fed by the Boise River, Lucky Peak Reservoir sat above the city and provided residents with forty-five miles of shoreline and three thousand acres of summer recreation. Surrounded by sagebrush covered hills, it truly appeared as an oasis. This time of year snowmelt would have filled the reservoir, and the summer season would be underway. The recent unusual cold spell had kept the boaters at home, so Matt knew any fun on the lake would be a few days premature.

At the top of the hill, he took a right onto the three hundred and forty foot high earthen dam, crossed to the other side, passed a boat ramp, and drove a half mile down the far shore. Flashing lights from patrol vehicles and the absence of the moon created an eerie amphitheater-like scene along the hills that bordered the lake.

There were two vehicles, both SUVs, with their search lamps pointed at a silver Mercedes CL Class Coupe. The identity of the owner of the Coupe was obvious. Not many people in Boise drove that kind of car.

One of the Boise County deputies, someone Matt didn't recognize, was pacing around one of the SUVs, and the other deputy, Duke Sholley, towered over the Coupe, staring down at an occupant in the front seat. Both men stopped and squinted into the headlamps of the approaching truck.

Sholley fingered his sidearm as Matt turned off the lights and opened the door.

"Duke, it's me, Matt Downing."

Deputy Sholley looked relieved, as if he'd just figured out he wasn't going have to shoot someone after all.

Matt made his way to the car, leaned down, and noted Fenton Cooper slumped over in the driver's seat, unconscious. He wore only a dress shirt and boxer shorts. "What've you got?"

Sholley looked thrilled to report something big. His booming voice cracked as he spoke. "The girl is in Zap's car. We got a call. Anonymous."

Through the rays of light, it was difficult to make out the occupant of the other police vehicle twenty feet away. "That's it?" Matt said.

Sholley patted him on the shoulder. "You told me if we ever had anything involving Post to give you a call. So I gave you a call."

"And I appreciate that, Duke."

"We got word this sixteen-year-old was abducted, and the suspect might be headed to the lake. We started over here and found the car straight away. Looks like statutory rape or worse. Girl won't talk. Traumatized, I suppose."

"How do you know she's sixteen?"

"Caller said so. She ain't got no ID."

Matt frowned. A gentle breeze started to ramp into a real wind. He walked back to his truck and put on his jacket, lifted the seat, pulled a blanket from the rear of the cab, and brought it over to Sholley. "Put this around Mr. Cooper."

Sholley bellowed. "The bum is dead drunk. You ask me, we ought to drag him a few times around the lakeshore."

Matt opened the door and tucked the blanket around Cooper. He patted the man's cool face a few times to no avail. There was no discernible smell of alcohol. He felt Cooper's pulse. It was erratic.

He headed for the SUV where the new officer had been pacing. It contained a young girl he recognized as Melody Westerfeld, a dropout from Boise High with a sporadic record that ranged from shoplifting to mild drug use. She appeared to be sober and clean.

"What's going on here, Melody?" he said gently.

Her appearance was typical—hip-hugging jeans with holes everywhere, a shirt two sizes too small, and enough mascara to make her eyes seem swollen. She couldn't have weighed more than ninety pounds.

Her head turned away, she stared out the opposite window. "Officers say this man abducted you," Matt whispered. "Seems like a wild story to me. You're too smart for that."

"She ain't sayin' much." The other deputy approached and held out his hand. "Sammy Zapeka. Started last month. Up from San Angelo."

They shook hands. Matt said nothing. He was thinking about how the situation might fit with the rest of the strange Post happenings of the last few days.

"Texas. San Angelo, Texas. She a bit young, ain't she?"

Matt motioned the new deputy toward the other SUV, where Sholley was now standing.

"This girl is always in trouble." Matt spoke quietly, though there probably wasn't anyone within five miles except for the victim, the suspect, and the three officers. "Any idea where the anonymous call came from?"

Both deputies shrugged. "We can check on it," Zapeka said. "Dispatch took the call."

"Did the car smell like alcohol when you got here?"

The two deputies glanced at each other.

"It wasn't strong," Sholley said.

"She say she was abducted? Raped?"

"She don't say nothing," Zapeka said, kicking dirt with his boots. "We found her in there, half-dressed, and that fella nearly naked. We put two and two together or one and one." Zapeka laughed and Sholley howled.

"Why didn't you call for an ambulance?"

"He's drunk," Sholley said.

"You boys taking them up to Idaho City?"

"This is at least statutory," Sholley stated, staring at his fellow deputy for confirmation. "Be bringing all this down to Boise anyway. Could be kidnapping."

Matt made the appropriate calls and then walked over to Cooper's car. He disliked Cooper, but he had the sense that all was not as it appeared to be.

The front passenger door was open. The keys were on the floor. He pulled out his flashlight and lit up the backseat. A pair of nicely folded pants sat on the seat behind the driver, and a coat jacket lay rumpled on the floor. He put on a pair of Latex gloves he carried in his pocket, opened the driver's side door, and pushed a button to pop the trunk. It was empty save a cheap ten dollar blanket.

"Where are the guy's shoes?" he asked.

The two deputies, in conversation near Sholley's SUV, shrugged their shoulders.

Around the area, he could find only the Mercedes tracks in the dirt. All around the car, there were boot prints, most looking as though they had come from the investigating officers.

The cool nighttime wind was becoming downright cold. Stars were out and abundant. Matt returned to his truck and got inside to wait for the investigative unit and ambulance to arrive from Boise. He'd be out here for hours. He looked at the torn carpet, the beat-up dash, and the heater vent hanging to the floor on the passenger side. Then he glanced back at the car caught in the bright beams of light and thought of Donny. And Penny.

Chapter 14
Boise PD Headquarters
Tuesday Morning

The morning was cool enough for Matt to keep his jacket on as he sailed through the parking lot of the Boise Police Headquarters at double his normal pace. He should've been tired, but he was pumped. Fenton Cooper would be in the Ada County Jail, and he had a few questions stored up after last night's investigation at the lake. He'd said nothing to the Boise County guys given the near certainty they were not involved in the incident, and he had been quiet when the Boise PD investigative unit arrived, yet he harbored doubts about Cooper's guilt.

He reached the front door of the jail. The entryway smelled like burnt coffee. A slight breeze sent some pieces of newspaper in a circle in front of the door. He swatted at one and missed.

Inside, he checked his gun at a window that looked like a convenience store setup in a bad neighborhood. He nodded to the cop behind the glass.

A loud buzz ensued, and he tugged on a door that responded with a thumping metallic clink. He entered another guard observation area, waved his hand, and stood in front of another door. Buzz and clink.

Down the hall, he passed three cells and turned to face Cooper in cell C4, where he had delivered him last night. The cell was empty. He examined the rooms on either side, though he was sure C4 was correct.

Billie Maxwell, a good-natured guard, waddled down the hall and disappeared into another hallway a few feet away from Matt.

"Hey Billie."

The man's head craned backward into view, as if someone pulled him with a cane. "Hey, Matt. Goin' home. I'm beat."

"Where's Cooper? C4. Remember, I brought him in last night."

"Some fellas came by, talked to him, then he got released."

"What fellas?"

"Bunch of high rollers in suits. Looked like Post company men. Maybe a lawyer or two." Billie came back into full view and scratched his chin. "I did recognize one of 'em. That camel jock crook. He talk a long time to that Cooper boy. I was in the guard station with Bo. They looked pretty intense. You should've talked to him last night."

"He was still a bit out of it," Matt said. "Maybe I should have."

Captain Lewis, Matt's supervisor, sat behind the glass of his office, staring at a pile of papers neatly stacked on his desk. Square-headed and a straight-shooter, Lewis was the only black cop on the force and the only black guy Matt knew well. Lewis didn't seem any different than anyone else on the force. He spoke a lot about escaping Atlanta and his new life as the ultimate minority in Boise. And he joked a lot about Idaho, but he sure seemed to like it.

Usually, Matt tapped on the glass and waited for Lewis's nod to enter. This time he threw open the door and nearly dislodged a cheap set of mini blinds attached to the inside.

"Where the hell is Cooper?"

Lewis folded his hands on his desk on top of the stack of documents. "Sit down."

"I'd rather stand."

"If you want to discuss Fenton Cooper, either sit down or get the hell out of my office. It's been a crappy morning already."

Staring at Matt, Captain Lewis sat with his hands clasped, his eyes unblinking. Matt remained standing for a few seconds and then sat down on an uncomfortable chair that purposefully put him below the height of the man on the other side of the desk.

Lewis stood up, walked to the door, and gave it just the right amount of push for it to close tight. He grabbed the stack of papers and shoved them across his desk. "Suppose you think my job is all ice cream and ponies."

Matt thumbed through the papers. The most important one was an order from Judge Craddick to release Cooper based on preliminary evidence of a botched investigation. He mumbled to himself. "They're not even charging this guy? All this before eight in the morning?" He raised his head and his voice. "How did they pull this off so fast? Judge C worked this in the middle of the night?"

Lewis shook his head, surveying the detective work area out his window.

"Cap, I came in here this morning to interrogate Cooper because I thought he might've been set up."

"I saw your report from last night. Nothing like that in it."

"Did you read it? The man's pants were neatly folded on the backseat, his shoes were missing, no bottles or evidence of alcohol in the car, and he passed my breath-smelling and field sobriety tests. You see what the station test showed?"

"Don't see we did one."

"I watched Stewart do it. Took two of us to get him to breath into the tube. He wasn't drunk. He was drugged."

"Maybe so, but I don't see it in this folder on my desk. Could be that's part of your botched investigation," Lewis said in a tone suggesting he didn't believe his own words.

"I'll find the test results. If you abducted somebody and were going to do them, you think you'd fold your pants in the back seat and lose your shoes?"

"Sucker's a little flaky."

"This guy is as smart as they come. And Melody. She might've gone with the guy voluntarily, but this was no abduction. You ask me, Cooper was drugged, driven out to the lake by someone else, and our girl was given some cash or drugs for her part."

"Who would frame this guy? The bad guys came to get him out. You find evidence of anyone else out there?"

"No, but there were prints everywhere. The county boys trampled the place and put their paws all over the vehicle. I wouldn't dismiss the possibility that Melody was the driver. I still need to check with Sholley about the anonymous call. Somehow the caller knew Melody was sixteen years old. Kind of detail that tells me the caller knew a lot more."

"Son, it's best you move on to other business. Sounds like your county boys didn't do much of a job out there."

"You're kidding."

"Come on, Downing. Move on. Every time something happens remotely related to Post, you're right there. Somebody is covering on this one, you're the only one who's concerned, and they ain't gonna pay any attention to you. Let it go."

"Just doing my job," Matt said, remembering Donny's similar accusation last night.

Lewis frowned. "Your job? You've been on the force about ten years?"

Matt stood, turned away from Lewis, and looked through the half-shuttered blinds on the office door.

"There's the time you stopped Rafi Thuban for running a stop sign. Before we could get a marked unit there, you had pretty much taken his car apart. Nearly got you suspended. Then you jumped into the Talbert case, and you were still a street cop. You were in Salt Lake before I knew what had happened. Had to get you back here before those white boys threw you in jail. You were convinced something serious happened to Evan Smith, the Post guy you befriended before he upped and went home to Florida. The Flaco conspiracy. The disappearance of Sonya Post." Lewis laughed. "Yep, you came out smelling real good when her royal highness showed up here, wondering why people were searching for her. You thought Post might've killed her. You want more?"

Matt sat back in the chair and rubbed his hands over his face.

"You were caught in unofficial surveillance of the Post residence last year. Fortunately, only Brevard and I know about that. Now this thing with Fenton Cooper. Pete Jones over in the Payette PD said you told him to contact you if anything to do with Post came up. Who else you got watching out for Post conspiracies? If you weren't so good at the rest of your job, I'd can your ass in a heartbeat." Lewis paused. "I thought you were getting over this."

"I get it. I get it." Matt stood again. He wanted to lash out. Shake the captain by the shoulders. Surely he could see the other side of this story—that Post circumvented the law once again for his own gain. "So you don't believe Post had anything to do with this Cooper setup?"

"Maybe," said the captain. "But that's part of their game. I know it's none of our business. My business or your business. The man has the green and the power that goes with it. He's going to win every time."

"You believe that?"

"Doesn't matter. I'm going to do something I should've done long ago. You are to officially keep your nose out of the Post's business for good. I don't want you near him unless he's running down the street, waving a gun in the air. Even then, you call me first. Got it?"

Matt said nothing. He slumped back into the chair.

"I've been ordered by the chief to cooperate," Lewis said. "Cooper's been released."

"Who showed up this morning?"

"Not at liberty."

"Come on. Sanchez Brothers?"

"Maybe," Lewis said, his eyes tracking something outside the office window. "Jesus, this morning won't end. The full package is on her way in."

Matt turned in time to see Donny approach the office door. He reached over, turned the handle, and let the door fall open.

She tapped her fingers on the stencil of Lewis's name on the glass.

"Captain. Mr. Downing. Or I guess I should address you as Officer Downing."

"What can we do for you?" Lewis said.

She reached down to the floor to pick up a Styrofoam coffee cup.

Her skirt hiked up a pair of dark hose to about mid-thigh. Both men followed the hem intently as it rose and returned to its home just above her knee. She tossed the cup into the trash can.

"Two points," Matt said.

"Cute." She smiled insincerely. "I was told by some flunky out front that Fenton Cooper was released this morning. I came to pick him up and rip you people from limb to limb about whatever bogus charges you've concocted. I've got a call into our lawyers." She leaned on the desk with both palms down, directly facing Lewis. Matt glanced over at her profile.

She ever so slightly turned her chin. "Like what you see?"

He ignored the comment. He thought it interesting Donny was not privy to this morning's proceedings and to the release of her latest conquest.

"You should fire that little twerp in the front. I don't think he even knew who I was—at first. Who bailed Cooper out?"

Lewis faked a smile. "Wasn't bailed out. The charges were dropped."

"Mr. Thuban was here this morning?"

Lewis nodded, uncrossed his arms, and leaned over the desk.

Donny moved forward to counter his move. They were only about a half a foot apart. Matt knew it was a challenge he wouldn't win, but the captain might.

"Who dropped the charges? Wicker?"

"You have a need to know?" Lewis asked.

"No, but you can tell me anyway. Let's keep this civil."

"It was Montrose and Judge Craddick."

Matt couldn't believe it. His own boss, seconds ago under some kind of gag order, was now a flood of information for the woman standing in front of him. And Max Montrose, the State Attorney General, had arranged to have the charges dropped in the middle of the night. He knew Craddick was in their pocket, but this was impressive.

Donny's phone blared out some rock anthem Matt couldn't identify. She grabbed the phone faster than he could draw his firearm.

"Roberto, what the hell is going on?" There were a few 'uh-huhs.' She interrupted. "Whatever. Are we going to sue these bastards?" She listened for a microsecond and then fumed. "The fucking cops! The city! They are trying to screw with one of my employees." She looked directly at Matt as she said it.

The conversation ended without a thank-you or a goodbye. She pocketed the smartphone with one expert swipe and was gone before the two men could say another word.

"Well, thanks. You can spill your guts to her but leave me in the dark." Matt started for the door.

"You want to know what I really think?" Lewis said.

Matt did want to know. Though the captain might follow the company line, he had a nose for the truth.

"Cooper's leaving town. What does that tell you?"

Matt shrugged his shoulders. "Seems strange. How do you know?"

"Billie heard part of the conversation in the jail this morning. Mr. Thuban told your friend Cooper to leave and not come back. Said if he showed his face again in the state of Idaho, he'd be back in jail."

"Yeah?"

The captain grinned. "Yeah. There's some good that came from this morning. He's leaving town. That tells me Cooper was set up and in return for his exit, he gets to stay out of jail. They want him gone. Nothing worse than statutory rape on your resume."

"Why wouldn't they just fire him?"

The captain thought for a minute. "Probably knows a few Post secrets. They want him running scared."

"So I was right. And you lectured me."

"What I said stands. You stay away from the Posts."

Chapter 15
Post Corporation Headquarters, Boise
Tuesday Evening

Rafi pulled a lighter from his pocket and lit the cigar. The sickly aroma hit Andrew from memory before the first puff came his way.

"Can't you take that Cuban death stick somewhere else?"

Rafi blew an impossibly thin circle into the air and watched it float and expand until it disappeared. "Honduran. You should try one."

Andrew took the seat at the other end of his office conference table. "I can breathe yours for free. What do you pay for those things?"

Rafi held the cigar out in front of him, examining it, a look of satisfaction on his face. "You, my friend, are a connoisseur of the finest garments and wine. You would insist on the finest cigars."

"Honduran?"

"They do not cost the most, but they are the best."

Andrew folded his hands on the table, unsure of what and how much to say to his longtime associate. They held reviews of the business day every evening in his office. The discussion centered on issues they did not want to talk about in front of the management team. They shared information and ideas freely and held back nothing. Until now.

Rafi was starting to show his age. His short dark hair and closely groomed beard featured as many streaks of grey as black. His eyes, points of darkness, seemed tired yet content.

The Post Corporation profits correlated nicely with the rise of Rafi in the organization. Andrew remembered their initial meeting in Sacramento on the loading dock of the first Post Sporting Goods store in California. The store had achieved remarkable profitability in its first year of operation, surpassing stores in Washington and Oregon that had been open for a decade or more. The store manager said much of the success was due to his young Arab assistant. He added that despite having a work visa, Rafi was being harassed and might be booted out of the country.

Andrew suggested an immediate introduction. At the time, Rafi was thinner, clean-shaven, and fresh with entrepreneurial spirit. Within the first five minutes of conversation, he'd relayed his ideas about inventory management and leveraging off the California lifestyle for marketing and promotions. Yet he spoke with a thick accent and seemed to be at odds with the West Coast aura. Later Andrew learned he was a Pashtun, not an Arab, and came from an English mother and an Afghani father. He had a wife—or wives if the rumors were true—and family somewhere in Pakistan, possessed a B.S. and M.S. from UCLA in Anthropology, but otherwise remained a complete mystery.

Within a few months, Rafi Thuban was relocated to the Post Headquarters in downtown Boise, Idaho. Within a year and at the insistence of Sonya, who seemed to hit it off with the young man, Rafi moved up to executive assistant and was on his way to becoming a citizen. Andrew had called in several favors, but the price was a bargain, considering the return on investment. Rafi never asked about the government's sudden change of heart. He simply morphed into the most loyal and valuable employee in the Post organization.

"Tell me about Denver," Andrew said.

Rafi placed his cigar on the edge of the table and put his hands behind his head. "Yes, yes. All under control. No worries."

"You said that in the staff meeting. What's happening? Who is this councilman Heber?"

An ear-to-ear smile appeared on Rafi's face. "He happens to be having an affair, a most fortunate situation for us."

Andrew paced the room, his hands behind his back.

"You seem worried, my friend," Rafi said.

"No."

"Preoccupied?"

Andrew did not answer.

Rafi reached for the cigar and tapped it until ashes fell onto the table. "Mr. Fenton Cooper has handed in his resignation. He will be taking the proverbial *3:10 to Yuma* tomorrow." He squinted into a contented smile, as if he had just finished a fine meal at a five star restaurant.

Andrew wasn't thinking about Fenton Cooper. His friend usually guessed right. Not this time. He stood with his back to Rafi, taking in the view of the city out the window. An occasional puff of the cigar and a distant buzzing telephone interrupted the silence.

"Does Donny know?" Andrew asked.

"She knows he was released. She believes the police tried to frame Cooper to get to you. She may even suspect Officer Downing," Rafi said, laughing. "According to Javier, she has a whole list of people and organizations we should sue."

Andrew grinned. "She is my girl."

"She will have some questions when Cooper disappears. Once she finds out there will be no story, no press, she will be fine. She will move on."

"Will he contact her?"

"No, our friend Cooper wants to put distance between himself and Boise as quickly as possible. He knows I made a deal to have the charges dropped as long as he departs. Even if Mr. Cooper decided to contact Ms. Donny, he'd have a tough time explaining how he got into the predicament at the lake." Rafi puffed a few laughs along with more cigar smoke. "Yes, yes, he is scared shitless."

"And if he does call? Cooper calls and claims he was set up?"

Rafi leaned forward and his voice grew serious. "We set up no one. We simply took advantage of a situation." He leaned back in the chair, his face easing. "You worry too much."

"Maybe. I think this is working out well."

"We think alike, my friend, though you should leave details to me. Speak no more of this. Leave it to Rafi."

"Sometimes we have to make hard choices for our children."

"Yes." Rafi puffed another ring into the air above him. "Goodbye, Mr. Cooper."

Andrew roamed the room.

"There is something else?" Rafi said.

"No. Nothing."

The hallway was empty save a few hardy souls working late in the facilities section, revamping plans for the Denver store. Andrew wandered the halls until he ended up in the vicinity of Donny's office. Even she had gone home. Her executive assistant, a twenty-something blonde firehouse name Destiny, was packing a purse the size of a small suitcase and logging off a computer.

"Mr. Post." He could see the tenseness in her face, as if she'd been surprised by a predator in the backcountry. "Ms. Post just left. I might be able to catch her."

"No, that's not necessary." Andrew's tone was purposefully polite. "But you can do me a favor."

"Yes sir."

"Call security and tell them to send my driver home. And find me a car."

The only company car in the basement was a white panel work van decorated with sports equipment and the Post Corporation logo. He would turn some heads if anyone noticed his ride. He'd probably driven less than a few thousand miles a year. Sitting in the driver's seat felt good.

The guard at the front gatehouse sat inside, chatting on a cell phone. Andrew pulled his keycard and waved it at the grey box. The gate started to lift. A young kid with a crew cut jumped up and stared out the window as the words "Andrew Post A01-0001" displayed on the screen.

Andrew pulled into the night, not having a plan of what to do next. What would he normally do? That was easy. His driver would take him home. He'd do his forty-five minute workout and have whatever Orlando deemed favorable for him to eat. The evening would be relatively quiet, though numerous items would come up, and he'd be on the phone with board members, politicians, accountants, store managers, or his senior staff. His phone might ring ten to fifteen times in the course of an evening. He'd turn the damn thing off about eleven, read the *Wall Street Journal*, the *Financial Times*, and thumb through the *Tribune*. Then off to bed.

Not tonight.

He reached inside his jacket, produced his phone, and turned it off. There was a Chinese food joint, the China Garden, that he'd passed almost every day on the outskirts of downtown. He'd stop there first.

He pulled into a small parking lot on the side of the building and almost clipped a signpost, trying to fit the van into the economy parking space. The restaurant was nearly empty. Two college-aged kids sat in a booth, sipping hot tea and ogling each other, oblivious to him or anyone else for that matter. A family of four surrounded a table in the middle of the dining room. They were the perfect four. Father. Mother. Two kids—a pretty but too thin girl in her teens and an antsy grade school son. They were engaged in conversation, and occasionally they all laughed together as if on cue.

"May I help you?" asked a very clean sounding man of Asian descent.

"I'd like to order something to go."

The man examined Andrew like they'd been introduced before. He pulled out a pad and waited.

"Listen, can you put together a meal for two? I don't care what you pick."

The man nodded, bowed ever so slightly, and disappeared.

Andrew sat on a red booth seat that had been removed from the dining room and pretended to read a menu. Year of the Horse. Year of the Goat. What seemed like two hundred possible entrees. And prices that had been scratched out and raised a bit.

Behind him, the glass front door opened, shaking a little bell he hadn't noticed when he came in. The new patron was Officer Matt Downing.

"Mr. Post?" Downing spoke quietly as if Andrew's whereabouts should be a secret.

"Officer."

"We seem to be running into each other a lot lately." Downing scratched his head and scanned the room, no doubt looking for bodyguards and an entourage. He moved a few steps closer and whispered, "What are you doing?"

"I'm ordering Chinese food," Andrew whispered back.

The thin Asian man was already returning with a bag and two little white boxes. He passed them to Andrew, bowed, and spoke, "Mr. Post, this is on the house."

"No, I insist."

The man bowed again and moved behind the register. Andrew reached in his pocket and grabbed his wallet. He pulled it out and flipped it open, exposing a five dollar bill and a few ones.

The Asian man held his hand out. "Eighteen thirty-nine."

Andrew removed a credit card and passed it over the counter. The man ran the card through a machine and examined the front and back.

The machine came to life and clattered as a credit charge printed. Andrew couldn't remember the last time he had charged something on a credit card. He signed the slip, entered a tip of ten dollars, and headed for the door.

Once outside on the sidewalk, through the window, he could see Matt Downing and the Asian man conversing. The husband from the family table had also joined the conversation. Downing returned a stare through the glass. His expression said it all. *What in the world was that?*

Chapter 16
Annie Lorda's Residence, North End, Boise
Tuesday Evening

Evening twilight near the summer solstice. It was the only time of the year when Andrew made it home with daylight to spare. This evening, a scattering of light below the tree tops was enough to make him plainly visible on Annie Lorda's porch.

He surveyed the street in both directions. A dog barked nearby and a couple of cars passed on a side street. An unintelligible conversation, somewhere between the adjacent houses, ebbed and flowed on a gentle breeze that caused the trees to sway just enough to be noticed.

He reached for the doorbell, stopped, and glanced down the street one more time. Staring in his direction, a shirtless man in a pair of khaki hiking shorts stood on a porch a few doors down. The man yelled something back toward his own front door and disappeared. Andrew was sure Matt Downing or someone from Post Inc. security would come out of the shadows as soon as the remnants of sunlight faded away.

"You'll regret this," he said to himself.

He reached for the bell again. Before he could complete his action, the door opened.

"Mr. Post."

"I brought Chinese food." He felt as foolish as a high school kid.

Annie Lorda stood expressionless in the doorway, dressed in a white cotton bathrobe and a plain face, hair loose to the shoulders. He glanced down at the food again and raised his eyebrows.

"Well, come in. It's 9:30," she said, stepping back, making a path for him to enter the house.

The statement about time seemed odd. Maybe this was late for her.

The house was in order. The first visit was no fluke. A dim nightlight over the stove in the kitchen and scant rays of departing sunlight from the outside turned the living room into a black and white photo.

"You were going to bed. Maybe I should go."

"I was reading. I can never get to bed early this time of year. Didn't expect to see you again."

Andrew had no response. He didn't expect to return either.

"Let's go in the kitchen and feed you," she said. "Should I call someone?"

"I'm sorry?"

"To help you with dinner. I've let all my servants off for the night." The jab was accompanied by a welcoming smile. He had expected something closer to outright warfare.

"Touché, I believe." He placed the bag and boxes on the kitchen dinette. "I might be able to manage with your help."

With efficiency rivaling the professional domestic staff of the Post Estate, the woman organized plates, dinnerware, hot tea, and napkins along with the food Andrew had brought. He tried to help but found himself standing next to the table, holding something until she put it in its proper place.

"You sit and eat," she said.

He sat as instructed and took a sip of hot tea. "Not alone. I won't eat alone."

"The rest of the world eats around dinnertime." She put her hands on her hips and stood over him in mock defiance. "I shouldn't have let you in. Last time you left like such an ass."

He tried a stretched look of innocence. "An ass? Must be mistaken."

"Look at me. I'm in a bathrobe, no face on, and my hair looks like crap." She laughed and let out a snort at the same time. He couldn't help but return the laugh.

"Stop." She snorted again.

"Ms. Lorda, I believe you have to eat, or you will snort like a pig all night long."

She covered her mouth with her hand, then mumbled, "I won't give you the pleasure again. And it's Annie, please." She smiled. It was a warm smile. "Before I forget, I want to thank you for the jacket. I let you get away without a proper thank you last night."

Andrew nodded.

They sat across from each other at the dinette. He ate twice what he usually had for dinner. Beef and broccoli. Orange chicken. Fried rice. Egg rolls. It was not up to his standards nor did he care. Annie picked at her own version of stir-fry she concocted from several of the entrees. Occasionally, she would sneak a peek at him, and he would peek back. They talked of the late season coolness, the Boise State University football team, one of the city councilman's trials and tribulations, and why gas prices were so ridiculous in Idaho versus Salt Lake.

Once the hot tea was consumed, they started to clean up. "Okay, here's something I should be able to do—clean up this mess," Andrew said.

Annie handed him a small kitchen garbage bag and laughed as he fumbled around with the plastic.

"Who designed this thing?"

She grabbed the bag, licked her fingers, and snapped it open. "Can you do anything for yourself?"

With the table cleared, Andrew carried the half-full bag to the back door and then stopped and waited.

"Yes, the dumpster is at the end of the carport," she said.

By the time he returned, the kitchen looked like it did when he'd arrived. The table was spotless, dishes and utensils were out of sight, and the nightlight was back on. The clock on the stove read ten-fifteen. It was finally dark.

"I need to let you sleep," he said. "I'm sure my boys are combing the town for me, despite my direction to let me be. They might even be waiting outside."

"Your boys?"

"Security."

"Must be nice to be wanted."

He grabbed his jacket off the chair and headed for the front door.

"Mr. Post?"

"I'm Andrew. As you said, Mr. Post is not a nice man."

"You sit down or don't come back. Now go into the front room, take off those expensive shoes, and sit for a bit. Not every day a billionaire comes to my home," she said as she disappeared toward the back of the house.

Andrew did as he was told. He tried to remember the last time he *had* to do as he was told. He chose an older chair in the corner, pulled his shoes off, leaned back into the cushion, and closed his eyes.

He contemplated this woman's changed demeanor. Maybe she was playing him. He immediately tossed that thought. Her lighter mood made some sense. She had made her case. He would either oblige her, or he would not. If he did go in a direction favorable to her, he would suggest a revelation of the facts or recommend a more secretive approach.

Annie returned, her grey hair pulled tight into a pony tail. She'd brought back a piece of fabric and a pin and proceeded to pluck out the stitching.

"I made a mistake." She held up the square. "It's a piece for my next quilt. Have you made anything yourself recently, Mr. Post? Hobbies? Besides money and fame and such?"

Andrew stood, disappeared into the kitchen, and returned with his hands out. Leaning down, he examined the area under the table. "The empty wine bottle. Where is it?"

She played along. "I beg your pardon."

"You must be plastered. I was here the other night, and the only one home was a cranky old woman." He returned to the chair.

"Wine? I would never on a first date."

"Date. You think this is a date?"

"You brought dinner!"

"I was trying to help the old woman."

"She's not here tonight."

The banter turned to silence, and then they both laughed a bit.

"Can you imagine what my daughter would think? She'd find you here and give you a few select words. She is your daughter, you know. You paid her off already."

"Don't ruin it!" The words escaped before Andrew could stop. He rubbed his temples with his fingers.

Silence ensued. Annie continued to pluck at the material. She never looked up.

After several minutes, she placed the piece of fabric on the table and leaned forward. "Right. You can't expect to come over here and not talk about this. We either have something very significant in common or some major differences or both. No matter which one, we can talk about it."

"Do you know you say 'right' a lot?"

"I don't think that's the subject."

"Okay, women love to talk. What difference does it make?"

"Difference?"

"Whether I believe your story. Your husband's story. Whether I buy into being your daughter's natural father."

Annie shook her head and returned to picking at the material.

Andrew continued. "From your perspective, that is. You got what you wanted. Surely your daughter can survive if I pay off her house and donate some rainy day money to her bank account. And your account as well if that will make you happy. We can even be friends if you want to go that route. I'll make it work. Besides, the appearance of you and me together will give the local paparazzi something to do."

"Why are you doing this?" She took the pin and placed it between her lips, never making eye contact.

"A gesture of goodwill. I told you that."

"Why is that so hard to believe? You know I've resigned myself to whatever you decide to do. I told you that you could just move on." She nodded at the front door. "Get up and go."

He looked toward the door.

"What's your angle?" she asked. "A man like you always has an angle."

Silence filled the room. Annie stitched. Andrew waited.

He finally spoke up. "We have to be friends to make this work. I could use some of that wine you are hiding."

"I don't drink much. There's a bottle of something in the kitchen by the refrigerator. Penny brought it over a few months ago. Opener is in the top drawer next to the stove. Be my guest."

The fact that she didn't serve the wine was not a good sign. He returned with a glass of domestic Merlot. Normally, he'd comment or make a future purchase suggestion, but tonight he didn't dare.

Trying to initiate more intimate negotiations, he thought it best to narrow the distance. He chose the closer wingback chair directly across the table from his hostess. Leaning forward to set down his wine glass, he witnessed the hands of a magician as she instantly produced a coaster and placed it in his path.

He grabbed her hand. She pulled it back like someone who'd been popped by an electric current.

"What do you want from me?" he said, surprising himself.

She met his gaze. "Truthfully? I'm not even sure. Maybe honesty. Maybe some trust in me. But more so, compassion for your daughter. I'm not sure these are qualities that would come easy for you. You obviously have something else in mind. I don't believe a man like you runs around and *does* gestures of goodwill."

"And my angle is?"

"You really want to know?"

"Yes."

"The gesture is a bribe or payoff to you. Lets you off the hook and ensures you won't have to deal with Penny. She doesn't fit into your plans, lifestyle, or family. Or maybe it's something deeper. Something so terribly important to you that you would come out here alone and deal with a mere commoner. Even flirt with me and suggest some kind of faux friendship for the masses to consume."

Andrew started to wonder if he wanted to be associated with this woman. She was close to a mind reader.

"Yes, but you stated you don't want to tell your daughter anything," he said.

"I told you, I wasn't sure what to do. I was hoping you could help. I forget that men like you always want that huge margin of safety." She reached across the table and patted him on the knee. "Just in case.

You could walk away and do nothing. You know I won't talk, but there is always the small chance. Just in case. Or maybe you can't walk away. That makes life interesting to you. Probably not very smart of me to even dream of involving Penny with your family."

"But you want me to care for her?"

"Yes!" She reached out and grabbed his hand. It wasn't a gentle touch. Her voice softened, "I don't insist. That's the difference between you and me. Do the right thing, Mr. Post."

"Last time we chatted, you were pretty insistent."

"Come on. You see through me. I'm an educated woman who married a truck driver. Now a lonely widow trying her best to cope with caring for her daughter. A church lady trying to play in your league."

He had no retort. He sipped the Merlot and waited. She returned to her project.

After another uncomfortable silence, she spoke. "Why were you so visible? You show up at Penny's. You come to my church. You've been here twice. All in front of the world. Aren't you the guy that avoids the public eye? I'm surprised cameras aren't set up in my yard already."

"The truth," Andrew said, "is that I was careless. No grand plan. Just careless." He reached out and cupped her hand. "You said it was up to me, correct?"

"That's right. Within reason."

"I think the best course of action is for me to get to know you." He paused, waiting for a reaction. There was none. "For this to work, we must develop a relationship that is absolutely convincing to the world as well as to your daughter. I can work on 'the world' and you'll have to convince Penny. But it must be absolutely convincing. Cameras, journalists, and people that want to see me fall down hard follow me twenty-four hours a day. As you said, there might be people watching us now. We'll need some kind of backstory, and I can't go to my usual sources for help. This will be all you and me. That's the only way we'll be able to keep your secret while helping your daughter."

"Your daughter," Annie said. She lifted her hand away and went back to work. "I'm not sure I could go through with such a thing. My husband died a year ago. You have a wife. Even as friends, people would talk. And I just have a problem with you not believing me. Plus I'm not real talented at deception."

"Calm down. No one said we have to sleep together."

"Thank God for that," she said, as if she were talking to her stitching project.

"You think about it. My opinion—we find some way for us to become friends. That should enable me to help your daughter when she needs it. That way, everyone assumes I'm helping out because we are associates."

"Associates?" Annie laughed hard enough that she had to stop her busy work. "Don't you have any friends? You mix terms like associates and friends, and I won't know whether we are in business together or what."

She'd sucker punched him and didn't know it. "Friends" had become a sticky subject. Rafi was a friend, but their relationship was mostly business. Andrew had thousands of acquaintances, though few fit the old childhood category of friend. There were old friends who wanted to associate with him since he became rich, political friends who would dump him with a change of the wind, business friends who were really colleagues or associates, and peers who had no time for friendship.

"You take your time to decide," Andrew said. "If you want to be friends, let me know. If you just want stealth financial support, that's fine as well. It's now your call, not mine. I'm not going to walk away."

"So I'm back to my original question. Why are you doing this?"

"Jesus! What else do you want from me? You asked. I'm responding. I don't have to explain myself."

"Trust doesn't come easy, does it Andrew?"

It was the first time she had called him by his first name. Her voice had softened when she said it. If she wasn't playing him intellectually, she was playing him on some emotional level. He felt a strong desire to either flee or give her something in return.

"Okay, trust," he said.

He heard a chuckle.

"It's funny?"

"Trust? Please. Look, I'll take the financial support for Penny. I will. The friend thing, I'm not so sure. I probably have a few open dates on my schedule. Convincing Penny would not be a cake walk, especially with Matt around. At least then, you would be there to help me through this. But trust? Again, I'm not real smart, but it's easy to tell there is a lot left unsaid here. I won't push you, and I guess I have to trust you to an extent. Whether I like it or not, you are part of my daughter's life."

Andrew walked over to the fire place, rubbed his hands together, and stared out one of the front windows into the night.

"There is something else you want to say?" she asked.

A sedan appeared under the streetlamp on the other side of the road and drove away at surveillance speed. Maybe it was Matt Downing or some idiot with a camera. Andrew knew he'd been careless. Everything in his gut told him to walk away. Correct his mistakes. Have Rafi clean up the loose ends.

"Tell me." Her tone was gentle and empathetic. Her aging hazel eyes begged him to come forth with whatever it was that ailed him.

He closed his eyes. "There's a reason why it doesn't matter," he stated in a tone of resignation. He moved toward the front door and contemplated turning the knob and walking away, shoes or not. He leaned his back up against the door. "There is…a reason why it doesn't matter if I believe your story."

Andrew knew he was teetering on something that might not be reversible. When he was a kid, he used to walk the wooden fence near the back of the local church, carefully balancing himself on the narrow two-inch wide supports between the fence posts. He and Josh Prater would challenge each other to walk the entire back fence as fast as they could without falling. One of those races had cost him eight weeks in an arm cast, the result of too much concentration on the legs of Missy Sulak in the nearby parking lot. He could remember the feeling as he fell toward the ground. There was a distinct moment when he discovered he would fall with no hope of recovering. The moment seemed to hang in time like a still picture on the wall.

He was losing his balance all over again. He was about to tell the story that had never passed by his lips or flowed from his pen. Only he and Rafi knew the truth, but the subject was taboo for the two of them. *What is done is done.*

"Neither your daughter nor my daughter are my flesh and blood."

Annie's eyes narrowed. "I don't understand."

There. He'd said it. He was falling and breaking his arm all over again.

"Even if they were switched, they bear no physical relation to me. It's well known that Sonya wasn't exactly faithful. Well, she's been that way a bit longer than the tabloids have indicated. You see, the twins were a product of Sonya and someone else, not me." Andrew cupped his face with his hands, pushed back his hair, returned to his chair, and sat forward supporting his arms on his knees.

"You don't have to—"

He waved his hand up and cut her off. He took another sip of wine. "Honesty. Trust. You throw the words around like they're foreign to me." He paused. "I was angry. Actually, enraged is a better description. Sonya was the love of my life. My business had taken off. Life was good. Almost perfect. At least for me. Not for her. When she announced she was pregnant, she also disclosed to me in private that I was not the father. When I found out she had been seeing another man, I was devastated. I had to make her pay."

Annie leaned forward and reached out with her hand. Andrew retreated to the fireplace. He stared at the door, the window, anywhere but her face.

"My family life growing up was less than perfect," he said. "My father left us when I was four, and I swore on my mother's grave I'd have a real family. I swore I'd be the perfect father, and I would be there. I'd marry the perfect wife, and we would raise perfect children.

"When Sonya announced her pregnancy and history of infidelity, I was sure she did it just to twist the knife into me for ignoring her. For the next nine months, I knew what hell felt like. The babies inside her were a daily reminder of my failed life. The truth is that I neglected my wife, and she returned the favor. I know that now, but then I was crazy with anger. By the time the twins were born, I wanted no part of them. Rafi had only been with me for a few years, yet I had already started to confide in him. The situation made us very tight. He tried his best to calm me down and take care of Sonya at the same time.

"At first, I was in denial. I didn't want to believe Sonya's story. You see, there was a slight chance the twins were mine, but very slight, if you know what I mean. Once the babies were born, there was a new paternity test that would erase my doubts.

"I asked Sonya to get an abortion. She didn't want kids. Her only interest in those twins was to provide objects of revenge. Something to shove in my face. Place the illegitimate ones in front of the world for all to see."

"She obviously refused," Annie said.

"Sonya suddenly was a born-again pro-lifer. It didn't help that Rafi vehemently and religiously argued against abortion. For Sonya, it was just a cover. The babies were born, and I had them tested against Sonya and me."

"DNA testing?"

"That wasn't available yet. It was something called HLA—some kind of test involving protein matching. Supposed to be eighty to ninety percent correct."

"And the test said you weren't the father."

"And Sonya was the mother."

"That's why it doesn't matter to you?"

"Yes."

"But you said the test could've been wrong."

"The test was correct. About the time Donny reached middle school age, DNA testing came along. By then, I wanted her to be my child. The results were the same. Donny is definitely Sonya's child and not mine."

The house went silent. Even the wind quit. The only sound Andrew could hear was his own breathing. Annie returned to work on her stitching project. He wanted to hear her thoughts. Right now, it was best to let her digest this news.

She finally spoke. "Who is the father?"

"Don't know and don't want to know. That secret belongs to Sonya. The only other person who may know is Rafi. He's been her one friend throughout all of our difficulties, and I've come to appreciate that."

"So why bother with me? Why bother with Penny? This makes no sense at all."

"Yes, it makes no sense. But maybe, just maybe, you have me wrong. Maybe I'm not the bad guy you want to believe I am. I could be here to help."

"I'd like to believe that, Andrew. I would."

"Now you know a more powerful story than the one your husband left you with. You could easily go straight to the tabloids and 'tell all,' as they say. Probably even sell the story for a lot of money. I've handed you a gift. A guarantee. I'm trusting you."

"What about your wife? She's Penny's mother."

"Trust me, that is one relationship you don't want to try and build. She rarely talks to Donny. With help from Rafi, I've pretty much raised Donita myself. I was correct in my assessment about Sonya's desire to have children."

"And your daughter doesn't get along with her mother?"

"She doesn't acknowledge her existence. Think about it. Have you seen a picture of Donny and Sonya together in the last decade? I'm quite surprised *that* story remains undiscovered by the press."

"Neither one of you wanted those babies." Annie looked up as though she had just discovered this fact. "Incredible. Here Frank and I suffered through two heartbreaking events to have one child. God gave your wife two children, and neither of you wanted them. My Jesse and little Samuel gave me a few blessed months, and then God took them away. Penny was my gift."

Andrew was spent. He stood there with his eyes closed, listening.

"You love your daughter?" Annie asked. The question was unexpected.

"Yes, absolutely, just as you love your daughter. With time I came to love both of the twins. I wish to God it had all happened differently." His throat dried and the words were becoming difficult.

"You still love your wife?"

He put on his shoes, picked up his coat and hat, and headed for the door. This woman was exhausting.

"Do you like me?" she asked. "Is that what this is about?"

He opened the door and stepped outside onto the porch. He looked back through the window. Annie sat in the same position, diligently stitching away.

Chapter 17
Boise PD Headquarters
Wednesday

Matt had spent the morning investigating a burglary at the City Side Deli, a small shop in a strip center near the University. It was one of those suspicious cases where the evening shift had conveniently skipped setting the alarm system after closing. Fortunately, it hadn't taken much time to nail down the identity of the so-called intruder. Matt sent some street officers over to pick up the kid, and then he returned to his desk across town to work the only case that mattered.

The first order of business was to contact Jesse Stickman, a clerk at the Bureau of Vital Records and Health Statistics. He'd already talked to Stickman late yesterday afternoon. The man was usually helpful and talkative, but the request for copies of the birth certificates of Donny, Katlin, and Penny had immediately shut down any casual conversation. Matt's requests typically referred to some petty criminal or some kid on a path to trouble, so he should've anticipated Stickman's doubt.

He dialed the number.

"Stickman."

"Hey Jess, just checked my email for those documents I requested yesterday. Don't see them yet."

There was a long pause on the line. "Well..." Stickman hesitated.

"I know this request is a bit unusual. Cut me some slack. It'll all make sense in time. Promise."

Stickman's response was businesslike. No chatting about the reason for the request. No discussion of Matt's cycling activities or Stickman's favorite pastime—baseball. "Okay." There was another pause. "I'll send unofficial copies to your personal email."

"Great. I owe—"

"Let's don't discuss this," Stickman said. Then the call was disconnected. Matt knew he'd just cashed in a load of chips with this guy. With time Stickman would understand.

He dialed the next number on his list—the Treasure Valley Regional Medical Center Records Division. This call might be tougher. He had no friends to trust down at the hospital. On the second ring, he thought better of it and decided to pay the records people a personal visit.

As he hung up, his mobile phone rang. It was Jensen, the arresting officer in the City Side Deli case. Said he had the kid over at the jail next door, and they needed Matt right way. Matt told Jensen to take care of the situation and hung up. The phone rang again. He ignored it. As he moved the mouse to log off his computer, he noticed a new email notification. As he suspected, Stickman had been sitting on the information. He opened the email and sent the attachments to the printer.

The slightly blurred documents confirmed his suspicions. Certified Live Birth: Donita Sonya Post on December 7th, 1981, at 11:55 P.M. MST. Six pounds, one ounce. Father: Andrew Donovan Post, age thirty-three. Mother: Sonya Van Cleburn Post, age twenty-nine. Katlin Lindsey Post born December 8th, 1981, 12:02 A.M. MST. Five pounds, ten ounces. Penny Lillian Lorda born December 8th, 1981, 1:37 A.M. MST. Five pounds, nine ounces.

Lillian. He smiled.

He placed the printout in a manila envelope and walked out.

The Treasure Valley Regional Medical Center had the feel of an old veteran's hospital. Matt took the stairs to the basement and made his way through a metal dirt-brown door labeled "Records." The place appeared empty except for a desk that looked like an old nurse's station and a single uncomfortable plastic couch.

He leaned on the counter and looked down hallways to the right and left. The left hallway led to another dented brown door. The hall to the right opened to a poorly lit room. He stepped down the right hallway, poked his head around the corner, and surprised a young girl with curly, dark red hair who was busily collating very old documents.

"Didn't mean to startle you," Matt said in the softest voice he could produce.

The girl put her hand to her chest. "Oh, it's kind of empty down here, you know."

She turned her chair toward Matt. She reminded him of someone forced to dress nicely, black slacks, pink blouse, and all.

"Can I help you with something?" As she said it, he flipped his badge out, leaving it open long enough for her to reach for it. Instead, she nodded.

"I need to find out about some twins born here a while back."

"What are you looking for?" She handed him a form. It was a two-page bureaucratic masterpiece with the title "Request for Records."

"I'm kind of in a hurry. Is there some way we can skip this? Me being a policeman and all." After a casual perusal, he offered the form back to the girl.

She hesitated, examined Matt briefly from head to toe, took the form, and reached for an old plastic phone. Just as she touched the receiver, she pursed her lips and pulled her hand back. Then she put the form away.

She tilted her head and stuck her finger to her lips. Raised her eyebrows. "I could get into trouble." Matt thought the implied suggestion was the last thing he needed right now. He hated to string this kid along, but justice was calling.

"What's your name?" he said, smiling but feeling like a rat.

"Amy." She reached out and gently shook his hand, her fingers lingering an extra second or so.

"Officer Downing. Matt. I'm looking for some birth records on December 7th and 8th. Attending doctors, nurses, names of kids born on those days. Anything related to the nursery or maternity."

The girl smiled and whipped around 180 degrees to an old keyboard and CRT monitor. "That's easy. What year?"

"1981."

The girl stopped typing.

"That's a long time ago. Got to go to the racks for that."

They spent about twenty minutes narrowing down the choices to two cardboard boxes jammed on top of ten-foot-tall metal racks. The records storage room was cold and dark, and according to Amy, it was kept that way to prevent deterioration. The contradiction of old, musty boxes stacked everywhere was hard to miss.

Matt placed one box labeled 12/81 MW-Stu on an empty shelf and started to carefully remove a couple of legal-size manila envelopes. He wasn't sure what he was looking for, and much of the jargon was foreign to him. Amy leafed through the other box with an agility that one could only gain by repetition.

After ten minutes or so, she stood, clutching a couple of folders. She wedged herself between Matt and his box. He tried to gain a little personal space by backing up, but the narrow aisles only allowed him a few inches at best. She pulled the folders up to her chest. Trying not to, he found her attractive.

"Here. I have what you want," she said, pressing her body forward until his personal space disappeared completely.

Matt took the folders and stared into her eyes. They were incredibly blue, the color of a filtered sky, aided by contact lenses to enhance the effect.

"Is that all you want?" she asked.

"I'm afraid so," he whispered. "Is there a place I can sit and look through these?"

The girl frowned. "Sure, follow me. Nobody comes down here. Sit over there." She pointed to a couple of simple desks covered with blue plastic containers about the size of the boxes in the back.

Matt rifled through a number of forms he didn't understand. He was able to glean a few items of interest. Doctor Norman Soloman had delivered Penny in room 3G10. A nurse named Christine Vasquez had initialed several documents that tracked the care of all three babies. She was listed on a nursery report as one of the attending night nurses. Two other nurses were listed on the report as working the day shift, but their signatures were faded and indecipherable. There was nothing about the doctor or doctors who had delivered the Post twins or any evidence of more than three children in the nursery that first night. Similar reports from the following day and night shifts mentioned only two patients: Penny and a boy named Dominguez. The Posts apparently had taken their twins home. He searched for anything resembling discharge records to no avail. Time was short. If he didn't get back and take care of this morning's break-in case, he'd get another lecture from the captain.

He carefully documented the names of the doctor and nurse and a few other pertinent facts in his spiral notebook.

Looking back in the box one more time, he was sure he'd overlooked a number of potentially important pieces of information. Given he'd just jilted Amy, she probably would not be too receptive to his taking the box or folders with him to make copies. He pulled out his phone and did his best to capture images of what he deemed most important.

Matt's phone rang as he left the basement. It was Erin Stahl of the *Boise Tribune*, a friend and fellow cyclist. She was returning his call.

"I need a huge favor," he said, hustling down the hall and looking in all directions.

The slightly nasal baritone voice of Erin came through almost too loud and clear. "Shoot."

"See what you can find in the rags from December 1981 through March 1982 on the Post twins, Donny and Katlin. You need full names?"

"You kidding? Donny Post? Who's this Katlin?"

"I'll tell you later," he said.

"What are you getting into now? You're like a kid reaching for the candy jar."

"Also, check on Penny Lorda. Same time frame."

The phone went silent for a second or two. Matt made his way up the stairs and out the front door.

"That's your friend, Penny?" There was no mistaking the surprise in Erin's voice.

"I'll explain later. This could be big. When it becomes a story, you'll have it before anyone else." This always worked with Erin. Anything to move her on a path to a big city market like Frisco or LA.

"Done. Is this urgent? I'm off to Maui for a week. Please say it can wait."

"It can wait," Matt said, thinking otherwise. "And thanks."

Chapter 18
Penny Lorda's House, North End, Boise
Friday Evening (2 days later)

"I suppose you'll keep avoiding the subject," Penny said, peeking around the corner, holding a tie-dye shirt.

Annie moved through Penny's house like a human vacuum, picking up magazines, Serena's dolls and books, and piles of clothes that might or might not be dirty.

Penny pulled the shirt over her head and walked back toward her bathroom. Annie could hear the voice trailing away. "I know he was at your house the other night."

Darn Matt, thought Annie. Right now, she just wanted him to show up and take Penny away to the movies. Then she'd have a couple of hours of peace and quiet with her grandchild.

She entered the kitchen. It was in better shape than usual. The stovetop needed a cleansing and the floor could use a mop, but at least there were no dishes stacked in the sink.

"Serena, come help your Grandma Annie."

Serena, pretty much a replica of her father—thin, dark-skinned, with long, straight, brown hair—came running from her room and landed in a hug at Annie's waist.

"Help Grandma Annie in the kitchen. Fetch the mop and the bucket in the garage."

"Again?" Serena whined. "Can we play Chinese checkers?"

"As soon as we clean up this mess."

Penny returned in a pair of her best holey jeans, sandals, and the tie-dye shirt Annie could've worn in her youth. She scanned left and right, shook her head, and disappeared back toward her room.

"You missing something?" Annie asked.

"Can't find my purse in this *mess*."

"Just trying to help."

Penny reappeared in the kitchen, an oversized purse on her shoulder. "You could help by telling me what's going on with Andrew Post."

Annie scrubbed the stovetop. "Aren't you late for the movies?"

"Go ahead. Dodge my questions. Hang out with a crazy man. Drive Matt nuts. Can't wait for what's next."

Three firm knocks echoed off the front door, and then it swung open.

"Where have you been? If we truck it, we'll catch the 7:25 show," Penny said to Matt as she hugged Serena.

Matt ignored Penny and made his way into the kitchen.

Annie pressed harder on the sponge until her fingers hurt. "Serena, I need that mop and bucket please." She finished the stovetop, rinsed the sponge, and neatly folded a dirty rag over the edge of the sink. She could sense Matt directly behind her. Moving toward the table, she maintained her position with her back to him.

Serena returned with the mop but no bucket. "I can't find it."

"Can you take Serena out on the porch?" Matt said to Penny.

"Hey, we got a freaking babysitter. I want to go out..." Penny's voice trailed off, the front door creaked open, and the sound of little and big footsteps left the house.

The door closed. Matt spoke. "Okay, I've held off on this subject for a couple of days, but I can't stay silent. What the hell are you doing?"

Annie spun around, mop in hand. "Don't come in here talking to me like that. I don't owe either of you anything."

"Andrew Post is a dangerous man. A convincing, dangerous man. What's he been telling you?"

"Why don't you go ask him?"

"You sound just like Post."

Annie leaned the mop against the sink and left for the garage, leaving Matt behind. The one-car stall was full of Penny's possessions. Boxes of old clothes she'd never wear again. Two old bicycles, a rusted tricycle she used to ride as a child, stacked cases of bottled water that belonged to Matt, an old motorcycle that died when she was married to Austin, every magazine and paper she had ever read, and the washer and dryer Annie had bought for her two years ago before Frank died. On the far wall, it was still there—Frank's workbench, tools still in order. Annie had tried to get rid of it. Penny had resisted. They'd quarreled about it for a week or two a few months after Frank's passing. Then Matt came by one day and carted the workbench off. Annie didn't know the destination was going to be Penny's garage.

She made her way through the clutter and picked up the mop bucket from its usual spot next to the clothes dryer. Frank's workbench, now within arm's reach, stared back at her, its worn surfaces evidence of the long hours of the solitary tinkering of her soulmate. All that time with such a secret held inside. She extended her free hand toward the nearest corner. Her fingers hovered inches above the surface. Had he spent more time on his projects after Penny came along? Her recollection was fuzzy, but it seemed true.

The opening of the door to the house startled Annie, even though she was half expecting it. Matt stood in the doorway.

"Can I try again?" he asked quietly.

She ignored the intrusion and lightly touched the edge of the workbench.

"Until a few nights ago, I'd never put together the connection between the Lordas and the Posts," he said. "Donny and Katlin Post and Penny were all born on the same night in the same hospital. I'm sure you know that."

Annie had no idea how to reply. Had Matt found out about the switch? There were only two ways he could know—either through Andrew or the letter. The former was out of the question. The latter was a possibility.

"It's an interesting coincidence that you and the father of the Post twins are communicating on a semi-regular basis, and that Andrew Post is helping Penny out. Be nice if you told me why?"

Matt paused and waited for a response. Annie looked away.

"I followed Post to your place the other night," he said.

"That explains how Penny knew Andrew was there."

"Andrew? My God, you are on friendly terms."

"Yes." She found no reason to stray from the truth. Hold back the facts, yes. Lie about it, no.

From the other side of the garage door, they heard a muffled laugh on the driveway.

Annie held her hand up. "Let's go back inside. I'd rather Penny not pick up on any of this discussion."

They returned to the kitchen and sat at the table directly across from each other.

"I don't really know how to say this, but I'm going to try." She reached out and cupped Matt's hands. "You're like the son I never had. You're part of this family. I'm worried this whole situation might become quite complicated, and I'd appreciate it if you'd stay out of it."

He shook his head. "I can't."

"I'm not in any danger."

"I'm not so sure of that. And I'm not liking this conversation."

The front door opened and Penny's voice blasted into the house. "You coming? We already missed the 7:25 show."

"Give us a minute!" Matt snapped.

"Okay, okay." The front door closed.

"Have you seen Frank's letter?" Annie asked.

"No, I wouldn't do that. I'd be happy to read it if you're offering."

The answer was all Annie needed. She was not ready to have the after-letter conversation with Matt now, if she ever would be. If he discovered the truth, he'd know his best friend—maybe his one true love—was a Post. The consequences were unpredictable and certainly not good.

She clutched his hands tighter. "If you want to help me, if you want to help Penny, stay out of this. Stop looking for trouble."

"So Penny has something to do with this."

She threw his hands back. "Go to the movies."

Chapter 19
Streets of Boise, Near Downtown
Tuesday Evening (4 days later)

The evening rush hour abated, leaving State Street with a gentle flow of traffic and a scattering of pedestrians enjoying the long daylight hours after work. Matt sat in the patrol vehicle, tugging at his belt, trying to relieve a bout of indigestion after downing a quick plate of Italian pasta from Leo's. His civvies would've been more comfortable, but the uniform was required for the extra patrol shifts.

He watched a group of women leave the small recreational center across the street. Annie was mixing in with the crowd of quilters—the "blue hairs" as Penny called them. Matt knew the routine from Penny's rants. These women had spent two hours engaged in some kind of meeting and would now spend an extra thirty minutes in conversation as they moved like snails back to their cars.

He wished they would pick up the pace. He needed to at least act like he was patrolling the area. His intent was to see if Annie was still meeting up with Andrew Post. If she was, he wanted to be there to see where they went, what they did, and how they acted together.

Since his discussion with Annie last Friday night, he'd kept his distance, though he'd spent some official and unofficial time tailing her. It was fairly easy to do since she stuck to a rigid schedule. If she'd not shown up tonight at her guild meeting, he would've known she was either sick or Post was back in the picture somehow.

So far, so good. Nothing to indicate any contact with Post. That didn't completely rule out the possibility, but it was encouraging.

He'd also kept his distance from Post. The captain had been adamant, and the passage of time would be good for the captain's angst. Matt's initial inclination had been to head to Post's workplace and confront him about the connection between the Lordas and the Posts. At a minimum, he would have enjoyed having Post on the ropes. But such a stunt would likely bring about another lecture from Captain Lewis, maybe even a suspension.

On the prowl for the opposite sex, a pack of junior high school girls passed Matt's open window and gathered at the curb, waiting on the signal to enter the cross walk. One of the taller girls, in an animated conversation with the pack, stumbled backwards into the street. A black Chevy truck approached the intersection at forty miles an hour, heading right for the girl.

Matt leaned out the window. "Hey! Out of the street!"

With its horn blaring, the pickup sped on by, weaving around the girl like a pylon on the police academy obstacle course. The girls giggled and waved at the truck, and then crossed en masse to the other side.

Matt turned his attention back to Annie. The spot where her car had been parked was vacant.

He contemplated swinging by her house. As he put the cruiser into gear, his radio came to life. "Charlie 4, 11-83, corner of West Fort and 15th."

He picked up the mike, "10-4, 11-83, West Fort and 15th. En route."

The accident was a fender-bender. A two-year-old red sedan had bumped into the back of a beer truck. The truck was fine. The sedan and the driver, a heavy teenage girl visiting from down valley, were a bit shaken. Matt ended up ticketing the young girl.

The vehicles and drivers gone, he sat in the patrol car and filled out some final paperwork on his laptop, wondering if he could follow-up on Annie before anyone else needed the services of the Boise PD.

Paperwork completed, he started to pull away from the curb when a black BMW 650i Coupe zipped through the intersection about five seconds after the signal turned red. Matt couldn't believe his luck.

He drove his foot into the accelerator, switched on his lights, and sped down 15th street toward the foothills. The speed limit was thirty-five miles an hour. The cruiser was doing almost fifty and barely gaining on the Coupe.

The Coupe swung left on Hill Road. A couple of blasts from the siren caught the attention of the driver. She pulled off onto a side street. Matt eased the cruiser up directly behind the Coupe and stopped. Big brown sunglasses in the vehicle's rearview mirror examined his presence. He dispensed with entering the license plate into the laptop. He knew the owner.

The side street was empty except for a guy working under the hood of a dusk-blue 60s-era Camaro a few houses away. Exiting the patrol car, Matt put on his baseball cap. He walked to the back edge of the Coup and stopped.

The window of the BMW rolled down in a smooth fashion. After several seconds of examining the vehicle's inner contents from the rear, Matt approached the passenger door. "Good evening, Mrs. Post. License, registration, and insurance please?"

Staring back and without a word, Sonya Post dispensed her license through the window. Sporting the same short haircut Donny displayed about five years ago, the woman's resemblance to her daughter was striking. The distinct aroma of fresh new car leather mixed with a hint of bourbon whiskey escaped through the opening. Sonya Post had lost her license some years back on a DUI charge. The newspapers and tabloids had had a field day with the story. Given the captain's recent edict, Matt didn't want to be responsible for a repeat occurrence of such a charge and the accompanying publicity.

He ignored the omission of proof of insurance and registration. "Can you step out of the car please?"

Sonya Post didn't protest. She turned off the car, opened the door, and lifted her long frame from the vehicle. Even in her sixties, she could turn a head. She wore black leggings covered by a scarlet tunic and a pair of tan sandals.

She removed her sunglasses. Her brown eyes were sunken and bloodshot, as if sleep had been an occasional bother. The skin on her neck and around her face was pulled tight.

"What's the problem?" The voice was throaty and tired.

Matt felt some sympathy for the woman. Up close, she just seemed to need help.

"You smell like you have been drinking," he whispered.

"Trust me, I'm not drunk."

"You ran a red light back there."

"Give me a ticket." She wasn't confrontational, just direct.

"I'm not worried about the red light. If I let you go, and you kill somebody..."

She pushed Matt aside and stood with her feet spread slightly apart. She reached out and touched her nose, and then walked a white line in the middle of the road like a tightrope artist.

Matt gently escorted her back to the side of the car.

"There," she said. "You convinced?"

"Yes ma'am. You can get back in the car."

She winked, slowly slid her frame back into the driver's seat, and shut the door. Through the open window, she asked, "Can I go? Or is there something else I can do for you, Officer?"

"Sure. There is something you can help me with. Did you know your daughters were born on the same night as Penny Lorda?"

Sonya Post hid her face again behind the big sunglasses. "So what if they were? Word on the street is that Andrew is hanging around with her mother. Is that true?" The tone sounded like a disinterested stranger.

"Maybe. Don't you find it strange that your husband is in contact with Angela Lorda?"

She laughed. "I stopped trying to figure out Andrew years ago. Listen, it's almost happy hour at my house, and I have a friend coming by later. Anything else?"

"That's it?" Matt said, hoping to coax something more useful out of a rare encounter with Andrew Post's wife.

"Listen, I didn't know who Angela Lorda was until that column appeared in the *Tribune* on Sunday," she said. "It's probably best for Andrew if the rumors are true. He needs to lighten up and have some fun. A priest has sex more often than my husband. Last time was that young girl, I suppose. Never got over it and won't discuss it."

"Lacy Talbert?"

"I don't know. Sounds right."

"Can I ask you a personal question?"

"What the hell were the previous questions?" She turned the key and a rush of power surged through the metal frame. "Oh, go ahead. I'm feeling nice today. Plus I guess I owe you for not giving me a ticket."

"What happened to Katlin?" The question was a little more direct than Matt wanted it to be.

Sonya Post appeared to carefully consider her answer.

"Listen, I'm not a mother. Never wanted to be one. Donny has come to terms with that. So have I. Andrew never will. Donny refuses to acknowledge me and that's fine. It would've been the same with Katlin. I got over it. Andrew did not. Whatever happened is deep inside my husband. So deep I'm not sure it's accessible to anyone. To me, she died, simple as that."

Chapter 20
Post Corporation Headquarters, Boise
Thursday Afternoon (2 days later)

"With the unfortunate loss of Mr. Cooper, we'll need to fill his position before we fall further behind on the Denver activities." Andrew glanced around the table at his management team. How many were naïve enough to think they were safer than Fenton Cooper? As far as he was concerned, only Rafi and Donny were guaranteed a job.

Donny's stare was ice cold. Most would have interpreted her posture as vindictive. Andrew knew it was more related to the delay in the store opening and any potential fallout affecting her reputation, not the loss of a two-bit East Coast guy.

It had been a week and a half since Cooper had left town and about as long since Andrew had heard from Angela Lorda. Several times he'd picked up the phone and started to dial her number, but each time he'd thought better of it. He had made a fool of himself. He'd been weak. Angela Lorda was looking for strength, not some old man spitting out his soul like a teenager.

"Any thoughts on Cooper's replacement?" Rafi said, directing his question to everyone at the table.

Gavin, one of the lawyers, tossed out the name of Michelle Petersen.

Andrew waved his hand aside. "Not a chance." Petersen was top-notch, but she and Donny together would be sparks and gasoline.

The accountants sat in silence, occasionally checking their smartphones. The CIO was absent and his nerdy assistant was useless for anything other than diagrams of expensive systems nobody could comprehend.

"What about Mark Houston?"

It was an excellent suggestion. Andrew turned to Cinderella Marshant, Cooper's former assistant, and smiled. "I don't know why I need the rest of these people when I have you."

Her face flushed with such a deep red Andrew thought she might pass out. He glanced at Rafi. His assistant was nodding his approval. Donny was the gauntlet. In the end, it would be her choice. She remained quiet, neither confirming nor opposing the suggestion.

Just as Andrew was about to ask those in the room to depart so he could have a private conversation with his daughter, Haddy appeared and handed him a message.

He stood. Everyone else looked as if they should follow his lead, the accountants standing up just enough as if a lady had entered the room.

"She's here?" he asked.

Haddy nodded.

"Have her escorted to my office."

"She is already in your office," Haddy whispered. "Didn't think it was a good idea to leave her in the front lobby."

Without another word, Andrew left the conference room with Haddy in tow. His departure in the middle of business was unprecedented, and the occupants of the conference room would be a little more than shocked. For years he had insisted on the Thursday weekly meeting at one o'clock prompt, a rigidly planned agenda, and one hour of his senior staff's undivided attention. He could not recall leaving the meeting in the middle of business since he set the tone some fifteen years ago.

Like it or not, he had their attention.

Annie Lorda sat in one of the two chairs in front of Andrew's desk, crossing and uncrossing her legs and folding and unfolding her arms, as if she were waiting on a job interview. Andrew watched her move about in a summer dress, mid-heels, and primped hair that had a subtle curl to it. She carried a black handbag and a wide-brimmed casual hat.

He was glad she was nervous. At her place, she was empowered by her surroundings, quick-witted, and able to counter his every move. He welcomed the deck stacked in his favor.

"I'm not sure I know you, Ms...." he said mockingly from his office door.

"*You* are taking me to lunch."

"I've already had my lunch."

"Too bad. You can watch me eat, and I'll assume it's my choice," she said as she stood.

He wasn't quite sure what to do next. It was as if he were standing in her kitchen again, holding the garbage bag.

She gave him a gentle hug in plain view of Haddy and a few other wandering Post personnel. She headed toward the elevators, and he obediently followed.

As he passed, he spoke to Haddy. "Have my car pulled around front."

It seemed the entire Post Corporation was moving about in the hallways. The bustle near the entrance was no different. If Annie had planned to make a scene, she had succeeded. Even Andrew's driver gave her a double take, making the connection between the lady he was assisting into the limo and the crazy woman rushing Andrew two weeks ago.

"You're acting a little forward for a friend," Andrew said, now comfortably in the back of the limo and out of sight of his staff. "I was starting to think I wouldn't hear from you."

"Don't get too encouraged. I'm doing this for Penny. Nothing more."

"Where do you want to go?"

"Angelo's on Broad. They have good Italian."

"Never been there."

She laughed. "Don't suppose you have. Pretend it is up to your standards. Kind of like me."

Chapter 21
Outside Angelo's Italian Restaurant, Boise
Thursday Afternoon

The sun beat down on Matt's Ford Ranger like it was a mid-summer afternoon. He'd rolled down the windows to try and catch a weak breeze. It wasn't happening.

Across the street sat a conspicuous black limo taking up several parking spaces in the lot of Angelo's Italian Restaurant, a medium-fare place popular with the university crowd. Standing outside the limo, two of Post's goons watched the area like Secret Service agents. Traffic into and out of Angelo's and along nearby Broad Street was heavy, and the men seemed nervous.

Matt had received a text message from Donny about a half an hour ago. She'd stated that her father had left with Angela Lorda. That he'd probably want to know that. Within minutes the age of instant communication had verified Donny's information. Several more text messages, one from Erin at the *Tribune* and another from a cycling friend, confirmed Post and Annie had been spotted going into Angelo's on Broad Street.

He'd considered popping in on the couple. Annie would crucify him for such an act. And his appearance would certainly get reported to the captain. Instead, he sat in the hot rays of the sun, waiting.

He checked his watch—2:25 P.M.—an hour and a half before the start of another evening overtime shift. Tuesdays. Thursdays. Every other Saturday. It was starting to wear on him.

Except for his encounter with Sonya Post, the last week had been uneventful. Matt had pieced together some names and a few more details about the night the twins and Penny were born. The pediatrician and the doctors who had delivered the three girls had all passed away. Christine Vasquez, the attending nurse from the nursery, was still alive and living down the Interstate in Nampa. He'd checked newspaper archives, gaining only two articles. The first was a birth announcement for Katlin and Donny, and the second, an obituary for Katlin Post. Neither added much to what he already knew. And surprisingly, there were no details to be found about Katlin's death.

Then there was Annie. He had done his best to keep an eye on her. Until today it had seemed unnecessary. She had gone about her week in the usual way. Sunday at church. Monday and Wednesday morning at the YMCA. Quilt guild meeting Tuesday night. Coffee with some of her friends on Wednesday. With little fanfare, she appeared to have dropped her mysterious relationship with Andrew Post.

Today's event was a game-changer.

The passenger door to Matt's truck clicked and opened toward the sidewalk. Uninvited, a large man in tan slacks and a light brown Mexican wedding shirt bent down and proceeded to take a seat on the passenger side.

It was Rafi Thuban.

He tossed a Panama Hat onto the seat. He said nothing at first, pulled out a cigar, unwrapped it, and started to chew on the end. He watched the restaurant like he was Matt's partner.

"Nice shirt," Matt said.

"Ah, it's a Guayabera, a traditional Cuban shirt. Very comfortable on a hot day."

"What do you want?"

"Cigar? I have one more."

Matt ignored the offer.

"You and I have something in common now, my officer friend. We both want to know what is happening between two people in that restaurant. And we have both been told to butt out. Imagine," Rafi said, punching Matt on the shoulder and laughing, "you and me."

An unfamiliar ringtone filled the car. It sounded like music in one of the Bollywood movies Matt and Penny had rented a while back.

Rafi pulled out his phone from his pocket and spoke. "Yes. Soon?"

Across the street, one of the goons was holding a cell phone to his ear.

"Very good," Rafi said, and he placed the phone back in his pocket. "They are leaving."

"You're spying on your own boss?"

Rafi smiled and chewed his cigar. "Protecting."

Within minutes Angela Lorda exited the restaurant and strolled arm in arm with Andrew Post to the waiting limo. Matt had seen her in a dress at church and at a few other formal occasions, but not like this. In addition to a sleeveless vanilla summer dress, she'd added heels, a fashionable hat, and a new purse. The purse was the real kicker. Annie never carried a bag she'd not made herself. She was clearly dressing up to attract Andrew Post. Matt could hardly imagine a more unlikely picture.

A Boise PD unit pulled alongside Matt's truck and stopped. One of the officers, a guy Matt wouldn't call a friend named Dresden, shouted, "What's up, Downing?"

It didn't take long for Dresden to recognize Rafi Thuban.

Matt made a bit of small talk and said nothing of his newfound companion. He could tell Dresden was looking past him at Rafi during the entire conversation. It wouldn't be long before the story passed through the department, and the captain would be somewhere in that chain of information.

The unit pulled away. The limo was gone.

Matt put his head on the steering wheel. "I've got to go to work soon. Do you mind?"

Rafi didn't move. He chewed the cigar and appeared to consider his next statement carefully. "Love that is not madness is not love. Do you know who said that?"

Matt stared out the front window.

"Of course you don't. Pedro Calderón de la Barca, the Spanish poet. I do believe he was correct. I did not see this coming. Mr. Post should be quite careful in these matters. Discreet."

"Careful. Discreet." Matt laughed. "He's not even trying to hide it. Running around with Annie. He paid off my girlfriend's mortgage in secret and just about everybody figured that out."

Rafi grunted and chewed. "This is why you are a small and insignificant person in this town. Mr. Post planned the information leak all along. He wants to plant the seed that he is doing nice things for Angela Lorda. He looks like he is trying to hide it. Any idiot finds out. Even you. His public loves him even more for such acts of kindness."

"So this is just a blossoming friendship? I'm not buying it."

"Maybe a love affair," Rafi said, appearing displeased at the prospect.

"Not a chance."

"A ruse then. Mr. Post has kept you off balance for so many years. You are simply the puppet, Detective. You will always be the puppet."

"Do me a favor and get lost."

The next thing Matt expected was some kind of forearm to his face. Instead, Post's handler exited the vehicle and then stuck his head back into the passenger window.

"For your health, you should do two things. One. Tell me anything you discover in your endless detective work involving my friend and Mrs. Lorda. Two. Don't fuck with me."

With that, he reached in and grabbed his hat, and walked away.

Interesting, thought Matt. Rafi Thuban was also in the dark on this budding relationship.

Chapter 22
Downtown Boise
Late Friday Evening

"You need to lay off a bit," Penny said.

"Yep, that's what the captain told me this morning. Fact is, I'm pretty much laid off from my job for a couple of weeks at the expense of my own vacation time."

Penny frowned and sipped her grande, three shots of vanilla, non-fat, extra-hot, latte. Matt sniffed his tall mild coffee, waiting for it to cool a bit. They'd found a table outside their favorite coffeehouse smack in the middle of downtown. Penny liked to sit inside and listen to the music, but Matt decided this type of evening could not be spent indoors.

He had wanted to go straight to Annie's after the scene at the restaurant. The plan was to stop by early this morning. Instead, he was summoned to headquarters for an unscheduled meeting with the captain where he was given an unambiguous cease-and-desist-or-else order and some time to think about it. He followed that up with a hard bicycle ride and then waited for Penny to call after her usual Friday evening dinner with her mother.

Surprisingly, after what had transpired over the last twenty-four hours, Penny seemed calm.

"So how is your mother?"

"Move right to the point, huh? Thought you were ordered to stop."

"I can't believe you are so okay with this. Your mother is hanging with Andrew Post. Doesn't that concern you?"

"Damn right it concerns me. But you should've seen Ma tonight at dinner. She was happier than I've seen her since before Dad got sick. I mean, she didn't really show it. She wasn't dancing or anything, but I could tell."

"This is serious. I can't believe you are taking this so calmly. Do I need to remind you about the situation?"

Penny reached out, grabbed Matt's nose, and twisted it until it hurt.

"No, I don't want to go over your list again!" She said it loud enough to attract the attention of the nearby tables. "But if you do, I have it memorized. Here's your damn list. Number one. Ma has a note from Dad. Number two. She nearly gets arrested for stalking Andrew Post. Number three. Post shows up on my sidewalk. Number four. Ma talks to Post at our church. Number five. Post comes to Ma's house, once or twice, depending on who you believe. Number six. Ma goes to lunch with Post."

"You forgot about the mortgage."

"Jeeessuss Christ!" Her voice carried enough to gather the attention of people traversing the nearby crosswalk.

What was really missing was the coincidence concerning the birth of the three girls. Matt had not relayed any of this information to Penny. He had been ready to discuss the issue after they found their table. Given Penny's present mood, he would wait.

"Get a little more excited. I'm sure there are a few people downtown that haven't noticed us yet," he said.

He glanced back to see Donny, her arms crossed, standing behind him in full business attire.

Penny glared in Donny's direction and then took another sip of her latte.

Donny put her hands on Matt's shoulders and squeezed. "Nice of you to drop by the other night. We should get together more often."

Penny's face reddened. Time for World War III. The patrons at the coffeehouse and the pedestrians in the vicinity appeared ready for a show.

Penny stood, placed her palms firmly on the table, and stared at her coffee cup. "Would you please leave us alone?"

Before Matt could intervene, Penny launched herself in the direction of Donny. They stood chest to chest. The most talked about girl-fight in Boise history appeared imminent. Matt managed to lodge himself between the two women. Neither was speaking. They looked like boxers at a weigh-in.

After a few tense seconds, Donny patted Matt on the shoulder and waltzed away. The hum of the audience was evident as he gently pushed Penny back toward her chair. She sat, head in her hands, staring at the ground.

"You slept with her? Jesus, help me." This time she was whispering.

"Not so fast. I went to visit Donny to ask her some questions about her father. I swear," he said, reaching out to grab Penny's hands.

She pushed him away.

"This is your problem," she said. "I see a situation that is pretty much all good. I don't understand it, and God knows I don't trust this Post guy much, but so far it's all good. Ma is at least not brooding. She may even be happy. My mortgage got paid off. I paid off my credit cards. And for the first time, if some bad shit happens, I might have enough money to cover it. The only bad part of all this is your obsession not only with Andrew Post but with little Donita too."

Penny rose from the chair and took one more swig from her cup.

"I'm going to go now," she said, holding her hands out as if that would control her emotions. She spoke slowly, steadily. "I don't want to see you again, tonight. Okay?"

Matt didn't answer. He and the rest of his audience sat and watched Penny move away in the opposite direction of Donny Post.

Chapter 23
Boise PD Headquarters
Just After Midnight Saturday

The email was from Erin Stahl at the *Boise Tribune*. Matt had meant to swing by her office Friday and check on his request for information, but Captain Lewis's unscheduled lecture concerning Matt's unofficial suspension and the surprise lunch date at Angelo's overshadowed everything else.

Subject line of the email said, "You asked for it." Matt scanned the normally busy Boise PD cubicle area. Half of the lights were dimmed, and all was quiet except for the muffled voice of a uniform on the phone somewhere in the back. He checked his watch. Ten minutes after midnight.

After the emotionally exhausting adventure earlier in the evening with Penny and Donny, he couldn't sleep. He was on some kind of forced vacation, but that didn't mean he couldn't swing by the office and check on things.

He clicked on the email. The text read:

Here you go. Nothing at all about Penny Lorda's birth. I found these three items about Katlin Post. Just happened across the fourth item by accident. Are you riding at Stanley on the 4th of July? ☺ Later. Erin

The message had an attachment entitled "Matt-stuff." He clicked again and text filled the screen. The first article, a story he'd already found during his own research, was the birth announcement of Donita and Katlin Post. The second story was more interesting. He should have been able to find it himself. That's why he had friends like Erin.

Post Infant Passes Away in Oregon

February 1st, 1982. Ontario, Oregon

Katlin Post, daughter of Andrew Post, the fast rising multi-millionaire and founder of Post Sports, died Sunday night at Malheur County Medical Center in Ontario, Oregon, of complications related to her birth. The eight-week-old infant was admitted to the emergency room just before 7 P.M. when she stopped breathing on her way to Portland for evaluation and possible surgery for an undisclosed condition.

"She was in trouble when they came in," said Dr. Lewis Vanoble, the emergency room attending physician.

A.D. Hewitt, a family doctor, was en route with Andrew Post, reportedly as a safety measure. Hewitt said the infant suffered cardiac arrest in the vehicle just as they passed the Oregon state line. Efforts to resuscitate the child were not successful.

"Katlin struggled from day one. It was tragic and for this to happen in Mr. Post's hometown makes it all the more heartbreaking," Hewitt said.

Sonya Post, the mother, was to fly to Portland and meet her husband on Monday for the medical consultation. It was unclear why the party was driving to Portland. Doctor Hewitt stated Mr. Post had some other business obligations, and this fit his plans.

Katlin was the twin sister of Donita Post, who is healthy and doing fine in Boise.

Hewitt said Mrs. Post had been notified and would join her husband sometime today.

The third article was a funeral announcement in the *Boise Tribune*. Matt had found it earlier. He read it again to be sure he'd not missed anything.

Katlin Lindsey Post passed away on January 31, 1982, at the age of eight weeks. She will be greatly missed by her family. The funeral service will take place on Thursday, February 4th, at St Phillips United Methodist Church, 754 16th Street, Boise, at 11.00 A.M. There will be no viewing and the casket will be closed. Floral tributes may be sent in her honor.

The fourth item was out of the *Ontario Daily* in Oregon.

February 15th, 1982.

Missing Doctor Located in Portland

Dr. Lewis Vanoble, a physician at Malheur County Medical Center, was located by police in Portland, Oregon, at the house of an acquaintance. Vanoble's disappearance had been reported by hospital personnel last Wednesday night after missing two shifts in a row and not responding to numerous phone calls and pages. Police had searched his apartment Thursday but found nothing out of the ordinary. Vanoble's car was in its assigned space. His father was contacted in Riverside, California, and was unaware of his son's disappearance.

Friday morning, Ontario Police Captain Samuel Reyes, announced Vanoble was being treated as a missing person at the request of his father.

Officer Cindy Watson of the Portland Police Department said Vanoble was edgy but otherwise fine. "He said he was going back to Ontario to get his things next week. Other than that, he was pretty quiet and refused to explain his disappearance."

Vanoble had worked at Malheur for approximately eight months. Hospital spokesman Nez Bailey said they would begin an immediate search for his replacement. "It's not easy to keep folks out here," Bailey said. "We're used to being short-handed."

Matt locked his screen, stood, and stretched. All was quiet. Even the uniform in the back either had left or was nodding off in his cubicle. He checked his watch again. Quarter past midnight.

He paced the room, considering the email. There was some connection between Post and Annie and these three girls born hours apart. What was it?

Katlin Post had died not long after coming into the world. One rule of detective work—death was always of interest.

A commotion out in the hall was headed in Matt's direction. Within seconds, Duane Selsnick, better known as Snick around the department, busted through the door, dragging a high school kid. The boy, about half the size of Snick, stumbled along, nearly falling every other step until the officer landed him in a chair next to a metal desk on the other side of the room.

"Hey, Downing. Thought you were shit-canned for a while."

Matt liked Snick. Everybody did. He was one of those big guys who didn't know it. A rural eastern Washington native who wore a persistent black shadow on his face and an equally persistent smile.

"I'm taking some leave. Cap wants me to take it easy."

Snick laughed, sat in his chair, and logged into his computer. "Everybody knows you're in the doghouse. I told you before. Stay away from those people. Those rich SOBs will slap you silly."

"What's with the kid? Don't recognize him."

The kid's face was resting on the desk. Snick pushed his forehead up and stared into his eyes. Then he let him back down. "Me neither. Some Colorado boy visiting his relatives in Meridian. Walked into a house up on the first bench and climbed in bed with some old woman. She screamed and the neighbors came running. Grabbed the kid and held him until lucky Snick came to the rescue."

Matt started to laugh along with his newfound company.

"You should've seen the old lady. She was ready to put one of her shoes across his head. Kid feels like crap now. Wait till he figures out what he's done."

Both men laughed. Snick said he brought the kid in to sober up and to protect him in case the old lady, Mrs. Anderson, was lurking close by.

"What are you working on?" Snick said, typing away on his computer.

"Nothing." Matt paused and then motioned Snick over to look at the email from Erin.

"Well, damn. You never quit. You should've been on my high school football team. We might've won a game."

Snick was right. Matt would never quit. He'd heard of cops spending their lives trying to solve an old crime. But this was different. He'd spent most of his young career trying to pin a crime—any crime—on one person.

"What do you think?" Matt said. "Anything stand out?"

Snick sat back on the desk, pointed his chin at the floor, and nodded his head. "Two things. One. Strange that doc just up and left. Two. Hard to believe the Posts would drive anywhere."

"It was a long time ago."

"He was a rich son of a bitch back then. He's a rich son of a bitch now. Besides, why the heck would he drive a sick kid five hundred miles through the middle of nowhere with a personal physician on a Sunday night? Hop on a plane and he's there in a couple of hours."

Matt had been thinking the same thing.

"Why are you interested in this stuff anyway?" Snick asked. "You gonna charge this guy with letting his kid die thirty something years ago? If that's what you're thinking, you better have a lot more than a few newspaper articles."

Again, Snick was right on the money. This pointed to something sinister. Why would they go to such lengths and put an ill baby in danger? Matt started to pace the room again. Didn't make much sense. Post obviously cared for Donny and would probably *kill* to defend her. Why put his other daughter in such a vulnerable position?

Then there was Annie and Post and the birth of the three girls. Maybe Frank Lorda somehow overheard Post or gained some knowledge about what Post was planning to do that night, and the information was detailed in the letter Annie possessed. Even so, some things didn't measure up. Why would Frank Lorda keep that a secret? And given this knowledge, wouldn't the Annie that Matt had known all his life go to the police? And now Annie and Post were together. The pieces of the puzzle didn't fit. Knowing the contents of Frank Lorda's letter sure wouldn't hurt.

"Why don't you ask this guy about it?" Snick said, seated at Matt's desk, pointing at the computer monitor.

The screen was filled with search results of Dr. Lewis Vanoble. Snick checked through a few links and found an announcement of Vanoble's retirement in Salem, Oregon, in 2009. They checked a few more links but found nothing of note.

"Well, a few years ago, the guy was still in Oregon. That's a start," Snick said as he headed back toward the kid. "He's waking up. Why don't you check on that doctor's driver's license records? Probably find a current address."

The phone buzzed several times and finally rolled over to the voice mail of Henry Kwiatkowski. "Hey, this is Henry. I'm not available—"

There was a click and a half-alive voice grunted.

"Henry. It's Matt."

Matt scanned the parking lot of his apartment complex, feeling like he was the object of the kind of surveillance he usually initiated. He should have hit the sack and called Henry in the morning.

"Matt?" The voice grew concerned. "Wassup?"

"Need a favor."

"At freaking one in the morning," the voice said. It belonged to a Portland detective Matt had befriended a few years ago when he'd accompanied a true bad guy back to Oregon for interrogation. The prisoner was a Hispanic man who'd apparently stabbed a guy in a Portland club for dancing with his girlfriend. The victim didn't make it, and Boise Police picked up the man after he broke down in a truck on Interstate 84 by the airport.

Henry met Matt at the Portland Airport with the suspect and offered Matt lunch if he'd accompany him back to the jail. Since then, he had come to find that Henry was a great detective from the standpoint of digging up information, but not much of a street cop. They were both cyclists and had shared some intense rides around the Portland area a few times a year. Henry might've been a little skittish around bad guys, but he could outride Matt like nobody else.

"Need to find out anything unusual about a guy and his current whereabouts. Dr. Lewis—"

"Hold on. God, I owe you a favor or two, but can't you wait until daylight like sane people?"

Matt could hear shuffling over the phone and then Henry returned.

"Dr. Lewis Vanoble." Matt spelled out the last name. "He was a doctor in Ontario, Oregon, in the early 1980s, and retired in 2009 in Salem."

"This have anything to do with that babe?"

Matt said nothing, knowing Henry meant Donny.

"I figured so," Henry said. "You're a persistent bastard."

"You'll do it?"

"Absolutely."

"I'll email you some background I found. One more thing."

"Yes?"

"See if there is anything on Dr. A.D. Hewitt. Probably from around Boise or Salt Lake in the 70s, early 80s. I'm checking here, but best to check your sources too. Besides, you'll dig up more than I will."

"Every time, buddy. Can I go back to sleep?"

"Goodnight, Henry."

The phone went silent, and Matt watched a car turn the corner of an intersection about fifty yards distant. A stray cat walked the fence near the stairs to his apartment. Otherwise, he seemed to be the only living presence around. He had a feeling some Post goon was watching his every move.

Hewitt was probably a stretch. He was betting more on Vanoble.

He'd come up empty on Hewitt back at the office. Of course, he'd only done a cursory search on the Internet and in the Boise Police records. Tomorrow he'd check the NCIC, the FBI database, and look up driver's license records of both Hewitt and Vanoble. Maybe even check out their medical licensing. If he was lucky, he wouldn't need Henry. But Henry was good. He had a way of finding that nugget of information Matt needed most.

Chapter 24
Smokes and More, North End, Boise
Saturday

Delay the inevitable. It seemed the best course of action. Last time Penny's boss asked to speak with her about her job, he'd reduced her hours to part-time and said he couldn't afford to provide insurance benefits any more. Penny had no way to pay if she or Serena got sick or in an accident. She hadn't admitted such a state to her mom. No way would she have that conversation now.

His name was Jake Robinson, but his nickname—The Rat—seemed a good fit for the moment. He hadn't appeared too concerned earlier when he said they should discuss Penny's hours again. But then again, Rat never seemed too concerned about anything. What more could he do? That was easy. Let her go. Fire her. Following the blow-up with Matt last night, she didn't need this right now.

Watching for a chance to procrastinate, Penny noted a customer walking straight to the counter. It was a regular in the same gray suit here for his cigars.

Crap, she thought. Why couldn't it be someone who needed some real help?

She grabbed the merchandise, rang it up, scanned the man's credit card, retrieved the signed copy, and threw it in the register.

As the guy started to leave, she jumped around to the front of the counter. "You always buy the same smokes. How about something a little more interesting?"

The man smiled. "What do you have in mind?"

"Just thought you might be interested in another brand of cigars. I don't smoke 'em, but I hear these are pretty good." She pulled down a box produced in the Dominican Republic that some of the young execs had been buying lately.

"Nah, not what I had in mind."

This time the man's smile was a little creepy. Talking to Rat about the further demise of her employment was almost preferable to dealing with a guy who wanted to get in her pants at the first sign of conversation. She placed the box of cigars back in the display and turned away from the man without another word.

The little chimes on the door clanged together announcing the man's departure. Maybe she should walk out the door too. Avoid the disappointment of being let go.

Instead, she waltzed back to Rat's desk—a big gray metallic thing that looked like it belonged in a 1960s police movie—and sat down.

The back of the store was really just a big warehouse full of everything they sold except for Rat's ugly desk; a computer; biker, liquor, and smoke shop pictures, some with stupid looking girls plastered on the front; and one restroom the size of a phone booth.

Rat fit the profile of the owner of girly pictures. Hefty guy, shaved head, a chin-strap black beard, a couple of piercings through his eyebrows, and a black biker T-shirt for every day of the week.

"So what's up?" Penny asked. She tried not to sound nervous.

"I want you back to full time."

She blanked on a reply.

"Forty hours guaranteed, maybe a few more. Also, you'll be back under the benefits plan."

"No shit. I thought you were gonna fire me."

"You want the job or not?"

"Business doesn't seem to be any better."

Rat gave her a look that would scare anyone else. "Is this a deal, or you going to fart around back here all day?"

She punched him in the shoulder, grinned, and danced back into the front of the store. She immediately pulled her phone out but then put it back in her pocket. Matt was still on the enemy list. He'd have to hear about it later. She could tell her ma after work. In person.

Suddenly she realized what had just happened. Surveying the store for any customers or shoplifters, she found none and then returned to Rat. He was moving some boxes around.

"This don't make any sense," she said. "Somebody put you up to this."

Rat was grunting as he pushed three boxes onto a hand truck. "What difference does it make? You're getting a sweet deal. If you don't want it, I'm sure I can find someone else." He stopped and pulled out a stack of job applications from his desk. "This is just from the last month. There's a lot of skin looking for work."

Life was good. The skies were blue, the wind wasn't blowing, and Penny was off until Monday. Her first order of business was to let her mother know of her good fortune, though she wouldn't be surprised if her mother was aware of the news already. The walk from work wasn't but a mile or so. Today she could walk forever.

She crossed State Street and headed north into her mother's neighborhood. Her neighborhood. She smiled. *Her house.* She owned it free and clear. It had come about in a most unexpected way, but it was her house.

Down the street, a vehicle was parked in front of her ma's place. It was a black SUV. A very nice Lexus SUV. Her ma didn't know anyone who had that kind of dough other than Andrew Post. She suddenly felt strange and distant as she approached the house. It was as if her mother no longer lived there. An image of her ma and Andrew Post, embraced and intimate, flashed before her. Her skin prickled and she walked rapidly by.

"God, this is too weird. Too strange. Ma's still in mourning," she said to herself. She clasped her hands together, stopped, tilted her head toward the sidewalk, and closed her eyes.

"Momma!"

It was Serena. She ran to Penny. "Where are you going? You missed Grandma Annie's house."

Penny squatted and hugged her child.

"I saw you walk by." Serena laughed. "I thought maybe you were trying to play a trick on me."

"No. I was just thinking, and I walked right by."

"Mr. Andrew is here."

Andrew Post and her ma stood on the porch, Post smiling, her mother's face painted with the usual look of concern. Even though it was Saturday, Post was dressed in a suit. Her ma was wearing a blue housecoat. She looked like his cleaning lady.

"Geez, the man must have one helluva laundry bill," Penny said under her breath.

They all went in the house without saying much other than the usual greetings and small talk. Her mother was busy making dinner for Serena. From the looks of the house, it didn't appear that Post had been there long, though it was tough to tell, considering her ma's penchant for cleanliness. When Matt came over to Penny's, anyone could tell how long he'd stayed based on the cumulative mess the two of them made. After an evening of TV movies, there would be blankets, food, drinks, beer, and other stuff thrown around plus the effects of allowing Serena full use of the rest of the house.

Serena ran to the table. "Yea, mac and cheese."

Penny paced the room. She needed Matt. She needed a smoke. She walked out on the front porch, sat on the rail, and produced a Camel Light and a lighter. As she lit the cigarette, Andrew Post came through the front door. He sat in one of the two wicker chairs and watched the street.

"I know this is a bit strange for you," he said as he stared down a curious jogger on the opposite sidewalk.

Penny's fingers shook. She dropped the lighter, then the cigarette. "Shit!"

"I tried to get Mr. Thuban to quit his cigars. I suppose when you cling to something that provides comfort, even if it is fleeting, it is hard to let go." The man's voice was remarkably smooth.

"Okay." Penny retrieved her cigarette and lighter. "You and Ma, it's weird. I just want to know what's happening."

"We've become friends."

"Bullshit. It's Dad's letter. Something about you in that letter, right?"

"Yes."

The direct answer shocked Penny. She expected at least denial or silence on the subject, the only result she'd managed from her mother.

"I won't tell you anything about the letter," he said.

"You've read it?"

"Yes."

"So Dad said something about you in the letter. Something that links you and Ma."

"You're quite perceptive. Your mother will have to determine when and if she ever tells you what is in the letter."

"And you became friends after reading it? I don't get it." Penny took a quick detour down to the sidewalk, leaving the man behind. She went to the mailbox, tapped on it, and checked inside to find it empty. Then she popped back up the steps and onto the porch.

Post sat patiently.

"You like my ma?"

"She is a good woman."

"She's happier lately. That's a good thing, right?"

He smiled. "It is a good thing."

Penny took refuge in the other wicker chair next to Post. They sat in silence for a minute or two. More neighbors drifted by on the sidewalk. The Johanssens from church. The tall man and his squat wife eyed them like a couple of gangsters. After they passed, Penny could hear the murmur of their conversation.

"These people always staring. Don't that bother you?"

"No."

"It would me. Listen, I want to thank you for helping me out," Penny said, surprising herself. She didn't expect to be so forthright with Post. He made it easy.

"Not a problem."

"I mean the job. You must've put some heat on Rat." She laughed.

"It's kind of like the mob, huh?"

He smiled again.

"You could just give me the dough. Then I wouldn't have to work."

"No, I could not. You need to work, even if it involves selling smokes."

It was the first statement where his tone changed. She couldn't tell if he was irritated because she worked at a smoke shop, or that there was such a business.

"Have you ever been to Colorado?" he asked.

She shook her head. "Not really. We drove through one time when Dad took me in his truck for a summer trip. Don't remember much other than truck stops and greasy food. I was about Serena's age."

"I've asked your mother to accompany me to Denver next week. I would like you to go. My staff will take you wherever you desire."

"Red Rocks?" Penny said as she grabbed his arm.

He gently removed her hand. "I assume you mean of the amphitheater fame?"

"Yes! My friends Lala and Benjie went a couple of years ago and showed me some bitchin' pictures. The Little Senators. Great band."

"Red Rocks? There are many other things to see around Denver. I don't even know if there is a show going on."

"I just want to go there. I don't care if I see a band," she said, out of breath with excitement. "But if somebody good is playing, I'd want to go, assuming we could get tickets."

This time she watched Post smile as if he knew a secret.

"Oh yeah! Bet you wouldn't have trouble scoring tickets, huh?" She popped her palm up against her forehead. "Son of a bitch. I'm back to full time. I can't go anywhere."

"I believe your employer will allow this one trip."

She jumped up and ran inside. Her mother was sitting at the table with Serena. Penny gave her the thumbs-up sign and shouted, "Red Rocks!" Her ma raised her eyebrows. Obviously she had no idea what Penny was talking about. It didn't matter. They were going on a road trip.

Chapter 25
Boise River Greenbelt, Boise
Monday

It was a bad day for a ride. Matt wanted to leave some frustration—in particular, his spat with Penny and his unofficial suspension—on the bike path. He had miscalculated how busy the Greenbelt would be on a summer Monday morning. So far, his trek had been spent dodging dog walkers, joggers, pedestrians, and other cyclists. And it was unusually hot. By late morning, he'd consumed more than half of his water ration only a third of the way into his planned twenty mile traverse.

Now this. A flat, and on the rear tire.

He grabbed his repair kit, removed the wheel from the frame and chain, and set about fixing the tire. His phone blared out Penny's ringtone.

He'd not heard from her all weekend. Past experience suggested it was best to let her come to him even if the dispute was his fault. She needed her time to heal, and no amount of premature discussion would help.

The ringtone played for a few seconds. Was she going to let him have it all over again or tell him the spat was over?

He tapped the screen and held the phone up.

"Hi." Penny's voice was gentle as if nothing had happened. "I'm going on a jet to Denver."

The bike wheel dropped onto Matt's lap. "For good?"

"Shut-up. I'm going to see Red Rocks. Post is taking me and Ma on his plane."

Matt had heard Penny talk about going to Denver to see a good band someday. He'd promised to take her. They'd just never gotten around to it.

"You can't go," he said, unsure of what else to say.

"Post is not so bad. He fixed my job so I'm back full time at the shop. Health insurance too, buddy."

Matt had been contemplating how much to tell Penny. He was hoping she might help him talk Annie into revealing the contents of the letter. He'd never considered Penny would turn into some kind of Andrew Post advocate.

"Don't go," he said.

"Stop worrying. I'll be back Wednesday night or Thursday."

"You're leaving today?"

"In about twenty minutes. Serena is staying with the Abernathys so she won't miss vacation bible school."

"Don't get on that plane! I'll be there as fast as I can."

"Chill. I'm coming back. It's not like he's some kind of murderer. Love ya. Bye."

Matt sat there with the phone up to his ear. He couldn't process what he'd just heard. He fell back into the grass and closed his eyes. Then the phone went off again.

It was the generic ringtone—the one programmed for most everyone else.

"I got some stuff for you." It was Henry, his police buddy from Portland.

Matt couldn't manage a reply.

"Matt, you there?"

"Yep. What've ya got?"

"I thought I had a lost connection."

"Just give me the news," Matt said, wondering if it was possible to fix his tire, ride six miles, jump in his car, and get to the airport in twenty minutes. Not likely. Have someone else go stop her? Who? He could call Penny back, but she wouldn't answer. He could tell by how she ended the call. Text her? She'd ignore that too.

"Geez, do a buddy a favor and get kicked in the teeth."

"Sorry."

"Okay, this A.D. Hewitt guy," Henry said, "I can't find squat on him. Either he's not or was not a doctor or the press got the wrong name. I checked similar names. Nothing. There were a couple of doctors named Hewitt back then, one in Twin Falls and another one in Salmon. One in Boise, Jack Hewitt, but he was an OB-GYN. Also did a quick search on the net and found nothing about a Post family doctor. So I called the Post empire this morning and said I was trying to contact an old friend named A.D. Hewitt, and he used to be Post's personal physician in the 70s or 80s. They said Post has had the same doctor for years, Dr. Marvin Hash, now in Cheyenne, Wyoming. There are several pictures of Hash and Post on the Web together at a golf tournament in 1986 and at a Republican fund-raiser in 1997. So the story fits. Post flies to Cheyenne for all his appointments now."

"That's strange," Matt said, gaining interest in the information.

"Best I can tell Hash practiced in Boise from 1978 to about 2000. After that, he left town to retire but still sees old patients. So that's the bad news."

Matt waited in silence.

"So you want the good news or not?"

"Sure."

"You could at least give me some acknowledgment. Some excitement. I spent a butt load of time on this for you."

"You love it, Henry. Yea for Henry. You're the best damn detective in Oregon. Now tell me what you have."

"Okay, drumroll. I found Vanoble!"

Matt waited.

"He's in a nursing home in Salem. Not doing well. Got in touch with his daughter. She was suspicious, so not sure we can just barge in and question him. The way she talks, he might not be able to tell us much. I'm heading down there in a few days for a friend's wedding. I can swing by and check him out. At least see if he's coherent enough to talk to you."

"That'd be great." Matt touched the red button on the screen and sat up, unconsciously hanging up on Henry. He felt like he was in the middle of the roadway trying to decide which way to go. One lane would take him to his issue with Penny, the other back to his Post investigation. The smart thing to do would be to keep riding no matter what direction he chose.

Chapter 26
Nurse Christine's House, Meridian, Idaho
Tuesday

The box house sat on an acre within shouting distance of the Interstate in Meridian, a bedroom suburb of Boise. Out front, Matt noticed a woman weeding a garden on her hands and knees. She halted the work, put her gloves in a bucket, and rose to meet him halfway up the walk.

She was short and plump with blond hair bought from a bottle at a discount store. Her hand was rough, but she had a polite smile that helped him stow some of his misgivings about approaching an old lady for information from three decades ago.

"I'm looking for Christine Miller, the former Christine Vasquez." He held out his police badge, though it seemed unnecessary. "I called last night."

"Yes, she is expecting you. I'm Sherry Miller, her daughter. Come inside."

The visit was the perfect diversion. Matt had spent Monday night in his apartment carrying around his phone, waiting for Penny to call. She never did. Finally, he called her just before midnight, but there was no answer. Texted her. No reply. Not long after, Henry called again with a startling piece of news only Henry could discover. Vanoble had received a financial payment of two hundred thousand dollars from a venture capital firm in California called Sentinel Partners. Henry was not able to connect the firm directly to Post, but the payment had been made about a month after Katlin's death and shortly after Vanoble had left his job in Ontario.

Matt had tried to contact Vanoble earlier in the day. A quick female voice had answered and said Vanoble was in no condition to speak to anyone on the phone. Matt would have to wait on Henry's visit to find out more about the good doctor.

Sherry Miller held open the screen door, and Matt entered a small living room complete with Early American furniture about as old as the lady he expected to see. The room had a pleasant flower-like fragrance and was clean. The daughter offered to prepare the drink of Matt's choice: iced tea, coffee, lemonade, milk, or orange juice. He opted for lemonade.

Christine Miller entered with a smile and held out a hand that appeared to be ravaged by arthritis. She was not quite as old as he was expecting, maybe a few years younger than Annie. He gently took her fragile hand and returned the smile.

"Let's speak on the porch," she said. "It seems a sin to waste such a nice day."

Outside, they sat on two wooden chairs suitable for the veranda of a Pacific Coast hotel.

"Great porch and view, Mrs. Miller," Matt said as he scanned the surroundings. The porch faced the foothills to the northeast and was bounded on both sides by operating farms. Mostly likely, the place was once an old farm house, and Christine Miller or some previous owner had bought it along with a little buffer zone of land on each side.

The woman reached out and touched Matt gently on the arm. "Please. Call me Christine."

Matt nodded. "How long before your neighbors sell out?"

"Can't tell. I thought when we bought this place nobody would ever move out here. Now we're just hoping to outlast the sprawl."

The daughter appeared with fresh-squeezed lemonade for Matt and orange juice for her mother, and just as quickly disappeared into the house.

The woman sipped her juice and then spoke. "I know you must be a busy young man. You said something on the phone about the birth of the Post twins."

Matt tapped his boot on the wooden floor of the porch. "I'm working on a case related to Katlin Post's death. I know that was a long time ago, and you probably don't remember much, but I'm searching for anything you might recall about the birth of the Post twins."

"Are you kidding? It was always a great conversation starter when I tell people I took care of Donny Post when she was born."

Matt pulled out his notebook and recorder. "Do you mind?" he asked, nodding toward the recording device.

"Not at all." The woman paused as if to recollect her thoughts.

He opened his notebook to a new page. "Donita and Katlin were born minutes apart on the night of December 8th. That sound about right?"

"Don't remember the exact date, but yes, about right. I was in the nursery that night, and they brought in three babies. It was a very slow month. Most people around here do their thing in the winter if you know what I mean. They have babies in the late summer and fall."

Matt liked this woman. Their conversation felt as though they'd sat on this porch and had similar discussions many times before. A perfect personality for a caregiver.

"To tell you the truth, I have a better memory of the third child. Can't recall her name. Her father came to the nursery and told me a heartbreaking story about his wife and the loss of their first two children. I'll never forget his face. He put that on me just as I was coming off the night shift. I was young and remember going home and having a good cry. I never did that in front of a patient," she said as she tapped Matt gently on the shoulder.

The discussion had taken an unexpected turn. Matt had never heard details about Annie's history with childbirth. He knew of the two children. Nobody ever spoke of either one.

"Did you see the Posts that night?" he asked.

"Yes, Mr. Post came in about an hour before the father I told you about. What a contrast. That's why I remember it so well. His behavior was reprehensible. He had no desire to hold either one of the babies. He only seemed interested in when they could leave. He demanded they be released as soon as possible. He had some kind of business to take care of. Said his wife was half sedated most of the time, so he'd have to deal with the children himself. It was like those babies were some kind of annoyance to the man."

"Pretty cold?"

"Cold? I'd call him an SOB to his face if I saw him today." She clenched her jaw, staring out into the distance. "All that money. Heard one of the twins died shortly after. I'm sure that was a minor irritation to him, like swatting a fly at the dinner table."

"That was Katlin. You know anything about her death?"

The woman took a deep breath, as if she were blowing the anger out of her lungs. "No, not really. Just what I heard through the grapevine and in the newspapers. Died somewhere out of town. Think it was some kind of heart issue, though that kind of shocked me. As I recall, the twins were pretty healthy."

She paused and stroked her chin. "You know, I would have remembered something like a cardiac issue, especially for such a high profile patient. From what I do remember, the other child in the nursery that night had some type of problem. They did some tests. I don't remember the details except that the tests were clean, so she must've come through okay. Never saw her again. Used to work four days on and three off, and that night was my last shift. I probably should've checked on her."

"She's okay."

"You know of her?"

Matt nodded.

The woman looked relieved. Then her face tightened again. "That man, Andrew Post. Something about him made that night stick in my head. I can remember being happy I didn't have to come back to work with him around the hospital."

Matt certainly identified with such a position. Everything Post did stuck in his head. He stood and drained the last sip of the excellent lemonade. "Thanks for your help and hospitality."

"I'm sure I haven't been much help."

"You know Penny, the other baby? I do know her. She's alive and well in Boise. A friend of mine."

"Wonderful!" Christine Miller stood and gave Matt a gentle embrace. "And her parents?"

"Her mother is fine. Her father passed away last year."

The smile vanished. "Oh my," was all she could say. Then the good-natured persona returned. "But they had a healthy baby. The Lord delivers. You do know that."

Chapter 27
In the Air, Return Trip from Denver
Wednesday Evening

Thirty-one thousand feet over the badlands of southern Wyoming, the executive jet streaked through the heavens at five hundred miles an hour en route to the state capital of Idaho. The weather was exceptional, though thunderheads upstream were producing what the pilots called a light chop. The flight plan listed the aircrew and six passengers on board.

ETA was fifty-seven minutes. Annie didn't understand half of the pilot-speak crackling over the intercom system and displayed in letters on a flat-panel monitor recessed into the wall behind her. She'd only flown a handful of times but never like this.

She didn't like flying. Every little bump felt like a car hitting an unexpected dip in the road, leaving her stomach somewhere in the wake. Frank had said it took him fifteen hours to make a delivery to Denver via Interstates 84, 80, and 25. This evening she would finish the return trip in an hour and forty minutes. Everything Andrew Post did seemed to be compressed into these smaller chunks of time. She'd had lunch with the man last Thursday and dinner at her house on Saturday, attended a local Republican fund-raiser and a show at the Morrison Center on Sunday, and now she was returning from a combined business/pleasure trip to Denver on Wednesday evening. All compressed into a week. None of it felt like the times she and Frank would go out to enjoy themselves. This felt like business.

The cabin reminded Annie of the executive motor coaches she and Frank had dreamed of owning. All luxury crammed into small spaces. Leather reclining seats that moved into virtually any position, tables recessed into the walls, a small but well-equipped kitchen and bar, and virtually any form of electronic entertainment feasible in a cigar-shaped room flashing through the sky at five hundred miles an hour. She wanted to keep her attention on the view out the window—the shadows of dusty earth, the highway with tiny matchbox cars and trucks, and the occasional patch of snow on the distant mountains. Instead, she focused on the scene inside the cabin. She would occasionally reach down to the pocket on the side of her seat and touch the tip of the little bag Penny had held up and proclaimed "the barf bag" at the beginning of the trip. So far, so good.

It was an awkward situation. Like a family on the last leg of a long vacation, the passengers were quiet. Annie occupied one of a quartet of chairs facing each other in the front of the cabin. Andrew sat across from her, examining some document on an electronic tablet on a foldout table, and occasionally, as if some alarm on his watch had triggered the action, looked up and smiled at her. On her right, across the aisle, Lanny—the public affairs lady they called L.A.—was sleeping with a magazine sitting across her chest. She'd been assigned to Annie in Denver during most of Tuesday and Wednesday when Andrew was away on whatever business had brought him there. Catty-corner sat Gavin, the lawyer, who had been consumed by his smartphone. Either he'd been reading, texting, or talking quietly, accompanied by an expression that suggested urgency. For the moment, he was staring out the window.

Annie glanced around the cabin, averting her eyes from anyone who looked up from their present distractions. Penny was seated in the back—actually lying in the back—on the only couch on the plane, dressed in her holey blue jeans and a T-shirt. At least this time, it was a plain blue shirt with no ugly saying or crude heavy metal band splashed all over it. She had earbuds stuck in her ears and was twitching to some kind of music Annie was glad she didn't have to hear. Donny, in great contrast, sat directly across the aisle in another one of the leather lounge chairs, spiffed up in a business suit, her black polished hair pulled back tight, staring through dark-rimmed reading glasses at a stack of papers. Her feet were going about as fast as the plane.

Sisters, thought Annie. The two of them had nearly put a stop to the trip before it started. Donny had no problem with Penny traveling along. She probably had been told in advance. But Penny. It had taken plenty of cajoling, the lure of a jet flight, and a visit to Red Rocks to see *The Finger Puppets* to get her on board the same plane as Donny.

Sisters. Annie thought they would make great subjects for some type of psychological study on the role of a kid's environment versus their genetic heritage. She sighed just loud enough for Andrew to hear. She put her hand to her mouth as he looked over his bifocals at her.

"I'm sorry," was all she could manage to say.

He took his glasses off and sat up. "Would you like something to drink? Eat? Something to read?"

She shook her head.

"I feel bad. Everyone seems to be busy except L.A.," he said. The woman remained asleep. "You must've worn her out."

That wasn't the case at all. The woman had worn Annie out. L.A. ran at top speed and reminded Annie of her realtor friend Betty

Sanders. The threesome—L.A., Penny, and Annie—had spent all day Tuesday with an agenda of things they "must do." All of it pre-planned and regimented.

The issue had been keeping up with L.A. and Penny. They'd visited the historic district near downtown, some place called the 16ᵗʰ Street Mall, the Denver Art Museum, and the Denver Aquarium. But the highlight, the place that had really perked up Penny, was Red Rocks Park, an area that jutted out of the hills to the west of town. L.A. had dropped Annie off at the hotel around dinnertime and had attended the concert Tuesday evening with Penny. Annie was grateful. She had not been too thrilled with the idea of dropping Penny off alone. Andrew had returned to the hotel to have dinner with Annie that evening around eight o'clock.

All day Wednesday, during a quick trip into the nearby Rockies, the word of the day from Penny was "bitchin." She'd been hyped-up since the concert. L.A. had seemed more pleased with herself with every repetition of the word. All the while, Andrew, Donny, and the lawyer had disappeared for another day of meetings.

The entire trip felt like a frantic, schedule-driven chore for Annie. In contrast, the return flight to Boise seemed a too quiet, almost boring affair. She leaned back in the seat, listened to the hum of the jet engines, and sighed.

"I can put this away," Andrew said, nodding to his electronic tablet. "There isn't much privacy, but we can talk if you'd like." He glanced down again, scribbled something with a stylus on the notepad, and then looked back up.

Annie stood. She would give Andrew what he wanted—permission to return to his work. "I'm going to go back and talk to Penny." She moved carefully through the plane, nudged Penny to move her legs, and sat at the end of the couch. Penny placed her bare feet on Annie's lap.

Off came the earbuds. She could hear a faint tinny version of some rap song playing on her daughter's chest. "Hi," Annie said softly.

"This is some freaking way to travel, huh?" Penny's voice was low as well. "My third plane flight in all my life. I could get used to it."

"Not exactly our style."

"Should I?" Penny asked.

"Should you what?"

"Get used to it."

Annie didn't answer.

"I mean," Penny said, moving her feet lightly to an invisible tune, "you two are like dating. Is this going to be the way it is?"

Annie tilted her head urgently toward Donny.

Penny understood right away. "Her? She's listening to her tunes and doing her homework."

Annie hadn't noticed that Donny was also wearing a white pair of earbuds connected to an outlet in the chair. Penny leaned over and punched Donny with some force on her forearm. "Hey, what are you listening to?"

Looking disgusted, Donny removed her headphones and spoke, "What?"

"Your tunes?"

"Some stream supplied by the leasing company."

Penny stared back as if she needed an interpreter.

"It's an eighties channel."

"Your company doesn't own this plane?" Annie asked.

Donny mellowed instantly. "No, Father's too cheap for that. We lease a plane when we need it. It does save money, but sometimes we get crappy flight crews and older planes. This one's pretty good. Father won't even splurge for a stewardess."

Annie had to smile again. Cheap and Andrew weren't often included in the same sentence.

"What other tunes do you like?" Penny said.

Donny closed the folder she was perusing and swiveled her chair toward Penny. "I like a lot of music. Even classical, though I doubt that's your style."

"Just trying to talk. Sorry."

Annie thought it might be a good time to escape. Maybe the two girls would start to converse. Even get to know each other. So far, they were at least civil.

"Can you excuse us?" Donny asked Annie.

The request was a surprise but just the escape Annie desired. She nodded and made her way through the narrow passage between Donny's chair and Penny. She was a little hesitant. The amount of estrogen, maybe more like testosterone, in the back of the plane was elevated. She wouldn't have been surprised if the two ended up in a tussle on the floor. So far, they'd avoided each other quite well the entire trip.

Annie nudged Andrew. "I'm tired of flying backwards." He tapped Gavin, the lawyer, and pointed to Annie's empty seat. The lawyer gathered his belongings and swiftly moved across from Andrew.

Annie just wanted to eavesdrop or maybe even referee. She would be closer in this chair, but her back would be to the girls. That might provide an environment more open to discussion. She sat and pretended to read a magazine she found in a file of reading material next to the chair. Andrew looked over, appeared pleased, and returned to whatever was of such importance on a Wednesday evening.

Annie tilted her head and could just make out the conversation. There was tenseness in Donny's voice. It was not going to be girl talk.

"God, you are easy not to like," Donny said.

"What's your problem?"

"For whatever crazy reason, Matt likes you. Why he picked you, I could never understand."

Annie inched her chair about a quarter of a turn sideways in order to keep an eye on the pair. Penny was leaning up on her elbows, staring at Donny as if she'd been accused of some crime.

"You don't even see it, do you?" Donny said. "He loves you. I assume you love him. But you don't show it. No commitment. That's your problem. Always has been."

"What the hell does that mean?"

The conversation was growing a bit louder, but not enough to wake L.A. or gain the attention of Andrew.

"It means stop worrying about marriage. Stop worrying about me. Matt won't even sleep with me."

Penny sat up. Annie inched the chair sideways a bit more to a position where she could intervene if necessary. Still Andrew did not look up.

"Any guy that sleeps with you ain't on my list," Penny said. "And stop lecturing me like you're my big sister or something."

The statement hit Annie like a slap in the face. Donny *was* Penny's big sister—by less than an hour.

Donny laughed, this time loud enough that even the lawyer glanced at her. "He did sleep with me. Sixteen years ago. Over and over in the same night. We were great together. But that was the end. He couldn't think about anything but getting back to you."

Penny's face was red. She flipped her dreadlocks back. "I'm not surprised. Just about everyone has slept with you at some point. Doesn't exactly lead to long term commitments. Emphasis on commitment!"

"All I'm saying is if you don't want the guy, let go. I'd take him in a heartbeat."

"You?" Penny started to laugh and a snort escaped.

Annie nudged Andrew in the knee. He placed his glasses on the table. She wondered whether he had heard any of the conversation.

"You think because I wear a suit and drive a car that's worth more than your little cottage that I can't whip the snot out of you?" Donny's expression never changed. It was as if she had this kind of conversation on a daily basis. In contrast, Penny's face appeared ready for combat.

Annie moved in and partially blocked the space in the aisle between the two girls. "I would ask the two of you to be civil. Penny, we are guests here."

"Penny? It's always me," Penny said in a voice trailing off.

Donny spoke at same time. "All I said was for her to marry her damn boyfriend. I'm trying to do her a favor. Then she calls me a tramp."

"Stop!" Annie said it loud enough to wake up L.A. "If you just knew how important it is for you to get along. Don't you understand the bond you have?"

"Annie!" This time it was Andrew's voice shouting through the small cabin.

Immediately she understood what had just leaked out of her mouth. Donny and Penny both went silent, waiting for some explanation. Annie returned to her seat and picked up the magazine. She could hear the girls whispering to each other. The conversation was still tense but behaved.

Andrew leaned over and spoke quietly. "What are you doing?"

Annie grabbed his hand and gripped it firmly. He returned the squeeze and went back to work.

A few minutes went by. She had been reading some article but had no idea what it was about. She leaned over toward Andrew. "Look back there."

He spoke without looking away from his documents, "I'm sorry. It's not an issue for me."

"Not an issue? Look at them. They *are* sisters."

He turned to look. The two girls stopped their conversation for a moment. Donny smiled at her father. Penny craned her head backwards from her prone position on the couch to see the object of Donny's attention.

Andrew returned to his work.

Annie thumbed through a few more pages and then whispered again. "You are so one-dimensional."

He turned off the tablet and put some papers back in a folder. "Okay. That one requires explanation."

"Your work. It's all you do. Even when you talk to me, you're working. Our outings feel like an entry in a planner. You do one thing. You are obviously one of the greatest people on the planet at it, but it makes you somewhat uninteresting."

"There are a number of people who find me fascinating," he said, leaning back in his chair.

"They are probably just as shallow," she said, agitated, but trying to hide it. She wanted to appear just like Donny. State her case in a matter-of-fact manner in a way he might understand.

He held up the folder. She stared at it until he placed it back on the table.

"You know what this is? It's a plan to buy seven stores in Southern California. We don't have a presence there, and I'm not big on acquisition as a business strategy. We've never taken a step like this. This plan is Donny's. She desperately wants to move this forward. This plan is everything in the world to her. That's why I'm so engaged at the moment."

Annie had no retort. No counterpunch.

Andrew put his items back in order on the table, turned on the electronic tablet, and went back to examining tables and figures.

Fifteen minutes later, over the intercom, the pilot's voice stated they would be landing on 28R in ten minutes and for everyone to be sure their seatbelts were fastened. The plane swooped down over Interstate 84, landed, and returned the passengers to the private jet area where they had started on Monday. Two limos were waiting. One for Penny and Annie and the other for the Post company passengers.

All the while, Penny and Donny had continued their hushed conversation until Penny entered the limo. Annie wondered what they had said. No matter what, the trip had accomplished two goals. Penny was talking to Donny, and at the very least, had gained a more favorable attitude toward Andrew.

Chapter 28
Annie Lorda's Residence, North End, Boise
Wednesday Evening

Mr. Choi, Andrew's limo driver, walked through Annie's house like an invader. Annie would have to become used to intrusion. Andrew had insisted his people check out her house, restaurants, even Sunday church and the YMCA before she would be allowed to settle in on her own. Choi was Korean and built like a bulldozer. Annie didn't like the idea of Mr. Choi taking someone down on her account.

Nevertheless, she was under the protection of the Post Corporation for the time being. She'd have to admit it was a comfort, given all the phone calls she'd received since being seen with Andrew at the restaurant last week. And she'd been away half the time since that very public encounter. The story, a kind of Cinderella for old people as Penny had called it, was accelerating in the media. She and Andrew had certainly hit the ground running.

While Choi completed his search, she checked her new answering machine. Andrew had told her to install the device and get an unlisted number, but she'd had the same phone number for three decades, and losing it would be like losing a friend.

The little LED screen showed forty-seven calls. Before Andrew, she might have received ten to fifteen calls a week, mostly from Penny.

She entered her bedroom to unpack the suitcase that Mr. Choi had hauled in minutes earlier. Something was wrong. The bed was made, her latest project was folded on a corner table, the curtains were pulled, and her bedroom slippers and nightgown were in order on the bench at the end of her bed.

It was the yellow bag by the closet. It belonged *in* the closet.

She wanted to shout to Mr. Choi, who was probably on his way down the sidewalk. She resisted. How would she explain she was certain someone had been in her house just because a yellow bag was out of place?

Mr. Choi would have noted any forced entry. He'd checked every door, every window, and each room. If she called him back, he wouldn't find anything unusual. She knew the identity of the intruder.

There were only three people with a key to her house. The only one that had not been out of town was Matt.

Annie heard the front door open again.

"Mr. Choi?"

There was no answer. Only footsteps heading her way.

She reached in her purse and grabbed the new smartphone Andrew had given her. She was new at this. Maybe she should've called Mr. Choi back. Dial one-five, he'd said, and someone would come quickly. He'd also said she could dial 911.

She touched the little picture of the phone, pressed nine, then one, and held the phone in the air in front of her. The footsteps had moved into the kitchen and were now heading her way.

Before she pressed the numeral one again, Matt appeared in the doorway. His face held an extra day or two of stubble, and his eyes lacked their usual sparkle. He was wearing a T-shirt, cargo shorts, and flip-flops.

"Annie?"

She threw the phone at him. He caught it.

"Have you completely flipped?" he said. "How could you take Penny with you? You guys just disappeared to Denver. It's one thing to run around with Post. That's your business. But leave Penny out of this!"

"Give me my key," was all Annie could manage. "I don't want you here anymore."

She couldn't believe what was coming out of her mouth. Matt had been her son. The son she never had. His parents had divorced when he was in junior high school, and the distress had caused him to grow very close to Penny and the entire Lorda family. All throughout the ups and downs with Penny and her marriage, he'd come and gone in the Lorda house as if he'd grown up there.

Annie was shaking. She wanted to slap him. "Did you find what you were looking for?"

His eyes scanned past her into the bedroom.

She turned her back to Matt, returned to her suitcase, and started to unpack. "Andrew suggested cameras and an alarm system for the house," she said. "I laughed. I said, 'Why would anyone want to break into my house?'"

"Don't change the subject." Matt's voice was less intense. "I told you that man is dangerous. You don't listen."

Annie spun around. "You won't find the letter. Now get out of my house!"

A knock on the front door interrupted any potential response. Matt disappeared. Annie could hear him talking to a reporter. He told the woman to take a hike and the door slammed. His movements were still evident in the front room. She wished he had left, but she also felt a tinge of guilt. Her discomfort was in the realization of a choice she might have to make—Matt, her adopted child, or Andrew Post, a man who was drawing her further into something she couldn't quite explain. She didn't want to make that choice.

Several minutes passed and the phone rang. Neither she nor Matt answered it. The machine clicked on. It was a reporter for the *Seattle Daily*. He wanted to do an interview in Boise in the morning or at her convenience. He seemed to be telling, not asking.

She put away a pair of slacks she'd taken but not worn on the trip and went into the living room. Matt wasn't there. She looked through the window on the porch. Not there either.

"*Seattle Daily*? That's a big paper." The voice came from the darkness of the kitchen. Matt was sitting at the dinette with his hands holding up his chin. Annie switched on the light and took a seat at the table.

"What can I do to put a stop to this?" he said.

"I know you have never liked Andrew. I know you think he is some kind of gangster. But I haven't seen any of that. Yes, he's an intense businessman, and I'm sure he operates on the edge of ethical behavior at times. He's helped me in the last few weeks. I needed the help. I needed a friend too."

The response was an internal confession. Annie was seeing a good side to Andrew Post. She'd rationalized "need" as the reason for their relationship. The reality was that she was lonely. Frank had been gone for a year. She'd lived for Frank. She'd lived for Penny. But there were so many hours in a day. So many hours alone. The pace of running with Andrew gave her little time to be lonely.

Matt stood and paced the kitchen. His breathing seemed to need a conscious effort. "This is a bad guy. You can't paint a skunk all black and expect it not to stink."

"I understand. I really do. You've spent your career trying to bring some kind of justice to Andrew Post. I know you feel justified, but it nearly cost you your job. It may still. Penny told me you were told to take some time off. I don't want you to lose your job over this, and I don't want this to come between us."

"He killed a woman. I know it was some time ago, but he did it. He had that creep Fenton Cooper set up and then ran him out of town. Those are just the first and last examples. There are a bushel of indiscretions in between."

"He was never charged with anything. Lacy Talbert died in his condo. He admitted that to me. He knows his affair with her was wrong. I could see it in his face when he spoke of her. He said it was

God's punishment for him."

Matt laughed. "God has yet to punish this man."

"You won't find the letter. I'm sure you felt you were protecting us, but its contents don't concern you."

"But it does!" He sat back at the table, his eyes regaining their sparkle. "I need that letter. It ties into Post's ultimate crime."

Typically such a statement would shake someone. Annie had heard these melodramatic words from Matt so many times that she just let it slide off. Maybe Andrew could help her find a way to bring some closure for Matt. She'd see Andrew Friday night at his house, her first visit to the Post Estate. Her intent was to discuss the state of their relationship and possibly easing up.

Her original plan had been to befriend Andrew for a time, probably another month or two, gain visibility and Penny's acceptance of Post, and then slow down and eventually separate. It was to be dating in the old-fashioned sense—as friends. Any more than that and her unstated guilt over Frank would consume her. She and Andrew could remain friends, and no one would think twice about Post occasionally helping her out or stepping in on Penny's behalf. She'd not yet broached the issue of telling Penny the truth. Right now her inclination was to keep quiet.

The fly in the ointment was the young man sitting at her table. She needed to find some way to break his obsession with Andrew. If he remained determined to poke into Andrew's affairs, the eventual outcome for Matt would be painful—the downfall of his own career. Matt might leave town or do something desperate in retaliation, neither of which would be favorable in regards to his relationship with Penny.

And by dating Post, maybe she could at least control Andrew's reactions to Matt's onslaught of attention to the Post family. Andrew had enough influence to keep the Boise PD from becoming too harsh with Matt. Of course, in the unlikely event Matt was right—Andrew Post was a bad guy—she couldn't begin to predict the outcome. She didn't have legions of spin-doctors and lawyers. Post could hang her out to dry even if things didn't go his way.

There was one more issue. Was this really her plan? Over the past week, she'd become more and more confused about her relationship with Andrew. Was she going to just walk away?

"Why don't you marry Penny?" Annie said.

"This is a diversion, right? Avoid the real issue?"

"Sure." She rose and pulled out a pitcher of orange juice from the refrigerator, poured a glass, and handed it to Matt. He held it up to the light and took a swig. "She won't commit."

"Maybe you should sleep with her."

Matt's face looked like a guy who'd just caught his parents having sex. "Geez, Annie." He rose and started to pace. "Since we're all friends here, are you sleeping with Andrew Post?"

She laughed. "Not yet."

"I don't like where this is going."

"Do something to make my daughter commit. I know she's afraid. Everyone knows you two belong together. I could even get Andrew to spring for a huge wedding."

They both laughed.

"Can you imagine?" Matt said. "Andrew Post at my wedding?"

Next, Annie did something she'd never done in the eighteen years Matt had been hanging around her house. She put her arms around him and hugged him tight. She'd given him the customary light hug many times, but not the one she reserved for so few. His arms hesitantly returned the gesture.

"You're my son. You may not have my genes, but you are my son. I want you to be my son-in-law. The sooner you get married, the better, and the sooner you forget about Andrew Post, the better."

Chapter 29
Snake River Plain, Southwest Idaho
Thursday Afternoon

The Snake River Plain defined desolation. It was a place no person would want to spend any amount of their life without modern conveniences. Matt watched the sagebrush and sand go by at what he guessed to be about a hundred and ten miles an hour. He couldn't help but think about the poor souls, one foot behind the other, sweltering in the summer heat, passing maybe ten to fifteen miles a day on their way to Oregon some century and a half in the past. He and Donny would cover ten days of wagon travel in the span of an hour, thanks to a Mercedes SLR McLaren Roadster, the Idaho Transportation Department, and federal government highway money.

Donny drove the two-lane highway like she skied—pedal to the metal, balls to the wall. The silver roadster slowed to ninety or so, dropped down a hill like a roller-coaster car, and entered the river canyon south of the community of Mountain Home. She pressed the brake, producing a deceleration that made Matt regret the cheesecake he had eaten at lunch.

They crossed the bridge at the upper end of CJ Strike Reservoir, the highway split, and Donny pushed on toward the west paralleling the river. Over a small hill, the lane was suddenly blocked by a giant farm machine hugging the shoulder. As Matt was about to protest the rapidly diminishing distance between the car and the machine, Donny accelerated and they passed as if the contraption had been going the other way.

Donny beat on the steering wheel to some classic rock, dancing in the leather seat while peeling up the white and yellow stripes on the asphalt.

"Dad used to yell at me about nearly killing us when I first learned to drive," she said. "I *could* kill us in this thing. I know it'll do way past one-sixty."

"I trust you," Matt said with wavering honesty.

She peeled off another twenty miles, seemingly irked that the road was dictating less than one hundred mile an hour speeds. A red light beeped on her radar detector, and she slowed to about eighty-five.

Matt peered over at the speedometer. "Don't you think you want to at least approach the speed limit?"

She winked, then sped up to one-hundred.

"Not great for a cop to get stopped out here, especially riding with you," he said.

They crested another rise in the road and passed a moving Owyhee County Sheriff's SUV as if it were parked in the right lane. Donny looked pleased. Matt leaned inward until he could see the ribbon of road out the passenger side-view mirror. The car slowed a bit. The SUV was beginning to narrow the distance, though the officer had yet to turn on his flashing lights.

"It was good to get you away," Donny said casually. "Best we don't get caught waltzing around Boise with your girlfriend nearby. You get kind of stressed around me."

"This is stress relief?"

"It is for me. Especially with Cooper gone. You won't give me any other kind."

The car slowed to its most leisurely pace of the afternoon, roughly the speed limit. The SUV pulled up alongside the SLR and a curly brown-haired kid of about twenty-five waved out the passenger window. He was yelling something, but Donny kept the windows up.

"Hold on!" she said.

She hit the brakes, turned off the road into a dirt parking area, and flung the wheel a half-turn. Suddenly the entire scene out the window was engulfed in a curtain of brown. Matt had no idea where the road had disappeared to or where the sheriff's deputy went. The tires caught and Donny slammed the accelerator down, then the brakes again. They broke out of the cloud, and the car came to a sliding stop.

A lanky kid with a few chin hairs masquerading as a beard found Donny's window. She rolled it down and proceeded to hug the stuffing out of him.

The kid nodded toward Matt. "Jimmy Wayne." He said it with a lazy tongue. Matt had seen the kid once in Boise for some kind of law enforcement workshop. He'd never spoken to him.

"Jimmy Wayne who?" Matt said, a little disturbed at the intrusion.

Both Donny and the kid laughed.

"That's it. Just Jimmy Wayne. When did you get this machine?"

The gullwing door opened and Donny exited the car. Matt watched her work the kid like an expert as she did suppliers, land planners, politicians, and the like. Except this time she did it in a pair of tight jeans, some kind of mid-heel shoe, and a blue tank top warmed by a loose work shirt. They laughed and examined the car from the front, sides, and back. The kid stole a similar peek at Donny.

Jimmy jumped into the driver's seat. "Man, this baby must've cost a hundred grand," he said, as he leaned forward, both hands on the wheel, pretending to fly down the highway.

Matt's door opened, and Donny started to climb in on his lap. "I told Jimmy he could drive up and down the highway once or twice."

Pushing her aside, Matt made his way out of the car. "Not me. You two can go."

After a short discussion, the deputy took off by himself. Matt couldn't imagine how Jimmy Wayne would explain driving a half a million dollar car around to Sheriff Jones, that is, if he ever got caught. That wasn't likely. Owyhee County covered an area the size of a small state. Yet there were a limited number of paved roads, so anything was possible.

Donny and Matt sat in the SUV to escape a rising west wind.

"Why do you mess with a kid like that?" Matt said.

"He stopped me about a year ago when I was driving Fenton's old piece of crap excuse for a car. Told him he had a choice. Either be fired or see me when I come by every once in a while."

"How'd you know it was going to be Jimmy Wayne?"

"A hunch. I think he waits out here every day in case I decide to drive by."

The Roadster passed going in the opposite direction.

"What do you know about Fenton Cooper's disappearance?" Matt asked.

Donny grinned, "What do you know about Fenton's disappearance?"

"It was time for him to leave. I believe he was set up by your father."

"Maybe. Cooper called me. Said he was leaving voluntarily. Then he said he was framed. Wouldn't tell me by who. Father is a bit protective, so it makes sense."

"You're not pissed about that?"

"Nah. Cooper was fun, but he was getting old. Besides, he screwed up big-time in Denver and was getting too big for his britches." She leaned her head back and laughed. "Britches. A word you'd understand."

"You're the one hangin' with Jimmy Wayne."

Donny pulled the work shirt off her shoulders and set it on the seat. "Getting hot in this tub of metal."

"Got any new thoughts on what your dad and Annie Lorda are up to?"

"That's the reason for this excursion?" She winked. "Took you long enough to get around to it." She closed her eyes and leaned her head back on the seat. "Why don't you talk first, Officer? Then I'll see if I want to talk."

Matt had little to lose by disclosing information to Donny. Andrew Post probably knew he was still running around asking questions. Apparently, Post didn't care much since the captain had not fired him yet.

"What do you, Penny, and Katlin have in common outside of being born around the same time in the same hospital? What does your dad have in common with Annie Lorda? The only answer is that she and your father are the parents of the three of you. Frank Lorda passes away, leaves a note for Annie, she reads it, and then becomes involved with your father."

"I already know all of that. Father and Angela seem to like each other. Not sure of the mystery there except for Father falling for such a plain person."

"What do you know about Katlin's death?"

"Just that I don't want to talk about it." Her tone instantly descended into a dark place Matt would never understand.

The Roadster came into view and pulled into the turnout. Out popped Jimmy Wayne with a huge grin. Matt could see his lips frame the word "damn."

Jimmy Wayne received his reward—a passionate hug from Donny—and he fled to the east back toward the town of Grand View.

Matt and Donny drove in silence for an hour or so. The washed out sage of the Owyhee Mountain's east slope gave way to the irrigated farmland south of Nampa. Matt napped for a brief time and awoke to the urban traffic of Interstate 84. The radio played soothing jazz.

"Katlin's death was kind of suspicious," he said, carefully broaching the subject again.

Donny's eyes narrowed, but she kept her focus straight ahead.

"I'm worried she didn't just die," he said.

There was no response.

"You think they would just let her die?"

A tear rolled down Donny's cheek. She reached for Matt's hand and he accepted it.

"That's bullshit," she said. "I wanted a sister. She died. Can that be the end of this discussion?"

"Can we talk about this at another time? I really need your help." Matt paused. "Look, I know we are talking about your father."

This time he felt the full strength of her muscles squeezing his hand. He was sure he heard sniffles. Then he was caught in the chest with a surprising backhand that felt almost like he'd been shot.

Donny swung wildly with her right hand, landing a few punches on Matt's shoulder and arms. "He's not my damn father!" she shouted.

The Mercedes started weaving across the highway lines on the Interstate, barely missing a minivan and a pickup truck. Horns blared. Even with his two hands, Matt couldn't avoid more punches.

"Damn you!" Donny yelled out. "Can't you lay off?"

Finally Matt was able to grasp her arm and hold it down. It took nearly all of his strength to maintain the position. "You're going to kill somebody!"

He felt the resistance fade and he let go. Suddenly Donny whipped the wheel, jammed the accelerator, and the car slid across the lanes into the shoulder. He was certain they would flip over the embankment. Again, she whipped the wheel, and the car straightened down the highway. She floored it, aiming at an exit about a quarter of a mile away.

The car slid to a halt at a four-way stop flanked by a service station. She pulled into the edge of the station lot, turned off the ignition, and put her head on the steering wheel.

"My mother screwed some other guy, and I'm the result. My mother is a worthless piece of trash. I don't even know who my father is. There. Now you have something big to use against Andrew Post. Maybe that's what Annie Lorda found out. He's not my real father. He doesn't even know I know. My mother, in one of her fits of verbal abuse, told me this gem of a fact when I was a teenager. She sits in the house boozed up all the time, and my real father is probably some aged ski jockey in some godforsaken place."

The news was startling, yet it made some sense. Why would a man let his own daughter die? Maybe if it wasn't his own daughter.

"You're right. You shouldn't have told me that," Matt said. It was so compelling that he knew he'd use it. She would hate him for it.

Donny started to laugh silently. "Go ahead. Tell the world. Maybe then, Father won't have to hide it any more. The world will find out he is the upstanding person in his marriage. I've wanted to tell you that for years. I've wanted to tell someone."

She left the car for the store. Upon her return, she tossed the keys to Matt and told him to drive.

They made Boise and headed toward downtown. A new round of silence persisted all the way to the coffee spot where they'd met hours ago. Matt pulled up to his truck in the back of the parking lot.

"I'm sorry," he said. They both exited the car. Donny pushed into his path and hugged him. It wasn't a sensual hug. It was more like the embrace of siblings.

He put his head on top of hers. He noticed the window to his truck was down. He'd not left it that way. Penny's head appeared, her eyes aimed squarely in his direction.

Chapter 30
The Post Estate, Boise Foothills
Friday Evening

In a setting that could only be scripted in Hollywood, Andrew and Annie had dinner on one side of the Post Estate while Sonya and her partner "did whatever they do on a Friday night" on the other side of the house.

Andrew had seen Devlon Scott's Cadillac hidden up in Sonya's private driveway. That was a good thing. Scott was still fool enough to think their tryst was just that—some kind of secret. With Scott around, there was no chance Sonya would venture into Andrew's part of the house, though there was little chance of such an occurrence without visitors.

Still Andrew was not completely comfortable. Sonya's version of cheating was so common, he passed over it like a visit from a neighbor. His affair—if one could call his passive courting with Annie an affair—was different. Similar to his six-month-long engagement a decade ago with Lacy Talbert, this relationship brought the troubling comparison with his mother's infidelity.

Yet there was also a surge of energy in his life lately that could only be explained by having another person to share simple pleasures, like dinner and plane trips. Someone with no connection or interest in his business. With Annie it was like it should have been with Sonya.

"You seem troubled," Annie said, sipping a glass of Owens Valley 2005 Merlot, seated at the end of a table that could seat twenty.

Andrew was finding she had a unique ability to correctly measure his mood at every turn. He couldn't decide if this was just a natural gift of hers or that she worked hard at attentiveness. His own philosophy of mankind dealt in self-absorption—people only thought about themselves no matter what they claimed. She was the first person he'd met in a long time that contradicted such observations.

Annie pointed to the lasagna on her plate. "This is good. I can see why you get picky when you have your own chef. I live mostly on salads, frozen stuff, leftovers, whatever."

"Orlando is not here tonight. I made this myself."

"No!"

Andrew nodded. "One-dimensional? I can cook. Haven't done it in years. You should have been here earlier. I did have to have Manny help me with the location of a few things."

They both laughed.

He picked up his wine glass in a toasting manner and she joined him, lightly touching his glass.

"Here's to us," he said.

He smiled. She did not.

"We should talk about us," she said. "Maybe it's time to start easing off a bit. Or at least think about it. Over the next month or two, of course. Penny is already taking a shine to you, so I don't see any reason to push this too far."

Easing up was the last thing on Andrew's mind. The past week had been good for his soul. He suddenly felt like doing something besides work. The inevitability of passing the reins started to feel like a good thing. He'd even let up on his top managers a bit and canceled yesterday afternoon's staff meeting. As soon as he'd sent the message, Donny had jumped at the chance to play hooky.

Before Annie arrived for dinner, he'd even talked about her to Manny, his longtime faithful house servant, who until tonight probably felt like another piece of the furniture. It was Manny who had suggested Andrew don his own chef's hat and provide the meal for his guest.

Things—life—had been better.

"Shouldn't we at least sleep together first?" Andrew said, a forced grin on his face.

"Right. I don't need my picture on the front of some tabloid, sneaking away from a hotel in the early morning hours. Besides, that would cost you a lot more than a few glasses of wine."

She was kidding, but he knew Annie must feel his growing attachment to her. She was letting him off easy. Giving him an excuse not to feel dumped, as the kids used to say.

"I don't have a plan," he said.

"Seriously? I find it likely you rarely utter such words."

After dinner, they retired to Andrew's home theatre. Annie suggested *When Harry Met Sally*, one of her favorites. Andrew ordered it through some Internet service Rafi had set up. She dozed while he watched the movie. Halfway through the picture, he nudged her awake and suggested a livelier film. An action movie or a western. Instead, she suggested sitting by the pool so they could chat.

Andrew dismissed Manny for the night, grabbed the wine bottle from dinner, and escorted Annie outside to a couple of comfortable lounge chairs. It was a calm night, though they could hear thunder somewhere distant in the mountains to the northeast. Occasionally, a flash of lightning would snap a picture of the nearby foothills.

"I love the rain," she said. "Can you smell it?"

He could.

"I think maybe we keep seeing each other but less often," she said. "Gradually. That way, there's no story of the big break up."

Andrew wanted to blurt out reasons for persistence or even progression of their relationship. He said nothing.

"You were right. The media, the phone calls, the people following me. I hate it. And it's only been a few days. How do you get used to that kind of life?"

"It's been that way so long I guess I don't think about it. I live in Boise because people here pretty much leave me alone. If we were in an East Coast market, you would have to move. Even when I go to California, I have to double my security detail. After the Talbert affair, wherever I went, the paparazzi followed me. That's when the attention ramped up. Once they were convinced I wasn't interested in women any more, they let up a bit. After so many years, you've made them happy again."

Annie raised her eyebrows and sipped her wine "So how do we unwind this?"

"The real problem with fame is you suddenly feel alone. It's strange, but when I was young, I had a number of very good friends. Now everyone is my friend, but I don't trust anyone."

She reached over and waved her fingers in the air trying to touch his arm. He brushed his fingers against hers.

"There's Mr. Thuban," she said. "And you have Donny."

"Family. And for the life of me, I don't know why Rafi has worked so hard for me. There is no way to repay him."

"You don't repay friendship. Feel blessed that you have it."

"All I did for the man was pull some strings to keep him in the country. It wasn't that big of a deal. He's not just dedicated his life to me and my company, he is good to Sonya as well. I don't know how to deal with that kind of friendship."

Annie put her wine glass on the cement and made her way to the pool. She took her shoes off and placed her feet in the water.

Andrew remained in his chair. "You can take a swim," he said, this time not smiling.

"I haven't had that much wine, sir." Her voice betrayed how much she had had.

He raised his glass in a toast. "No one would see you."

"You would. Then you would want to finish this little charade tonight."

He watched her stroll around the pool area in her summer dress. She approached a door that led to Sonya's part of the house. Behind the door, the faint sound of a television could be heard.

"Is she in there?"

"Sonya? Yes." He saw no reason to hide anything.

"She is here tonight?"

"Yes."

"You have your part? She has hers?"

"Yes."

"What if she comes out here?"

"She has her own pool area. She won't come out here."

"And if she does...come out here?"

"She wouldn't stay. We bump into each other occasionally but rarely are words spoken."

Annie shook her head. She turned her back to the door, wobbling slightly. "And you take care of her?"

"Yes."

"Why can't you be together? I'd give anything to be with Frank again."

The statement hurt. He was trying to gain favor. She was promoting a guilt he didn't want to explore.

For the next few minutes, Annie drifted through the pool area, deep in her own thoughts. He guessed she was wondering how she arrived at this juncture in her life. What it was like when her husband was alive. Maybe how she could have everything now except for her husband.

Andrew only thought of her. Sonya was nearby. But that was it. He had no want of his wife.

Annie paused and sat on the end of the cushion of one of the reclined pool chairs. "The other issue is Penny," she said.

He'd been wrong again. She'd been contemplating her own child.

"She and Matt are having a hard time. Don't suppose Donny told you Penny caught the two of them embracing in a parking lot yesterday."

The news was a surprise. Donny had said she was leaving early to go for a ride. She hadn't said anything about Matt Downing.

Annie leaned forward, her voice determined. "I need to do two things. One. Get Penny and Matt married. Two. Get Matt to let go of you."

"It appears you have a plan."

"Nope. You're the expert in planning and negotiation. Surely your business savvy can provide some sort of 'Matt and Penny' plan."

"I'll work on it," he said, lacking outward enthusiasm.

"Putting distance between you and I would help. Our relationship seems to make Matt's desire to take you down all the stronger. I'm planning on suggesting a trade to him. I quit Andrew Post and so does he."

"Sounds like a plan."

"I enjoy all of this, don't get me wrong. You have been great. We should remain friends. Maybe distant friends. Invite me to a party once in a blue moon."

"I don't party."

"Can you have Mr. Choi take me home?"

"Mr. Choi is off tonight. I'll take you, but first, a question."

Annie waited.

"Nothing was accomplished by you coming here tonight," Andrew said, "I mean as far as anyone seeing us together."

She shook her head as if she didn't understand.

"Why have this dinner?" he asked. "Were we here to plan our demise? Was that the purpose?"

Annie stood and kissed him on top of the head.

She never answered the question.

Chapter 31
Table Rock Mesa, Boise
Midnight Saturday

The huge brightly lit cross, a sentinel the city would protect regardless of pressure from the secularists, sat above the valley on the edge of Table Rock Mesa a thousand feet or so up in the foothills. Surprised to find a locked gate on the road, Andrew and Annie had to hike the last quarter of a mile. Despite the midnight hour, they'd scared a couple of kids who'd scurried away like mice.

Andrew recalled, years ago, hiking up to the cross from the old penitentiary on his first date with Sonya. They'd sat on the wall next to the cross for hours, watching the sun as it fell into Oregon to the west. He'd not known much about her that day, but in retrospect, Sonya seemed more familiar back then than now—forty years later.

He had met her at a fledgling outdoor shop called "The Experience," his first job in retail. Ahead of its time, the store targeted a new crowd of kids who would soon discover the mountains were more than mining and timber. He was trying to install a stubborn roll of register tape when she laid a pair of shorts on the counter. She watched him for a few seconds while he struggled to complete the seemingly simple task. Then she spoke.

"Problem?"

Before he looked up to see who owned the voice, he'd fallen for her. Her shoulder length dark hair and wide brown eyes allowed him to overlook the fact that she stood four inches above him. He remembered how stupid he must've looked. He didn't even ring up her shorts. Just asked her out on the spot. She said she wasn't thrilled going out with someone who couldn't fix a cash register. But then she wrote her phone number on a business card lying on the counter and walked out. The shorts, apparently, were free.

Andrew had not been up on the mesa since that date so long ago. He'd intended to take Annie straight home. By impulse, he'd turned up into the foothills and made his way up Table Rock Road. Annie had not protested the diversion. It was a good sign.

A mild breeze blew through the sagebrush, a little cool for the beginning of summer, courtesy of an outflow of air from distant, decaying thunderstorms. The view and Annie's grip on his arm took Andrew's mind off of Sonya.

"I've been told on a good night one can see the lights of Oregon. I don't really believe that, but if true, it would be from my hometown," he said as they both stared into the twinkling lights.

The breeze picked up a bit. A small animal hopped around a few yards down the hill. An occasional car passed by in the distance on Warm Springs Avenue. The airport stood to the south, the white beacon on the tower inviting planes to the ground.

Annie released her grip and perched on a low wall of rocks with her back to the city below.

"Is there something special about this place?" she asked. "I mean to you."

Andrew walked over to the cross and looked up. "I'm usually not a man who lacks clarity in what to do." He didn't look in her direction, but he felt her eyes examining him. "Do you really want to follow the plan?"

"Do you?"

"I enjoy your company," he said.

"As I do yours."

Neither spoke for a minute or two. Andrew drifted around the area, deep in thought, trying to gauge what was happening. Annie turned toward the lights and let her legs hang off the wall.

She broke the silence. "I'm a bit confused. My husband died a year ago. I spent a long time with Frank, and I still miss him. And you—you're married, and your wife still lives in the same house. I wonder if I would be pushing the two of you further apart. That maybe there is some chance for your marriage without me."

"It's been over for a long time."

"I think you still love her."

"I do. But we will never be together again."

More silence followed. The wind relented except for an occasional wisp flowing up from the bottom of the hill.

"I think 'slow' is the key here," she said. "I've enjoyed the last week. Maybe we go with the flow. I'm still worried about Matt, but maybe let's not have a plan."

Andrew nodded. "The plan is not to have a plan. I like it."

She patted the top of the wall next to her. He obeyed and sat down.

"I brought you up here because I didn't want to take you home," he said. "I feel like I'm back in high school."

She hooked her arm through his. "Ah, to be a girl in high school pursued by you."

"Harmless. I was harmless."

They stayed for a few more minutes before a police car appeared down the road in the vicinity of Andrew's SUV. They met a young officer halfway back to the car and explained they had come for the view. The kid recognized Andrew immediately and rambled on like he was in a job interview. He offered to follow them back down the hill to make sure they were safe. Andrew declined the offer but said he would call the chief and thank him personally for Officer Brandon's help.

The short trip to 14th Street was uneventful and quiet. Andrew walked Annie to the door. She hugged him like a relative and he went home.

At the entrance to the Post Estate, the guard started to speak to Andrew as he drove up. Andrew held his hand out and rolled it, signaling to "just open the gate."

Inside, he drifted back into the theatre. He played with the remote until he landed on Bogart playing Sam Spade in the *The Maltese Falcon*. He turned the sound down very low and closed his eyes. Sleep would not come, so he poured a glass of wine and stared at the movie.

At some point, he must've dozed off. Bogart, Mary Astor, and Peter Lorre had morphed into another classic movie he couldn't identify. He switched off the screen and wandered into the pool area, the dining room where they had had dinner only hours ago, and finally the kitchen. The persistent television was still playing on Sonya's side of the house.

In a rare intrusive act, he returned to his living room and opened the hallway door that led into Sonya's enclave. He hesitated. What would he say to her so early in the morning? She would be so soused, groggy, or both that normal conversation would be out of the question.

Given the press coverage, she had to know about Annie. Maybe that was it. Maybe he was feeling guilty.

Passing through the hallway, he opened the far door and stepped into her side of the house. As he made his way into the bedroom, fifty inches of six talking heads spewing conservative babble flooded his ears from a flat-screen television in the far corner. Clothes littered the floor, and a tray table with a bottle of bourbon and the remains of a cheese and cracker plate sat next to an empty bed.

Yet there was another noise—a low humming sound. It was the shower running in the bathroom.

He reached down and picked up a pair of men's trousers. The discount store brand instantly identified the owner. Scott, like clockwork, should've left the house before midnight or by one o'clock at the very latest. Andrew glanced at his watch. It was a little before four in the morning.

The urge to leave was absent. On the edge of the bed, he sat, watching the steamy shower scene as if it were a movie. There was a woman, a tall woman with a slight paunch, and a man equal to her height and built like an ex-linebacker, embracing and doing other things that favored the frosted-glass Sonya had chosen for the shower stall.

On the bedside table sat a handgun in a black shoulder-holster. Andrew took the gun from its cradle. It was cool to the touch and lighter than expected. Placing his fingers around the grip and rubbing his forefinger on the trigger, he aimed the weapon at the shower door. He alternated his aim back and forth between the two bodies. Then he placed the gun back on the table and returned to his side of the house.

He should sleep, he kept thinking to himself. He really should.

Chapter 32
The Post Estate, Boise Foothills
Early Saturday Morning

Sonya Post drifted backwards and fell onto the bed, as though it were a target in motion. This night, like most, was a rush to beat back the impending depression with booze and flesh. Her latest partner, Devlon Scott, was sufficient in that he pretended love and stayed with her until she eventually passed out, or the bliss of sleep replaced the darkness of her waking hours.

She closed her eyes and let the room spin. Sometimes, it brought nausea, and she would have to immediately sit up. Other times, it came with a euphoric feeling, like an amusement park ride at the state fair. Dry air drifted in from an open door leading to the pool area, raising goose bumps over her still-soaked body. Heavy bare feet approached on the wood floor and a cloud of cheap cologne invaded her space. A soft towel fell onto her hips and legs.

"Babe, at least dry your butt off before jumping into the sack."

His voice was like his cologne.

Reaching blindly, her hand came upon a pair of men's pants hanging unoccupied on the edge of the bed. One of the pockets contained a multitude of keys on several metal rings daisy-chained together. The other pocket held a set of nickel-plated police issue handcuffs.

"Baby, you're spilling my shit on the floor."

The bed quaked as he sat on the edge of it. Throwing the towel aside, Sonya sat up and reached around his shoulders. She had to stretch to dig her fingernails into the center of his chest, where a generous mass of peppered hair lay. Her bare breasts pressed hard against his back.

"My boss—your old man—is on to us," Scott said.

Sonya couldn't control her instant laughter. "He doesn't care. I want another drink."

"The place already smells like the inside of a bourbon bottle. Look, I need this job. I should've left hours ago."

She pressed her hands lower under the white bath towel he'd wrapped around his waist. "Get me a drink."

"Suit yourself. I'm not dispensing anything from down there again tonight. He let out an abbreviated guffaw that stopped instantly, as if someone had jammed a hand over his mouth. He jumped up, knocking Sonya back on the bed, and headed to the liquor cabinet next to the big screen TV. With his belly hanging over the towel, he looked like one of those Olympic power lifters.

"Unless you want Gin or some bottle of wine with a Frenchie label, we've emptied this thing," he said.

"Go get some of Andrew's stash."

"You kidding? Not even at this time of night."

"You chicken?" She stood and zigzagged her way toward the middle of the house, steadying herself from time to time along the walls.

"Put something on for Christ's sakes," he shouted from behind her.

Giggling, Sonya passed through a door into the "demilitarized zone" and then into Andrew's part of the house. His liquor cabinet was supplied like a cache for the end of the world. She put her hand around a bottle with a fuzzy label that appeared to say bourbon whiskey and pulled it to her chest. She put it up to the light. It was at least two-thirds full, enough to do the job.

Back in the bedroom, she danced over to Scott and placed the bottle on the table. "I want it in a glass if you don't mind. I'm a little classier than what you're used to."

"Yep, real classy babe," Scott said.

He grabbed the bottle and took a swig.

"Get the glasses and bring them to...a...bed."

"You're plastered."

She returned to the bed and spread out like a snow angel. Cool metal pressed against the skin of her lower back. She rolled over, retrieved Scott's handcuffs, and dangled the pair over her head. Scott was changing channels. He settled on watching some idiots playing poker. She jingled the cuffs again.

"Hey, don't lose those." He took another swig of whiskey.

"Come lock me up. If you don't, I'll tell your boss."

"Lock yourself up. I'm telling you, I'm spent. Nearly pulled my arm out of socket in the shower."

Sonya fell back on the bed and pressed the cool metal of the handcuffs on her forehead. Out of the corner of her eye was Devlon's pistol. He called it a 357 something or other. She turned on her side and watched it. It didn't look like the pistols she had handled at the store back when Andrew let her keep her fingers in the business. It was more like a toy, like the guns in the old arcades.

But it was no toy. A few weeks ago, they'd taken a cruise in Devlon's prized burgundy Cadillac CTS into the sage country of the Snake River Plain. Normally, she had no idea what kind of car she was riding in, but Devlon kept bringing up the name each time they took a drive. They'd found an isolated spot and made love in the heat of the day. Afterwards, Devlon set up a couple of targets and let Sonya pop the gun a few times.

She wasn't bad. On the first shot, she held the pistol too close, and the recoil narrowly missed her face. She could still see Scott, keeled over laughing, leaning against the Cadillac CTS. On the second shot, she held her arms at length, squeezed the trigger, and put a hole into the caricature's head on the little cardboard box some twenty yards away. She held the pistol up and pretended to blow the smoke away from the barrel.

And here it was again, an arm's length away. She could simply pick it up, stick it against her head, and be done with it. Didn't take much of an aim to do that.

Somewhere in the back of her closet sat a small silver pistol she'd bought at least twenty years ago. She had intended to shoot it once— right into the heart of Andrew. If he'd ever found it, there would be hell to pay just for having a gun on the premises. Yet as the years passed, the urge was not revenge, but relief. That required a strength she couldn't find in herself. Not even with the help of booze, valium, weed, or promiscuity.

She made her way to the closet. Tucked up in the corner sat a small black security box. She pulled it off the shelf, nearly dropping it on her foot. Sitting on the floor, she fumbled with the combination until she was ready to give up. She slammed her hand on the top of the box and the lid popped up as if it had never been locked. There it was. Sitting by itself with a small box of bullets. She picked up the weapon. It seemed so small compared to Devlon's 357. The metal was cool. She pulled the gun upward, brushing the bulge of her belly with her forearm. It wasn't much of a pooch but her condition was a far cry from her youth. Andrew had told her years ago she looked to be in better shape than some of the Olympians. Now she was fading, dying—a cruel, slow march to the end of life.

Sonya pressed the barrel up against her temple and felt the small ring of metal on her skin. Her finger toyed with the trigger. Was it loaded? She didn't care.

Like a defense mechanism, Andrew's image flashed in her mind. He was smiling. *Why doesn't he come in and take the gun away?* She could still hear him preaching about gun control. He hated guns since the day that young Talbert girl shot herself. The chance he had a gun in the house was slim to none.

A tear rolled down her cheek, and she lowered the weapon. She tossed the gun back in the box, closed and locked it, and returned the container to its proper place.

Back in the bedroom, she found her way to the brown bottle. Pressing it to her lips, she inhaled the stuff. It could have been water. There was no kick, no bite. A large hand reached around her waist, and she fell into Devlon Scott's lap. He kissed her on the forehead.

"You've had enough. Time to put you down."

He stood, picked her up in the same motion, and deposited her on the bed.

"I'm not finished," she mumbled. She flopped around and found the cuffs while Scott stood over the bed.

"Let's use these," she said.

Scott pulled the cuffs away. He picked up his disposed socks and slipped them on her hands like some kind of puppets. Then he expertly slapped a cuff on her left hand and bellowed again.

"That's to keep you from making marks on your wrists. Don't want the boss to think I'm some kind of animal." He laughed again and headed out the door toward the pool. He said something about being too hot and to cuff herself wherever she wanted to.

Sonya rolled over and her elbow jammed into Devlon's gun. She wasn't finished.

Fumbling with her hands, one of them bound to the dangling cuffs and both covered by foul black socks, she managed to pick up the weapon. Rolling over, she tried to plop her feet on the floor but somehow missed and landed next to the bed. Gripping the pistol tightly, she managed to get to her knees and then stand. Everything in the room seemed to be moving to the right.

The cool breeze from the patio blew on her back. She turned and found the door to the pool.

Outside, Scott was sitting in a wooden chair a few feet from the water, puffing streams of smoke in the air from a Marlboro. Sonya closed in on him. He made no motion to indicate knowledge of her presence. Her shadow betrayed her as she tiptoed up behind him. He seemed relaxed but instantly tensed up as she pressed the barrel against the side of his head.

"I'm not done yet," she said, laughing and holding the handgrip with both hands, struggling to stick her webbed fingers against the trigger.

"Careful babe. That piece is loaded and so are you." This time it was a nervous laugh.

"I'm not your rich whore." She pressed the gun harder into his skull. "I *told* you I'm not done."

He reached back and wrenched her arm with a powerful grip. The ground felt like it disappeared, and she floated to the cement. A pop filled the air and her ears started to ring. It was as if someone had hit her on the side of the ear with their palm. The grip on her arm released.

She made her way to a sitting position. Devlon Scott's big body had spilled to the ground just a foot away. A mix of gunpowder and cheap cologne along with some other sickening smell acted like a stimulant.

The scene was difficult to comprehend. Red fluid was flowing from Scott's head. Sonya could only think of the active lava tubes on the Big Island of Hawaii. The gun was a few feet away on the ground. A painful faint sound like a low frequency gurgle could be heard. Suddenly, like a whale surfacing, Scott's massive chest filled and evacuated in one last breath of life. Then his body went limp.

The realization that she had shot Devlon Scott was equivalent to five cups of coffee.

She should call the police.

Call Andrew.

Rafi.

The last swig of bourbon in her stomach started to rise into her throat. She stumbled to the bathroom just in time. The heaves seemed endless. She fell back against the wall and started to shiver. A man had been shot, and she had watched his last breath. *In Andrew's house.*

She tugged on the socks on her hands and managed to pull the uncuffed one off. She needed to go out and get the key, get the cuffs off, and escape.

Stopping for a minute, she listened. Still no sirens. Surely the security guard or Andrew would come running in at any moment.

Back at the bed, she searched for Scott's big key ring. Then an idea struck her. *Scott shot himself.* She was cuffed to the bed, and he simply went out and put the gun to his head. She'd been passed out and had no idea what had happened.

After placing the keys back in the pants pocket, Sonya positioned herself on the bed, reached over her head, and managed to wrap the cuffs around one of the bars on the antique wrought iron frame. After several tries, she managed to snap her free hand into the other cuff.

She kicked at the covers, wishing she'd at least partially covered her body first. It was of little use. She could only wait.

Chapter 33
Annie Lorda's Residence, North End, Boise
Saturday Morning near Daybreak

"Pack a bag." The beams of Annie's porch light backlit a man breathing heavily. Annie, in her white cotton robe, stood frozen in the doorway.

Andrew squeezed by and entered the house. He was dressed in khaki pants, lightweight hiking boots, and a brown flannel shirt.

"Rained a bit overnight," he said. "Feels more like Seattle outside. We'll have to take your car."

Annie closed the front door and stood, arms crossed. "I'm going somewhere?"

"Yes."

"We were together a few hours ago." Her eyes were baggy as if the night had robbed her of all rest. "I would assume you can afford a car of your own?"

Andrew walked through the kitchen and peered out the door to the carport. "Less conspicuous. Snuck out this morning. Hope they didn't see me."

"Who?"

"I told the guard at my house to gas up my car. He was hesitant, to say the least, but he likes his job. Once he left, I hightailed it out the back. Security camera may have caught me but too bad. I'm gone now." He held out his smartphone, pressed his fingers on it, and felt the buzz that announced its discharge. "Even if they want me, I'm not answering."

"And you're going to take my car somewhere?" Annie entered the kitchen and started to clean off a spot on the counter with a folded rag. "I'm a little lost here."

"We can talk later. Pack a bag for a few days. You'll love it."

"I can't just leave—"

"Come on, Annie. I ran away from home. If you don't run away too, I'll look stupid. And pack a few warm things. It's summer, but where we're going, it'll be cool at night."

"Suppose you're whisking me away to Sun Valley? Assume you have done this before." Her tone had a hint of playfulness.

Andrew put his hands on her shoulders. He grinned and winked. "Never."

He had done this before. But it seemed like centuries ago in a life lost to deadlines, deals, store openings, quarterly earnings, and 10-K reports.

Right after they had first met, he kidnapped Sonya and whisked her away to Sun Valley. Whisked might've been a strong term. With twenty-five dollars and a change of clothes, they packed into a five-year-old rose-colored Dodge Lancer he had borrowed from his brother.

It was the summer of 1972, and he thought the allure of Sun Valley would impress his new girl. The image was like a snapshot he could pull from his pocket at any time. Sonya, leaning back in the passenger seat, windows down, swaying her lean frame as she sang "Mashed Potato Time" with Dee Dee Sharp. Her fists pushing into his ribs as she appointed the tune "The Idaho State Song."

Carefree was inadequate to describe the pair. They were closer to habitual misdemeanor criminals. They toured the famous Sun Valley Hotel, pretending to be a well-to-do but scandalous California pair cheating on their spouses. They snuck into an unoccupied room behind the maid service, stole a bottle of Champagne from a room service cart, and charged their lunch to someone named the Nelsons.

Andrew had to pull Sonya away from the place before they went too far. They managed to find a small motel by the river in Hailey for fifteen bucks, a bottle of wine for two, and a trail up the side of the famous Bald Mountain. They reached roughly the halfway point, sat on a log, and drank the whole bottle while watching sun rays escape the valley below.

He'd thought if he could get her back to the room before they both fell off the mountain, they might make proper use of the elevation and contents of the empty bottle. They made love twice before they found the motel—once at a ski lift tower and then again in the Lancer in the parking lot as she hummed "Mashed Potato Time."

He had returned with Sonya to the Sun Valley Resort once about twenty-five years later. She had been there many times but only twice with Andrew. Upon arrival, she disappeared with some of her crowd. He spent two days talking business with people he could have dismissed without a thought. He could've rented half the hotel, purchased crates of Champagne, and bought everyone at the resort a fine meal. He didn't. And he made love to no one.

Before Annie could stop him, Andrew had invaded her bedroom. The bed was undisturbed, and a quilt lay draped over a rocker. A small table and a sewing machine sat in the corner, illuminated by a small lamp. No wonder she was tired.

A duffle bag sat in the corner of the closet. He pulled it out and emptied an assortment of dull colored fabric onto the bed. In the top of the chest of drawers, underwear was neatly arranged similar to a shelf at a clothing store. It was all the same color and brand.

Footsteps approached from behind. "What are you doing?" Annie demanded as she reached out to close the drawer.

"You don't have much in here to excite anybody. Pretty dull."

"I wear it under my clothes. Suppose you were looking for some kind of dental floss stuff." She fused her way between Andrew and the chest. "You get what you see here. No surprises."

He placed his hands on her hips. "Come with me. I promise you'll be glad you did. No expectations, just fun and good company."

"You can have anyone in the world for company. Someone exciting, not a bore like me."

"I'm into boring. Consider me one-dimensional." He gently moved her to the side, opened the drawer, grabbed two pairs of panties, and threw them in the bag.

"Okay. Okay. You better not turn into some kind of pervert." She grabbed the duffle bag and put it back in its place. From the closet, she produced a red roller bag. She meticulously packed the red bag, rolling her shirts, folding her jeans just right, and fitting it all into a space seemingly too small for the contents.

"Fix some breakfast," she said as she left for the bathroom, "if you know how."

He opened the cupboard to find two boxes of cereal, bran and some sort of generic fruit mix. He pulled the boxes off the shelf and placed them on the dinette. In the refrigerator, the milk sat on the shelf labeled "dairy products." He placed the carton on the table and went in search of bowls.

"They're in the cabinet to the right of the stove."

He looked over his shoulder. His newfound companion was dressed in blue jeans, a gold Rocky Mountain National Park T-shirt covered by a red flannel shirt, and a pair of worn hiking boots. He stared at her feet and then examined her up and down. "Not bad."

She smiled, and he quickly added, "I was talking about the boots. We sell those in the store."

"Yes, I suppose you do."

Andrew grabbed the bowls, set them on the table, and sat down. "I made breakfast. I like variety." He poured the two different kinds of cereal, mixed the contents in the bowl with his fingers, and added a generous portion of milk. He pushed the bowl in front of Annie.

"See, I can cook."

"You were a bit wasteful with the milk. The dinner the other night was delicious. I don't doubt your culinary skills."

"Go ahead, eat up. We've got to go."

"I'd need a spoon." She twirled her hair with her forefinger and he liked it. "Ah, maybe the Posts have never had cereal for breakfast."

Andrew held his palms out. Then he repeated the pouring of the cereal and milk into his own bowl, cupped the bowl in his hands, and started to drink the milk.

Annie snorted a laugh.

"There you go again. Kind of a Porky Pig thing," he said.

"You're cruel." She smiled and placed a spoon in his hand. "You'll have manners in my house, Mister."

He was amazed to find less than forty thousand miles on the odometer of the decade-old yellow Subaru in the carport. Andrew started to back it into the street. Annie objected every time he came close to a pole or to the sides of the driveway.

As the car swept into the street, she reached up to unlock her door. "Wait. I have to do something."

He pressed the lock button on the armrest. "Forget it. Let's go before our parents catch us."

"The trash, it goes out on Monday."

Andrew put the car in gear and pushed the pedal. Her hand closed around his wrist. "Please. They only come once a week." Easing the car to the curb, he exited, walked to the black plastic trash bin at the back of the carport, and held his hands out. She nodded, and he pushed the bin out to the curb.

"I hate to ask, but won't your neighbors be a little pissed when they see your trash can out all weekend?" he said as he buckled back into the driver's seat.

She glanced back at the trash bin. "Well, I don't know. We can push it back in—"

"Not a chance. We're out of here."

The Subaru sped along Highway 55, north of Boise, hugging the world class rapids of the Payette River. Huge boulders provided explosions of water and mist as they tried to block the force of a current that was dropping over a hundred feet per mile on the way to the Snake River. Later in the morning, kayakers and rafters would be filling the highway, ready to try their skills below the town of Banks, on the Cabarton stretch below Cascade, or for a few true experts, right in the Class V rapids out Andrew's window.

Annie sat quietly in the passenger seat, reading a novel.

"Spend much time up here?" Andrew asked.

"Some."

He waited a few seconds for more information. She kept reading.

"Nervous?" he asked.

"I'm not much on twisty roads."

"I'm not much on raging rivers. I used to kayak in these waters— with Sonya."

He hesitated, waiting for a reaction to the mention of his wife's name. None came.

"Almost drowned up here right around this bend," he continued. "I was pretty green and got stuck in a hydraulic current. Water pushed me under and back, and I panicked." He shook his head, reliving the moment. "You ever kayaked?"

She shook her head no.

"The force of this water is incredible. It can pull you under or slam you against a boulder and have no remorse."

"That's silly. Rivers don't have feelings."

Andrew maneuvered the car around turn after turn, the endless rapids clinging to the road wherever it went.

"You try sticking your head under that water in a kayak," he said. "It wants you. Will chew you up and spit you out—or worse—it will suck you in and try to keep you. Then the river will go about its business."

"Well, you best watch your driving and quit talking so we don't find out."

"Change of subject. You ever heard of the song 'Mashed Potato Time'?"

Annie let out an almost inaudible laugh and turned the page on her book.

They left the rapids and arrived at a smooth stretch of water at a town called Smith's Ferry and crossed a bridge over the river. The climb up the Payette had transformed the view from sagebrush water-starved hills to a forest canopy held together in rock and dirt under clear, crisp air. After another couple of miles and a short climb over a hill, Andrew pulled the Subaru off the road and announced they had arrived.

Annie put the book down and examined the surroundings. The

view was obstructed by trees and brush.

"We have to hike a short distance," he said. "It's not far."

"This is where you bury the body parts?"

"That would be a little further up the road."

The hike was short. A few muddy patches lined the trail, the result of recent storms. Through a small meadow, an aged log cabin emerged within the trees on the opposite side. There was a porch on the front and an outhouse fitted into the bank of a hill some twenty yards to the rear.

"This is yours?"

Andrew didn't reply. He breathed in the air and closed his eyes.

Annie crossed the clearing and threw her bag on a wooden bench on the front porch. She reached for the door and found it unlocked.

"Not exactly secure," she said.

The inside was Spartan. A kitchen with a propane stove, a homebuilt sink and counter, and a picnic table. There was a couch and two chairs built from local materials covered by yellowed cushions with Zia symbols. Another door off the kitchen led to a pantry. A rustic four-post bed sat in the opposite corner with blankets wrapped in plastic bags piled up in the middle.

The one conspicuously absent item was a light fixture. Andrew smiled as he watched his guest search for a switch along the walls. "How do you turn on the lights?" she asked. He stepped back onto the porch, laughing.

"Seriously, it's still kind of dark in here."

He pulled Annie outside. "Look around. Do you see power lines?"

She dropped her head into her hands and laughed. "Is this the best you can afford?"

"This is my place." He spoke as if he were announcing it to the meadow and a pair of black birds pecking in the clearing off the front porch.

They sat on the bench and he told the story of his cabin. He'd been up here about fifteen years ago looking for a place suitable for Andrew Post. He found a place for Andy Post. A realtor had picked out twenty-five acres on the edge of Round Valley, and Rafi closed the deal on construction of a beautiful two million dollar "cabin." On a weekend jaunt to check out the area, Andrew and Donny had hiked up an abandoned lumber road on the edge of the property and found an old forest ranger cabin built in the 1930s. It sat just inside the Boise National Forest boundary and was barely better than a pile of logs.

"I'd love to experience this cabin the way the rangers did," he'd said to Donny. "No television, phones, power."

Of course, Donny had thought he was nuts. Privately he had Rafi work a small land swap with the Forest Service. He still owned the fortress a mile and half down the hill, but it was here he felt most alive. At times, he'd actually brought family and guests up to the Round Valley cabin, thought of an excuse to go back to Boise, and spent the night here.

"You have a palace nearby?" Annie said.

He nodded.

"And you brought me here?"

He turned his back to Annie and stared into the sky. Her hand touched his shoulder.

"I'm impressed," she said.

He blew a light laugh through his lips.

"No, really. I expected a palace. But this brings a whole new side to Andrew Post."

He reached up and touched her fingers. He feared looking back into her eyes. "I would tell you no one ever comes here but me. That's not quite true."

She pulled her hand back and sat on the bench. "I don't understand."

"An outfitter I know uses the cabin as a warming hut in the winter and a stopover in the summer. That's probably why it was open. Sometimes they forget to lock the place."

Andrew disappeared for a few more trips to the Subaru, returning with some groceries and water they had bought in Horseshoe Bend. He showed Annie where he stored the lanterns and sleeping bags. She made quick progress producing a stew of carrots, potatoes, and beef chunks and left it to simmer. By the time they had put the cabin in order, the sun was high enough to provide some comfort for their explorations.

They packed a couple of granola bars and apples and set out on a trail into the national forest. It was Annie's first time hiking in years, and she seemed to be having fun. They reached the top of a hill about a mile from the cabin, sat on a fallen tree trunk, and took in the view of the Round Valley countryside below.

"See that house right over there on the edge of the tree line?"

She searched and shook her head.

"Right there." He guided her head with his hands.

"Near that inn?"

Andrew stood. "That's my other cabin. We can go there if you'd rather."

"We'll see how cold it gets tonight."

"It's summer. Probably won't drop below forty or so."

Annie stood and nearly tumbled over into the dirt as her boot caught a snag. He reached out to steady her.

"I want to ask you something, and I don't want you to get mad," she said.

He waited for the question.

"Why are you doing all of this?"

"You ask that question a lot." He paused. "The cabin is mine. I take care of it. I mend it. Chop firewood. Clean it. It's all mine. Sometimes I think it is more of what I am than a thousand retail stores."

"No. No. No. You don't understand the question. I sat up all night contemplating your behavior. Why go through the dates, the publicity, the support? Far as I can tell, you have no responsibility here. No incentive to help out. Oh, I guess you might have thought I could go to the press about your wife's shenanigans and the issue with the real father of your daughter. Maybe I might tell all, but if you schmooze me, I won't." She shook her head. "But that's not what this is about."

No defense came to his mind. It felt like he was on trial, and the prosecutor had finally caught him.

"Does Donny know that you are not her father?"

He said nothing and proceeded to gather his daypack.

"Okay," she said. "That's unfair of me. None of my business."

He placed the backpack on his shoulders. He'd never said a word to Donny and that was for the best. Sonya had never talked about the twins since Katlin died, so it was next to impossible that she had told Donny anything about her birth. Like Annie, he didn't want to burden his child with such a disruptive truth.

They hiked for another couple of hours, resting frequently, and then ate their snacks on a saddle between two hills. Despite a temperature in the seventies, the intense mountain sun beat on them, as if they had been hiking in a desert. They walked back down a trail used by the outfitters that skirted the back of the big cabin and returned to their rustic quarters. When they arrived, the sun had managed to climb directly overhead, opening up the pine forest that surrounded the meadow in front of the cabin.

Annie took advantage of the perfect afternoon to read and nap on the porch. Andrew spent time mending the outhouse roof, which had been damaged by some unseen weather event. Thunderheads started to grow to the north, and he stopped from time to time to see if the rain might sweep down his way.

Just before dinner, he piled some firewood on the porch while Annie cleaned the kitchen and readied the cabin for sleeping. He told her to take the bed. He would sleep on the couch.

The hiking and afternoon chores made the stew taste like it came from a five-star restaurant. They shared stories of growing up in the Northwest, their parents, their jobs, and even their spouses. Andrew always felt relieved of the world's burdens at the cabin. With this lady, he confirmed a new sort of life, if only she understood that as well. She was common, but intelligent. Hard-nosed, yet emotionally sensitive. At first, with the letter and her inaugural visit to the Post building, he'd only been curious, like the deer that pops its head up to see the origin of a strange noise. He had no idea what to expect. He'd not expected to like her.

The potbellied stove put off an amazing amount of heat, almost too much, and Andrew kept the front door half-open. He pulled a bottle of liquor from a box in the back closet and placed two shot glasses on the kitchen table. The bottle had a dirty yellowish tint but no label.

"Moonshine?" Annie asked.

"No, some whiskey a friend of mine brought me. Smooth stuff."

"Thought you were a hifalutin wine person?"

"Usually, but this will put hair on your chest."

She put her hands up to her chest. "You won't get to verify that. You first."

He poured a shot, swirled it a tad, and threw it down his throat with one motion. He put the glass down with a thump and turned to his companion, who was pouring her own shot.

She looked at him, raised her eyebrows and then the glass, and did her best to mimic his quick motion.

Andrew repeated the feat with another shot.

"Mister. I won't be able to keep this up long," she said as she filled another glass. "I don't drink much. Never have."

She threw down the second shot, coughing a bit. He followed with another.

By her third, Annie was starting to giggle. She drank her fourth and Andrew had to intervene. "Let's pace ourselves. It's only eight o'clock." He grabbed a wool blanket and led her out to the porch.

She looked up, seemingly surprised to see the clouds had arrived. A few large raindrops were landing like miniature artillery fire. Her eyes had a faint glaze, and her words started to run together.

Standing on the porch, gazing into the darkness surrounding the cabin, he held her hand. She wrapped her free arm around his neck and leaned her head into his chest. "Keep me warm or I'm going to the palace," she said.

"I'm at your service," he whispered. "I'll do whatever you want."

She didn't respond nor did she let go.

After a minute or two, they sat on the porch bench. Wrapped together in the blanket made necessary by the cool air from the nearby rain shower, they engaged in a steady stream of conversation. Annie spoke of her marriage, Penny's troubles in high school, her job at the store in Hyde Park, lonely times at home while Frank was on the road, and Penny's failed marriage. Andrew sat back and listened.

"Let me ask you a question," she said, "since I've been doing all the talking tonight."

"Shoot."

"What's it like to be able to have anything you want?"

"Come again?"

"You know. You're a rich bastard. You can buy anything."

"Bastard! Did I hear the word 'bastard' from you?"

"If it fits." She giggled.

"I don't have everything I want. As they say, money doesn't buy happiness."

"Bullshit!" She giggled again and put her hand to her mouth.

"No more booze for you. You're turning into a gutter mouth." He gave her a light hug under the blanket and grinned. Then his face turned serious, and he stared off into the growing shadows of the late evening. "This is what I want."

Her warm body shifted nervously next to his. "You mean the cabin?" she asked. "A retreat from the hustle and bustle?"

He didn't answer. It was *her* that he meant. Surely she knew this. She knew his thoughts as soon as he did. She was likely frightened or unsure, or maybe suffering from guilt due to the loss of her husband. Maybe it was too soon.

Just like that their conversation ended. Annie sat staring vacantly out into the dull light. Andrew remained silent, stoic.

The raindrops had become steady and were falling straight down. Thunder bellowed through the mountains to the east, yet the storm and its rain couldn't quite cover the silence on the porch. He could hear and feel every breath of the woman he'd tucked into his side.

He broke the lull. "What is it you can't buy?"

"That's simple, but it'll cost you another drink," she said, her head falling to the side as if she'd be sleeping within seconds.

He brought out one more shot and made her swear this was it. She downed the shot. He held his shot glass in the air. Just as he was about to throw it to his lips, she jerked it from his hands, spilling half of it and stealing the other half into her mouth.

"Honesty. You can't...find...buy...find...uh"

He put his hand around her neck and drew her against his shoulder. He couldn't help but think how nice it was to hold a warm body.

"Okay. Honesty." He sighed. "Last night I wanted to shoot my wife."

He waited for a reaction. There was none. He went on to tell her about the shower, the two lovers, and the gun. How it should've enraged him. How he should have busted into the shower and beat the man to a pulp. How he should've put a bullet into both of them. How, in the end, he didn't care. Annie drifted away as he spoke. He knew she'd not remember much of anything he said, but he told her anyway.

Chapter 34
The Post Estate, Boise Foothills
Saturday Morning

The body lay arched with one arm twisted behind the back in a painful fashion. Matt's instinct was to reach down and yank the appendage back to its natural position. He squatted a few feet from the upturned chair and examined the cool cement where the gun was found. An "X" was chalked on the ground with the word "weapon" written next to it. A black body bag, ready for its occupant, sat off to the side.

The pistol, a .357 semi-automatic that no doubt belonged to the victim, was already comfortable in an evidence bag. The officer said they'd lifted several sets of prints from the gun, one clear set on the handle likely attached to the fingers that pulled the trigger. Attached to Andrew Post, thought Matt.

The pool sparkled ignorantly a few feet away. Matt peered over the edge. A small object sat on the bottom in the shallow end.

He waved over one of the uniforms and motioned his eyes into the pool. The officer nodded and then disappeared.

This was new territory. Boise wasn't exactly the murder capital of the world. When someone was murdered, the killer and the victim always knew each other and many times intimately.

The victim was prone, parallel to the pool, his feet close to the chair. The exit wound was not large, but the smell of blood and scattered fragments of Devlon Scott's head made Matt a little uneasy. He'd seen many an accident victim in his days. This was the first person he'd seen shot in the head. It was only the second murder scene he'd visited in his nine years on the force.

The first murder had been much cleaner. The Munson brothers, a couple of kooks that lived in trailers on the edge of town, had decided they were both in love with the same woman. After a 21st century duel, Jester, the older brother, ended up in jail for life. Justin, his younger sibling, was shot through the chest, the bullet lodged in his spine. The entry wound was small, and the case was clear-cut with no issues regarding the identification of the murderer.

This case would prove to be much uglier in that pieces of skull and dried flesh lay spattered by the poolside, and it had occurred on the private estate of Andrew Post. This was one event no amount of money could brush under the carpet. Post was missing and his wife had been found passed out, cuffed to a bed in her birthday suit.

"Detective, she's a bit more coherent." It was one of the uniforms calling out from the back door.

Sonya Post looked as if she'd been shot herself. Dressed in a nightgown and cover, she sat on the edge of a sofa chair in her living room with her head in her hands.

Matt was gentle. "Mrs. Post, you ready to answer a few questions?"

Their eyes met. It was clear she wouldn't know who shot the victim even if she'd been present. Her face was smeared with tears and day old mascara tire marks. Her appearance bore little resemblance to the elegant woman he had stopped on Hill Road a few days ago.

Matt exchanged a glance with the female uniform assigned to her. She rolled her head as if to say, "You can try."

Even easy questions seemed a stretch for Sonya Post. After a few attempts, Matt thought it best to wait until she recovered a bit more.

The front door opened and Chief Pettigrew made his entrance. Too bad the captain wasn't with him, thought Matt. Lewis could run interference. But then again, the captain would bust Matt out the door if his presence at the scene was discovered.

Pettigrew was a plain, forgettable man, more politician than lawman. He'd been associated with most every Post investigation in some way or another as he ascended the ranks of the Boise PD. Matt was sure if he reached in the chief's pocket, he'd find Andrew Post's picture in his wallet.

"What are you doing here, Detective?"

Before Matt could answer, the chief stepped away and yelled across the room. "Can some of you guys get out there and corral the freaking TV guys? Let's have some control over this scene."

Matt smiled. The control had just been lost.

He ignored the chief's original question and started to report on what he knew. "Name's Devlon Scott. Post Corporation security thug."

"Thug?" The chief rested his smooth palm on Matt's forearm. "I expect you to keep this investigation professional. I thought you were on leave."

"Likely murdered but could be suicide," Matt continued.

"Murder? You're jumping the gun a bit here, son. Prints? Powder burns?"

"Yes sir. Several on the—"

Pettigrew raced toward Mrs. Post upon identifying her through the door in the next room. Matt finished his summary alone. "—murder weapon. Positive on the powder burns, so he was definitely shot at close range. Died about two hours ago. Both he and his 'friend' were drunk as a skunk. Mr. Post isn't here for you to kiss his ass."

"Sir?" A young uniform named Stemmons appeared.

"You got something?"

"Yes sir. Something you should come see."

The security room was on par with a secure business environment. There were a number of computers in a black metal rack off to the side and at least ten video displays curved in a semicircle around a modular vanilla desk. A guilty looking security guard waited in a mesh chair.

Officer Stemmons took up a position behind the man while Matt stood over him a foot or so in front of the chair.

"Sir, this is Jim Watkins," Stemmons said. "He was on duty overnight. Won't say much without talking to Andrew Post or the Post team of lawyer-types."

Watkins was not a caricature of a security guard. He was rail-thin and couldn't have weighed much over a hundred pounds. His shaky voice matched his frame. "I'm just doing as I've been told," he said.

"By who?" Matt asked.

"It's in my contract."

"Not to cooperate with the police?"

"Sort of. They told me not to talk to anyone without a lawyer."

Matt laughed and kicked gingerly at one of the black castors on the guard's chair. "So you're involved in this murder?"

The guard sat back in the chair, looking to put some distance between Matt and himself. He scanned the doorway and a hall which led toward a door that emptied out to the guard shack.

"You waiting for someone?" Stemmons said.

The guard's head swung back and forth between Matt and Stemmons and then back to the hallway.

Watkins spoke in a whisper. "Listen, I wasn't even here when this happened. Mr. Post came in around four o'clock and asked me to go fill up his Lexus. Said to go down to the GasMart on the Interstate— the one by the airport. That was a strange request, but I do as I am told."

"So he took off in his car?" Matt said as if he didn't believe it.

"No, I came back and buzzed him. He didn't answer, so I figured he went back to sleep. Changed his mind."

"Buzzed him?" Stemmons asked.

"Yeah, there's an intercom system. Also sent him a text message."

Matt inched closer to the man and leaned down slightly. "You didn't know he'd left the house?"

"No. Besides, I've been ordered to report Mr. Post if he leaves..." Watkins scanned his surroundings again, not making eye contact with Matt.

"And?" Matt said.

Watkins stared at the floor and tapped his cowboy boots by the back heels. He shook his head.

"Who do you report this to?" Matt asked.

"I've said enough. You guys could get me in a shit-load of trouble." The guard raised his eyes up to Matt as if he was hoping for some promise of discreteness.

"Well, let me help you." Matt flipped through some pages in his notebook. "You called the police at 5:27 A.M. You were one of two people in the house when our boys arrived. I wouldn't be holding back."

Watkins squinted. "What?"

"You could be a suspect," Stemmons said.

"Now wait a minute. I don't even carry a gun. Besides, I was told this was a suicide."

"You know how to shoot a gun?" Matt asked.

"Sure, but—"

Stemmons shoved the chair, and Watkins spun into a position directly in front of him. "If you got something to tell us, do it."

"Look, I was fooling with camera number nine—the one that shows the fence by Mrs. Post's pool area." Watkins speech was very quick. "Zoomed it out a bit and saw the edge of a puddle of blood on the ground."

"So all you can tell me is that this happened between four in the morning and 5:27 A.M.?" Matt said.

"Between four and a little after five. That's when I got back. I'd of heard the shot. Surely somebody around here heard it."

Stemmons nodded at Matt. "We're still checking on that. Nothing yet."

"Double check then."

Stemmons left the room. Matt sat down on the edge of the desk right next to Watkins. "You were gone for an hour to get gas?"

"Told you I had to go all the way up by the airport."

Matt raised his eyebrows and said nothing.

"Okay, so I ran back to my house on the west side to get a couple of things. Mr. Post made a point of it to tell me to take my time."

"You said you zoomed the camera out a bit. Why was it zoomed in? Wouldn't you want to monitor the widest area possible?"

Watkins reached in his pocket, and then pulled his hand out in a surrendering gesture. "Can I smoke?"

Matt nodded. "Not my house. I don't care."

Watkins retrieved a cigarette and was barely able to light it. "Hey, I'm a security guard. One thing they told me was to keep my mouth shut. Can this be off the record?"

"I promise I'll only use what I absolutely need. You can wait for your lawyers if you like."

"No way. They'll be Post people, and I'd rather them not hear what I have to say."

"Get your own lawyer."

"You know these people. Better that I pack up and head back to Seattle."

"Don't be leaving just yet."

Watkins stood and paced in a small circle. "I was told to keep that camera focused on the gate any time Mr. Scott was in the house."

"Scott here often?"

"He and the old lady Post have been painting the town so to speak. One night they drifted into the pool area, and Mrs. Post fell in the pool. I ran out to help, and Mr. Scott held a session with me later that night."

"A session?"

"Yeah, that's what he called it. Popped me in the gut a couple of times before lecturing me on the meaning of privacy. Told me if he ever appeared on any camera at this house, he'd loosen a few of my teeth to compensate."

"How could you guarantee that? He has to show up on some camera when he comes here."

"He calls either me or Landers, the other guy who works on my off nights, and tells us he's arriving. We turn off the camera on the west entrance of the house. That's the one they built for Mrs. Post so she could come and go without seeing Mr. Post. She has her own garage, and Mr. Scott parks his car either in it or in front of it. We also zoom in camera nine, the one on the pool, cause they come out there a lot. Sometimes even when Mr. Post is here. Those are the only two shots where Mr. Scott might show up."

"How long has this been going on?"

"Bout six months."

"You don't think Post knows about it?"

"He knows. He's rich. Doesn't give a flip."

"Where are the cameras?"

"Mostly on the outside of the house. Five perimeter shots, plus two at the front entrance, another shot of the main garage, one outside Mrs. Post's private garage, and one on the back gate by the pool."

"That's the one you saw the blood on?"

The guard nodded.

"What happened to the guy in the guard shack?"

"Once everyone is in for the night, he goes home. Sandy left well after midnight after Mr. Post got back."

"Is that unusual? For Post to be out that late?"

Watkins nodded and puffed on the shaky cigarette.

"Anything else of interest on these cameras?"

"I've said enough."

"Okay." Matt sighed. "We'll want to speak to you again. Don't be going anywhere."

Matt sat in the security guard chair and watched the monitors. Two of the displays gave different views of the front of the estate. Media types were milling around outside the gate in both images, gawking and aiming ridiculously long lenses at the house in hopes of getting the perfect shot. Another view displayed the driveway and the main garage. Still another kept watch at the guard gate. Another camera—number three—was dark. Matt guessed this was the one with Mrs. Post's private garage in its field of view.

"Private garage," he said to himself. He rented a two-bedroom apartment and was too cheap to pay for a covered parking space.

Camera number nine was the key. It displayed the backyard and a chalk semicircle denoting the body position and the dried pool of blood in the very lower left of the screen. The body bag and the body were gone. At the top of the screen, one of the uniforms had stripped to his underwear and T-shirt and was stepping down into the pool. Matt would have his bullet soon. The other cameras gave varying views of both sides of the house.

Matt nudged a mouse on the table and a center console screen came to life. The image had ten boxes along the top and a vast array of icons below it. He clicked on the first box and a red outline appeared around it. He pressed a joystick next to the mouse and rotated the camera view. Playing with the mouse, he determined that by rolling the thumbwheel he could zoom into and out of the scene.

Alternately, he could get a much bigger view by looking at the individual monitors.

He moused-over to camera number three, highlighted the box, and clicked. A message appeared at the lower left of the main console screen, asking if he wanted to enable the camera. He typed in a "Y" and the screen came to life. A two-car stucco garage with a wooden door came into focus.

He maneuvered the joystick and found the driveway that joined with the main entrance road. He swept the camera further and located Mrs. Post's private entryway into the house.

Though he was quickly adapting to the system, he'd need some expertise. He picked up his phone and called the station.

The man from EJM Security Systems looked irritated, as if someone had kept his daughter out late. He was short and round, filling out a huge Hawaiian shirt and a pair of casual pants. He slicked his black and grey hair straight back with some sort of gel—the spitting image of some Italian mobster, completely out of place in Boise.

"What the hell is going on here?" the man asked.

"I need you to retrieve everything on these cameras from last night," Matt said. "Everything."

"Well, that'd be about twenty-four hours of video, pal."

Matt smiled. This guy *was* a mobster. "I want it all. Is there some way of knowing when someone left the premises besides the video?"

"Sure. This baby logs everything."

Matt raised his hands outward in a questioning gesture.

"The alarm system. The logs will tell us when someone turned it on or off. Pretty good proxy for somebody coming or going. Usually we can match that up with a video image taken at the time the unit was disarmed."

The man sat in the chair and started to operate the controls at a dizzying pace. After several grunts, he turned back to Matt. "Hey, put your face down here."

Matt leaned down to the monitor. The man stuck his hand out. "Name's Joe Smith." Matt shook his hand. A report with a number of fields appeared on the screen. A few rows were highlighted.

"Right here. You got the alarm disarmed and then armed around 4:02 A.M., then at 4:36 A.M., again at 5:04, and finally disarmed at 5:32. I'm guessing that's when you boys showed up cause the alarm system has been off ever since."

To Matt the sequence made some sense. Post had had enough. He saw Mrs. Post and Scott doing their thing sometime in the night. Maybe snuck into their room, grabbed the gun, and waited for Scott. Sonya Post was likely passed out the whole time. Maybe that's what set Post off. Seeing your spouse chained to the bed isn't exactly mainstream. Scott was drunk, maybe even fell asleep on the chair. Post snuck up from behind and popped him, threw the gun down, and fled.

Typically Post was anything but irrational. He had been acting a bit strange lately, so an emotional act like this was not out of the question. If he'd planned it in advance, he would have simply hired someone to do his dirty work. No, this was the way somebody like Post would go down—from an emotional error in judgment. An out-of-character irrational act. Or maybe Post wasn't so irrational. Maybe he had reached such a level of arrogance that he thought he would pull this off right under everyone's nose. Under Matt's nose.

"I want to view all of the cameras from four in the morning until five twenty-seven," Matt said.

Joe Smith looked especially irritated. "You and I'll have to get married to spend that much time together."

"Just do it."

"Each one? It's the weekend. You're paying me 125 bucks an hour."

"Take that up with the department. Can you speed up the playback?"

"Yeah, but somebody's gonna pay me for this."

"Let's give ourselves a break and go at four times the normal speed."

"That's still several hours glued to these monitors."

Matt waved his hand to begin.

Viewing the video was a mind-numbing affair. Frame after frame of near motionless scenes made Matt think about what it was like to be an airport security screener. Bag after bag of the same stuff, looking for that one needle in the haystack of the universe of airline transportable items.

What to look for? A picture of Post blowing smoke from the barrel of a gun? An argument? Someone sneaking in the house? Someone sneaking out? Post likely left through Sonya's private entrance. He'd leave no trace on the cameras that way. Matt made a mental note to have the door handle checked for fresh prints, though that might not mean much since Post owned the house.

Camera number nine, the camera Watkins claimed he panned to discover the body after returning from filling Post's car with gas, displayed a monotonous scene for an hour and twenty-one minutes. Matt could make out the grey shades of the edge of the concrete patio and a white stucco fence that partially surrounded the pool area with a five foot strip of dark grass separating the two. This unchanging scene played out from four o'clock until 5:21 A.M., and then the camera shot suddenly widened enough to show the pool of Devlon Scott's blood in the left corner. The tips of Scott's fingers were barely visible on the edge of the image. Then the camera rotated and zoomed in on Devlon Scott's body. Matt had Joe Smith slow this part of the video to real-life speed. After watching it over and over, the absence of movement or breathing confirmed Scott was already dead. Matt thought of Watkins and his reaction to the scene on the monitor. The poor guy sat in the same chair every night, dozing off, reading magazines, smoking his cigarettes, and wishing something exciting would happen. It did.

Joe Smith backed up the video to a position thirty minutes prior to the discovery of the body, and they watched the monotonous scene in real time. They saw nothing of consequence.

"Son of bitch left without a trace," Matt mumbled.

The statement seemed to shake Joe out of a trance. "I can tell you which doors were used if you're looking for somebody coming or going. Might help."

"Jesus, why didn't you tell me that," Matt said, leaning over and shaking his head toward the ground.

"You got to ask for this stuff. Go to Coney Island if you want a freaking mind reader."

Joe clicked and typed, and another report popped up on the console screen.

"The 4:02 alarm was triggered at the main garage access door. Same for the 5:04—"

"How bout the one in between? Mrs. Post's private entrance. Am I right?"

Joe puffed out a laugh. "You ain't no real detective, are you? Score one wrong answer. That was triggered at the back gate. Looking through this log, that exit ain't used much. That'd be this camera here." Joe knocked on number eight with his knuckles.

"Can you control access to that gate?"

"Yeah."

"Open it. How do I get there?"

"Beats me. I just program this shit."

"Wait here."

"I ain't going nowhere until I get paid."

Matt walked back into Sonya Post's side of the house. The chief was still there, holding Mrs. Post's hand and speaking to her like some kind of counselor. Matt passed through the living room unnoticed. He made his way to Andrew's side and then to the main garage access door, passed through the garage, and ended up on a long driveway. To get to the front entrance, he traveled all the way around the house, through a front garden area, and up to the guard shack. As he approached, he heard the click of several cameras and a voice or two calling out his name. The mysterious gate was not to be found.

He returned to the garage and eventually back to Sonya's living room. Stepping back out into her pool area, he noticed a dark open space with a narrow pathway surrounded by ivy covered stucco walls. He walked through the opening and entered a fenced area occupied by a couple of roller trash bins and a selection of garden and lawn maintenance tools.

There were two gates. One pointed toward Andrew's side of the house, probably to his pool area. The other more substantial gate was up against the outside fence. A camera sat on a metal pole pointed down at the latter gate. He opened it and walked out of the compound to a dirt patch alongside a dry drainage ditch. Down the side of the ditch and about twenty yards distant lay a bridge on the street leading out of the neighborhood.

Back in the security booth, Matt sat back with a cup of coffee and watched the lonely light on the fence gate. Joe ran the video of camera eight up to 4:32, minutes before the log indicated activity, and let it roll at normal speed. The light was low but bright enough near the gate to capture an intruder. Or in this case, a murderer leaving the premises.

After a few minutes, Matt and Joe both sat up and looked at each other.

"Let me roll that back."

Even in reverse, the image of a person passing through the gate was clear. The mobster started the video playback again. Matt watched the time. At 4:36 A.M., a person appeared briefly, back to the camera, opened the gate, and disappeared.

Joe rolled it back and started playing the video at half speed. The person was definitely a man, and he was carrying a small bag. He appeared in the first frame at 4:36:15 A.M. The image started to move frame by frame and then stopped. Joe clicked a few more times, and the image zoomed to the man approaching the gate.

His contrast to the gate was minimal, and he only appeared in a limited number of frames.

Matt set his coffee down and approached the monitor. "Okay, go slower. Right there."

The man had turned his head slightly for a few frames. Even with the low light and the fuzzy image, there was no doubt that the man was Andrew Post.

Chapter 35
The Cabin, Round Valley, Idaho
Sunday Morning

There was a soft knock at the door and a female voice called out Andrew's name. Annie started to pull the covers off her face, but a numbing pain hit like somebody had squeezed her temples with a vise. Her stomach screamed for her to keep still.

She could hear the door open and close and a conversation commencing outside. The female voice spoke first. "Saw a car in your spot and thought somebody might have been borrowing the cabin. Glad to see it's you."

"Come on inside." It was Andrew's voice. "I can offer you some coffee in about ten minutes."

The door opened again. Annie's stomach started to rise into her throat. She threw the blanket to the floor, raced past Andrew and a young muscular brunette in hiking shorts and a yellow skintight top, yanked the door open, and reached for the railing. The retching repeated. She felt Andrew's hands and the young woman's eyes on her.

"Maybe I should go," the young woman said.

Annie waved her hand backward as if to say, "Never mind me."

The relief from emptying her stomach was replaced by a feeling of being wrapped in ice. Andrew threw the blanket around her and led her back inside. She made her way to the couch. The brunette offered up a damp but warm wash cloth. Annie put the cloth to her head and raised her eyes to the girl.

Her beauty was shocking. Annie expected to see Andrew behind the woman, examining every nuance of this specimen's perfectly structured body. But he was busy putting coffee together on the stove. He'd obviously left out a few facts on why he wanted this cabin so badly.

"Can I get you something else?" The face was friendly—brown-eyed, mountain-bronze, and fresh.

Andrew brought a couple of steaming cups of coffee to the table. "I'm sorry, this is Lynn Sofel. She's a partner in the outfitter I told you about."

"Actually, I *am* the outfitter. Denny sold out last summer." The woman nodded toward Annie, probably not wanting to shake her hand after the porch incident.

"Splendid!" Andrew said.

"Seriously. You knew that. I told you last time you were here."

"I'm testing you," he said, a big grin painted on his face.

"Sure you are," said the woman with a knowing smile.

Annie didn't like their banter. What other tests had Andrew done on this woman? Annie lowered the washcloth and examined Andrew's friend a little more closely. She wasn't as young as Annie had first thought. She had lines on her face and the start of the crinkles—one of Penny's descriptive terms—around her eyes. Probably in her thirties, still half Annie's age. And there was no competing with a girl who had the thighs of a figure skater.

The dark beauty and Andrew sat and talked as they sipped coffee like a pair who'd gone through college together. There seemed to be no intimacy, only serious friendship. Annie looked around the cabin for some quick escape, but the pantry was the only other option.

So she sat and waited.

The woman finally left. Andrew warmed some more water over the stove so that Annie could clean herself up. She washed her face and gargled with some chillingly cold water. The banging in her head was steady. As if on cue, Andrew delivered two aspirin. She washed them down and made her way back to the bed.

Under the covers, she couldn't stand it anymore. "Who is she?" It sounded immature and accusatorial.

There was no answer. She peeked out into the room to find it empty. "Thank God he didn't hear me."

"I heard you." The voice came from the pantry. "She's just what I told you. She's an outfitter down on the Payette. Operates out of Cascade. Nice girl, huh?"

"Nice isn't the word for her."

Annie napped and woke-up to a nearly pain-free head. She was wearing only a T-shirt and underwear. She had no idea whether she had climbed into bed last night that way or had some help. She must've looked like a real fool.

From her suitcase she pulled out another flannel shirt and a pair of jeans. Outside, the pop of splitting wood blended with the chorus of wind in the trees.

She rinsed out the washcloth and placed it back on her face. It felt refreshingly cool. Her stomach was still a bit knotty. Through the front door, a blazing sun bounced off the porch. She held her hand up to block the light, looking for Andrew. Around the back of the house, she found him working up a sweat in sixty degree weather over a pile of wood sufficient for the rest of their visit.

"Don't you think that's enough?" she asked.

Andrew placed the ax on a big stump he was using as a base, wiped his brow, and stood with his hands on his hips. The wisps of white and grey on his chest and some wrinkles of life gave away his years. Yet he appeared to be in fairly good shape, a slight gut barely spoiling his tanned and shirtless upper body. Annie imagined him as a powerful, young man—short but lean and forceful. Unconsciously, she reached down and felt the slightly protruding handles disguised by her brilliant use of a wavy flannel shirt.

He placed another log up on the stump and split it with one stroke.

"You're right," she said. "Maybe not so one-dimensional. Can I get you some water?"

He shook his head.

"Lunch?"

He shook his head again, this time looking at her as if he wanted something. The look made her nervous.

"Are you angry with your husband?" he asked.

"What?" She barely said it loud enough to hear.

He pushed the debris off the stump and sat, throwing his head back, releasing tension in the back of his neck. "I've been angry with my wife for a long time," he said. "So long, I tend to forget why."

Annie sat down on the edge of the porch. "I'm not angry with Frank. I see his action as an act of love. How could I be angry about that?"

"If I'd seen your husband switch the children, I'm not sure I would have said a word. To me, Donny and Katlin were strangers. They belonged to someone else. I lost Katlin and I felt so little."

"But you redeemed yourself in Donny. You've raised a very successful young woman."

"Redemption? Maybe." He stared out into the meadow. "Now I sit here thirty-three years later in the ruins of what feels like one long bomb blast. Thirty-three years in a destructive relationship with a woman I wouldn't let leave. Then you appear out of nowhere."

"I didn't—"

"Don't," he said, cutting her off. "Don't say anything."

Chapter 36
Next Door to the Post Estate, Boise Foothills
Sunday Evening

Andrew Post had spent the last two days hiding from the law. Matt had spent the last two days waiting for Captain Lewis to call him out on the Devlon Scott investigation.

So far so good. No sign of the captain. But also no sign of Post.

Matt had tried to get someone—Rafi Thuban, Donny, one of the Post security types, anyone—to open up and tell him where Post had gone. So far, no one was talking. Actually, they had claimed ignorance of Post's location. Matt wasn't buying it. He'd obtained Post's mobile number from Donny with some protest but repeated calls went unanswered.

Post was a fugitive and was somehow keeping Annie Lorda with him. Maybe she had no idea he had shot someone. Maybe she was being held captive. Maybe he'd done her in, too. The latter seemed unlikely. At least that's what Matt kept telling himself. Surely Annie had heard about the shooting. It was impossible to avoid the story.

Matt's occasional partner, Frank Saras, had kept him informed of the details of the official investigation. Saras had said the department only wanted Post for questioning and that Jon Fransen, the detective officially assigned to the case, was promoting the suicide theory—a preposterous conclusion in Matt's mind. Nobody shoots himself in the back of the head with his non-shooting hand. That was especially true with a pro like Devlon Scott. The victim had been shot by someone else, and there were only three suspects—Andrew Post, Sonya Post, and the security guard on duty. Matt had ruled out a stranger. Too difficult to avoid the cameras or someone in the house. Given Scott's past behavior toward the man, the security guard was a marginal possibility. Matt's gut said no—the guard was telling the truth. Sonya Post had been cuffed to the bed. That left Andrew Post pulling the trigger in an irrational act or in cold blood, knowing he could walk away a free man.

Saras had also said the department wasn't interested in the most damning piece of evidence—Andrew Post's fingerprints on the weapon. They had also ignored the video of Post leaving the premises. Such irresponsible police work pointed to an internal cover-up. Matt would have to be careful from here on out.

Most troubling was a neighbor who'd told Detective Fransen he could pin down the time of the shooting to exactly 4:52 A.M. The cameras had shown Post leaving the premises at 4:36, some sixteen minutes earlier. The neighbor's statement was not helpful to Matt's theory of a homicidal jealous husband. In Matt's mind, either Post had come back, the neighbor's time was wrong, or the witness was helping Andrew Post stay out of trouble.

Determining the credibility of this witness—Andrew Post's next door neighbor—was next on the agenda.

The neighbor's house was basic modern—uncomfortable chairs and couches, ugly colors, low lights, lots of glass, and incomprehensible art all over the walls and tables. The man fit the house. Despite the hour, well past nine o'clock, the middle-aged "accomplice" could've been on his way to work. He wore a loud-red dress shirt, skinny slacks, thin glasses with dark frames, and a solid brown tie worn loosely.

"Mr. Lopresti?" Matt shoved his badge in the man's face.

The man examined the badge and handed it back. "That's right." He made no attempt to welcome Matt past the front entryway.

"We had a bit of a conflict between your statement and another one of the neighbors. What time did you say you heard the shot?"

"Jesus, how many times do I have to recount the story?" Lopresti retreated a few steps and leaned back against one of the uncomfortable chairs, trying to appear relaxed.

"There have been some statements made that might change the complexion of the case."

"Such as?"

"I'm not at liberty to say. Now"—Matt pulled out his notebook and flipped to a random page of notes—"you stated you heard a sound between four and five that morning?"

"That's right."

"And you were sure it was a gunshot?"

The man appeared to carefully consider his answer. "I've already been through this three times."

"Just one more time. Your statement is very important, and we want to be sure of every detail before this goes to trial."

"Trial?"

Matt remained silent and waited.

"I stated it sounded like a gunshot, yes."

"You shoot guns?"

"Absolutely not."

"You an expert on guns…what they sound like?"

"I think it might be best for you to talk to my lawyer."

"You need a lawyer?"

"Believe that's all, Officer. Good night."

The man stepped forward and put his hand on Matt's shoulder to turn him back to the door. Matt held his ground.

"Mr. Lopresti. I'd like to do you a favor."

"And what would that be?"

"To keep you out of trouble." Matt paused. "The Posts can be formidable enemies. I can assure you, they'll protect you when they need you. When they don't, they'll step on you like a cockroach."

"What's going on here? I was told it was a suicide."

"You tell me. You might've been mistaken about the time or your certainty about the sound. Maybe you felt compelled to help."

Lopresti rubbed his fingers through his hair. "Look. That's all I have to say. I'm in the middle, if you know what I mean."

Bingo. Matt's line of questioning wasn't exactly in the detective handbook, but Lopresti was following his lead.

"Let me help you a bit," Matt said. "There's some new evidence that says the gun might've been fired earlier. And that it wasn't a suicide. There's also some evidence of last minute maneuvering."

"A cover-up?"

"Maybe. I hope you have a good lawyer." Matt started for the door.

"Hold up."

Matt stopped. Waited.

"Sometimes you get in a position that screws you either way. I made my money in the markets. You hedge your bets the right way, and it can make you sinfully rich for a while. Then somebody tips one of the dominoes, and they all fall down. Your bets, both ways, sink you. You understand?"

"Not really," Matt said. "But I do know you can limit your losses."

Lopresti left Matt at the entryway and returned to the front room. He sat down on a lime-green plastic chair.

"They have me," he said.

"Who?"

"Come on. I know why you're here. Just because my business depends on Post and I'm a bit in the hole doesn't mean a darn thing."

Bingo again. "Mr. Lopresti, I can help you. I just need to know if you're sure of your statement about the gunshot."

Lopresti stared at the floor. "Honestly, I heard something yesterday morning. Was it a gun? Probably. Did it happen at 4:52? That's what my clock said when I got out of bed."

"Is that when you heard it? When you got out of bed?"

"That's when I got up. Can we be done now?"

"I'd think very carefully about this," Matt said in a voice meant to sound understanding. "Maybe you'll be lucky, and you won't have to testify. The evidence is not favoring that outcome at this time."

Matt pretended to write a few more details in his notebook, nodded toward the man, and walked out the door.

He knew the club across the street—Rochee's—was harboring the love of his life. What condition she'd be in was anyone's guess. He was pretty sure she had no idea her mother had been missing for the last two days.

An obstacle of a man stood in the doorway, completely dressed in black, shaved-head, numerous tattoos poking up around his T-shirt, and a V-shaped beard pointing toward the sidewalk.

Matt approached the bouncer. "She in there?"

The man nodded and made no effort to hinder his progress.

Inside, the place was dark and smoke burned his eyes. Blinding lights flashed on a stage where a poorly skilled retro-punk band screamed into the recesses of the hall. A young girl bumped into him, spilled some kind of concoction on herself, and nearly fell to floor. Matt pulled her upright and sent her across the pit toward a dozen or so kids standing in front of the singer.

He strolled throughout the building, occasionally shining his flashlight at kids commingling in some remote spot. An unfamiliar tall woman with spiked red hair stood behind the bar and watched him closely. Despite the hair, she appeared to be a generation older than the clientele.

A dark outline of a well-chiseled man also appeared to take interest in Matt. He couldn't see much except for the muscular shape, a baseball cap, and an earring in the shape of a cross. It was Johnny Lowell, the preacher's son, an old friend of Penny's from her seedier high school days.

"She's over there." The voice came from the dark outline.

Matt moved closer and couldn't see Johnny's hand until he came within a foot or so.

"How is she?"

"Fucked up. Big time. She called me about an hour ago to come party. I told her I don't party anymore, but something about her voice made me come over. Got here and it was like fifteen years ago."

"Thanks for calling me." Matt patted Johnny on the shoulder and took aim into a corner where a single red light shown on three people sitting on an old couch, examining something on a beat-up coffee table. The one in the middle was Penny.

"You need any help?" Johnny asked.

Matt waved him off. He was responsible for the mess, and it was his to clean up.

He was angry with Penny, but he was also angry with himself. Penny had been so wasted, she had barely recognized him. Her condition likely saved Matt from some kind of a tussle. He'd been able to lead her out the door and drive her home with no push-back.

She lay under the covers, occasionally talking to some unknown hallucination. Matt decided it would be best for him to stay until the next morning, when the effects of the drugs and alcohol wore off.

He called the Schneider's and confirmed Serena's whereabouts. Serena would stay the night and Monday at their place. That would give Penny some time to recover. He dialed Annie's home number again only to get the answering machine. Annie's new smartphone, the one Post gave her for protection, went straight to voicemail.

Penny's place was dark and empty. He found a spot on the couch in the front room and fell asleep.

The buzzing on the table wasn't instantly recognizable. Matt had been dreaming that Jimmy Wayne had been found guilty of pulling the trigger on Scott, but Jimmy kept turning into Donny.

He swatted at the phone and knocked it on the floor, retrieved it, and touched the answer button.

"Matt? It's Henry."

"Yep."

"You need to get out here. I visited your doctor guy—Lewis Vanoble. He's in Salem, but he won't be here long."

The news brought Matt out of his slumber. "It's been a freaking week."

"Yeah. Yeah. I'm not even supposed to be here. Should've gone home after the wedding yesterday. But I stayed for you, my friend."

Matt listened. Said nothing.

After a few seconds, Henry started again. "Found his house pretty quick through his driver's license records. Nothing special."

"He's at home?"

"No, I told you he's in a terminal care facility. His daughter says he could go at any time."

"Is he able to talk?"

"He comes and goes, but he's still got all his marbles. Got some interesting things to say—"

Matt hung up and immediately called the airlines. He was able to get a nine hundred dollar center seat on a seven A.M. flight to Portland in the morning. It was worth it. He'd pay nine thousand dollars to get Andrew Post.

He briefly considered calling Henry back...find out what the doctor said. No, he'd hear it firsthand. Vanoble would be worth the trip. He had to be there. Face to face. Hopefully, Post wouldn't come out of hiding while he was gone.

Chapter 37
The Cabin, Round Valley, Idaho
Sunday Evening

Facing the open meadow, Annie sat in silence.

They had spent the middle of the day hiking to a pristine mountain lake across the valley. Upon their return, Andrew had decided to walk down to the big cabin for some food supplies. He'd been gone about a half an hour.

A mosquito or two buzzed near Annie's face. She hated mosquitoes more than any creature on earth. Yesterday they didn't seem to be as bad. Maybe the rain had stirred them up.

The sun was closing in on the steep hills to the west. That would be the signal for the little blood-suckers to eat her alive. Andrew better hurry or there might not be anything left. Annie heard the faint crunch of his boots pushing up the dirt road. The sound moved closer while she swatted the buzzing devils away from her ears. Rather than sit around and be blood bait, she decided to go out to meet him.

Andrew came into view at the top of a small rise in the road, carrying a couple of paper bags full of food. Annie laughed.

He held his hands out under the bags. "What?"

"My personal grocer, the billionaire," she said.

"Uh huh."

"Just funny."

She hopped over and took one of the bags.

"Let's do something fun," she said. "Outrageous. Something you don't think I've done."

He raised his eyebrows.

She pulled his free arm toward the cabin. "And you better have something to blow the mosquitoes off the porch."

Inside, Andrew put away the foodstuffs and folded the bags.

"Okay," he said. "Outrageous. What would that be?"

"Surprise me."

They drove at least ten miles on a dirt road up and over a mountain to the east of Round Valley, leveling out to follow a stream of white water in a broad canyon. The sky was still bright, but the canyon was fully in the shadows. It reminded Annie of the forest in "Little Red Riding Hood." After a few miles of hugging the stream, Andrew pulled into a gravel lot next to a small meadow. Another vehicle, an old Volkswagen Bug, was parked there as well.

Andrew exited the Subaru. Annie wanted to question his intentions but decided to remain quiet. She was the one, after all, that had asked for something outrageous. He opened the hatch and pulled out two towels and a battery-powered lantern.

They stepped down the riverbank. A dam of variably spaced rocks awaited their next move. With towels under his arm and the lantern in one hand, Andrew skillfully moved to the rocks in the middle of the stream and turned to wait.

"What if I fall in?" Annie said. She was very deliberate with each step. He grabbed her fingers with his free hand, and she followed his feet to the other side. A foursome of college-aged kids came down a narrow trail along the edge of the river.

"It's great," said a skinny, shirtless boy with a lumberjack's beard. Two girls and another kid passed and nodded their heads, acknowledging the cool old people.

Fifty yards further, they reached a slow area in the river with rocks strategically placed like the outlines of little rooms along the bank. Steam rose into the waning light.

"Now what?" Annie asked.

Andrew set the lantern on a rock close to the stream. "We'll need that for our return trip. Get in." He sat on a big rock next to the one supporting the lantern and started to loosen his boots.

"You're kidding."

"You said outrageous."

"Shit."

He put his hands to his ears and keeled over. "Such language."

She watched him place his flannel shirt, T-shirt, pants, and his underwear on the rock with his shoes, as though he were laying them out on a hotel bed. He walked carefully into the water, lowered his white butt into the steam, and let out a sigh.

"They were right," he said. "It's great."

"Geez. Did I ask for this?"

He smiled.

"Don't look." She found her own rock and followed her companion's lead. She made her way into the water. It was hot. Almost hot enough to scald.

Andrew honored her wishes and kept his head pointed away, downstream. "You're going to have to come down this way. Too hot over there," he said.

"God, I'll get you for this."

She moved to within a foot of Andrew and sat in the water. It did feel good. "We should've had some of that whiskey of yours before coming out here."

"That we should," he said.

They rested in the soothing heat. Annie closed her eyes and listened to the stream. A gentle wind played in the pines and an airplane hummed somewhere high over their heads.

"What do you think Penny would say if she read your husband's letter?" Andrew asked.

"Why?"

"She asked me if I'd read the letter and I said yes."

"Penny would believe the letter. Beyond that, I have no idea how she would react. You think I should tell her?"

"No."

Annie reached her hand out as far as she could and touched Andrew's elbow. He reached backward and touched her fingers. She grabbed his hand and held on.

"I'm not giving you permission to turn your head," she said.

He laughed.

"What about Donny? What if she knew you were not her father?"

"I doubt it would matter much."

"That's a bit hard to believe. It would be pretty intense news to bear."

"Donny is a rock. I've raised her that way."

"Do you ever miss Katlin?"

She immediately felt his hand tense up. She waited for an answer, but only the wind and stream replied.

"Do you want to talk about her?" she asked.

"No."

"Okay."

"I let her go." It was the first time she heard a crack in the confident voice of Andrew Post. She waited for and wanted more. But she would not pry into such a sensitive issue. She'd react the same way if he brought up the deaths of her first two children. She waited. He said nothing. She waited for what must've been ten minutes. He held her hand and stared at the river. Then it was time to go.

On the return trip, Annie leaned back in the seat and relaxed. That *was* outrageous. She'd never tell Andrew, but her desire had been to crawl up next to him and have him pull her close. Not for the stimulation, but for intimacy.

At the very least, she wouldn't have to worry about the silly confidence-draining moments when lovers see each other "in that way" for the first time. She could run around the cabin naked and not worry about it now. The thought made her shake with laughter. Andrew smiled back but kept his attention on the dark road and the never ending trees and curves.

The cabin was cold and pitch-black. Andrew started the potbellied stove and lit a couple of lamps. Annie pulled a chair up close to the stove, waiting for the warmth.

"Don't get so close," he said. "You'll burn yourself."

She heard a couple of glasses clink. He pulled her chair back with her in it and placed two wine glasses on the wooden table. "Maybe something a little less toxic tonight."

He filled the glasses with a Merlot. She sipped hers slowly.

He swirled the wine and sipped it a few times. "Now for dinner."

They divided the chores of cooking the great American meal— steak and potatoes. Andrew had put together his secret marinade before they left, though it looked mostly like Worcestershire sauce and a few additives. Annie readied some broccoli for steaming and set the potatoes inside the door of the potbellied stove. They pulled a couple of pieces of French bread apart and ate it.

Andrew grabbed a blanket, and they sat on the porch while the potatoes warmed and the steaks simmered on a small grill he had brought out from the pantry. It was cool, but not as cool as the previous night.

"What are we, Annie?" he said. "I mean the two of us."

"Where are the mosquitoes?"

"They're like tourists. They disappear after it gets cool enough. Now my question. It doesn't feel like we are slowing down to me."

Annie forced herself into a natural fit against his body. He was warm. She was warm. She decided not to reply.

Chapter 38
River Run Senior Center, Salem, Oregon
Monday Morning

A deck of low clouds knifed into the side of the hills lining the Willamette Valley as Matt pressed south from Portland in a rental car. Fine beads of rain played with the windshield enough to force him to constantly tinker with the wiper delay. The plane ride had been uneventful. The scathing text messages from Penny upon his arrival meant she had awoken from her stupor and remembered at least some of what had happened last night. He had a nagging feeling that not calling her right away would cost him. For Penny his motto was "Give her space, but never ignore."

Crossing the Marion Street Bridge, he drove into West Salem. After ten minutes of searching and backtracking, the River Run Senior Center faced him through the front windshield. The place had an uncomfortable appearance of permanence.

The complex consisted of a common building and two wings attached in a V-shape. It looked like a cross between a hospital and a modern motel. Being Monday, the small parking lot was empty except for one of those nursing home vans parked directly in front.

Inside, he found an empty front desk, a leather sofa, and several oversized chairs lining the walls. A dining room that resembled a school cafeteria stood behind a glass wall directly opposite the front door. Two hallways branched off to each side, leading to the two residential wings. A handful of elderly residents were eating a late breakfast, most alone, a few moving along like their bodies were in a swimming pool, struggling to push forward against the water.

At the front desk, he noticed a serious thirtyish woman bearing down on him from the hallway to the right. She wore a blue women's business suit, hair pulled tight into a ponytail, narrow silver-rimmed glasses, and a hard expression that could be Donny's.

He pulled out his police ID and held his hand outward. As he was about to open his mouth, the woman put her hand in the air and beat him to the punch.

"I suppose you want to put the good doctor out of his misery."

"I'm sorry?"

"Suppose you are Detective Downing?"

The woman was older than she first appeared, maybe closing in on forty or forty-five. Her whole face seemed to be pulled backward as if someone had yanked on her ponytail. A good coat of makeup masked a less than fair complexion under the hood.

"Yes, that's me." Matt scanned the woman for a nametag but didn't see one.

"Doctor Vanoble probably won't make it much longer. He was doing a little better until your friend from Portland came by. Ever since, he's been about as agitated as a dying man could be."

"And you are?"

"Deidre. Deidre Vanoble, his daughter."

The woman pulled a white handkerchief from a small black purse and wiped her eyes. "I could have easily stopped all of this, but Father wouldn't let me. Said he needed to talk to you. He won't tell me why."

"Your father's information is crucial to a murder back in Idaho."

"Murder?" The word seemed to shake the woman. "He's never lived in Idaho, and it's not the kind of place he would visit much."

"Actually, it was back when he worked in Ontario, Oregon. Thirty-three years ago."

The surprise on Deidre Vanoble's face could not be faked. "You must have the wrong doctor. He's been around here his whole life. I was born in Portland."

"And your mother?"

"She's still there. They divorced when I was young."

"Well trust me. Your father worked in Ontario at the Malheur Regional Medical Center thirty-three years ago. I know it's been a long time, but he may have direct knowledge of the incident in question. If it would make you feel better, you can come with me, take me to his room."

The offer didn't stand a chance. Deidre Vanoble was not going to cooperate. Matt would have to obtain permission from the center and locate Vanoble on his own.

He found the director's office hidden behind a wall of curtains down the left hallway. A secretary dispensed Vanoble's room number, never taking her eyes off of a computer screen.

Matt found room A113 and its occupant. Physically, Dr. Vanoble was a mess. He was confined to a hospital bed, dressed in the standard hospital gown, tubes crisscrossing like some kind of lab experiment. Two sticks protruded from sleeves similar to the forearms of a malnourished child. Breathing appeared difficult, though nearby oxygen equipment was dormant. His eyes didn't follow Matt into the room. They followed Deidre Vanoble trailing a short distance behind.

Before Matt could speak, Vanoble pointed his finger at his daughter and coughed one word, "Out."

His daughter obeyed. Vanoble pointed at the door. Matt closed it.

The room was hard and grim. No carpet. Floor-to-ceiling vertical blinds that effectively blocked out any vestige of the outside world. There was an antiseptic smell faintly mixed with urine. It made Matt want to open the window.

Vanoble had probably refused to return to a hospital, and this was the last place he would ever see. There was no sign he'd left the bed recently. No magazines, books, clothes, personal items anywhere. Everything neatly packed away in drawers and hung carefully in a half-open closet. It was as if they had prematurely started to pack his belongings before his bed was even cold.

"She's been real helpful since she found out I have some money," Vanoble said. His voice was very rough.

Matt pulled out a small recorder. "Do you mind if I use this?"

"Mind?" That was all Vanoble could say before a coughing fit suggested it might be too late. After numerous deep heaves, the doctor spit into a towel sitting on a table across his bed. His face was now deep red.

"Throat cancer. Couldn't quit smoking."

Matt pulled up the only chair in the room—a flimsy plastic thing that reminded him of the ones at the DMV. Vanoble hacked again. He stared at Matt through foggy specs that had probably diagnosed and helped thousands of patients. Matt wondered how a man devoted to medicine could smoke.

"I'll try and make this quick."

"You better." Vanoble laughed.

At least the man still had some sense of humor.

"I'm trying to—"

Before Matt could get to the first question, Vanoble reached out and grabbed his shoulder. The grip was weak but determined. "Are you going to get those bastards?"

"That might depend on what you know and who you are talking about."

"They're murderers."

"Who?"

"Post and his thugs. You know who."

The next thirty minutes were difficult. The man was struggling to speak and was quite emotional. His memory, however, was excellent.

Vanoble stated he had divorced just before he had left for Ontario. Deidre and his ex-wife had remained in Portland. Vanoble had wanted a fresh start. A friend suggested he do some time in eastern Oregon, far from home at the Ontario hospital. They needed an emergency room physician for about half the money he was making in Portland. He took it.

He'd been there a little more than a half a year when Andrew Post showed up one night several weeks after Katlin Post was born.

"I remember the night well. I was napping and one of the nurses woke me. She said some men had taken over one of the examination rooms. Of course, those men were Andrew Post, some man who claimed to be a physician—and I doubt he was—and an Arab-looking man with a couple of thugs under his command. The Arab turned out to be Rafi Thuban. I didn't know of him at the time."

Vanoble stopped to spit blood into his towel. Matt reached for the pitcher of water. He waved him off.

"When I arrived, the infant was on the examination table. Over in the corner of the room, Thuban and Post appeared to be having a quiet argument. About what I could only guess. The two thugs countered my every move as I tried to make my way to the table.

"Thuban came over to me, pulled me back into the hallway, and spoke quietly into my ear. He said the baby had stopped breathing on their trip to Portland and had died in the vehicle as they crossed the Oregon border. He stated Mr. Post's personal physician would handle everything. I made my way back into the room and inched toward the table, but it was obvious they were not going to let me diagnose the child.

"My cursory examination from a few feet away confirmed their story. The infant appeared unresponsive. No indication she was breathing. Their doctor stopped his work and took Thuban's place between me and the child. He told me she had a congenital heart defect. Given the man was supposed to be a physician, he seemed incapable of telling me what any physician would want to know. She may have had some kind of stenosis. The emergency room nurse told me the child was bluish when they whisked her by the front desk, making me believe she was alive when they brought her in or shortly before that. No matter, they took no action to revive the child. I tried to question their doctor again, but Thuban's thugs pushed me back into the hallway. From the doorway, I could see Andrew Post wrapping the child in a blanket and taking her away.

"I left and called the police. The officers arrived like they had been waiting in the parking lot for my call. They briefly spoke to Post and Thuban, who had since claimed a private patient room, and then they left immediately afterwards."

The story was incredible. Matt was so engrossed he'd not taken a single note. He looked at the recorder and hoped to God it was capturing every word.

Vanoble drank a small amount of water, rested a minute, and continued. "Thuban found me, took me back into an office off the front lobby, and closed the door. He shoved a piece of paper in front of me. It was a death certificate. In no uncertain terms, he said I would call the time of death, sign the form, and forget any of this ever happened. He said if I said one word, he would ruin me and my family. I believed him.

"So my options were to fight Andrew Post and his money or walk away. I walked away and I relived that moment over and over ever since. The next morning, I came back to the hospital to make sure it wasn't just a nightmare. The place was buzzing with people. Lawyers. State Police. A few reporters. The minister from the local Methodist Church. More Post Corporation types. I couldn't get near Post or Thuban."

"So you felt you had to pack up and leave town?"

Vanoble stared at Matt as if he wondered if the young officer had fully grasped what he'd just said.

"I read it in a newspaper article," Matt said. "They stated you just upped and left the hospital in Ontario."

Vanoble nodded. "A couple of lawyer-types came to my house about a week later. Said Post was considering malpractice charges against me. They were even contemplating criminal charges. I was floored."

Vanoble stopped to cough and spit again. Matt checked the recorder.

"They said I was sleeping in the backroom, and due to my incompetence, precious minutes were lost that would have saved the child. They said I did nothing. And you know what? They were right. I did nothing.

"I started to think back on that night and look for nurses, attendants who would back my story. The one nurse who clued me in on the whole thing refused to get involved. She suddenly seemed convinced of my guilt."

"Someone got to her?"

"Who knows? I just know it was me alone against them. They told me to disappear. That was the last I saw of those bastards."

"Why do you call it murder?"

"The child was alive when she arrived. I'm convinced. The doctor had a syringe on the table. That was it. No leads hooked up to the body to monitor the child's condition. No action I could see that a normal doctor would take in such a situation."

"They claimed she was dead already," Matt said.

"Whatever. At the very least, they let the child die. Why keep me from the child? The only reason to keep me away would be to let her die or murder the poor thing. Plain and simple. These are heartless, evil men."

The words launched another coughing attack. Vanoble spit more blood into the towel, threw it on the floor, and grabbed a clean one off the table. Matt glanced at his eyes. Bloodshot, almost yellow, but angry.

"What about records of the event?" Matt asked "Wouldn't the hospital have to have some kind of documentation from that night?"

"Good luck. You won't find a thing. I'm sure the records were 'lost' long ago."

Some of the displays on the monitor by Vanoble's bed started bouncing around and a small yellow light started to blink.

"Your name is on the death certificate," Matt said.

"Goddammit, don't you think I know that! Yes, I signed it! I was young and scared. It's probably the only document you'll find."

More hacking led to a staccato rhythm of beeps from the medical equipment. A nurse entered the room, followed closely by Vanoble's daughter. The nurse inspected the monitor and gave Matt a forceful look. Deidre Vanoble was pacing, ready to pounce.

"The doctor needs rest," said the nurse, injecting something through a tube that led to his arm.

Vanoble shook his head. He coughed over and over. He motioned for Matt to come close.

Matt leaned within inches of his mouth. Vanoble whispered. "Tell me you will put them away. Leave the money out of it."

"Money?" Matt whispered back.

"They gave me a lot of money. It's in an account in Portland. I never spent a penny. It's worth millions now. My daughter only came back because she found out about it. But I still want her to have it."

Matt leaned back and nodded. Vanoble's daughter had stopped pacing and was leaning against a far wall. She was impatiently waiting for her father to pass on. Matt wanted to honor the man's request. He knew he would not.

Matt sat in his rental car in the parking lot and looked at the recording device. He played a few snippets. Vanoble's voice came in loud and clear. He had what he wanted. It wasn't clear what he could do with this kind of evidence so many years later, yet just the exposure would vindicate him.

Of course, the good doctor's recording was not enough. The Post machinery would find ways to crush the credibility of the story, and once published, make Matt and Erin look like fools. He'd need to find more evidence to back his case. That would be easier now that he had the story in hand.

At the very least, he was closing in on a formidable and all-out public and legal attack on Post. The Devlon Scott murder would send Post to jail. The killing of Scott might be seen by Post's supporters as the action of an emotionally charged man defending his honor. Some might even go as far as defending the killing. Yet the addition of the circumstantial evidence of the Lacy Talbert murder and the killing of Katlin Post would show the world that Post had been a common criminal all along.

Chapter 39
Cabarton Stretch of the Payette River
Monday

They had spent three days without any outside contact—no phones, television, or radio. The rest of the world had passed by, and they were both okay with that. Annie had left a brief voicemail on Penny's phone Saturday morning, so she assumed her whereabouts were known. Surely Andrew's people knew where he was and that he was okay.

Annie stood in the sun, its warmth in sharp contrast to the chill lurking in the shadows. Activity buzzed around her. A half-dozen or so rafts were in various stages of preparation to make the ten mile journey along the North Fork of the Payette River from the Cabarton Bridge to Smith's Ferry.

Andrew and Lynn tossed paddles and supplies into the eight-man raft while a bone-thin teenage boy kept the boat tethered with a nylon rope. Four other boat riders had already put on their life jackets and were busy taking pictures of each other on the bridge a few feet away. There was Natasha and Dennis, a couple of college kids from Texas who seemed to be just friends, and Phillip and Jackson, two young men who were more than just friends. Annie thought the latter would've been more at home in a coffeehouse around the Bay Area than romping around in a cold river in southwest Idaho. Natasha and Dennis spoke to each other in a continuous two-way stream, as if their minds were joined by some persistent connection. It would have been annoying had their conversations not been interesting and filled with humor.

Then there was Lynn Sofel. At the cabin, she appeared stunningly fit. Now in white cotton shorts and a tight one-piece bluish camouflage swimsuit, she possessed the form of someone who tested the limits of her body for a living. Even though she appeared to be thirtyish or so, there was a hint of premature aging from constant sun exposure. There was no sign of makeup or anything unnatural. She didn't need it. It was a fresh complexion, full of life.

The one thing Annie couldn't miss today was her arms. The woman had triceps for God's sake. She was the woman all women loved to hate. But Lynn Sofel made that task difficult.

Their boat was distinct from the others at the bridge. Though the vessels exhibited a variety of colors and sizes, all at odds with the colors God had given to this part of the world, the one with Cascade River Company stenciled on its side was the only boat with a frame mounted in the interior and the only one that blended into the pine green foliage and brown cured grasses of the local environment. The frame was secured by several cords attached to small evenly spaced rings on both sides of the raft. A padded chair rose from the middle of the frame to a height just above the sides of the boat.

The skinny kid had given up his rope to one of the San Francisco guys. They were in a whispered conversation as they scanned the rest of the rafters. They had probably made the connection they were about to go whitewater rafting with one of the richest men in the Northwest.

The kid retrieved two yellow paddles from the boat trailer. The paddles were so long they didn't seem to fit the raft. Andrew met the kid as he reached the boat, and they proceeded to slip the long paddles into rings attached to the left and right of the padded chair. Andrew touched Annie on the shoulder as he passed by on his way back to the van and spoke quietly, "Lynn is an expert. You're going to love this trip."

Annie wanted to help. But she just stood there as the commotion around her continued. Pretending to take interest in a tree that was having trouble holding its ground next to the river, she turned her back to the loading operation and fought the urge to beg Andrew to take her home.

"This guy won't be here much longer." It was the voice of Lynn. "Too many people drive off the road to load up their boats. I've asked the Forest Service guys if they could put up some kind of barricade. No luck yet."

She kneeled down, cupped what little dirt she could gather, and packed it over the exposed roots.

"This tree gets no respect. We call it a Doug Fir, but it's really a hemlock. Imagine the insult of being called one thing, but you're really something else."

Lynn patted the trunk and returned to her work.

"Damn," Annie said under her breath. "Smart too."

The time to leave had arrived. At some point, this woman would lower those shorts, hop in the boat, and plant herself on the chair. The perfect shape would be on display for the world to see— including Andrew. How could anyone compete with that? Annie would keep her shorts and T-shirt on at all costs. Underneath was an ill-fitting one piece she could have used last night in the hot spring. Being self-conscious was silly considering Andrew had probably caught a glimpse of her in her full glory. She should have left her swimsuit at home. With the proper excuse, they'd be back at the cabin doing something else. But Andrew had been so excited by the prospect of her first raft trip, she couldn't say no.

The other passengers made their way into the boat. Natasha and Dennis, nipping at each other about who would scream first, took up the front two spots. Phillip and Jackson loaded quietly and sat forward of the elevated chair. Andrew stepped in and took one of the only positions left—the very rear of the raft, the closest spot to Lynn.

Annie stepped into the river in her borrowed water shoes. The water was only a few inches deep, but the cold was numbing, and within seconds, painful, as if someone had stuck pins in her toes. Andrew leaned over the boat and reached out to guide her. Lynn appeared at her side and provided extra support.

She felt like a little old lady. She looked back at Lynn, who now sported a Boise Hawks baseball cap, sunglasses, a white nose courtesy of zinc oxide, and a friendly smile. This woman was on a mission to make it impossible for Annie to dislike her.

Lynn climbed up into the chair and kept her shorts on. The kid did some fancy magic with the rope and tossed the bundle back into the boat. With one shove, he pushed the boat into the current and headed back to the van so he could meet them later in the day at Smith's Ferry.

"What's his name?" Annie asked.

"Bradford," Lynn said, busy adjusting herself in the seat and stretching her back and neck. "Bradford Pinchot, like the forest. He's from Boise. Lots of trouble in high school. Dropped out and came up here looking for work. He's still a handful sometimes, but so far so good. He's one of my two employees."

Annie sat back in the comfort of the sun with Andrew's arm supporting her, watching nature's best pump and slide the oars like a machine. The east side of the river remained dark in the shade of a sloping tree canopy. For the most part, Lynn was able to keep the boat in the sun. Every once in a while, the entire river ducked away from the warmth, causing a burst of conversation centered on the air temperature. Dennis and Natasha quibbled about whether it was in the forties or fifties and argued something about measuring temperatures in the shade. Phillip, who apparently saw the Texan's banter as argumentative, assured them it was closer to sixty degrees. He said he'd lived most of his summer life in the damp and cool of the California coast. Somehow that made him an expert on the interior of the Rockies. Jackson ignored the group and spent his time readying an expensive waterproof camera.

The river dutifully flowed downhill but at a relaxed pace, saving its energy to burst through the rocks somewhere in the distance. Lynn appeared to be doing the same. They rounded a short dogleg, cut to the right, and entered a series of short rapids. The ice water occasionally escaped the river and jumped into the boat, arousing a round of gasps from the Texans and Annie. Phillip remained quiet as if the cold water were something he dealt with every day, but he ducked and shifted to miss the spray like everyone else.

"These are pretty easy, Class I," Lynn said. Her voice lacked the slightest hint of exertion. "We'll hit Trestle, a class III, right after lunch. The canyon narrows down a ways. It'll be fun, but I'll want some help."

"What does she mean?" Annie said to Andrew.

"She wants us to paddle. But don't worry. She'll tell you what to do."

"Is it dangerous?"

He didn't reply, but Annie could feel his silent laugh.

After a break and another hour or so of a mix of what Lynn called baby spills and lover's water, they stopped at a beach for lunch. Annie decided to be proactive and started to unload the lunch supplies. She sent Andrew into the shade with a bottle of sunscreen. The sun had climbed enough to change a comfortable day into a relatively hot one. Phillip, the consummate weather expert, said it was only seventy degrees or so, but it didn't matter to Annie. What did matter was Andrew's increasing resemblance to a boiled crab and Phillip and Jackson's constant whispering as their eyes tracked Andrew.

Lynn, with help from Dennis, retrieved several boxes and drinks from inside the cooler. Natasha found a space on the beach. Even at a distance, she and Dennis kept up their inseverable communications link. They were debating the difference between the pine trees in southwest Idaho and those back in East Texas. Lynn explained the effects of the dry climate and how ponderosa and lodgepole pines lived and reproduced.

Lynn handed two boxes to Annie and waved her off toward Andrew. "We can do this. You two enjoy yourselves."

The woman was impressive. She wasn't just some kid who had escaped to the wilderness. She knew about the environment around her and could converse on a number of topics.

And she was scoring a few more style points now. She seemed

honest in her desire for Andrew and Annie to be together. It was almost as if Lynn had set them up on a blind date and was trying to force the issue. Maybe she and Andrew were just friends.

Annie left the raft area and joined Andrew. He'd found a spot in the shade where they could place their blanket on the sand and lean up against a granite outcropping. Given their damp clothes, it was cold in the shade, but Annie insisted Andrew stay out of the sun for a while. The sunscreen sat in the sand, unopened.

As Annie made herself comfortable, Lynn appeared with a couple of bottles of water. She smiled, handed the bottles to Andrew, and made her way back to the boat. If she was fatigued from two and a half hours of steering and intermittent rowing, she hid it well.

"I'm so glad you got to see Lynn in action," Andrew said, opening the water and the plastic lunch box. "She's wonderful, you think?"

"A little too wonderful," Annie said. A nod would have been a much better answer.

She felt Andrew's hand on the back of her neck as she watched Lynn in the distance partake of her own lunch at the boat with the Texans. All three were talking, laughing, and pointing at the trees, the rocks, and the river.

"You're jealous," Andrew said.

"I am not."

"Trust me. Lynn and I have been friends for years. We have good conversations, and she doesn't expect anything from me. I did help her out in getting this business going. Every once in a blue moon, I come up here, and she gets me away from it all. That's it."

"I'm sorry. Young, beautiful, and smart is tough to compete with." Annie started to eat the ham and cheese sandwich supplied by the Cascade River Company. At least *it* was average.

"Don't tell her that," Andrew said.

"Hmm?"

"That she's beautiful. She'd laugh. She thinks she is a bit too boyish."

"That's a laugh," Annie said, wiping a stray drip of mustard off of Andrew's upper lip. "There are four men up here, and she's not one of them."

"Everybody has confidence issues. Even me."

"I hardly believe that."

Andrew finished his sandwich, took out an apple, and stretched out flat on the sand. "This is beautiful. Perfect."

They sat in silence and finished their lunch, enjoying the fresh scent of the pines and a gentle upstream breeze.

Annie took up the same position in the sand and watched a cloud trying to make a place for itself in a lonesome sky. "Can I confess?"

"We're not Catholic. I'm not sure what good it would do, but go ahead."

"You and me together, it's great. But when I start thinking about Penny, Matt, your wife, my Frank, your business, the outside world—it's almost like a panic attack. And I have so much to do this week back home. It's like I should go back immediately."

The statement didn't seem to faze Andrew. "I understand."

"No, I don't think you do. I'm supposed to be in mourning. Frank has only been gone a year. I'm having the time of my life here, and I enjoy your company."

"So relax. I'm an upstanding guy. No pressure here."

"You're also married. I feel like I've lost my way. If I had it to do over again, I'm not so sure I would have come to you. It's just that you deserved to know."

Andrew sat up and placed his hand on Annie's. "You did the right thing. You were desperate for help, and I know what it means to be alone."

"I would've survived. So would Penny. Before we met, my first inclination was to come clean with Penny about her situation. You would be her natural father. Then I wondered what kind of change that would bring. What kind of damage I might inflict. She's had a bit of a tough go, and things are pretty good now. I thought it best not to interrupt that."

"Just as I have never told Donny that she is not my flesh and blood. It's a good feeling to help you and your daughter. I want to right the ship, so to speak. And I'm good with it, I really am. Besides, whatever I do, it won't be enough."

"Enough for who?"

"Me. God. Whomever." His voice became quiet, contemplative. "I always fall short."

"Short of what?"

"It's just not enough. God won't forgive me. Redemption isn't possible."

"Redemption for what?"

"Nothing." He paused. "Something terrible."

And with that, Andrew shut down. She tried to coax more conversation. He'd been in a great mood. Everything was perfect and she had spoiled the moment. She seemed to have a knack for that. He wanted to tell her something. Something important. Today wouldn't be that day.

"It's just around the corner, past the bridge," Lynn said. "Grab your paddles."

She slowed the raft to let a few kayakers move under the Trestle Bridge immediately before the water plunged into some of the best Class III rapids they would see before the take-out at Smith's Ferry. Annie noted a little more tenseness in Lynn's voice as she doled out instructions. Andrew assured her this was a piece of cake for their guide.

The river made a cut to the right as it dove under the bridge. A small hill laden with boulders supporting the upstream side of the railroad tracks blocked the view ahead.

Annie could hear it—echoes in the narrowing canyon of water crashing over God knows what.

As they passed under the old blackened steel trestle, the boat came alive with whooping and hollering. It was the Texans leaning over the front of the boat, paddling with all their might. Jackson was fumbling with his camera case, and Phillip was urging him to paddle. Andrew handed Annie one of the small red paddles and said it was optional. Said Lynn could handle this alone, and that it was pretty much for the excitement of the guests.

Annie didn't want to be left out. She jammed her paddle into the water. Suddenly the Texans were in the air above her head, hanging onto the rope on the side of the boat. Dennis was paddling in the air and screaming at the top of his lungs. The raft seemed to be climbing straight up out of the water. As the bow crashed down, a wave blasted over the boat as Lynn directed the two Bay Area guys to work their paddles. The stern rose and fell back into the current like a roller coaster ride.

Annie, oblivious to the icy cold splash hitting her in the face with every rise and dip, was fixated on Lynn. The woman leaned one way and then the other, ripping at the oars with an intensity not seen until now. Her muscles pulsed through her shoulders and arms. The scene was chaotic, but the boat remained straight and true to the current.

What seemed like minutes was measured in seconds. They emerged into a slower section of easy rapids. Lynn glanced around the raft to make sure her paying guests got a good ride. Andrew was right. Though he kept saying that the rapids were only Class III, it was a marvel to watch this woman with such skill, power, and confidence.

And her reassuring smile remained etched onto her face. Annie could see why Andrew had taken such an interest in her. Maybe he didn't have a thing for Lynn Sofel, but if Andrew was half his age, this woman would have everything he would want.

After another hundred yards, Lynn directed the boat toward the shore. From Andrew's expression, it seemed an unplanned stop.

Dennis jumped out and nearly fell, trying to direct the tip of the raft into a little cove of backwater behind a boulder the size of a house. Natasha clapped and yelled out useless instructions to Dennis as he brought the boat to a stop. Lynn told everyone to take a short break, reached into a compartment under the chair, and removed a first aid kit.

"What happened?" Andrew asked. He'd made his way forward and was looking down at Lynn's leg. He grabbed the first aid kit out of her hands.

"Nothing. Somebody popped me with a paddle. Need to clean it off and put on a bandage."

Annie shot up as Andrew kneeled. She wedged herself between the pair and snatched the first aid kit out of Andrew's hands. "You're not touching her."

Out of the corner of her eye, she could see Lynn and Andrew exchanging what were likely either incredulous looks or a laugh at her expense or both. She took an alcohol wipe and scrubbed a shallow one inch cut below Lynn's right knee. She fought the urge to look up. It was better to finish the job with the bandage versus being subjected to death by embarrassment.

The rest of the trip was a little less perfect. Andrew spoke enough to show he was not upset. Annie remained quiet.

They made their way over Howard's Plunge just upstream of the take-out point. There was considerable tension in the raft before they reached what most people considered the scariest part of the Cabarton stretch and much rejoicing when they landed in the flat water on the other side. Annie didn't pay much attention to any of it. She wanted to be home.

The kid was waiting at the pull-out point as the river opened up into a small lake upstream of Smith's Ferry. Several kayakers and a couple of other rafts were also completing their journey.

A large group of patrons stood by the road, pushing their stories of the day's trip beyond the truth. While Andrew and company unloaded the raft, Annie took a walk down the edge of the river, looking for a place to hide.

The current was deceptively slow here. It hardly looked to be moving. She tossed a small rock into the water.

"You know, Mr. Post has been a godsend to me." The voice belonged to Lynn. She sat down a few feet away and tossed her own pebble in the water.

"I wasn't a good girl in my youth. Too many boys. Booze. Stayed away from drugs, though. At least the heavy stuff."

"I'm sorry." That's all Annie could think to say. "I mean for my stupidity back there."

"Not a problem. You might want to apologize to Andrew. I think you hurt him. He won't show it."

"Why me? Look at you—" Annie placed her hand to her mouth. "God, my foot is permanently stuck up here today."

"Seriously. The whole point of today's adventure was for you two to have fun. Andrew told me he was bringing someone special. He has never brought anyone special. He has never brought anyone." Lynn paused as if she was carefully crafting what to say next. "I'd do anything for him."

Annie nodded.

"He showed up on a raft trip about like this one roughly ten summers ago. Came by himself. We were down below Banks. Jeppy, one of my long lost partners from back then, kept telling me that Andrew had the hots for me. He was one of those screwy boyfriends that seemed to think it was funny to say those kinds of things. After the trip, Andrew told me if I was down in Boise, I should come visit him. I didn't know who he was. I mean, I knew he was a rich guy, but not some zillionaire."

"How could you not know about Andrew Post?" Annie said.

"Just wasn't into Boise. Civilization. Business. Whatever." She held her arms out. "This is my world."

Lynn rose to a squat position and scanned the dark currents off the bank. A couple of horns tooted behind them—probably a few of the other vans and trucks starting back to wherever they began their adventure this morning. The kid was walking toward them.

"Load everybody up," Lynn shouted. The kid waved urgently for Lynn to come. "Give me a minute," she said.

"So did you go see him?" Annie asked.

"Not right away. He came back, though. Several rafting trips, an occasional overnight on cross country skis, and one or two guided trips into the Frank Church. They were all group trips, and he would show up alone and pay everybody's cost. I think it made him feel good. Then one day he appeared in the middle of the week, which was strange. Almost always came with the crowd on the weekends. Asked my boss for a solo snowshoe trip with just me. Mr. Dickson, my boss back then, said no way. I was a little hesitant, but Andrew and I had many a great conversation on the previous trips and I trusted him. Besides, I thought it would be pretty strange for a rich guy to come out here to make a play for me or bury me in the snow somewhere. He took me to his cabin. Told me he wanted to consummate a business deal. Three things he wanted. I was to dump Jeppy, go to college, and start my own business. All I had to do was say yes, and he would make it happen."

"And you agreed?"

"Not exactly. Took about a year before I got pissed off one day working for Dickson. Decided I could do a better job. Picked up the phone, and the next thing I knew, I was in the business school at Pullman for three and half years. Graduated and came back to Cascade and started the Cascade River Company with a couple of partners."

"He paid for everything?"

"Sort of. School was gratis. But as Andrew says, business is business. He was one of the partners. I think it was more of a teaching moment."

"You mean he's an owner?"

"Not any more. He made me prove I could do it. Run the business for a profit. Each year I made money, he gifted me a little bit of his share back. I own it free and clear as of last summer."

A horn tooted. It was the kid at the van. Lynn reached out to Annie, indicating it was time to go. "My assistant gets a little impatient."

As soon as they reached the van, Andrew shouted, "Let's have a group picture." Despite Annie's behavior, he seemed pleased with the whole adventure.

Though no one said a word, it was clear they all knew the identity of the cheerful old man. Annie was sure Phillip and Jackson knew all along. Apparently the conversation had spilled over to the Texans.

One of the lingering kayakers took a picture of the whole crew with Jackson's camera—Dennis and Natasha, Phillip and Jackson, Annie and Andrew, and kneeling in front, Lynn and the kid. After a few shots, the group disbanded. Andrew handed a small point-and-shoot camera to the kid and insisted on a picture of himself with

Annie, and then another one with Lynn included, and a last one of just Lynn and Annie.

In between takes, the kid kept glancing back in the direction of the highway toward Cascade. Annie didn't notice anything unusual other than a few vehicles passing carefully through the narrow section of the road coming out of the canyon.

As Andrew and the others aided the kid in his task of stacking the last trip items into the back of the van, a car pulled up on the far shoulder, hidden from their view. The kid peered around the van and then went back to work as if he was suddenly in a hurry.

An easy-looking man with straight dirty blonde hair and a forester's mustache approached, alternating his eyes between the crowd behind the van and the road.

"Folks," said the deputy as he removed a well-worn Valley County Sheriff's Department baseball cap.

Everyone in the group stopped in their tracks except for the kid, who kept packing up.

"What do you want, Sandy?" Lynn asked in a not-so-friendly tone.

The deputy ignored Lynn and spoke straight to Andrew. "There's been an incident at your house. Your people have been trying to reach you for a couple of days."

The kid kicked the dirt. "Mr. Post, I'm sorry. I saw it on TV last night, so I called the sheriff's office as soon as you guys left. They said you were missing, so I thought it best to let someone know where you went."

"I told you we should have called somebody!" It was Jackson, who was walking away. Phillip threw his hands up and followed his partner to the other side of the highway.

Post never looked away from the deputy but spoke to the kid. "It's alright, Bradford."

The deputy waited on Andrew's response. Annie grabbed his arm. "Maybe you should talk about this away from the group."

Andrew huffed. "It was apparently on the news. Let's have it, Officer."

"A man killed himself Saturday morning by your pool. One of your security people." The deputy pulled out a folded piece of paper. "Name is Devlon Scott, age fifty-one, an employee of SecureCom NW. Shot himself in the head with his own gun. Pretty inebriated as well. They need you to return home ASAP."

"Thank you, Deputy," Andrew said, dismissing the man.

Lynn squinted and shook her head as the officer returned to his car. "What a jerk. Why didn't the police just call you?"

Annie spoke up. "My fault. We turned our phones off. They've been off since we left Saturday morning."

"Good idea," Lynn said. "Always a good idea."

Jackson stood on the other side of the road with Phillip in exaggerated conversation. Annie was sure they'd known about the incident before now. Why hadn't they said anything? Why hide something as horrible as a suicide at Andrew's house? Maybe they had doubts about his identity. Hush-hush conversations, mysteries, and such seemed a natural part of Andrew's world—something she would never be comfortable with.

The whole affair only seemed to fuel Dennis and Natasha even more. As the van left, they were in an animated conversation about some Texas multi-millionaire who had shot himself a few years back. Given everything they knew had flowed freely from their mouths over the past six hours, they obviously had no prior intelligence on the Post incident.

The last three days had been magical for Annie. Hopefully, they had been for Andrew as well. Now they were heading back to a horrible situation. And given they'd been together the entire time, she'd be in the thick of it.

Andrew, still in conversation with the rest of the riders, held her hand. He appeared unfazed by the news.

Chapter 40
The Post Estate, Boise Foothills
Monday Evening

Remnants of yellow crime scene tape hung across the glass door leading out into the pool area. The house was silent, the truth trapped inside its walls. A chalk outline of Devlon Scott stared at Andrew—one-third larger than the size of Lacy Talbert but the same position.

Earlier, as Annie had negotiated the curves of the Payette River with fingers dug into the steering wheel, Andrew had held an extended phone conversation with Rafi that framed the incident into an unspoken cover-up of an accidental shooting. Rafi was too clever to say such things on the phone. Instead, he'd relayed pertinent facts to make Andrew understand. He said the angle of the wound had been the subject of much speculation, yet the "powers that be" had determined the event to be a suicide. That a "select few" had considered Andrew a suspect until cooler heads prevailed. That Sonya had been "minimally involved." Those words were a sort of code they had developed over time. "Powers that be" were friends of the Post Corporation, usually public officials who owed Andrew, or in the case of elected officials, those who wished to be well-financed in the next election. A "select few" were known unfriendlys. "Minimally involved" meant Sonya did it or at least had some hand in the shooting.

Andrew made his way to the patio. Next to the pool, he took a seat in one of the chairs, wondering if it was the last place Devlon Scott had sat. What had Scott been thinking when the gun went off? Had he been surprised or had he been ignorant of the threat? Andrew closed his eyes.

Lacy Talbert, a face of desperation staring at him from across the room, had known exactly what was coming. He'd not believed she would pull the trigger.

That was his thinking when he opened the door of the Park City condo on a cold early November day some nine years ago.

He had accompanied Lacy to Salt Lake City for a meeting on some potential property in Sandy, a suburb a short distance to the south. He rarely traveled with his real estate team unless there was some unusual circumstance or thorny issue that required his presence. Neither was the case this time.

What drew him to Utah was Lacy. Their six month tryst had ended a year earlier amid a barrage of press coverage. Even after their break-up, the media had continued to cover non-existent secret meetings evidenced by touched-up photos and fake witnesses. He'd had enough. He couldn't imagine what their very public affair had been like for a young, introverted woman like Lacy.

She'd requested his presence in Salt Lake with no explanation of why. At first he declined. A female acquaintance subsequently told him Lacy had become withdrawn and sullen after receiving the news that he would not be going. She said Lacy still harbored feelings for him, and she was concerned for Lacy. That was enough to change Andrew's mind, so he made the trip.

The meeting in Sandy was routine. Lacy's behavior remained as it had since their break-up—cordial and businesslike. At the conclusion, she disappeared in the rental car, leaving Andrew stranded in the front lobby of the building where the meeting took place. Instead of searching for her, he left by limousine for the airport and his flight home. Upon arriving at the executive terminal, he received a simple message from Lacy on his pager. "Please come" was all it said. She didn't have to give a location. He knew where to go.

He'd relived those moments over and over. He'd questioned whether he should have called the police immediately, why he had not recognized her distress, and why he hadn't realized earlier that she was headed to their old rendezvous point—his condo in Park City.

The final scene replayed in his head like a movie he'd seen many times. She stood in the kitchen of the condo, her back to him as he closed the door. Her body blocked the gun sitting on the kitchen counter. The condo was ice cold, yet she'd removed her jacket from her standard blue business suit. His first instinct was to remove his coat and wrap it around her. But he just stood there.

Lacy turned to him, her face painted with weeping mascara lines and a lost expression. Then she raised the gun to her head. He didn't say anything. He tried but his voice failed him. She mumbled something he had for years tried to decipher in his memories of that evening.

Watching her hold the gun to her head, Andrew felt no fear. He was certain she'd called him for attention. She would not pull the trigger. If her intent was to die, she would not have called. As this young woman displayed her last gasp of life, he was thinking rationally.

He saw himself walk slowly across the room, coming within a foot or two of Lacy just as she pulled the trigger.

It wasn't like the movies. She was blown to the side of the room and the gun fell to the floor at his feet. Covered with parts of Lacy's head, he reached down and placed the gun in his hand and stared at it.

That's how the local police found him. Sitting in a chair, staring at Lacy, holding the gun.

At the station, they'd asked him if he'd pulled the trigger and he'd answered "yes." It had taken hundreds of thousands of dollars in legal fees to straighten out the truth. He still felt the same way. He *had* pulled the trigger, or he might as well have. Either way, he'd killed Lacy. He'd never touch a gun again.

Andrew opened his eyes. A gun had shot Devlon Scott. The gun he had aimed at the lovers in the shower the other night.

Sonya was on her bed, staring into space. It was not too hard to understand what had transpired early Saturday morning. She was no killer, and yet she was "minimally involved." Somehow she had shot Devlon Scott accidentally.

"I'm so afraid." She never looked at Andrew. Her face appeared to be cried out. Here was another woman he had wronged. She had the same expression as Lacy. This time he would be there for her.

He sat on the bed next to his wife and pulled her into his arms. Despite an uncomfortable stuffiness in the room, she was cold and shaking.

"I don't want people looking at me. Asking me questions. Taking my picture." Her voice cracked.

"You don't have to tell anyone. Rafi and I will take care of this, and I will take care of you."

Chapter 41
Boise PD Headquarters
Monday Evening

Matt peered through the one-way glass of the interrogation room and watched one of the most powerful men in Idaho tap his fingers on the table. Post had to know he was there.

It had been a whirlwind of a day. Matt had just arrived at the Boise airport on his return trip from Oregon when Erin, his *Boise Tribune* contact, messaged him that Post had been found and was at Boise PD headquarters. He could barely contain his excitement on the way to the office.

Upon his arrival, he'd learned from Billie that Post came to the department to answer questions voluntarily—that his handlers wanted him to appear to be fully cooperating with the investigation. And so far, no one had spoken to Post or his lawyers. Billie said the word on the street was Post had disappeared with Annie Lorda and had kept everyone, even Post's own people, in the dark. That the company line was Post's disappearance was an unfortunate coincidence.

Billie said the word was out that Devlon Scott had been sleeping with Post's wife. And the media frenzy had just begun.

What Billie couldn't answer was how Post thought he would get away with murder.

Matt's typical tactic for setting up an interrogation was to let the guilty simmer awhile before questioning. A kid would break into five or six vehicles and scream his denials from the back of a patrol car. He'd mumble his innocence during processing at the jail. They'd let him sit in a dimly lit cell for a few hours to preheat and then bring him to A12 or A13, one of the two interrogation rooms.

Both were identical—bright ivory walls and a Navy-ship-grey cement floor, four uncomfortable chairs surrounding a single metal table in the middle of the room, and a fairly large mirror, the function of which was common knowledge. The interrogation area defined claustrophobic discomfort, and it worked most of the time.

Not that everyone Matt questioned was guilty. He had a knack for sizing up the suspect through the looking glass and knowing guilt or innocence with about a ninety percent accuracy rate even before he spoke to the suspect.

This time he was one hundred percent sure. Even Rafi Thuban couldn't save Post.

The one fly in the ointment was Matt's presence here. The last thing the captain would tolerate would be the sight of Matt and Andrew Post engaged in conversation. He was so far out of bounds he'd have to hope all the evidence he had acquired would make Captain Lewis forget about his conduct.

Matt entered interrogation room A12. Post was flanked by the Sanchez brothers, the top corporate legal defense team. Their clothes were as polished as their reputation.

Javier Sanchez, tall and fit, broke away. Before Matt could speak, he was shaking the lawyer's hand. The smile under Javier's bristling black mustache reminded him of a car salesman. Roberto, a well-trimmed but shorter and heavier man, took his place in one of the two remaining chairs. The lawyer squirmed a few times, trying to find a comfortable position and placed a black leather briefcase on the table.

"Against our advice," Roberto paused and waved his hand toward his client as if he were introducing the players in a theatre, "Mr. Post has agreed to talk to you, answer your questions. He is aware you are not officially on this case."

Officially on the case, Matt thought. He might not be on the job. They probably knew that too.

Javier touched Matt on the shoulder as he passed, taking a seat next to his brother. "He will speak in our presence, of course."

The voices of the Sanchez Brothers were interchangeable— smooth and relaxed, tuned by years of expensive education and experience. They'd arranged the chairs so that Matt had no option but to either stand or sit next to Post instead of taking his preferred place directly across the table.

Roberto opened his briefcase and removed a notebook and a gold pen. "Proceed."

It felt like an order. Matt decided to sit rather than stand. He turned his chair to face Post from the side. The man stared straight ahead.

"Where were you Saturday morning around...say 4:36 A.M.?"

"Mr. Post is not a suspect. Do you expect a change in his status?" Javier said.

Matt expected the interference. "Depends on what he says." He turned his attention back to Post. "Saturday morning?"

"We were under the impression he is present simply to answer a few questions," Roberto said, "as a favor to you".

Matt ignored the interruption. "Saturday morning?"

"We'd advise against answering until we know your intent," Javier said. Roberto nodded.

Post turned his head and seemed to be waiting on a response. He was playing Matt. This standoff was just another way of showing who was the alpha male, who would win, and who would lose. They owned the chief, the DA, and even the Lieutenant Governor. But they didn't know what Matt knew.

"You said you would answer my questions," Matt said.

Roberto started to speak, but with the wave of a hand, Post washed away any potential reply.

Matt repeated the question. "Where were you on Saturday morning at 4:36 A.M.?"

"On the way to my cabin," Post said.

"Up in Round Valley?"

"Yes."

Matt glanced at his notes. "Your security man took your car at 4:02 A.M. and came back around five. We correlated his statements with the surveillance videos and the alarm log files." Maybe the little hint about the videos would shake Post. Surely the man was aware the police knew the exact time he had left.

"I went with a friend. Decided not to take my car."

"Who might that friend be?"

"It's irrelevant."

"Irrelevant!" The word slipped from Matt's lips. He was supposed to keep with the cold monotonic voice—the one that unnerved the suspect. "That might be your alibi."

"I'm only speaking to you as a favor to Mrs. Lorda. Both of us want you to stop. I know you find me distasteful. I know that you alone want to put this death on my hands. I didn't kill Mr. Scott. Captain Lewis has informed my staff that you are not supposed to be here. He told me you have seen fit to inject yourself into the investigation. That you were at my home Saturday morning. I personally asked the captain for some latitude in this matter. Otherwise, you'd not be allowed in the building. In exchange for keeping you out of trouble, I want you to go, forget about me, and forget about this case. For your sake, and most importantly, for Annie's sake."

Post was as calm as the day Matt saw him walking away from Penny's house. The man exuded confidence. And why shouldn't he. He always walks. *Not this time.*

"We have video of you sneaking away from your house around the time of the murder," Matt said. "Your prints are on the gun."

Post held his hands out as if to say, "So what."

"It was a suicide. What time did Mr. Scott take his own life?" Roberto asked.

"He was killed between four and five. Probably just before 4:36," Matt said, staring at Post's profile.

"You don't know?" Javier said.

"We know Mr. Post was up and about near the time of the murder. His fingerprints were on the murder weapon, and he certainly had a motive, given the lust-fest going on under his roof."

"You have evidence of Mr. Post leaving?" Roberto asked.

Matt ignored the question. "Why would you sneak away in the middle of the night to go to your cabin? That's a bit odd, even for you."

"You ever want to be alone, Detective?" Andrew's eyes turned to Matt's. There was something different in his expression. A hint of humanity. Matt looked away. He wasn't about to be manipulated.

Post continued. "For someone like me to be truly alone, I have to run away. People want to protect me. I pay them to protect me. I ran away and shared a beautiful three days with a person I have begun to care for. The only reason I haven't shown up before this is that the two of us agreed to cut our connection to the outside world on our short vacation."

A knot started to grow in Matt's gut. The thought of Post and Annie together hurt.

"Hard to fathom. Both of you having no knowledge of the incident for three days...and...the fact that you felt you had to run away when you can do what you want."

"Precisely. That's what I wanted and I did it."

"Okay, for grins, let's assume you ran away. What about your prints on the gun?"

Post nodded. "Yes, you might have found my prints. I came home late Friday night and found the gun lying on the bedside table. I picked it up and put it down."

"You picked it up and put it down?"

"Yes."

"Where was Mr. Scott at the time?"

"In the shower with my wife." Post said it with no expression. No anger. No sadness. Nothing. Even the Sanchez brothers let the statement bounce away as if Andrew Post had just discussed the weather.

"I should have shot him right then and there. But the fact is, I didn't. Anything else?"

"I spoke to Mr. Lopresti. He's not so sure of his original statement about the time of the gunshot. He's not even sure it was a gun."

"I don't need Lopresti."

"Like you didn't need Katlin." The statement slipped from Matt's mouth. He didn't intend to show his cards.

"This is not relevant," Javier said.

Post ignored his lawyer and Matt. "I'm not happy Mr. Scott is gone. Seems he shot himself. It's a sad day for the Post family."

Just then, the door opened. Rafi Thuban and the chief entered the room. Rafi smiled. The chief did not.

"This man is not on the investigation. Anything said in this room cannot be used against Mr. Post," Rafi said. "We can go now."

"I'm not finished," Matt said.

Rafi approached and put both his palms on the table, leaning down close to Matt. "Officer Downing, I trust you misunderstand these circumstances. Mr. Post will talk to the detectives who are working this case. He was speaking to you out of courtesy."

Post smiled at Rafi. "It's fine. I would like a chance to speak to this young man alone."

Nearly everyone in the room objected. Post sat quietly until the protestations ceased, and Rafi had escorted everyone but Matt into the hallway.

The door shut.

Post was deliberate. "I know you are running around asking questions about Katlin's death. You are also trying to pin this unfortunate suicide on me. It's not hard to follow your tracks. I would suggest you abstain from these activities. There are ghosts that you may dig up that could be detrimental to your health."

Matt scoffed. "You sent them away so you could threaten me?"

"I don't waste time on threats," Post said, patting Matt on the shoulder. "Given you have no intention of letting go, I believe the chief and Captain Lewis will be looking for you. Feel free to use me as a reference and have a nice evening. Tell Annie I tried."

Chapter 42
Boise PD Headquarters
Late Monday Evening

Chief Pettigrew sat at his desk while Captain Lewis paced, passing the time examining pictures of the chief with various Idaho dignitaries. The room was unusually warm and smelled like stale furniture. Stacks of papers were distributed everywhere, as if the chief had been readying his belongings to be relocated. Matt knew it was the usual state of affairs for the chief.

After waiting for Pettigrew to say something, Captain Lewis finally had to speak up. "You directly disobeyed my orders."

"I did." Matt said. There was no reason to deny it.

"Officer Downing, Mr. Post has an alibi. A good one," said the chief, his eyes staring into the ceiling.

Matt noted the avoidance of eye contact. If the chief had been a suspect, he'd be guilty.

Pettigrew continued as he focused on some documents scattered on his desk. "A neighbor—a Mr. Lopresti—said he heard the shot around five A.M. or just prior. Thought it was a loud car backfiring until he heard the news."

"Maybe it was a car backfiring," Matt said, trying to retain a hold on his emotions. "Or maybe the guy is mistaken about the time."

The chief shook his head. "Says it was definitely a gunshot. Also, his alarm rings at 4:50 to get up for work. Said he heard the shot right after he got up."

"He's not so sure about that," Matt said. "I spoke to him last night."

The chief and the captain exchanged glances.

"Officer Brandon spoke to Mr. Post around 4:40 A.M.," said the chief. "Saw a man walking along 13th street near Ridenbaugh and pulled over to check him out. Was surprised to find it was Andrew Post. Mr. Post told him he couldn't sleep and was out for a walk. Then Ms. Annie Lorda told us Mr. Post came to her house just after five, and they left in her car around 5:30."

Lewis remained silent. Matt wanted to know what his boss thought about the case, but there was no way he'd force the issue given the presence of the chief and the captain's scowl.

"Lots of alibis for Post unless you have questions about Lopresti's statement," Matt said to the chief. "If he was mistaken, and I believe he was, that leaves the possibility open for Post to be the guy who pulled the trigger."

Pettigrew made eye contact with Matt. "The medical examiner says Scott shot himself. Angle of the wound and such."

"You're kidding. Nobody shoots themself with their off-hand in the back of their head. Any rookie cop could spot that discrepancy."

"That's enough, Detective," said Captain Lewis. "It's over." The captain paced for a moment and then approached Matt.

"I was ready to haul your ass out of town when I found out you went to Post's house during the investigation. Not only that, you continued to ignore my orders and started asking lots of questions. The only reason you're here is that Post requested we take it easy on you." Lewis and Matt stood face to face. "I like you, son. You've been a good cop and a good detective. I was able to let things go until you showed up tonight to interrogate Post. I'd have stopped you myself, but that crazy bastard said he wanted to talk to you."

Lewis's tone was sharp. Several times since this morning, Matt had rehearsed how he would tell the captain about the evidence he had uncovered regarding Katlin Post's death and the Scott murder. Now he wasn't so sure the captain had the guts to back him up.

Lewis put his open palm in front of Matt. "I'm going to need your gun and badge."

The words didn't register.

"Your gun and badge," Lewis repeated.

"You're firing me?" It hit just as if Lewis had slapped Matt on the side of the head.

"We're going to let you resign. That, too, is courtesy of the man you are trying to put in jail. If you don't, you'll be terminated."

Matt glared at the chief, who pretended to examine some kind of report on his desk. He handed over his badge and his sidearm.

"Captain?" Matt said.

"*You* made this decision, Matt." Lewis reached out and grabbed his shoulder. "If you want to try your hand somewhere else, I'll put in a good word for you, but you're finished here."

Matt stopped hearing the captain. He had no hard feelings. He seemed to have no feelings at all. He turned and left the chief's office. He walked through the halls of the department wondering if this would be the last time he'd be there. The loss of his gun felt like a lost limb. He kept reaching for it in his shoulder-holster to make sure what had happened was real. No one seemed to notice the absence of his badge or firearm as he reached the long hallway off the desk area. Maybe they already knew. Maybe they didn't. They'd all know soon enough and Post would have his last laugh.

Chapter 43
Penny Lorda's House, North End, Boise
Late Monday Night

A solo evening. Penny had smoked a joint and was on her second shot of bourbon. She should change to something a little less toxic like a glass of White Zinfandel, the kind of wine that made Matt launch into an expression of someone who had popped a Sweet Tart into his mouth. Tonight Matt could have his high fashion wine. She'd stick to the warmth of the bourbon shots.

She cracked a window to let the smell of her sins dissipate into the summer air in case this was the one night in a hundred Serena awoke and drifted into Penny's room to share her bed. On a small TV on her dresser, some late night guy was doing a monologue. He seemed to be particularly funny.

She'd watched the late news and caught a follow-up story on the shooting at the Post residence. Everyone in town was talking about it. The death had been ruled a suicide. Why would someone do such a thing at their boss's house? But then again, this was the Posts. Andrew Post seemed like a decent guy. Her dad used to say, "Out of the ordinary was ordinary with the Posts."

Matt had phoned earlier and mumbled something about losing his job. Surely she'd heard wrong.

She'd spoken to her mother briefly a few hours ago. Her ma had no comment on the suicide story or her whereabouts lately.

The whole Post thing was bizarre. Her father had hated Andrew Post and his empire. Penny recalled her dad sitting at breakfast, chopping his over easy eggs into a gooey mess, examining the *Tribune*, and detailing to anyone who would listen how the Posts were above the law and in cahoots with every political hack in the Northwest. Her mother had been silent on the shenanigans of the Post clan, but she'd not disagreed with her husband either. Now her ma and Andrew Post were beyond friends, and Penny had been pulled into the whole affair. It was flat-out strange.

The late night TV guy was doing some skit like Jeopardy. Two women and some guy who must've jumped into the studio right off of Hollywood Boulevard were answering ridiculous questions. Penny wondered how anyone could be so stupid. Or so funny. The wind outside had shifted and was pouring cooler air straight into the half-open window. The force of the air slapped the bedroom door shut. Penny pulled a sheet from the foot of the bed across her legs. She should get up and check on Serena. Maybe the bang of the door woke her up. But the buzz was satisfying, and she leaned back against the headboard.

She must've dozed for a few minutes. The TV Jeopardy game was over, and the late night host was talking to some girl with holes in her jeans, a tight T-shirt, several hundred dollars of enhancement surgery, and long blonde hair streaked with dark strands. Penny liked the hair.

She lightly slapped her own face and moved out from the protection of the sheet. Closing the window, she sniffed the air but couldn't tell if the sweet remains of the smoke were gone. She'd check on Serena.

Lying sideways on top of the covers, her kid was curled up into a fetal position. It would be useless to move her. Ten minutes later she'd be right back in the same spot.

As Penny backed into the hall on her tiptoes, she heard a clicking noise. It was the sound of a key entering a lock on a door. Her front door.

"Oh shit," she said softly. "It's Ma."

The sound of the protesting door hinges froze Penny. What to do next wasn't clear. One thing was certain. Her mother would come in, take one look at her, and know she'd been smoking and drinking. There was no hiding it. She could remember a number of times in her youth when she'd been found guilty by appearance alone. Her mother would follow her around the house on an endless crusade until Penny would finally have to leave. She'd run away to Jon Fendly's house or over to Camel's Back Park. To escape the guilt trip, she'd get even more stoned.

But that was then. The almost daily bout with alcohol and drugs had ended after Serena was born, or more correctly, after Serena had been conceived. Penny had made a personal pact to stop. She'd been mostly successful but had fallen back off the wagon late in her marriage to Austin—the prick. He'd just walked away.

Her second born-again moment had been waking up in the emergency room, suffering from what the doctor called heart irregularities at four in the morning and having no recollection of how she got there. The police claimed they found her next to a trash dumpster with a pipe and some ice—a smoker's version of meth—painting the side of the building with her fingers and walking in circles. Matt told her the cops had called him as a favor and were taking her home when she started to freak-out in the backseat, screaming she was having a heart attack. She pledged to herself it would never happen again. She could still remember Matt sitting with her in the hospital room and then taking her home. He never said a word. He just took care of her.

She was lonely. Tonight was a once in every two or three month event. She needed to relax. Nobody needed to know.

Heavy boots traversed the wooden floor of the living room as the sound of the closing door echoed through the house. The combination of boots and her mother made no sense. Maybe the last shot of bourbon was a little too relaxing.

"He's going to get away with it again," said a familiar male voice from the front of the house.

The dark silhouette of Matt appeared at the other end of the hallway. Then he disappeared back into the kitchen and reappeared. Penny stood next to Serena's door, unconsciously tugging downward on her T-shirt.

"Suicide! Why would that joker kill himself next to the pool at Andrew Post's house?" Matt asked as he walked by again, appearing to be talking to someone else.

Penny laughed. "That's what I said." She put her hand to her mouth. She had no idea why that seemed funny.

Matt stopped in the hallway, staring at Penny. "What are you doing?"

"Sshhh! I'm checking on Serena. Who's out there with you?"

He ignored the question. Next thing she knew he was in her bedroom flat on the bed, smelling of beer and talking non-stop to the ceiling. If she didn't know better, she would have thought he was stoned too. More likely it was just the effects of a six-pack. She giggled again at the thought.

"I'm fucking high," she said.

The statement didn't appear to register with Matt. His rant continued. She couldn't recall seeing him so agitated.

"I wasn't expecting you. Thought I'd pissed you off too much," she said.

He lifted his head up from the bed. She examined him from the bedroom doorway.

"They fired me," he said.

The late night guy was introducing some band on the TV. Penny could still smell the remains of the joint in the air. If she smelled it, she was certain Matt could too. He'd said nothing in the hospital that night a few years ago, but since then, he'd become her mother's ally in regards to any vice whatsoever.

But he just sat there talking to the broken ceiling fan.

She turned off the TV. "Let's smoke a joint."

"You already have."

Penny laughed again. "Oops. I've been caught."

She leaped onto the edge of the bed, pulled on the belt loops of Matt's jeans, and forced him over on his stomach. She straddled his butt and pushed the desert camo shirt up until his arms were held prisoner. She started to massage his shoulders but stopped and pushed the shirt up over his head.

Surprisingly, there was little resistance. The ranting had subsided, though he was still conversing with himself. Something about Post and an alibi and a lying-ass uniform.

She loved his physique. Austin, her ex, was short and built like a truck. Matt was long but not skinny. Strong but not ripped. Tan but with a sprinkling of freckles that grew in number toward his shoulders. His back reflected a serious cyclist with muscles to support the cause, but nothing more. Yes, she did like it.

Reaching under his hips, she managed to undo his belt and jeans and slide them downward just enough so that he looked like one of those kids with the baggy pants walking down Fairview Street. Next, she slid her fingers under his boxers and pulled them until they were halfway down his butt.

"Hand me that lotion," she said, pointing to a tall pink bottle on the bedside table. He grabbed the bottle and tossed it backwards, hitting her in the shoulder.

He went on about a tape and something about 4:36 and Post leaving by a gate.

Penny picked up the bottle and spurted drops of lotion along his spine and across his shoulder blades. She laughed again. The drops looked like the pigeon poop under the eaves of the back entrance of the smoke shop. A little more than she expected plopped out of the bottle. Major pigeon poop. She giggled and then squirted some more.

The pools of lotion squished between her fingers as she started to spread it out. She made fists and jammed her knuckles into Matt's lower back. He let out a groan. She moved her hands down into an area that would surely create a protest, but none came.

This is it, she thought. Stop screwing around. Actually, start screwing around. She laughed again.

She jumped backwards off the bed and closed the bedroom door. She threw her plain white T-shirt and underwear on the floor and climbed back on top of the body on the bed. She hesitated. Would this be some monumental mistake she'd regret for years to come?

Maybe, but the combination of the pot, booze, her loneliness, and everything else was too much. She pressed her breasts down onto his back and slid the lotion around. It was intense.

If Matt minded, he didn't mention it. For some reason, she started to pay more attention to his conversation.

"Freaking Brandon. He couldn't have seen Post on his way to Annie's. I looked at the dispatch logs. He gave a ticket to a guy over at the airport ten minutes before he saw Post. He spent his whole evening on the south side of the Interstate, where he was supposed to be on patrol, but somehow he ended up in the North End to conveniently see Post. Brandon's been spouting off about helping the old man at Table Rock. He's either on the take or working with the chief. That Thuban thug could've killed Scott or had him killed. Post still could have done it. An act of passion he'd have to cover up? More likely a planned murder right under my nose. The little jaunt with your mother was planned to be sure Post would have an alibi. Like the Talbert case, he wanted a solid one. And just to be safe, he doubled down."

The statement about her mother startled Penny. "My mom's with Post again?" She stopped the skin to skin massage and lay motionless on Matt's back.

He turned sideways, flipping her onto the other side of the bed. "Your mom has been gone for three days."

She shook her head as if the motion would clear her mind. She knew her ma was away with Post. She knew it.

"Your mother says they ran off to Round Valley for a few days. I spoke to the caretaker at Post's cabin, and he says Post wasn't there. Your mom could be covering for him."

Penny laughed. "You mean like lying? My mother doesn't know how. You know that." She paused and examined Matt's face. He seemed oblivious to her present condition. "Do you even know that I'm sitting here in the buff, half covered with lotion?"

"I can see that." He said it in such a matter of fact tone that she thought she had no chance of ever exciting Matt Downing. He continued, "Maybe Post forced her to lie or charmed her into doing it. He has a way of pushing people into doing things for him."

Penny wiped her hands on the bed sheet and reached up and touched Matt's face with the back of her fingers, tracing his chin and lips. She spoke softly. "You are obsessed. Let go."

"I could go public. Erin would be ecstatic to do this story. Make that freaking cardboard chief eat his words."

"Jesus, stop! Tonight, be obsessed with me. I know I said we function better as friends, but I want more than that tonight. Prove to me you want me, not her."

The distance in Matt's eyes disappeared. He reached out and pulled Penny toward him.

Chapter 44
Post Corporation Headquarters, Boise
Tuesday

His back to the security desk, the figure on the video screen scanned the lobby. The guard at the desk was busy on the phone, likely speaking to Haddy Benson, Andrew's executive secretary, trying to convince her that a Boise detective needed a word with Mr. Post. Of course, Haddy would have none of it unless the detective was accompanied by Rafi or had prior permission from Andrew. She'd be suspicious of a lowly detective showing up without a captain or the chief in tow.

Andrew feared the resolution to the Matt Downing dilemma would come at a terrible price. He didn't want to lose Annie, but that was secondary to his fear of reopening any discussion of Katlin's death. His own life was less important. And Sonya. For the first time the other night, he'd felt responsible for what she had become. All this time he'd rationalized that he was caring for her. He'd enabled her behavior, and now she had accidently killed a man. She would not go down for this. He would care for his family.

Andrew would have to silence Downing, but for Annie's sake, he'd try reasoning with the boy one last time. He reached over and punched a button on his phone. "Have Officer Downing escorted to my office."

The speaker emitted background noise from Haddy's work area. After ten seconds or so, it went silent. Andrew imagined the frown on Haddy's face as she paged the front desk.

Andrew closed the office door. He stepped behind his desk and placed his hands on the back of his chair. The leather felt as cold as the scene before him. Downing sat on the couch and leaned forward, his forearms resting on his knees.

Neither man spoke. Andrew caught a glimpse of Haddy peeking through the half-closed blinds of the window next to the office door.

He and Matt Downing could've been lions or wolves circling in advance of a bout for domination of the pride or pack. Andrew, the old alpha male, challenged by the young, aggressive intruder. As in nature and in business, one would win and one would lose.

"You looking for a job?" Andrew said, not smiling.

Downing glared back.

"You've put me in a tough position," Andrew said. "I would ask you one last time to cease and desist. Nothing you do or say will implicate me in the murder of Devlon Scott."

"You bastard. It's not Scott's case that forces you to have a discussion with me. It's Katlin."

The very mention of her name angered Andrew. He wanted to be very careful with his words, yet the eventual resolution to this dilemma was becoming more and more clear.

"Let's humor ourselves with the Scott case," Downing said as he hopped up and turned his back to Andrew, peering at an image of an empty front lobby on the video screen.

Andrew sat in his chair. "Be my guest."

"The way I figure it, you found Scott with your wife and you finally cracked. In a fit of rage, you corked the guy. Your wife was too drunk to notice until she sobered up the next morning."

"Why would I wait until now? Scott's been around for months."

"Annie," Downing replied.

"Again?"

"Annie. She showed you what a relationship should be. You came home and rediscovered what a disaster your marriage has been. Popping Scott helped you to resolve the issue."

"I'm not unhappy that Devlon Scott is gone. Not that I wanted him dead."

"Of course you're happy. You shot the man and you get to walk away. But this time, even though you have the police and the courts in your pocket, I'm not going to let you walk. You see, the issue is not just Scott. It's about the death of Katlin too. Does Dr. Vanoble ring a bell?"

Andrew sat stone-faced. He'd not give the young man the satisfaction he craved.

"It's also about Lacy Talbert," Downing continued. "Even if you get away with another murder, once your fawning public sees the cover-up on the front page and evidence that you had something to say about Katlin's death, they'll never buy another product from the Post Corporation again. Even better, they'll finally know who you really are."

Andrew was amazed at the confident, cold voice of Matt Downing. He was usually an excitable kid.

"You find your alibi not so tight," Downing said, "so you conjure up Lopresti's statement and Officer Brandon's account of you walking the street in the wee hours of the morning. Fact is, Brandon couldn't have been at two places at once, and Lopresti is a pretty stinkin' bad witness."

"That I can't vouch for. No matter. I didn't do it, ex-Officer Downing." Andrew rose and moved in front of his desk, closing the distance between him and his nemesis. "For Annie, I will try this one last time. Cease and desist. Marry Penny Lorda. Have a happy life. No regrets. No grudges."

Downing avoided Andrew's eyes. "You know I can't do that. Despite the mess I'm in, I've devoted my career to justice. I took an oath."

"It's not justice. You are a vengeful, torn man. You don't have to be. All you will do is hurt the people you love."

Downing shook his head.

"You leave me no choice," Andrew said. "I suspect you'll spread your stories to Annie and Penny, if you've not already. Doesn't matter. Go ahead. I love Annie Lorda and my family enough to do the right thing. I don't believe you love anyone enough to do the right thing."

Andrew went to the door and held it open. Downing stood motionless, looking as if he wanted to say more.

"I assure you," Andrew said, "I will do whatever it takes to protect my family. Whatever it takes."

Chapter 45
YMCA, Downtown Boise
Wednesday Morning

Out of the corner of her eye, Annie could see Matt staring through the glass door of the sterile workout room. His presence rippled through her aerobics class, generating a wave of conversation from women lying on their backs and twisting like cruller donuts.

She did her best to avoid eye contact, but it was tough to ignore his beaten-down appearance. He sported several days of growth on his face, a half-tucked wrinkled dress shirt with the sleeves rolled up, a pair of dress slacks without a belt, and sandals. He may as well have spent the night down by the river.

A growing round of chatter forced the leader of the class, a thirty-something replica of the perfect aerobics instructor, to end the session. The instructor left the room, eyeing Matt on her way out. The entire town had heard about his dismissal and speculation was spreading faster than the flu. Annie had discussed the matter with a few of her best friends, but she'd mostly been quiet about the subject.

An array of women of various sizes and shapes dressed in muted colors of sweats and nylon or cotton tights filed by Matt as they exited through the glass door. Their whispers were loud enough for Annie to catch a word or two.

Now alone in the room, Annie pulled her hair back into her standard grey pony tail and proceeded to stretch. Matt stepped inside and closed the glass door behind him. The hum of gossip faded away.

Annie glanced toward the door. The departing throng pretended to ignore her but they couldn't help casually looking back into the workout room. The eyes of the world seemed more obsessed with her every day.

"I'm impressed," Matt said from the far side of the room. "Always have been. You're as limber as a thirty-year-old."

Annie said nothing. She sat up and forced her legs outward in what they used to call "Indian-style" before the world became politically correct. Then she put the bottom of her feet together and pressed down on the inside of her knees. The stretch felt relaxing.

Several large rubbery blue and red balls, having a life of their own, rolled around on the floor near Matt. He stuck his foot out and halted the rocking motion of the closest one.

"I'm sure you can find those in a Post Outfitters store," he said.

Annie put her hand up with her palm facing Matt as if it would stop him from saying anything else. "What are you doing?"

"You don't look the type," he said.

"What type?"

He made his way across the room and nodded toward her shirt. She glanced down at the extra-large holey black shirt with some band on the front.

"The punk crowd," he said.

"It's Penny's. You know that."

"Appears I'm something of a novelty around here. Guess it's tough not to gossip."

Annie stopped her stretch and looked up. "None of this is funny. Someone dropped a line to one of the local TV stations about your abrupt resignation. People think maybe you're on drugs or something. I spent the morning defending you. Your slovenly appearance isn't helping."

"So Post isn't finished with me. It wasn't enough to get me fired. He's trashing my reputation as well. Erin might know the source of the TV story. Might come in handy."

"Seriously. Stop with the Post stuff. It's time to think about yourself."

"Can we talk?"

"Not here." Annie stood and wiped her forehead with one of the little white towels and tossed it a few feet into a laundry bag.

"Two points," Matt said with a nervous smile. "It's something a friend of mine says a lot."

Two women sized like Laurel and Hardy knocked on the window and waved as they backpedaled toward the door. They seemed hesitant to interrupt.

"My brunch dates," Annie said.

Matt walked over to the glass and watched the ladies exit the building. "I don't think they're expecting you to join them."

"Penny told me you'd gone off the deep end. Your job, for Christ's sakes. Is this worth it?"

"Little late to quit now. I've got nothing left but the proof of his bullshit life."

"We are *not* talking about this here. Let me get my bag in the locker room. I'll meet you at the house."

"I'll wait in the parking lot."

"I can't believe you left with him." Matt paced back and forth on Annie's porch like a cat, clutching a paper-sized envelope under his armpit. "He's dangerous. He's a killer."

Annie had played her conversations with Andrew over and over in her head. The two nights at her house, dinner at the Post residence, the trip to Denver, and the cabin trip. He'd been so calm. He couldn't be this person Matt had conjured up.

Since Frank's revelation, she'd started to doubt where trust existed before. The one constant in her world had been Frank's honesty. Maybe that's why he had been so truthful, so wonderful. It had been his penance for "the lie." And the real damning part of the story was that he had been right. Had he not switched the babies, Penny would be dead. Or at least the real Penny. And the girl she raised would be living such an incredibly different life, it was hard to fathom. She and Frank would have remained childless.

Frank's final act had been honesty. He must've suffered greatly, but forgiving him was still so difficult. Now she'd become involved with a man who had a questionable reputation. A man the papers trashed and praised at the same time. He was not a person to openly trust. Yet she had trusted him.

"He's no killer," she said. "He may not be a saint, but he's no killer."

Matt stopped his pacing and stared directly at Annie. "You're so sure. Are you positive he showed up at 5 o'clock in the morning? Maybe it was 5:15 or 5:30."

"The police are convinced Andrew is innocent even without my statement. They said they didn't need me."

"That's how they work. I spoke to one of their key contacts, a Mr. Lopresti, and he waffled big-time. Someone told him to manufacture a story that gives Post an alibi. Also too, Lopresti makes his money as a supplier for Post."

"Can you come inside and sit? I'd rather have this conversation in private." Annie put her hand on Matt's shoulder. He resisted her touch and walked into the house. She followed, though she had acquired a habit of looking up and down the street before closing the door.

Matt set the envelope on the kitchen table. "Brandon, that scumbag who works the south side, was lying. Said he saw Post walking to your house right around the time Scott was shot. Brandon would have no reason to be patrolling the North End. He gave a ticket to a guy at the airport minutes before he said he saw Post."

Matt pulled out a piece of folded paper from the envelope and handed it to Annie. She scanned the photocopy. It was a speeding ticket for a Mr. Carlton Anders on Victory near the Interstate. Time of the violation was 4:35 A.M. She knew it took about ten minutes to get to the North End if you caught all the lights from up on the first bench.

"Could these times be off on this ticket?" she asked.

"As opposed to Lopresti's exact nailing of the time of the shot or Brandon's casual arrival to flag Post down at 4:40 in the morning? Four forty-one to be exact."

The incredulous appearance of Matt's face told her he'd not considered other possibilities. So certain of Andrew's guilt, he could only follow a line of reasoning that led him to that conclusion.

Matt moved to the couch. His legs were going fifty miles an hour.

Annie didn't know what to say. She stood indecisively between the kitchen and the living room.

"Suppose you were going to shoot yourself," he said. He popped right back up from the couch, grabbed her arm, and gently pulled her into the kitchen. He placed one of the kitchen chairs in the middle of the floor. "Sit."

Annie shook her head and sat on the chair.

"If you were going to shoot yourself in the head, show me how you would do it." He placed a wooden knickknack shaped like the state of Idaho on her lap. She had bought it at the State Fair years ago. For the first time, she realized its shape resembled a handgun.

"Pick it up and shoot yourself." Matt nodded toward the knickknack.

"Please stop!" she said.

Matt kneeled directly in front of Annie. His voice softened. "If you grant me a little time to tell my story, I'll let you decide what I do next. I know you think I've pretty much lost it. If I don't plant at least some semblance of doubt in your mind, I'll give up. I'm so certain of this that I swear I'll stop if you tell me I'm wrong. That's why I had to come here. I couldn't do what I'm about to do and have you and Penny hate me forever."

He sounded confident. If there was a shred of hope of heading Matt off at the pass, Annie would do just about anything. She picked up Idaho and held it to her temple. Then she put it back on her lap.

Matt nodded. "Precisely. Now put the gun in your left hand and pull it around to here." He guided her to a position that forced her to twist her head a bit to point the gun in the right place and pull the trigger.

"The bullet entered here." His index finger touched her skull a few inches behind her ear. "And exited here." He touched her just above the right eye on the eyebrow. "Someone else pulled the trigger. I'm convinced. I have copies of the police report complete with pictures and diagrams if you want to see for yourself."

Annie put the state of Idaho back on her kitchen table. "I'll pass. Even if someone shot the man, why are you so sure it was Andrew?"

"Motive," Matt said, pacing the room, "and his prints on the gun." He handed her a report stating the prints on the murder weapon belonged to Andrew Post.

This was the first she'd heard about the discovery of Andrew's fingerprints on the weapon. Such a fact was unsettling. How could his prints get on that man's gun? He'd spoken of his aversion to firearms, so why would he be holding a gun in the first place?

"There are only four possibilities," Matt said. "There's the security guard. Considering he has no motive, he's pretty safe. Besides, he chatted with the station attendant at the GasMart up on the Interstate. Timestamp on a credit card charge slip backs up his story. Suppose I could verify him on some kind of video camera at the gas station, but that's not necessary. Then there's Mrs. Post. She was chained to the bed."

Annie had not heard the details. She wore her surprise on her face.

"Mrs. Post was handcuffed to the bed." Matt paused. "This is *not* a normal family. She doesn't remember a thing."

He strolled into the living room and back into the kitchen. "Then there's the possibility of a stranger. Maybe someone like Thuban. I'd believe that, but he'd be setting his boss up and that makes little sense. If he were doing this for Post, he'd choose a time when Post was far away from the scene. Last is Andrew Post. His wife was screwing—"

Matt stopped abruptly and looked at Annie.

Then he continued. "Well, she was doing Devlon Scott. Post probably knew it, had had enough, and in the heat of the moment, popped him with Scott's own gun on the patio. Or, more likely, given Post's strange order for the guard to leave, it might have been pre-meditated. On the other hand, he was sloppy and his prints were on the gun which points to an act of emotional rage. Or, since he disappears for three days with you, maybe he planned it in advance. Either way, his people build a case of alibis, everyone goes into cover-up mode, and he walks away."

Matt sat down on one of the kitchen chairs. "His alibis are shaky, and that's being nice, yet nobody wants to pursue this case. He is showing the world—mostly me—that he can do whatever he wants, whenever he wants, and he can do it while befriending you and Penny

at the same time. He's seeing how far he can push me before I'll do
something really crazy. This is not you and him, it's him against me."
Matt put his head down on the table. "Is that enough?"

Annie wasn't sure how to respond. As always, Matt had been
thorough and had done his homework, though he'd viewed the entire
issue through a tunnel that forced him toward Andrew's guilt. He had
placed some doubt in her mind. What she wanted was for Andrew to
appear and explain all of this away. And somehow fix *this* issue sitting
right in front of her. Andrew was powerful and smart enough to do
that, and she had asked him to try. He was also powerful and smart
enough to do what Matt had just discussed.

They sat in silence. She listened to the trees outside, a siren blaring
in the distance, and a plane cruising overhead. Out there, life went on.
In her world, she was becoming consumed by confusion.

One thought started to repeat in her head. *Could Andrew really be
playing me?* Not long ago, she'd have said, "Absolutely not." Now there
was some doubt.

"Okay," Matt said, sounding agitated. "I don't think I'm getting
through to you."

He left the house and returned from his truck with a backpack. He
removed another large folder overstuffed with newspaper articles and
computer printouts. He laid the folder on the table and produced a
small recording device from one of the side pockets of the backpack.
He set it on the table alongside the folder.

"Thirty-three years ago, three girls were born in the Treasure
Valley Regional Medical Center. I think you know who they are. There
was a set of twins, and the other one was Penny."

Annie suddenly wanted Matt to leave. How could he know this?
Had he seen the letter? She was frozen to the chair, unable to act or
speak.

He punched a few buttons and a voice of an elderly woman told a
story of twins and another child born the same night. The voice
seethed as she spoke of the father of the twins—Andrew Post. She
recalled his reprehensible behavior and how he didn't seem to want
his children. She spoke of the father of the other child and how his
story of the deaths of their first two children tugged at her heart. That
the obstetrician had felt his child might have had some issues but that
further tests had refuted the original diagnosis. Matt played with the
buttons on the front and the recording stopped.

"That was Christine Vasquez, the nurse who took care of Penny,
Donny, and Katlin on the night they were born," he said. "I spoke to

her when you went to Denver."

"I don't want to hear any more," Annie said, her voice cracking.

Matt seemed oblivious to her protest. He appeared to be speaking to the air inside the house.

"Roughly eight weeks later..." He stopped and placed an article in Annie's hands. It described the death of Katlin Post in Ontario, Oregon.

When she finished, Annie handed the article back.

Matt continued where he left off. "It was a bit strange for a man of Post's wealth to drive a child to Portland for treatment. Especially a child he didn't care for. Also, he had a Dr. Hewitt with him that nobody seems to be able to track down thirty-three years later. Dr. Hewitt was no doctor. Or at least not a licensed one. The child died before reaching the hospital—at least that's the story. Then this."

He slipped another piece of paper into Annie's hands. This one detailed the disappearance of a Doctor Vanoble from an eastern Oregon hospital.

"Doctor Vanoble was the ER physician who called the death of Katlin that night. He disappeared about a week or two later. He also mysteriously came into a large sum of money. I found him and I want you to hear what he had to say."

Matt pressed buttons on the recorder.

Annie couldn't imagine what was to come. It was apparent all of this was not about Frank and the switch.

Vanoble's ragged voice echoed in the room. She heard him speak of his entrance into the ER, how the child was not breathing, his conversation with the emergency room nurse who said the child was blue when she had arrived, his doubts about the Post family doctor, and how the men in the room seemed to be purposefully hindering him from helping.

The story bounced off of Annie like a book on tape. She knew what she was hearing. It just wasn't processing in her head. Without warning, her throat went dry and she started to shake. Hands grabbed her shoulders as a stream of involuntary tears erupted and slid down her face.

Vanoble's voice was gone. She was glad for that. Her heart told her not to believe any of it. But she remembered Andrew's words about his daughter—"I let her go." His words about redemption and never doing enough. His words about doing "something terrible." And the doctor's voice—it was full of remorse and anger, and she believed him. The voice on the tape cried out for its own redemption.

Matt kneeled beside Annie, embraced her, and placed his head on her shoulder. "I'm sorry."

She pushed him away, gathered herself, and went to her bedroom. She contemplated shutting the door and locking it, remaining hidden until Matt left. Instead, she opened the closet, pulled out a bolt of fabric in muted shades of red and orange, unrolled it completely, and picked out the envelope. She'd not seen the letter since she'd given a copy to Andrew.

Back in the kitchen, she pressed it into Matt's hands. Her energy was fading. She shook as if she had a fever. She sat on one of the chairs. Her mind kept repeating, "How could this be?"

Matt concentrated on the letter. His jaws clenched. His face tightened. Suddenly his head arched up.

"Jesus, Annie!"

She had listened to Matt describe the real Penny Lorda's death or possibly her murder. All of the evidence she'd overlooked in Andrew's favor now haunted her. Had he killed Lacy Talbert? Set up Fenton Cooper? Shot Devlon Scott? Killed what he thought was his wife's illegitimate child? And all along, during their dates, their outing to the cabin, their trip to Denver, he knew he was responsible for the death of her natural child. *How could this be?*

Barely able to string the words together, she spoke. "Why would he do this?"

Now Matt spoke quietly. "Donny told me Andrew Post was not her father. That her mother had fooled around. All I can surmise is that Post really didn't want his children. Maybe it was revenge. Get back at his wife. I don't know."

Donny knew about her mother, thought Annie. Was Andrew lying about that as well? Trust had been thrown to the wind. "What do I do?" she pleaded.

"Never go near him again," Matt said, tapping Frank's letter with his forefinger. "I'll take care of Post."

Andrew knew his innocence would not be an issue. The papers were treating Scott's death as an unfortunate occurrence and Andrew as a troubled victim of circumstances.

Immediately after hearing the news, he had thought maybe Rafi or one of his men had done this deed, or maybe the man had really shot himself. Sonya could drive anyone of the male persuasion crazy, especially after an evening of alcohol, though they usually didn't resort to blowing their brains out on his back patio. Rafi despised the situation at Andrew's house, but putting Scott away made no sense. Everything Rafi did was calculated, and though his friend could be cold, he was no murderer. He would simply make Devlon Scott disappear by running him out of town. Just like Fenton Cooper.

But Andrew had picked up on the truth quickly. Sonya had pulled the trigger. As with Lacy Talbert, he felt responsible. By rationalizing their separation and distancing himself from the truth, he'd enabled Sonya's behavior. Now the only person who could hurt his wife was Matt Downing. Everyone else had moved on.

He stared at the two file folders on his desk. They were marked "Executive Correspondence" and yellow sticky signature tags protruded from documents inside. The first folder came from the plans group and contained a revised schedule for the Denver store.

He grabbed the gold executive pen out of his briefcase and held it up in the air. The inscription "To Dad from Donny" was as clear as the day she'd bought the pen some years ago.

The pen represented everything he owed his daughter. Not physical items or money but the emotional sharing he could not outwardly display. And somewhere trapped behind that wall of intellect was a confirmation of her love for him too. A child of another but claimed by him. The past still hurt, yet he'd kept those horrible days out of his mind.

"I could drop that by Jenson's office on my way out if you wish," Rafi said, making himself comfortable in his usual chair.

Andrew initialed the slip and tossed the pen and folder into the briefcase. "I'll do it myself."

"You have been doing too much yourself lately." Rafi flipped on the video screen behind him and craned his neck to scan the security cameras.

Andrew rubbed his temples, leaned back, and stared at the ceiling.

"I'm a bit worried about Scott's death. I don't like a mess at my house, and I sure as hell don't want Sonya dragged into this."

Rafi pulled a cigar from his breast pocket, sniffed along its length, and placed it in his mouth. "She has been both hysterical and somber. She is on some potent medication."

"Hand me one of those death sticks."

"You do not smoke," Rafi said as he tossed the remaining cigar from his pocket onto the desk.

Andrew imitated Rafi's attention to detail. He examined the cigar in its plastic sheath, then opened it, and took in what was a particularly sickly sweet aroma. He stuck it in his mouth and chewed the end, mirroring his counterpart. "I'm feeling adventurous these days," he said. "Almost as much as my daughter."

Both men smiled.

Rafi stood and leaned forward over the desk. He kept his voice low. "Scott was garbage. I have taken care of everything."

Andrew sat up and leaned toward Rafi. The two men were only a foot apart, chewing the cigars. "Maybe we should light these things."

Rafi pulled the cigar out of Andrew's mouth and proceeded to carefully cut off the end like some kind of surgeon. He did the same with his own. A lighter appeared in his hand. Andrew retrieved his cigar, grabbed the lighter, and coaxed an orange glow with a few puffs. Rafi smiled and did the same.

Andrew blew the first burst of smoke over Rafi's head. "You're correct. Mr. Scott was a man who belonged in the gutter."

"I had to do some fast work to ensure your guaranteed innocence. You make this difficult for me. I was not so sure until I discovered the truth." Rafi let out a forced laugh. "I had thought, 'If you wanted Scott to disappear, it could have been much cleaner.'"

Andrew leaned back in his chair. "You and I have walked the tightrope more than a few times. We're not criminals. We're not murderers. My wife is no killer."

"Yes, she says the gun just went off. She panicked and handcuffed herself to the bed. Did she tell you this?"

"No. She doesn't tell me much. What about Officer Downing?"

"Yes, yes. He has been terminated. No one will listen to him."

Andrew blew another puff up in the air. "Annie will hate me. I promised I would find a way to put an end to our little battle. I promised her I would try to persuade Downing to stop his escapades." He shook his head. "No, I think Downing is going public with some contradictions and that could be a problem."

"We will discredit him. Considering his recent loss of employment, this should not be too difficult. People never believe a disgruntled former employee. Instead of quitting, his record can denote a termination. Who knows, he may even be a bit unstable."

"I can't allow that," Andrew said. "I'm already in trouble."

"Ah, women are the seeds of trouble."

"Any chance he could dig up the truth about Scott?"

"Always a chance, my friend, especially if we do not fight back. The evidence is stacked against us. It all points to Scott being shot by someone else. Even a rookie like Officer Downing has seen this."

Perfect curls emitted from Rafi's lips and flowed through the air like some drifting organism.

"So how do we deal with the risk?" Andrew said.

"If Matt Downing calls his little newspaper friend and anyone buys the story, Mrs. Post might have to go public as well. We can build a case for the accident, and she can spend some time in rehabilitation, which might not be bad for her."

Andrew raised his eyebrows and puffed heavily on the cigar. As usual, Rafi had considered all the possibilities. The facts conspired against Andrew that night. Rafi had taken care of business. A neighbor had heard what he thought was a gunshot and maybe he did. Andrew had not seen an officer on the North End. That was pure fabrication. To protect Sonya, he had allowed it.

"I can't let my wife to go to prison," Andrew said. "Rehab maybe. Prison? Absolutely not. I'll admit to the murder myself first."

"As I would too, my friend."

For the first time in Andrew's memory, all of the posturing and playing with the facts was troublesome. His wife had accidently killed a man, and she sat in fear in their house. He was as guilty as she was, maybe even more so.

It all seemed rational until he thought of Annie. It was as if she were sitting across from him, blowing smoke into his face. The ethical woman with morals. The little woman on his shoulder. The contradiction was ugly. He'd have to allow all of this monkey business to protect his family—the moral and ethical path for him. Annie wouldn't buy any of it.

"I need you to do me a favor," he said.

Rafi leaned his head back and closed his eyes.

"A favor?" Andrew repeated.

Rafi nodded. "I am here."

"I want you to find out what Matt Downing knows."

The video screen behind Rafi went black. He placed the controller on Andrew's desk, grabbed a pen, and started to cycle it through his fingers. "You have said for me to stay out of his business."

"Suppose he digs into Katlin's death?"

"He has already," Rafi said as he puffed another circle of smoke. "Are you quite sure you want me to do this?"

Andrew didn't reply. Didn't need to.

He stared at the phone on his desk. It was Wednesday evening, Rafi had gone home, and he needed to finish some work. The Board of Directors would be meeting again by teleconference next week and he should prepare. They would be pleased at the twenty percent year-over-year revenue growth. They would be even more pleased at the announcement of bonuses.

Instead, he just wanted to get away. Preferably with Annie.

Andrew picked up his cell phone and tapped her name. Her line buzzed several times, and the voice that now comforted him came on the speaker.

"Yes?" There was painful tenseness in her voice.

"You okay?" he asked.

The line went silent.

"Annie?"

The line went dead.

He tapped her name again. The phone rang and rang until the answering machine picked up. He hung up.

He dialed her cell phone number. She answered. A dispirited voice emanated from the tiny speaker. "Please don't call me anymore."

Before he could say a word, the line had been disconnected.

He dialed the house again. The machine picked up after several rings. He left a simple message, "I'll be over in five minutes."

Andrew picked up his briefcase and headed toward his office door. His cell phone rang. The screen showed the caller as "Annie."

"Hey, what is—"

"Just listen." It was a male voice—Matt Downing. "She knows you killed Devlon Scott and murdered her child. That's right, you son of a bitch! She showed me the letter. You were evil enough to kill your own illegitimate child, only you didn't know it wasn't your wife's baby either. Don't worry. I'm still working on Fenton Cooper and maybe the Lacy Talbert case isn't quite over yet. Even if nobody else believes me, Annie does and you two are finished. Game, set, match!"

The phone went silent.

Chapter 47
Rafi's Place, Boise
Very Late Wednesday

The Lexus protested slightly as Andrew pressed up the driveway to the black iron gate. The house—a small version of a Southern plantation on ten acres surrounded by dirt-colored sage on the Boise River Plain—always made him smile. He told people if they wanted to find Rafi, look for the most conspicuous home southwest of the airport in the middle of nowhere below the second bench.

He pressed the red button next to the keypad on the gray box. The gate opened and he drove onto the grounds of Rafi's place. The world transformed from brown and gray to a living landscape that defied the semi-arid terrain. A lush lawn of Kentucky bluegrass carpeted the inner acre topped with enough concrete statues and birdbaths to start a yard store.

Every ten feet or so, lamps on each side of the drive pointed the way. There were no signs of security, though the cameras were there and no doubt Rafi was watching. The driveway split, one branch headed toward a barn and six-car garage, the other, a curve with the apex located below the steps of the front door. Andrew took the curve.

As he exited the vehicle, the front door opened, and Rafi appeared wearing only a white T-shirt and jockey shorts, an unlit cigar dangling between his fingers. Despite the darkness and a light wind, the pavement oozed warm air stored from the long daylight hours.

"It is late, my friend," Rafi said, waving Andrew in the door.

The inside was no match for the Southern exterior. Each room was decorated in some exotic mix of furniture, paintings, and various but significant pieces of floor art. They entered the Egyptian Room.

"Something serious has happened, no?" Rafi said, sitting on an uncomfortable-looking wooden arm-chair, its frame inscribed with images of deities and legs ending in replicas of human feet, making it appear almost alive. The room seemed incomplete. There was only a single table, an ornamental chest against the far wall, the chair Rafi occupied, and one other similar chair with legs carved in the form of animals. The entire room was carpeted with blue and red rugs also with intricate patterns that one could believe had been pieced together thousands of years ago.

"Matt Downing. He told Annie everything," Andrew said, trying to find a comfortable position on the other chair.

"What is 'everything'? Mr. Devlon Scott?"

"Well, your cover-up work was a bit sloppy."

Rafi's usual smile faded.

Andrew put his hand out. "That's not the issue. Let him believe what he wants to believe. As long as he doesn't link Sonya to the shooting, I don't care. The real issue is Katlin. He found Vanoble and I'm certain our good doctor friend relayed his story of how I killed her that night in the hospital."

"This is troubling." Rafi reached over, grabbed a box filled with long matches, and lit his cigar. "We need to put an end to this."

"I need to put an end to it," Andrew said.

"You need to talk to Mrs. Lorda. Tell her what happened. It was long ago."

"I will not! I will protect my family. No matter the cost."

Rafi's smile returned. "You need me."

"No, I came here to tell you something of critical importance. Whatever happens, you must take care of Mrs. Lorda and her daughter. And, of course, Donita and Mrs. Post."

Rafi frowned. "I do not like the sound of your voice. You should rest. It is very late. We can talk in the morning."

"And just in case, you protect Matthew Downing as well."

"I do not understand. Just this morning you asked me to find out what Downing knows. Now protect him?"

Andrew stood and put his hand on Rafi's shoulder. "You'll know what to do. Mrs. Lorda will hate me no matter what I do. And she should. As you said, I manage to mismanage my personal life. My only concern now is with Matt Downing."

"It is not wise for you to go after this boy. You are an amateur."

"I've made enough mistakes in my life, and too many people have suffered. You do your part. That's all I ask."

"This makes no sense. What are you protecting? Mrs. Post is stronger than you think. Donita is fine and Katlin is gone. *What is done is done.*"

"No, it's not done!"

"My friend, you remind me of that night. The crazy look in your eyes. You must let this go. Let Rafi handle it."

"Not this time," Andrew said. "Not this time."

Chapter 48
Bogus Basin Road
Thursday Morning

The road to the top was a dizzying set of one hundred and eighty-three curves over sixteen miles, ending at the ski area parking lot. This morning Matt's energy level was so high he had no trouble putting away the first six miles despite an unusually warm morning. At this rate, he would reach the tree line in record time.

In a rush to clear his head, he'd been careless and had only brought one small water bottle. He usually carried a spare in his pack, but at the first rest stop, the spare was not to be found. With temperatures approaching eighty degrees by late morning, water would become the limiting factor.

This was the big day. Soon he would run by the *Tribune* and talk to Erin Dubois. He would lay out all of his evidence and hope she would come through. There was no question he would need the help of the press, and if anyone could force the issue, it was Erin. Publishing the evidence would serve a number of purposes, including placing pressure on all of Post's cronies in town and forcing the politicians, lawyers, and the police to do the right thing. And the *pièce de résistance*—the beginning of the fall of Andrew Post.

Penny was off today, providing protection for her mother at Annie's house. She was the impetus for his ride up the foothills. She had told him this morning it was either that or sex. If he refused both, she said he'd drive her crazy. Given what Post knew, Matt was apprehensive. He had even dreamed of several black SUVs pulling up at Annie's in the night and taking her away.

Penny had berated him when he'd suggested she might not be able to deal with Post's men if they came to the house. Laughing as he glided in a temporary downhill section, he knew Annie might have the best protection possible. Penny was not one to confront.

The road was nearly empty. As Matt coasted through a corner, he could hear the roar of big truck tires closing in on his position. It would be easy for the Post thugs to trail him and gently bump him off the road. They could turn around and return to Boise, leaving to chance that someone would actually see him hundreds of feet down a steep embankment. He recollected the story of a motorcyclist who'd been hit by lightning a couple of years ago. Nobody had seen the man when the bolt hit, and it had been a couple of days before his body was spotted by some weekend hikers.

A big black Ford truck, raised off the ground about two feet, passed well to the left of Matt almost in the opposing lane and sped up the road out of sight.

That was enough. Time to turn around.

He stopped, drained the rest of his water bottle, and put his feet on the pedals, intending to make good time on the downhill. He'd gone less than twenty feet before he heard the drumming of his phone in his pack.

The default ringtone meant it was not Penny. The screen on his phone displayed the message "No caller ID available."

"Downing," he said, stepping off the bike.

"I believe it is time to put an end to this." The voice surprised him. He wasn't expecting to hear from Andrew Post. He scanned the horizon for danger.

"Post?"

"Very good," the voice said. "I know you think you finally have me. Don't underestimate what I can do to you."

The threat was irritating. It sounded desperate, confirmation that Andrew Post was worried.

Matt paced in the dirt of the turnout, trying to think of just the right thing to say. He'd imagined this moment for years. He had Post. Yet he never thought about what he would say once he had one of the most powerful men in Idaho on the ropes.

Andrew Post handled this issue for him. "You meet me at my cabin in Round Valley. Just you and me. If you don't show, you will regret it for the rest of your life."

The challenge raised the hairs on Matt's neck. Was this real? The threat started to make him angry.

"All right, you rich asshole. You may not go to jail, but all those people out there will know what kind of evil—"

The phone had gone silent. Matt looked at the screen. The call had probably ended before Post heard the first word of his rant. Didn't matter. He'd say it to his face in Round Valley. He wasn't afraid of Post. The ride had helped to calm him. Right now he could hardly get the phone back in his pack. He'd probably do the downhill at record speed. In three hours, after a brief detour, he would be face to face with his nemesis.

Erin Dubois, black-framed glasses hanging precipitously on her nose, was engaged with her laptop. New Age music played in the background, as if Matt had entered a Native American museum. She wore a biking outfit in the colors of the Swiss flag with an unzipped fleece jacket hanging over her shoulders. Behind her, a small white gym towel sat on the credenza. Despite the fact she worked for a newspaper, there wasn't a single sheet of paper in sight.

Erin had the unfortunate luck to have a last name spelled like the eastern Idaho town that was pronounced locally as *Duboys*. Her press buddies shortened her name to *Boyz*, and she carried the nickname everywhere she went.

Matt had met her on one of his first cases, a kidnapping of a child by a white trash guy from Caldwell who had served a little time and had a record of domestic abuse. Erin had just arrived from Chicago, fresh out of the University of Illinois with a journalism degree, ready to right the free world. Matt had recently made detective after serving a near record short stint as a beat cop. He would find out with experience that the case—really a domestic dispute between unmarried parents—was not that unusual. Yet both he and Erin treated it as though the Governor had been abducted. Their colleagues in the press and in the department were unrelenting in their ridicule of her articles and his rapid use of personal overtime on the case.

That event and her serendipitous membership in Matt's cycling club had cemented their relationship.

"You said this was good. I have a date with a shower and some clean clothes," Erin said, leaning back in some kind of modern ergonomic chair. "You riding next weekend?"

"Doubt it."

"Don't be a hermit. You've been nixing us for the last couple of rides."

Matt dropped the envelope on her desk. She looked at it like she detested it. Then she put her fingers under the flap.

"Let it be for now," he said.

"You said this is the big stuff, baby," she said with a French twist.

Placing his hand on top of hers, he spoke firmly, "This is serious. I need you to hold onto this. It's my insurance policy."

"Can we skip the crap? You said this was big. I want a blow-by-blow, and I want to see your incontrovertible evidence."

Matt shut the door to the office. He sat in the chair and methodically summarized the information. The Devlon Scott cover-up. The Lacy Talbert murder. Fenton Cooper's setup. And finally the Katlin Post case. He was going to confront Post. It could be a trap, and if so, he wanted Erin to have the evidence.

She said nothing and didn't seem surprised.

"Jesus, I expected a little more enthusiasm," he said.

"Just taking all this in. Yes, it's big all right."

"Keep this under wraps until I return."

"Okay. Probably best to tell me where you two will meet," she said, sticking a pencil sideways in her mouth. "Just in case."

"You planning on following me?"

"Suppose you don't come back. You claim this guy killed at least two people, and you have the evidence."

"You have your story right here." He patted the envelope. "I'll take care of myself and I'll be back."

The pencil dropped from her mouth onto the keyboard. "You disappear and I'll be investigating *your* case."

"I think the man is going to try and scare the crap out of me. Maybe bribe me. He's desperate. He's not—"

"You said he killed two people, maybe three. That means he's crazy."

"You know his cabin? Round Valley?"

Erin nodded. "I know of it. Never been there, but read about it in some home design magazine. Some place."

"We're meeting there. Just the two of us."

"Shit! You are crazy!"

"I'll be fine. Just protect this with your life. Here are a few names in the department that can help you. I'm sure you can force the *Tribune* editors to print this story."

"If this all checks out, somebody will print it."

Matt stood and Erin followed suit.

"Don't worry. If I don't come back, you'll know where to find the body."

"That's not funny."

An array of similar patterns lay on Annie's dining room table. She rearranged the squares like a puzzle with an infinite number of connecting pieces. She and Matt were not all that different. In her quilting, she spent considerable time determining how the geometric patterns she had designed might fit to her satisfaction. Matt did the same. A pattern of actions by Andrew placed into a final product only Matt could design. Others might gather the same evidence and see a different placement of the pieces, depending on their viewpoint.

Annie wondered how the pieces of evidence fit together for her. It was best to just let it go. She had the place to herself, and she could occupy her time working on the quilt she'd promised Penny. She didn't want to see Andrew, Matt, Penny, or anyone else.

Penny had managed to see her mother's need for privacy. She had left a half an hour ago to check on Serena, who was staying at the neighbor's again. Judging from her edginess, she was likely out buying cigarettes as well. Annie had heard Matt tell Penny, in no uncertain terms, to remain at the house. Given all that had transpired, Annie still couldn't make herself believe she needed protection from Andrew Post.

Happy with the current pattern on the table, she sat at the sewing machine and started to stitch the first two pieces together. The hum of the machine masked the sounds of the outside world. Then she took her foot off the pedal and listened.

The sounds came back. A car passing by, turning into a nearby driveway. A couple of young kids yelling and laughing in one of the yards behind the house. The low roar of jet engines as a plane headed north to some destination like Spokane or Missoula.

Still something was wrong.

She set her bifocals on the table and then stood but made no movement toward the door.

He was there. At the window. Rafi.

He was dressed in casual slacks, a black shirt, and a red tie. His eyes were particularly deceiving. A friend.

She moved to the edge of the kitchen and watched the man.

He nodded his head. "Open the door."

The voice on the other side was encouraging, as if he were trying to talk a child into unlatching the lock.

Annie's first thought was to call Matt. Or Penny. Or anyone.

Maybe the police. Maybe even Andrew. Her hands shook. It seemed to take a Herculean effort to make a decision.

She dropped a piece of fabric on the floor. Shook her head. Surely this man would not simply come up the walk and do away with her. Even if he was part of the evil empire, he'd be smarter than that.

She walked to the door and opened it wide enough so her body blocked any invitation inside.

Rafi's eyes twinkled. The gentleness in his face put her at ease.

"I want to take you somewhere," he said.

"Where is Andrew?"

"May I?" he asked, his arms suggesting she make way for his passage into the house.

"Not a chance."

"My boss told me to care for you. He said no matter what happens I should do that for him. And I will."

"I don't need your protection. Matt will be back soon."

"I am not so sure of that. I believe he and Mr. Post are about to collide."

Annie stepped out onto the porch and closed the door. Her neighbor, Mr. Stanley, was watering his lawn and taking great interest in her meeting with Rafi. Stanley was an ass but at least he was a witness.

"They're meeting somewhere? How do you know this?"

"I do not know this with certainty. It is my guess." Rafi sat on one of the porch chairs, reached into his pocket, and pulled out the remains of a cigar that looked like a puppy had attacked one end of it. "None of that is of immediate concern to me. I need to show you something."

"What has Andrew put you up to?"

Rafi chewed the cigar and started to focus on Mr. Stanley, who'd been watering the plants near his mailbox much too long.

"Your neighbor will flood the streets," he said with a chuckle. "Mr. Post has not put me up to anything. He would be furious with me if he knew what I have planned for you. But I must protect you and I must protect him, and I see no other alternative."

Annie sat on one of the two porch chairs. An unknown couple moved by on the sidewalk with nary a look.

"You see," Rafi said, "Mr. Post will be reckless as long as he thinks he is no longer in your graces. I could have helped him clean up this mess. Protect his family. But he insists on handling it himself."

Annie knew Andrew and Matt were both beyond reason. Matt

would follow Andrew to the end of the earth to confront him. And Andrew—he had turned out to be something she'd never dreamed of. He had played her and he was dangerous. That meant he'd use any means necessary to get Matt off his back, regardless of her feelings about the matter.

"You can follow me in your own car if that would make you feel safer," Rafi said.

"What is so important that I have to come with you?"

"You must. If you refuse, I cannot guarantee bad things will not happen. You must come with me."

"Can we wait for my daughter? She should be back soon. I can phone her."

"No, it must be only you."

"I don't know."

Rafi kneeled in front of Annie. "It is so important to me that I thought about taking you by force this morning. But I am a gentleman. You are a lady. I give you your choice."

"Okay," she said, knowing deep down it was the wrong thing to do. "But I want to let Penny know where I'm going."

"It is best you do not."

Chapter 50
The Cabin, Round Valley, Idaho
Thursday

The Old West.

Just two men, grit, and pistols.

Andrew had seen a number of westerns. He knew the plot well.

No good choices. One man walks away. The other lies dead on a dusty street.

Would it come to that? He didn't think so.

Matt Downing stood at the opposite end of the cabin near the entrance. A sliver of bright sun invaded the room from a crack in the partially open front door, leaving his facial expression hidden in silhouette. He wore a plain brown t-shirt, worn blue jeans, sandals, and a shoulder holster.

"You don't look like a cop," Andrew said. He looked down at his own khaki hiking shorts and trail shoes. Not exactly John Wayne. He smiled.

"This is funny?"

"Not even," Andrew said. "I see you found the note."

"Pinned to the front door of that hotel you call a cabin down the way," Downing said, holding up the note. "Is this your place too?"

Outside, the sunlight faded temporarily, allowing Andrew to see a mix of determination and fear on the young man's face. "Yes, it's my place."

"So what now?"

"This has to end," Andrew said. "Nice gun by the way. Your own?"

Downing glanced at the weapon in his hand. "You know damn well it's my own."

"I'll try one more time. Go home. Marry your friend. Have a nice life."

"Not a chance."

They stood ten feet apart, face to face. Andrew reached up and stroked the day and a half's worth of grey stubble on his chin.

"As you wish. Simply point your"—he squinted at Downing's gun—".38 Special, I believe, directly at me and pull the trigger. It's your only choice."

"The one with the gun usually calls the shots."

"Then what did you come here for? You're not going to arrest me. You have no authority." He turned his back to the boy and headed for the indentation in the wall that served as a closet in the bedroom.

An open kitchen window, its white curtain flapping like a flag, surrendered the smell of rain to the cabin. On cue, a steady knock of heavy raindrops hit the green metal roof.

"I came to tell you what the world will discover about you in the next twenty-four hours," Downing said, "and there is nothing you can do about it. I wanted to see your face."

In a cigar box sat a blue metal Colt Single Action Army Revolver, the "equalizer" in the West. Rafi had bought it for Andrew at an auction years ago as a souvenir. Since Lacy's suicide, Andrew had refused to keep a gun in the house. He'd gone as far as suggesting prohibition of the sale of weapons in his stores. He had capitulated to the only person who could change his mind—Donny. Now Sonya's accident reinforced his disgust. His willingness to pick up the gun betrayed his state of mind.

He was surprised the weapon was still there. Some intruder or errant hiker could have hauled off the Colt. Seems hikers were not interested in Rafi's cigars, or maybe he'd misjudged the morality of the mountains.

Andrew pulled down the weapon and a green box of ammunition. The box read "High Performance Centerfire Cartridges," ".38 Special," and "Keep Out of Reach of Children" on the front.

"You know they have all this stuff plastered on this box. The only real issue is whether these bullets would kill someone, don't you agree, Mr. Downing?"

Downing said nothing. Andrew could hear concentrated breathing along with creaks of the floor as his adversary inched closer. Would Downing simply fire his weapon? Seemed unlikely. Certainly the boy had never shot someone in the line of duty. This would be in cold blood.

Andrew picked out six bullets and loaded them one by one before returning the hammer to the safe position. Would the Colt fire? He'd never attempted to load it, much less shoot the antique. He lowered the Colt to his side and faced his opponent.

"Long time ago, I was pretty good with a sidearm," he said. "In fact, I was damn good. We're even now. Don't want the police coming in here and taking one of us away for murder. At least this way, one of us can claim self-defense."

He fingered the trigger. Downing's eyes followed his every move.

"Son, do you understand who you are harming with all of this? I'm sure you think it's me. Trust me. We'll settle this now, so no matter the outcome, I'm good. It's Annie, Penny, and my family who are in your sights. I'm just standing in the way."

"Don't try and negotiate your way out of this, Post."

"Ah, but that's what I excel at. You know the first night I went to Annie's house, she said she didn't have a plan. I don't have one either. But I do know that if I can't get through to you, one of us isn't leaving this cabin."

"Scare tactics as well. Nice." The fear and angst in the young man's voice was unmistakable.

"You understand you are both right and wrong about Devlon Scott," Andrew said. "Yes, he was shot by someone else. No, I didn't shoot him. Pretty much everyone in the Boise PD has already figured out who did it. You've just been blind to the possibility. It was a complete accident. My wife pulled the trigger and I'm protecting her. Are you really interested in taking down my wife, a woman who will be headed to rehabilitation anyway? She is scared to death. You would do that to her? You would do that to Donny?"

The name seemed to fly out and pinch the young man. He slipped his gun back in his holster—a positive sign. "Mrs. Post never cared about Donny. I know Donny doesn't think much of her either. You know that. Besides, your wife was handcuffed to the bed, and your fingerprints were all over the handle of Scott's gun. How do you explain that?"

"I told you before. I could've killed both of them that night. I walked into Sonya's room, picked up Scott's gun, and aimed it at the shower. Those are the simple facts."

"What about Officer Brandon's lies and that Lopresti perjurer?"

"I had nothing to do with either of them. I suspect my people wanted to be sure I had alibis. You already know this. It doesn't mean I pulled the trigger."

"Let's say your story checks out. I should just forgive your wife after she put a bullet into a man's head?"

"If you decided to go forward with your information, I suspect Mrs. Post might be forced to confess to the world, and there would be numerous angry and embarrassed people. You might win the first round, but you'd be out of law enforcement for your entire life. So to save you, but more so to save Sonya, I'm not going to let that happen."

Downing laughed. It sounded forced. "You save me? You're too late. My contacts have a copy of all of my evidence. It may not implicate Mrs. Post directly, but there's enough there to lead to the truth if she is involved."

Andrew sat down on one of the two rustic chairs that stood like bookends to a heavy oak table. He placed the pistol across his lap. "Ah, yes. Erin Dubois. She's a little green for the press business. Not very safe with evidence either."

"What does that mean?"

"You might want to contact her. Right now, she's probably frantically searching for the envelope you left on her desk. You see, I too have friends at the *Tribune*."

"You son of a bitch!" Matt Downing's hand reflexively reached for his pistol. He put his hand on the stock but left the gun in the holster. "I still have my copy and one to spare."

"You assume you'll get to leave here to retrieve them. The only way that happens is if you shoot me. Or give it all up. And I don't believe you have the guts for either choice. You see, you have something to live for. You can marry Penny Lorda, have a family, and with my generosity, live a worry-free life. I only have my family left to protect. And you're the bad guy."

"You act like someone who doesn't mind pulling the trigger. Even if your wife killed Scott, there's still Lacy Talbert, Fenton Cooper, and Katlin Post."

"All cases in the past. All history. The simple matter is that you and I are at a crossroads. You won't stop until you put my reputation away. But you risk my family and I won't have it. That leaves me with few options."

"Two murders and a setup and all you can say is 'all history.' That's cold. It only proves who you really are." Downing's breathing was acute and the veins on his neck stood out. "You killed the true Penny Lorda—Annie Lorda's natural child. And you expect me to go home and leave that on the table?"

"You are so sure of yourself. Yes, I see you've read the letter, and you've driven a stake into the heart of my relationship with Annie. You've won that battle. I concede. You can quit now."

Downing laughed nervously. "Not a chance. Whatever I do, it won't be enough for all your crimes and all of your victims."

Andrew had contemplated Annie's actions over the past day. He had been stunned at Matt Downing's proclamation on the phone. Annie had shown Downing the letter. That explained her intense state of anger. A mother convinced that her child had died at his hands. Lacy's mother had the same thought for years after Lacy took her own life. He thought how brutal his fate had been. But he wasn't innocent either.

The sidearm out of the holster and pointed squarely at Andrew's face, Downing closed the distance to within a few feet. Andrew put his fingers on the Colt. He watched the dark metallic circle of the barrel of Downing's .38, waiting on a flash. He'd be dead before his mind could compose such an image. But the chances of Downing firing the weapon were remote at best.

"Shoot me," Andrew said calmly. "It solves everything."

The gun in front of his face started to shake.

Andrew brought the Colt up and pulled the trigger.

Chapter 51
Boise River Valley, West of Boise
Thursday

The farmland of the Boise River Valley passed by in the window of Rafi Thuban's Mercedes G-class SUV. Against every ounce of common sense she possessed, Annie had decided to accompany Rafi. He had come with an offering and had been willing to leave. No doubt the man could have forced his will upon her. If Rafi Thuban was after someone, it would be Matt, not her. And maybe this trip would lead her to Matt's location.

She used to tell Penny that at some point you have to trust people. Lately that advice seemed ridiculous. Trust had been disfigured into the unrecognizable, a close relative with an all-knowing smirk on his face.

Nevertheless, today she had taken her own advice. Her only regret was leaving without so much as a note.

The house sat below the bench on the Payette River east of the town of the same name. It was a ranch-style farm house surrounded by furrowed fields with some type of sprouting plant Annie couldn't identify.

Instant summer had invaded Idaho, and she generally suffered under a full sun. Today would be one of those days. She knocked on the front door. No one answered. Tried again, this time a little harder. Still nothing.

A rusting blue Ford Taurus sat in the driveway, and a white Chevy pickup in need of a paint job lay dormant in the dirt on the side of the house. She examined the area for a tractor in the fields or some other sign of life.

Annie and Rafi had spent the midday driving around Ontario, Oregon, touring Andrew's childhood stomping grounds. There was the wooden single room schoolhouse of Andrew's grade school years, not the usual church frame one might picture, but a simple rectangular building with barely a pitch in the roof, tilting over like a tree caught in the wind. There was the small campus of concrete block structures that had served as both the intermediate and high school. A medical center rebuilt on top of the old hospital where Andrew had taken his first breath and Katlin Post had died so long ago. And the shack—a little beige box presently occupied by a Hispanic family on the end of a white gravel road—where Andrew had played with his brothers, watched his father walk away, and atoned for his father's departure by working as hard as any grown man to keep the family together.

Rafi had stopped several times to examine the fields and the far away barren hills. He had not explained why Annie needed to see where Andrew had spent his youth. All she could surmise was Rafi had wanted her to know of his friend's humble beginnings. And humble they were. Much more so than Andrew had let on to.

After an hour or so in Ontario, they had driven for another twenty minutes in the farmland north of the Interstate before Rafi dumped her off in front of a set of twin mail boxes and told her to go talk to the owner of the ranch house she now stood before.

She walked over to an open barn and saw an old man tinkering with a faded red tractor. He wore greasy coveralls, a sweat-drenched white T-shirt, a worn John Deere hat, and work boots so old they probably couldn't be replaced.

"Excuse me," she said.

The man moved under the machine as if he had no idea he had a visitor.

This time she was more forceful. "Hello!"

A dirty face, worn by sun and wind, popped out from under the tractor. He had a half-mustache made from a swipe of grease, bushy white eyebrows, and a wild mop of matching hair crammed into his hat. The man winced as he pulled himself up. He grabbed a rag and wiped his hands and face. He said nothing.

"My name is Annie Lorda. Rafi Thuban said I should come see you."

The man squinted and shook his head. Annie was beginning to think she either had the wrong address or was part of some cruel joke.

"Do you know him?" she asked. "Or his boss, Andrew Post?"

That did it. The man spoke immediately. "Is Mr. Post okay?"

"Yes." She felt like her answer was not quite truthful. "How do you know him?"

"Same back to you. How do you know him?"

"I'm just a friend. He and I had a falling out. I'm not sure why I'm here. Mr. Thuban thought I should see you."

"People don't like Mr. Post. He's a good man," said the farmer.

She stuck out her hand to try again. "I'm Annie Lorda."

The man raised his eyebrows, held up his dirty hands, and smiled. "Paul Talbert."

"Talbert?"

"Yes, I'm Lacy's father if that's what you're wondering. Wife passed away last year."

Annie thought carefully about what she should say next. "Andrew and I were good friends for a short time."

"Then you made a mistake, ma'am. Don't go losing a friendship with Mr. Post. He's about all I got left out here. Shows up every week or so. He told me about you." Talbert wiped his cheek with the dirty rag. "He's smitten with you."

The man flung the rag back on top of the tractor and walked past Annie. "Come with me. I want to show you something."

They crossed the driveway, and Talbert opened the passenger door of the white pickup. Annie glanced toward the main road. Rafi was gone. She entered the vehicle, and they took off down a series of checkerboard farm roads. After roughly three miles or so, they turned into a well-kept but small cemetery covered by big cottonwoods along the edge of the Payette River. On the drive, they'd said virtually nothing to each other, though it didn't feel awkward.

Paul Talbert opened the passenger door of the pickup and then walked away toward the far end of the cemetery and sat down on a wooden bench. Annie followed.

A standard tombstone decorated with fresh floral arrangements sat under one of the larger trees next to the bench. It read:

Lacy Marie Talbert
January 8th, 1979 – November 21, 2006
God Rest Her Soul

Talbert traced the traditional Catholic Sign of the Cross and bowed his head. Annie didn't know whether she should pray, sit, or speak. She opted to give the man some distance.

The wind blew just enough to wake up the cottonwoods. She closed her eyes, felt the cooling breeze wisp across her arms and neck, and listened to the peaceful flow of water nearby. The only other sound was traffic, far, far away. The moisture of the river brought freshness to the air that made her want to fill her lungs.

Her peace was interrupted by the man's voice. He had risen from the bench and was kneeling near the tombstone. He spoke as if he were still speaking to his maker. "He comes here every week. Never misses. Places flowers on her grave like these. After she passed, Mr. Post came to my house. Lacy had already told me about their relationship. She called it 'a little fling.' Mr. Post admitted what he did. Said he'd had problems in his own family. Lacy was young and ambitious and worked in the headquarters there in Boise. Mr. Post had taken her under his wing, and they both made an error in judgment."

Talbert paused, touched Lacy's tombstone, and stood up.

"He comes up here more than I do," he continued. "Told me he was responsible for her care. The papers said they were having some sort of love affair the night she passed. By then, their relationship was long since over. Mr. Post really wanted to make up for his mistake. Never blamed Lacy, though I can tell you she wasn't exactly an angel. We all missed Lacy's problems. Mr. Post took it hard. He said he's done some bad things, but I think the man is too hard on himself. God forgives, you know, and so do I."

Talbert stepped away and headed back to the truck. Annie took one last look at the flowers and followed.

As she opened the door, he spoke, "He's a good man. Don't pay no attention to all that newspaper gossip."

Like the trip over, the trip back to the farm was silent. Annie thought about what she had witnessed. It wasn't a play on her. It was faith. It was life. Even though it seemed a stupid word, she couldn't get "smitten" out of her mind. She wanted to ask the man what Andrew had said about her, but it didn't seem appropriate.

Rafi reappeared like clockwork after Paul Talbert returned to his barn. Neither man saw each other. Annie thought it could've been a show, a setup just for her, but not likely. No man with a conscience could fake what Talbert had just done. She asked Rafi to drive her back to the cemetery. She sat on the bench and closed her eyes. The air was still fresh, and the quiet was intoxicating. She wanted to speak to Lacy Talbert. Ask her why she got involved with Andrew Post. Ask her why women would risk falling for a man they could never understand.

After lunch at a sandwich shop in Caldwell, Rafi headed to Boise. He said very little, giving Annie the opportunity to think about what she had witnessed. When she asked if he was taking her home, all he said was "not yet."

Chapter 52
The Cabin, Round Valley, Idaho
Thursday

In the confines of the cabin, the ignition was more like a concussion than the pop Andrew was expecting. Matt Downing's weapon fell to the ground. He grabbed his right thigh, grimaced, and fell backward onto the floor.

Andrew rose out of the chair, bent down, picked up Downing's pistol, and held it in the air in front of Downing. "That's how you pull the trigger. Fortunately, I just grazed you. You had your chance. You see I'm quite serious. Ready to negotiate?"

"You're crazy," Downing said, glancing at his weapon, but not reaching for it.

Andrew placed the boy's gun on the table and reached out to help him up. Downing scooted backwards on his butt, his eyes never leaving the Colt in Andrew's other hand.

Andrew grabbed a towel from the kitchen and tossed it to Downing. With some difficulty, the boy stood and made his way to the chair near the door. He pressed the towel against the shredded section of his blue jeans.

Returning to the chair at the other end of the coffee table, Andrew paused to get his words just right. "Okay, let's talk Lacy Talbert. Grab your gun."

Downing stared at his pistol, three feet away on the table.

"Alright," Andrew said. He stood and approached the boy. He grabbed the barrel of the Colt and held it in the air directly in front of Downing.

"Let me show you how Lacy held the gun." He reached down and picked up Downing's free hand and stuck the weapon in it. He wrapped his own hand around Downing's and lifted the gun up to the boy's temple. Before the barrel touched his head, Downing let go of the towel and shoved Andrew backwards, twisting the gun sharply, forcing Andrew to let go.

"Suit yourself." Andrew wiped his hands together. With little resistance, he retrieved his Colt from Downing's fingers and returned to his chair.

"Lacy was about this far away," Andrew said, nodding to the distance that separated the two men. He placed the Colt up to his own temple, the ring of metal cold to the touch. "Do you know what it's like to shoot someone in the head? Like this? I could pull the trigger right now, and they'd think you did it. Your prints are on the gun.

People think you're crazy. Your life would be finished."

Downing inched closer to his pistol on the table as he spoke. "Jesus, put the gun back down."

Andrew lowered the weapon and placed it on his lap. "I tell you I've never shot someone in the head. But I watched an innocent young woman do it. I couldn't move. Couldn't help her. That's why I told the police that I pulled the trigger. I may as well have." He leaned forward. "You ask me if I killed Lacy Talbert and I'll admit to it. She physically pulled the trigger but it doesn't matter. So, yes, I killed her. I watched her brains blow across the room. Her blood all over my clothes. My face. My hands. I washed it off, over and over, but it never goes away."

"There's still Fenton Cooper and Katlin Post," Downing said.

The diversion to a new topic made Andrew feel like he had at least planted some doubt. "Fenton Cooper wasn't set up. He was stupid. You saw what you wanted to see. And as far as Katlin is concerned, you have no idea what you would unleash with a story like that."

Matt Downing leaned out across the table and retrieved his gun, never taking his eyes off of Andrew. "I think it would be best if I just walked away."

"I can't let you do that. Not sure what I expected by coming forward with some of this stuff. Annie said I needed a reversion to honesty and trust. I was hoping you'd believe me. However, if you said, 'Okay, I believe you,' then I would have a tough time believing *you*. Guess I'm not up to Annie's standards. And unfortunately, it's like that first night with her. I don't have a plan. But I do know you're not just getting up and leaving."

Downing stood up, his right hand carrying his gun and his left hand holding the blood-soaked towel against his leg.

"Maybe we should leave it to fate," Andrew said. "Or to God. Or skill. Whatever makes you happy." He picked his weapon back up from his lap and rose up off the chair. "How about the count of three and we fire?" he said, stepping forward to match a slight retreat by his opponent. "An old fashioned duel."

He let the Colt fall to his side. "You see, at this point, I don't care much about me. Go ahead and shoot me. It would take all the satisfaction away from your hard work. I'd be dead. Nobody would care about your story. They'd actually be investigating you because of your crazy obsession to put me away. You want to scream to the world that I killed my own daughter, or Annie's, if you decide to sidestep her trust. If I shoot you, then it's in self-defense. Or I just admit to it. You've made sure Annie won't come back to me. But I love her and shooting you would not buy me any points with her. This all sucks, doesn't it?"

"I'm not going to duel with you. That's insane." Matt Downing's voice cracked. "You could own up to the truth. Maybe Annie would like that."

Andrew laughed and stepped back until they were in their original positions when Downing first stepped through the door. Ten feet apart. Two pistols. He wasn't so sure about the grit.

"One."

"You won't shoot," Downing said.

"Two. I suggest you ready yourself."

"Put the gun away."

"No way," Andrew said. "You must've expected this from a murderer. If not, then you might believe a little of what I've said. Be a man. You came here for this. Fire your gun. Pretend I already said 'three.' Who's to know?"

"You *are* insane!" Downing said as he turned and hobbled toward the door.

Andrew raised the pistol and aimed it at the boy's back. Downing must've either heard Andrew's movements or by instinct, knew a gun was pointed at him. He stopped in his tracks.

Chapter 53
Boise, Idaho
Thursday

They pulled up to a middle-class two-story house on the southwest side of town near the airport. Rafi exited the vehicle and escorted Annie up the walk.

A man in casual work clothes with peppered hair and a dark mustache peered through the window, nodded, and opened the front door. He shook Rafi's hand. He had a work badge hanging by a lanyard with his picture and Stanton Electronics on the front.

"We appreciate Mr. Post and his offer to help," said the man.

Rafi made no effort to introduce Annie. He examined the distant family room as if he was expecting someone else.

"She's upstairs," said the man.

Annie and Rafi were left to find a seat on a worn couch in the family room. After several minutes, a scrawny teenage girl with stringy black hair dressed in holey blue jeans and a black T-shirt entered the room. Her hair hung in her face, making it difficult to detect facial features. Without a word, she plopped down on a recliner near a big screen television and stared at her bare feet.

"Hello, Melody." Rafi's voice was gentle but firm.

The girl did not reply. Her father stood nearby at the kitchen island, watching.

"I told your father Mr. Post would help you if you helped me," Rafi said. "You don't have to go back to juvenile. No more drugs. Agreed?"

The girl nodded.

"Trust me, Mr. Thuban," said the father, "Melody does not want to go back. I've told her about the school in San Jose. We all want her to go. I can't tell you how much we appreciate you setting this up."

Rafi nodded to Annie, stood, and approached the girl. She made no effort to look up. He kneeled, put his finger under her chin, and gently tilted it upward. With his other hand, he brushed her hair back.

The child's face was used-up as if she had not slept for days. There was no trust in her eyes.

Rafi smiled. The girl struggled but returned a hint of a smile, her lips trembling slightly. He pulled a picture out of his pocket. "Do you remember this man?"

Melody nodded.

"Tell me about him."

The girl glanced at her father.

"It's okay," Rafi said.

"He used to give us money." She said it so quietly that Annie could barely hear her.

"Who?"

"Me and Sharee. He'd give us money to go on rides with him. Lots of money."

"Did anyone ever ask you to go with him? Somebody else?" Rafi asked.

The girl shook her head.

"You were never forced to go?"

She shook her head again and tilted her eyes toward the floor.

"You used the money for drugs?"

She nodded.

"You remember the night the police caught you at the lake?"

The girl nodded again.

"Who helped you at the police station?"

"You did."

"What did I say to you?"

"You said to tell the truth."

"Who'd you tell the truth to?"

"The other man."

"The judge?"

"Don't remember, but he was nice to me. He told me they had to let the man go because the police messed up."

Rafi bent down and looked into Melody's eyes. "You did well. I want to come back and see you someday, free of drugs and ready to work for me.

Back in the SUV, Annie stared out the window as Rafi drove in silence. He'd said nothing since leaving Melody's house. He didn't need to. She now understood that Fenton Cooper was a bad person, Rafi had taken advantage of the situation to get Cooper out of town, and he'd turned bad into good. End of story.

The last stop was Andrew's house. Rather than pull into the driveway and through the gate, Rafi eased up to the curb.

"I will take you inside if you feel it is necessary," he said. "First, I would tell you something about Devlon Scott. Hopefully, it will be enough to convince you, and you will not have to go in the house."

Rafi described Scott's shooting from beginning to end in full detail. He mentioned a few actions he had taken to ensure Andrew's innocence.

"Mr. Post takes the blame for Mrs. Post's behavior. He has taken her plight very hard, even to the point of possibly admitting to the shooting himself. Without Matt Downing, there would be no issue. Yet your young friend suspects the wrong person, and the evidence to protect Mr. Post is sketchy at best."

Annie found the story incredible. Sonya Post had killed Devlon Scott by accident, and Andrew was protecting her. Annie had told Andrew, in not so many words, to take care of his wife. And he had done so.

"Do you need to see Mrs. Post?" Rafi asked. "I would like to avoid it if possible."

Annie shook her head and quietly said no.

Rafi left for the house to check on Sonya Post and had been gone a good ten minutes. During that time, Annie contemplated the last few hours. Mr. Thuban had provided striking evidence of what she wanted to believe—that Andrew Post was not the monster Matt had conjured up. But if Rafi Thuban could convince the little girl to admit her guilt to the police, scare Fenton Cooper into leaving town, and generate enough alibis to sweep the Devlon Scott killing under the rug, why couldn't he do the same for Andrew's character? Rafi was very convincing, but he'd also shown he could be convincing in covering up a bad situation. And there was still the issue of Katlin Post. Annie had heard the tape of the doctor. Andrew had admitted to something bad from his past. Something he was unwilling to discuss. Something terrible.

Annie thought of Frank. Her life was upside down, and she was losing faith in most everyone. She was becoming just like Andrew Post.

Rafi returned. He made no move to start the vehicle. His face, colored with indecision, pointed straight over the steering wheel. Annie waited for some kind of statement, yet the awkward silence persisted for a minute or two.

"Why did you—"

Rafi interrupted. "Have you seen a woman in distress?"

"I…I don't know. Yes, maybe."

"My intent was for Sonya—Mrs. Post—to confess to you. Place more evidence in Mr. Post's favor. Show you he is not what others say he is. I could not do that to her."

"I completely understand."

"She is frightened. Mr. Post told her she did not have to tell anyone until she is ready. Actually, she never has to confess. He has promised her complete protection. This is one reason why his meeting with Matt Downing is a poor idea." Rafi paused. "I would only ask one thing."

"Yes?"

"That you trust me on this. I cannot push Sonya to tell you, for her sake and for Mr. Post's."

"He still loves her," Annie said.

"Yes, he does."

"And he has the power to make this go away?"

"Yes, he does."

Chapter 54
The Cabin, Round Valley, Idaho
Thursday

Andrew moved his hand to the right slightly, squeezed the trigger, and a bullet raced past Matt Downing's head into the wall.

Downing turned abruptly, the shock of hearing the gun fire and *not being shot* showing on his face.

"Three comes after one and two," Andrew said.

A muted version of some rock anthem started to play. Andrew nodded toward Downing. "Go ahead and answer your phone. Tell whoever it is that you are having a duel with Andrew Post and you will get back to them." He chuckled at the absurdity. "Go ahead. In the meantime, I'll try to think of some way out of this."

Downing retrieved his phone. The conversation was animated and seemed to involve Annie being taken somewhere. It was obvious the caller was Penny Lorda.

Downing hung up, his fear replaced by determination. He pointed his pistol at Andrew's chest. "I should shoot you, you son of a bitch. While I'm up here playing games with you, your henchman came by and kidnapped Annie."

Andrew's phone buzzed in his pocket. He let it go.

"Where is he taking Annie?" Downing demanded.

Andrew didn't answer. He couldn't imagine why Rafi would take Annie away. He pulled out his phone intending to call Rafi. Before he could swipe the screen, his phone chimed once, indicating an incoming text message. It was from Annie.

PICK UP YOUR PHONE, PLEASE!!!

The phone chimed again.

Rafi took me to see Lacy Talbert's father, Sonya, and Melody.

"What the hell is he doing?" yelled Andrew. The phone chimed once more.

I'm confused, worried you will do something stupid. Headed toward Banks. Are you there? Call me!

"Who is that?" Downing said. "It's Annie, isn't it?"

It was unraveling.

Rafi never did anything without carefully understanding the consequences. There was only one reason to take Annie to the town of Banks on the Payette River. In order to bring Annie and Andrew back together, Rafi would be leaving a trail of dispelled accusations about Andrew. Banks was the end of the trail.

Suddenly the confrontation with Downing was a distraction.

Andrew started for the door.

Matt Downing pointed his pistol. "That's enough of this charade! Trying to scare the crap out of me. You're not going anywhere. Put your weapon down, or I *will* fire this time!"

Without hesitation, Andrew brought the Colt up and pulled the trigger, sending a bullet across the boy's forearm. Downing's gun flew onto the floor and slid under one of the chairs. He fell in pain, grabbing at his arm.

Andrew nearly lost control of the Lexus crossing the old Rainbow Bridge as he passed from Round Valley into the narrows of the Payette River. Fortunately, his back tires slid into the mountain side of the two-lane highway that left no margin for error. Swinging the wheel, he regained control and sped through a series of tight curves hanging above the river. He nixed following the usual route since it required ten minutes of washboard dirt roads before arriving at Smith's Ferry. This route, at least at top speed, would wipe three or four minutes off of the trip.

The race to reach Annie sobered his mind. He couldn't shake the thought of what would have happened had she not called or if he had ignored her messages. He could have pulled the trigger. He would have been Lacy Talbert. Yet, at the time, Lacy had been severely depressed and mentally exhausted. Maybe he'd reached that point too. Or maybe he would have shot Matt Downing. He had no plan other than to ensure his family's safety. That's all that mattered.

The Lexus cruised through Smith's Ferry on one of the few straight segments of the highway at close to eighty miles an hour. He blindly passed a large RV and a pickup, forcing a motorcycle in the opposing lane off the side of the road.

His phone buzzed again. It was Annie. He hit the decline button and dialed Rafi's number. He'd tried to reach Rafi earlier as he drove away from the cabin. Like then, this call went straight to voicemail. He hung up, pocketed the phone, and drove on.

The next twenty-one miles between Smith's Ferry and Banks couldn't have been more of an obstacle than any other paved highway in America. Following the froth of the Payette, the road constantly twisted back and forth as it descended unmercifully toward lazy stretches near the towns of Horseshoe Bend, Emmett, and Payette. He usually drove at a leisurely pace, using the pullouts and passing lanes to let impatient kayakers and rafters reach their destinations.

Not today.

Despite his focus on reaching Banks before Rafi and Annie, his mind started to diagnose Rafi's logic. Rafi's travels to Talbert, Melody, and Sonya were an obvious effort to defend him. Show Annie he was not the beast Matt Downing had conjured up in her mind. A late attempt to bring them back together. Reconciliation.

He'd told Rafi to take care of Annie, and his friend was obeying those wishes in his own way. Andrew had never considered "the truth" as the solution to bringing Annie back.

He was determined to keep this secret. He'd broken the agreement he and Rafi had crafted so long ago, and somehow Rafi knew. Somehow his protector always knew.

He was panicked by what Annie was about to face. He had to be there. He needed to explain, as she had said, how important it was to just let life go on. It was best for everyone. She'd never understand. If he could only get there first. Maybe stop everything.

His phone continued to chime in his pocket. Likely messages from Annie or maybe even Downing. The only person he needed to talk to was Rafi, and Rafi was not answering his phone.

Chapter 55
Along the Payette River, Banks, Idaho
Thursday

For most tourists, Banks was a place along Highway 55 to stop and use the restroom, a bridge where the North Fork and the South Fork of the Payette River join, or a blip of civilization between Boise and McCall. For river runners, it was a stopping point for the most adventurous and a starting point for the amateurs.

Annie stood in the middle of a dusty parking area, watching Lynn talk to a crowd of spent customers near an overlook fifty feet away. They all had the same look of accomplishment on their faces. In between handshakes and chatting, Lynn and Bradford, her young assistant, adjusted life preservers, coolers, and ropes in the Cascade River Company van for the return trip. Even from a distance, she appeared imposing next to the crowd of city dwellers.

Annie wished she had reached Andrew. Maybe he'd at least read her text messages. He'd said it was an automatic response—to check his phone. If so, he must be without it or had not seen a need to respond. Or maybe he really was through with her.

She'd spent the day understanding the man in a way she hadn't seen until now. She wasn't sure what she wanted to hear from Andrew. She just wanted to hear something. It didn't help that Andrew and Matt were going to "have it out," whatever that meant. She'd phoned Penny on the way to Banks. Of course, Penny was furious about her disappearance and had no idea where Matt was. Penny said she was going to call Donny to see if she knew anything. Annie checked her phone. No new messages or calls.

"Why did you bring me here?" she asked, talking over her shoulder.

"It's the last piece of the puzzle." She felt a gentle touch from Rafi's hand.

"Andrew did not do something terrible so long ago," he said. "We did something terrible together. You see, I had the perfect plan. He didn't want the children. Such rage, I cannot forget. Mrs. Post, Sonya, would never be a mother."

Rafi stepped in front of Annie and spoke softly. "My family lives thousands of miles away in a place so distant in space and culture that you would never understand. But I am a family man. The children were not to be savaged by such a cruel couple as Andrew and Sonya Post. I would not allow it. But Mr. Post would never consider sending them away, especially to my family, which was my original plan."

"Yes, I believe that would be a stretch for Andrew."

"Mr. Post had a public image to protect. How would it look if the Posts voluntarily gave up custody of their children? Mr. Post would not allow this. Yet as long as the twins remained with him, they would be pawns in a vicious battle—a conflict few knew about. There was only one way to separate these innocent girls from their heartless parents. So I planned Katlin's death. Every detail. Miss Donny was to be next."

The confession sent a shiver through Annie. The killer was right in front of her. Matt had the evidence but the wrong man. *Why would Rafi say this in front of all of these people? And why here?*

"I didn't plan on such an incompetent fool as Benjamin Hewitt."

"I don't think I want to hear any more of this," Annie said, reaching into her purse for her phone.

Rafi arrested her wrist and held it tightly. "Do not be afraid. Hear my story. Look around you. You are not in danger."

She pulled away from his grip. Her hands trembled.

"Mr. Post believed we were going to Portland that night. He told me he would go to the experts, but he had no intention of letting them treat his sick child. I tell you, he was not right in the head. I believe he wanted the child to die."

"Annie?" It was Lynn Sofel waving from behind a rock wall. "What are you doing here?" she shouted.

Annie didn't acknowledge the woman, and it showed in Lynn's face.

Rafi glanced in Lynn's direction and then continued. "You see, Hewitt made an egregious error. The child was supposed to appear dead when we entered the hospital. But she was awake. He'd not given her the right dosage. As Hewitt displayed his incompetence, I was busy telling Andrew that Katlin had passed on. There were no tears. No remorse. His reaction to the entire affair was as if he'd had to stop at a grocery store on the way home from work. Then he noticed Katlin moving. He snapped and dragged me into the corner of the room. I told him to calm down. We argued while Hewitt pretended to know something about medicine. A young doctor arrived, and I could see disbelief on his face. So I pulled the young man away to"—Rafi paused as if considering what to say, then continued—"counsel him. When I returned, Mr. Post and the baby were missing. The room was empty except for Hewitt, who sat in a chair with his head resting up against the wall. He told me Mr. Post left with the child. That he walked over, wrapped her in a blanket, and left. I found him in a dark room down the hall, tears streaming down his face. He said, 'This child I will protect until the day I die.' Something cracked in his armor that night."

"I don't understand," Annie said.

"No one killed Katlin Post. Andrew is not a killer. Neither am I. That is the end of the story." Rafi bowed slightly and headed for the store. As he walked away, he turned and smiled. "He will be furious with me."

Annie turned to see Lynn, busy, but occasionally peeking back in her direction, a look of concern painted on her face.

She contemplated such a bizarre story. Such a bizarre world.

Then it hit her.

Her own child. Standing thirty feet away.

It was too much. She wanted to run. She wanted Frank. She wanted Penny.

A cloud of dirt sprayed into the parking lot. People shouted from every direction. No longer could she see Lynn or the store. Only voices in a white dusty fog.

Her lungs protested. Her eyes protested.

She coughed and pulled a tissue from her purse to dab the dirt from her eyes.

The cloud settled. Andrew's silver Lexus was sitting across the lot. Andrew was out of the vehicle.

In a semicircle, a gathering crowd was watching. He appeared to look right through them. His eyes found Annie.

The three formed a triangle. Andrew at his car. Rafi at the store. Annie near the center of the parking lot. They all exchanged glances. No one moved.

Annie's face spoke the truth. He was too late. *She knew.*

Rafi stood at the entrance to the store, a pretend look of surprise on his face.

Andrew knew the damage had been done. He made the first move and walked deliberately toward Rafi. For only the second time in their friendship, he was truly angry with his friend. Halfway to the store, he noticed Annie heading in his direction. She started slowly and then gained speed. Her purse fell off her arm to the ground. She ignored it.

He stopped and shouted at Rafi. "How did you know?"

Annie's fists hit his chest. Tears flowed down her face. He wanted to hold her. He wanted to explain. He wanted to tell her how happy Katlin had become.

"Damn you! You knew the day you walked into my house! My daughter is alive! Damn you!"

He did nothing to stop her. Her wild swings landed on his chest and arms, but there was no pain. She slapped his face. Still no pain.

The semicircular crowd had not closed in but was increasing in size. Looking past Annie, he could see Lynn creeping closer.

"Did you tell her?" he asked, speaking in a firm tone.

The tears continued but Annie shook her head.

"She mustn't know. Does she know?"

Lynn made her way through the crowd and moved to within ten feet of Andrew and Annie.

"How could you? How could anyone do such a thing?" Annie said.

A tear rolled down Andrew's face. "I thought she was dead! I was ready to let her die."

Annie shook her head and looked at the ground. Andrew moved closer. "Don't you understand? I would have let her die! That would have been my revenge and my way out. What kind of person could have such a thought? I believed she was dead, and that was just fine. Then I saw her move. My head snapped. God swatted me and said, 'That's enough!' I grabbed her and took her away."

Annie tried to back away and stumbled. Lynn swiftly moved in to support her.

Andrew wanted to shout out his guilt. "I had no idea it was a setup. In that room that night, after God stepped in and stopped us both, Rafi and I came to an agreement. He convinced me it was best for Katlin that we carry out his plan. To the world, Katlin would disappear. We would send her away, let good, decent people raise her and care for her, and keep our distance for the rest of our lives. Only I broke my promise after Lacy died. For twenty-five years, I'd let myself believe that Katlin was better off without me. And I was right, and I swore she'd never be tainted by me or my family again. But I couldn't just walk away from her life! Not then, not now."

Annie continued to shake her head as if she couldn't stop.

"Andrew?" Lynn looked totally confused. She held onto Annie's shoulders as if Annie would tumble without her support.

"I'm sorry." It was all he could say. He moved toward both of the women. Annie put her hands up to block his approach and then grabbed the keys out of his clenched fist. She shook off the grip of Lynn and ran to the Lexus.

Lynn stared at Andrew. She wanted some kind of answer to the puzzle in front of her. He tried to speak to no avail. He looked over to Annie just in time to see her gain the driver's seat.

The SUV roared to life. Rocks and dust sprayed the crowd, and they yelled their displeasure. Andrew took off to catch the fleeing vehicle.

He was able to reach the passenger door as the traction control took over. He popped the handle open and held on. The door nearly pulled his arm out of socket as the Lexus moved away. Yelling for Annie to stop, he was able to grasp the inside passenger handle above the window and gain some leverage inside the door frame with his left foot.

Then he lost all feeling in his right arm and fell away to the ground.

Matt's good hand could barely steer the Ranger through the twisting turns. Just getting the truck back to Highway 55 was a major accomplishment. In his condition, chasing Andrew Post at high speed was a poor idea, yet Post was upset with Annie and had taken off with his pistol in hand. The man had already shown he was capable of pulling the trigger. Matt wouldn't take any more chances.

On one of the straighter segments of the road, he'd tried to pull his phone out to call Penny, maybe the captain, or the sheriff, but it wasn't in his pocket. He'd probably dropped it in the cabin when he was shot.

The wounds were not life threatening, but enough blood leaked through the towel wrapped around his arm to keep his hand wet. At times, he'd painfully gripped the steering wheel with his bad arm, and it was now coated with a combination of wet and dried blood. He no longer felt pain from his wounded leg.

He'd contemplated stopping in Smith's Ferry to use the phone. He had chosen to forgo that option. Explaining his condition would take too much time and attract attention.

Even with his wounds and the battered Ranger, he was convinced his driving abilities were much better than Post—a man who rarely drove himself anywhere. He'd probably catch the man before Horseshoe Bend, certainly by Boise if that was Post's destination.

If he didn't find Post, he'd head straight to Annie's. That's where he had left Annie and Penny. Then he'd try and pick up the trail of Rafi and Post. It was a good plan. He was thinking clearly.

He slowed as he moved through the last turn before the bridge at Banks. The place would be crowded and cars would be turning off and on the highway. He wanted to catch Post, but not at the expense of knocking off some innocent kayaker.

Rounding the canyon wall, he noticed a crowd in the parking lot across the bridge. In the middle of the lot sat Andrew Post's Lexus. And Andrew Post. Reaching to his shoulder-holster with his injured hand, Matt felt the coolness of the handle of his pistol.

He pulled across the bridge and pressed the brakes hard. Rafi Thuban was standing in front of the store.

The truck stopped about fifty feet short of Post.

No one seemed to notice Matt's presence. All eyes were on Andrew Post, a young woman, and Annie.

Matt opened the door and winced as he stepped from the vehicle. For the first time, he felt dizzy enough to suggest the possibility of a blackout. He leaned back up against the truck. Taking a deep breath, he squinted in the direction of Post, but he saw Annie instead. She was running away toward Post's SUV.

Post sprinted after her. Suddenly a spray of rocks and dust erupted behind the SUV. Through the rising cloud, Matt could see Post hanging on to the door handle of the vehicle, yelling something. He wasn't certain, but Post's free hand appeared to carry his Colt revolver.

Despite the searing pain in Matt's injured arm, he managed to pull his weapon. With all his concentration, he put his hands together and fired a shot at the moving suspect.

Post let go of the truck, and Annie sped away safely. Post fell to the parking lot. Then, with some help, he sat up. He had a red stain on the side of his shirt under his right shoulder. Matt had nearly missed. It was tough to be a marksman in such pain.

People were screaming and running away toward the embankment and the store. Rafi Thuban was no longer in sight. The Lexus had disappeared.

Matt steadied the gun again. Surely the sheriff would be coming soon. The crowd would see to that. All he needed to do was to keep the man here. He would fire again if Post tried to leave. If Post was crazy enough to shoot Annie in a crowded parking lot in broad daylight, he was crazy enough to fire again at Matt.

As Matt took a few steps forward, Andrew Post turned into a double image. Matt shook his head, but that only made the dizziness worse. Instantly the parking lot turned into a black and white scene reminiscent of an old style photographic negative.

Then there was nothing as Matt slumped to the ground.

Despite the roar of the engine, Annie heard the pop. At first she thought it might be the vehicle. In her rearview mirror, she caught a glimpse of Andrew falling away.

The Lexus grabbed the pavement and rocketed toward the far side of the highway—an embankment of dirt, rocks, and a few pine trees. The passenger door slammed shut on its own, startling her even more. She looked forward and turned the wheel fast to the right, nearly tipping the SUV on its side. In a panic, she jammed her foot on what she thought was the brake. The vehicle seemed to be under its own control. It screamed forward, aimed toward the other side of the road and the river.

She stared down in disbelief at her foot on the accelerator pedal. She jabbed hard at the brake pedal with her other foot and screamed.

The SUV tried to slow, but it would not stop before jumping off of a small cliff.

The next ten seconds were a lifetime. She was on her side, then upside down. Trees slammed into the rear of the vehicle, and it spun halfway around while sliding down a mixture of rocks and dirt. Airbags popped all around her, briefly holding her to the seat. The SUV flipped again, the roof groaning as metal gave way. She heard a scrapping noise and a splash.

Her head whipped back into the seat and then hit the side window. The last thing Annie could remember was the sound of water everywhere.

Chapter 56
Payette River, Banks, Idaho
Thursday

The crowd had dispersed, some disappearing into the store, but most tripping, sliding, or falling down the dirt embankment to the boat launch area below the parking lot.

Andrew rose up in a daze. Through the trees, he'd just seen his Lexus flip through the air and disappear toward the Payette River.

He brushed the stinging area under his shoulder. His fingers were wet. Pieces of gravel stuck to his legs and arms. Blood seeped from a gash on his right leg.

An arm steadied him just in time to stop his own descent back to the ground. It was Lynn. She was taking her T-shirt cover off, attempting to press it up to the leak near his shoulder. Voices nearby kept saying something about being shot. Rafi's voice was mixed in the conversation.

Pushing Lynn's arm away, Andrew gathered all the strength he could muster and took off down the road. The voices trailed him.

Annie knew.

He'd failed.

Despite his love for Annie, he'd never intended to tell anyone about Lynn. That had been his rock-solid promise after Lacy had killed herself. He'd screwed up every relationship in his life. Lynn was happy, one of the few truly good human beings he knew. Stories of that night in the past and the realization Lynn was a Post would have only complicated her life, their relationship. The possibility she might be related to Annie didn't change a thing. He'd die to protect her secret. Somehow Rafi had discovered Andrew had broken his promise to stay away from Katlin. How long had Rafi known?

Sonya had shot a man in their house. Andrew had allowed their living situation to persist for decades, rationalizing away the disease that infected his wife by believing their arrangement was best for the both of them. Devlon Scott's death fell on his shoulders. Lacy Talbert's too. Sonya's fate as well. And Katlin's life—he wouldn't screw *this* up.

Thirty yards or so down the road, he could see the path of snapped pine branches and a fresh broken trail down the embankment. Sitting in the water, the Lexus sat motionless, upside down, braced against a rock of nearly the same size, steam rising off the undercarriage. The water was deep enough to cover the windows. Annie was nowhere to been seen.

The embankment was steep, especially the first twenty or thirty feet, and then it smoothed out to a very small beach with rocks scattered about. Andrew hopped down the small hill and started to slide. In an effort to control his descent, he managed to tear a gash in his left hand and shred the bottom of his hiking shorts. Pain pierced his right shoulder so thoroughly that he thought he might've been shot again.

Lynn was making her way toward him like a deer hopping through the forest. Just as he made it to his feet and stepped into the water, she jumped in front of him and pushed on his shoulders.

"No!"

Andrew let his forehead fall to touch Lynn's. He breathed heavily. "She's in there!"

Lynn said nothing. She must've deduced his determination to go into the water.

He reached down to pull off the trail shoes he'd been wearing. She grabbed his arm. "Leave 'em on. Otherwise, you won't get two feet on these rocks."

They both stepped into the strong current.

It was impossible to walk to the vehicle. By the time the bone-chilling water reached their calves, both Lynn and Andrew, just to remain steady, had to resort to taking a few steps and then reaching out on all fours to grip rocks jutting up above the current. With the water reaching his knees, Andrew started to fall with nearly every step. Lynn's luck was only marginally better.

"We're going to have to float to it," she said.

The crowd had reappeared on the highway above the river. Rafi was pacing up and down the edge of the road, his phone stuck in his ear, no doubt calling anyone and everyone to help.

"Let me do this," Lynn said, laying herself gently into the fast current.

Andrew didn't wait. He did the same and his body floated directly toward the vehicle. Twenty feet away and approaching rapidly, the Lexus was acting like a big rock, steering water around it on both sides. He'd have one chance to grab on. If he missed, he might not make it out of the current for hundreds of yards.

Just ahead, Lynn was steering her body by directing her feet like the bow of a boat, trying to arrive at a place she could latch onto. Her aim was directed toward the back wheel well. Andrew tried the same tactic, but by the time he steadied himself, he was already at the pile of water just upstream of the vehicle.

Lynn had disappeared. She'd likely missed the SUV and was
floating in the current downstream somewhere. Andrew knew he was
Annie's last hope. With all his might, he tried to launch himself
toward the side of his truck. The water forced him hard right toward
the front of the vehicle. He was rapidly being pressed away from his
target and toward the middle of the river.

Somehow he grasped the edge of the front wheel well with his left
hand. The force of the water was incredible. He remembered the old
days of kayaking, listening to instructors speak of dangers like
hydraulic holes, undercut rocks, and sieves, and how the water was in
control. *Better to go with it than fight it.*

He reached out with his right arm and a ripping pain shot through
his chest. Even with both hands, he was losing the battle.

His fingers clawed with every ounce of strength he possessed. It
wasn't enough. He was slipping away. He'd failed her.

The current threw him around the front of the Lexus and the rock
holding it in place. Something wrapped around his ankle and bit
through his sock into his flesh. His motion stopped. His chest was
right next to the big rock—in strong current—yet he was motionless.

He flapped his hands wildly, trying to keep his head above the
water. The pain in his ankle was paralyzing. Turning toward the rock,
he was able to seize a handhold and stabilize himself. He couldn't
muster enough strength to improve his situation.

A hand grabbed his right leg. Above the roar, he could hear Lynn's
voice, but he couldn't understand her. She'd pulled herself up on the
SUV and had made her way to the rock. On her stomach, she'd
managed to catch Andrew's loose leg. Holding onto his ankle with
one hand, she secured his belt with her other hand. Together, they
managed to pull him up on the edge of the rock, though his left leg
was still caught on something in the current.

He lifted his ankle up to the top of the water. The black custom
bug net he had installed last year was wrapped tightly around his sock
just above his soaked shoe.

Lynn crouched and then launched herself back toward the SUV.
Her feet landed perfectly on a crossbeam. Like a gymnast on a balance
bar, she moved toward the front of the vehicle, carefully avoiding still
steaming parts of the engine, transmission, and exhaust.

Andrew shouted, "Is Annie out?"

She gestured that she didn't know, or that she had not attempted
to help her yet.

"Go get Annie first!"

She ignored him. She made her way to the very edge of the vehicle, grasped a stabilizer bar with one hand, put a small pocket knife in her teeth, and fell over the side of the SUV. Andrew would've normally marveled at such strength. He could only think of Annie, upside down in the water.

"Go help her!" he screamed. "Help your mother!"

Lynn was able to grab a piece of the bug netting still attached to the front bumper. Within seconds Andrew's leg loosened. He pulled his entire body up on the rock and unwrapped the severed netting. Through the sock, it had cut into his skin and sharp needle pains shot through his foot. For the first time, he noticed a heavy smell of gasoline mixed with other fluids leaking from the undercarriage.

Lynn regained her position on top, or rather, the bottom of the vehicle and hopped across to the far end of the rock. A kayaker pulled alongside the SUV and shouted at her. She plopped in the water near the back of the Lexus. Dragging his dead weight with his arms, Andrew made his way to the point Lynn had just occupied. Peering over the edge, he could see she had jumped into a col in the water. He sat up and then slid down the rock into the river, landing atop Lynn's back. He bear-hugged her to gain his balance.

The water was hip-deep, and the current was pushing him back toward the vehicle. Here, the floor of the river was sandy.

Lynn disappeared into the water. Andrew wanted to do the same, but there was very little room. Lynn's head re-emerged.

"She's unconscious. Bill, you got something to break the window?"

The kayaker handed her a small crowbar he'd obviously grabbed for such a job.

"I'm going to need some help," she said, ignoring Andrew and looking directly at the kayaker.

Andrew surprised Lynn by grabbing the crowbar. He was responsible for all of this. Time was running out.

He dove straight down. The shock of the cold made him want to surface immediately. Underneath the froth, the water was fairly clear. Fighting his own buoyancy, he grasped the side view mirror with his left hand. Remnants of an expended airbag partially blocked the view. He could at least make out a protective bubble of air surrounding Annie's head and shoulders. He tried to strike the window with the crowbar. As he did, he let go of the mirror and involuntarily surfaced. The tip of the crowbar barely touched the window on his way up.

He started to dive again, but he surfaced quickly. Lynn held his shirt with both hands.

"Stop! Andrew, listen to me. We have to do this together. If you bust that window, then the cab will fill with water, and we'll have to work fast to get Annie out."

"What do you want me to do?" It was the kayaker.

"Get a rope so we can tow her over to shore as quickly as possible."

Andrew fell back into the water and made his way down to the window. He started to jab at the glass again, holding on to the mirror with his left hand. Lynn's face appeared. She put her hands over Andrew's, and they both sent the crowbar into the window. This time he could see an indentation and a spider web of cracks in the glass. Somehow Lynn was able to keep herself from floating away. Andrew had to regain his position after almost losing his grip on the mirror. With three hands, they thrust the bar forward again. Then, Lynn flipped backwards, pushed her back against the rock for leverage, and kicked through the window with her feet.

Andrew needed to breathe, but his need to get Annie out was greater. His body screamed at him to surface. His head popped out of the water and air filled his lungs at such a rate he couldn't help but swallow some of the river. He started to cough violently, all the while trying to recompose himself for another dive.

As he started to go down, Annie's head popped up next to him. Then Lynn surfaced. Unlike Andrew, Lynn seemed to be in no distress.

"I don't think she's breathing." Lynn placed her fingers on Annie's throat. "She definitely has a pulse. Bill, hurry with that rope!"

The kayaker skillfully maneuvered back to the vehicle towing a line held by several people onshore.

"What did you mean by 'my mother'?" Lynn said to Andrew as she held Annie's head clear of the water. "And what the heck was all that back in the parking lot?"

Andrew continued to cough and shook his head. He'd not remembered saying any such thing. Strangely, his wounds no longer hurt. Maybe it was the cold of the water. He barely noticed he was shivering.

The kayaker finally made their position. Andrew could feel Annie's hand wandering aimlessly under the surface of the water. He reached out and held it.

"I'm sorry," he said in between coughs.

"We'll be back for you in a minute," Lynn said, her eyes as alert as ever.

She held Annie in a hold Andrew had seen in lifesaving demonstrations. What was different was that Lynn didn't swim. She hung onto the rope and a couple of men onshore started to pull her inland. She gained some footing, but it was obvious she'd not make the shore without the help of the rope. The kayaker hooked onto the rope right behind Lynn.

They moved away with an urgency to get Annie ashore. Andrew finally was able to control his coughing. All he could think about was Annie. She had to make it.

Within thirty seconds, Lynn had Annie on the beach. Numerous bystanders and the rope-pullers stood in a circle, blocking the view. After a short time, the group started to clap.

Annie was okay.

A strange groaning noise came from the SUV.

Lynn was already heading across the current with the kayaker and the rope.

Andrew felt a strange peacefulness. At the same time, his little area of calm real estate appeared to be diminishing. Then another groan emerged from the Lexus, and it started to swing around toward him. He instinctively reached out for the wheel well.

"Andrew!"

It was Lynn's voice, but he couldn't see her. His feet were being pulled under. The river had decided to take him. He held on with both hands, clutching at the tire, the fender, the wheel well. He arched his back and neck, straining to keep his mouth above the water.

The kayak came into view as the metal screamed again, and the SUV started to round the rock. He was yanked under the water. His feet were then crushed into the river bottom as the Lexus rolled slightly and came to a stop.

He couldn't move and he couldn't hold his breath any longer. Lynn's face came into view—this time in absolute distress. Panic. It was then that he knew he would die. She pulled at him. She kicked at the SUV in desperation.

Andrew reached out and grabbed her hand. She pulled. He managed to pull her back to him. His last sight was Lynn's face. Katlin's face.

Chapter 57
Treasure Valley Regional Medical Center, Boise
Sunday

"They're all here?" Annie struggled to gain some comfort in the hospital bed.

"All three are here," Rafi said, standing at attention.

She noted the nervous look. The man was not used to being subject to the whims of a female, much less four of them.

So many things had happened since she had been revived alongside the river. Her memory of that moment was particularly sharp. A crowd around her. Lynn's stone face of concern. Shouts of commotion.

She had searched the faces for Andrew. She had pleaded with the faces about Andrew. Their expressions had been as clear as if they had put him away themselves.

Now, days later, she sat in the same hospital, one floor away from where it had all started. A broken hip. A separated shoulder. Lacerations to the side of her face. Tubes snaking into her arms and a host of beeping, buzzing machines behind her.

"Mr. Thuban, you look worse than me. You've been here three days straight. Go home."

He held his hands outward. "This is what I do. My instructions are clear—take care of you. You will be going home soon."

"Well, you can't just follow me around."

He smiled. "I will do as you please."

Annie's head felt a little light and she lay back. "You said Donny would run everything, but I could be involved at my own discretion. In the business, that is."

"It is your choice."

She retrieved an envelope off the bedside table. "I had Mr. Choi bring this to me yesterday."

She opened the envelope and handed the letter to Rafi. He pulled his glasses from his shirt pocket, sat in the chair next to the bed, and read Frank's letter. He took some time to finish it as if he was reading it over a few times.

She watched him closely. His face was drained of color, and his mouth hung open. He politely handed the letter back and spoke nary a word. Standing again with his hands behind his back, he stood at the partially open door, staring into the hallway.

"Will you tell Donny and Penny?" Annie asked quietly.

Rafi turned, looking at once both puzzled and shocked. "That is not my place."

"You are their father."

He stroked his chin, closed the door to the room, placed his hands behind his back, and paced. "What would make you say such a thing?"

"While we were tearing up the countryside that day, I wondered what motivated you. Why you chose to remain here with Andrew. So much was happening that I completely missed your role in this whole affair. It was first apparent in the way you spoke about Mrs. Post. Plus she was not Mrs. Post to you, but Sonya. Then it was how you looked at Lynn and how you pursued my importance to Andrew. You had no idea what you had done. You thought you were showing me Andrew's long-lost daughter—your long-lost daughter. You said it was the last piece of the puzzle. But there was one more piece—your face after reading Frank's letter. It was not the look of concern of a friend for a friend. It was so much more. It *is* so much more."

Rafi stopped and stared at Annie from across the room. The shock and surprise gone, hidden by a squint and a forced smile. "I cannot speak of this."

"Oh no! I'm not giving you a pass on this. I've got a lot of confusing information in my head, and I don't have anyone to share it with."

He nodded but said nothing.

"You said you did something terrible. You both did. But that something terrible started with you and Mrs. Post, and I suspect it spun out of control." Annie paused. The emotions were gaining the upper hand again. "Did Andrew know?" she asked.

He raised his eyebrows. "He did not."

"You could not let those children live under the roof of Andrew and Sonya because they were *your* children."

"Family is very important."

"It was important to Andrew too. You planted ideas in his head. Egged him on to get him to think he wanted the children gone, didn't you? Maybe you should have tried the truth."

"You see conspiracy everywhere. Is it too difficult to believe I simply wanted what was best for Donita and Katlin?"

"My God, the last few weeks have been all about what to say and what not to say. Had we all been honest, I wonder how this might have turned out. Andrew might be alive, at least."

Rafi bowed his head. "Yes."

Annie blinked a number of times, trying to avoid another tearful breakdown. She breathed slowly, fully. "I'm not liking you much right now, you know."

"Yes."

"I suppose you need time to digest Frank's news just like I did. So the question remains. Will you tell Donny and Penny?"

"If I could, I would do many things differently. I'm not a good man or a bad man. Just a man."

"You won't tell them?"

"Mr. Post said you can be a persistent person. I will say nothing. They will not know. Unless, of course, you decide to tell them."

"I plan on having a discussion with all three girls, but your place in their life is your secret to divulge. Not mine."

Rafi nodded, opened the door to the room, and scanned the hallway, his back to Annie.

Neither spoke for some time. She drifted off to sleep and then awoke. She had no idea whether seconds, minutes, or even hours had gone by. Rafi stood as he did earlier.

"Even though he's gone, I'm not sure I can forgive him," Annie said, "or you for that matter."

"Did you forgive your husband?"

Before she could reply, Rafi swung around and held his hands outward to halt any response. "It is an unfair question. How you think of me is of no importance. Mr. Post has lived with his conscience for a long time. He could not forgive himself. From the moment he picked up his daughter in that room, all that followed were acts of love. You have told me what your husband did. He was, how should I say, a little less than innocent too, yet I am quite certain you believe he was acting out of love. You should forgive both men."

"And you?"

Rafi seemed to carefully consider his answer. "My life has been devoted to redemption. How can one ever do enough?"

"Andrew would have forgiven you. I know it."

"It is not his forgiveness that haunts me. It is my own."

"What happened with Donny?"

"I do not understand."

"You sent Katlin away to live her life with another family. Donny remained with you."

"Ah, as most men do, we both fell for her. She became our project. We raised her together. We sent one child away. We could not send another. The decision was never discussed."

"I'm still angry at him, but I'd trade all the money he willed to me to have him back. All of it."

"Then you forgive him," Rafi said quietly. "Mr. Post used to tell me it was a burden to be rich. I find it quite satisfying myself. You will soon be either burdened or satisfied."

"What does one do with a billion dollars, Mr. Thuban?"

"With your inherited investments, a portion of the Post Corporation, and your part of Mr. Post's personal wealth, it is closer to three billion dollars."

Annie huffed. "One, two, three billion. It's a little hard to tell the difference when you were living on a check for two thousand eight hundred and sixty-two dollars a month."

There was a long silence. She occasionally caught a glimpse of Donny moving back and forth on the other side of the doorway, phone in hand, animated in gesture. Rafi stood motionless, his back to the door.

"What will I tell them?" she asked.

Rafi did not reply.

"And Matt?"

Rafi's smile returned. "No charges will be filed. According to the sheriff, it was an accident. Mr. Downing is said to be quite distraught over the entire incident. Trust me, we will ensure his innocence and help him regain his life."

"Yes you will," Annie said.

The three women surrounded the bed. Annie had hesitated for another thirty minutes until Rafi finally agreed to go home in exchange for allowing the women permission to enter the room.

Penny reached out and held Annie's hand.

Donny tapped her foot on the floor, as if she were attending an unnecessary office meeting.

Lynn placed her hands on the end of the bed and appeared to force a smile.

"It's difficult to know where to start," Annie said. "Thirty-three years ago, the three of you were born in this hospital one floor above where you stand today. Due to a mix-up, two of you were switched not long after you were born."

Penny squeezed Annie's hand. Her face was contorted, perplexed.

Annie turned to Penny. "You, my beautiful daughter, are actually a Post. You are Donny's sister."

She expected a chorus of doubts. Something suggesting a drug reaction or head trauma. Instead, Penny and Donny stared at each other as if the other would speak.

Suddenly Penny's hand released, and she turned her back to Annie. "Jesus! The letter! Dad found out!"

Annie saw no reason to poison the girls with the absolute truth. She would let Frank's secret remain his secret. "Yes, your father knew."

"This is bullshit," Donny said, though the uncertainty in her voice evoked an unfamiliar fear.

"It's true," Annie said. "I told your father. This is why he came to me. This is why he wanted to get to know Penny."

Donny backpedaled to an uncomfortable chair in the corner and sat, shaking her head.

"That's not the end," Annie said.

"You're my mother," Lynn said quietly. "Andrew said 'Help your mother.' I thought he'd lost his mind in the cold water." Lynn sat on the edge of the bed and looked out the door. "I know I was adopted. You gave me up for adoption?"

"No. You were switched with Penny. You're Katlin Post."

Penny stood beside Annie, staring at Lynn. "That's impossible. Katlin Post died. Katlin. The other sister. Matt said she was killed."

"She nearly died, that's true," Annie said. "Andrew and Mrs. Post were having a very difficult time. He wanted Katlin to grow up away from their troubles." There she went again, speaking in half-truths. She felt an obligation to bring these girls together. Unite the sisters. Have a connection with her lost child. Maybe Andrew was right. Maybe she should've kept quiet.

"Andrew hid you, Lynn, from the world. He was so happy that you were happy. He died trying to keep you a secret from a world that might disturb your life."

"But I'm your daughter?" Lynn said.

"Yes, my husband discovered you were switched with Penny. Until recently, Andrew didn't know this. Neither did I."

"How did dad—"

Annie cut Penny off. "You're father discovered the switch some years ago. He kept it to himself. End of story."

The four women sat in silence. Annie watched the girls. She couldn't imagine what was going through their minds.

She thought of Andrew. A tear fell down her face. She broke the silence. "If he had lived, we would have fought over this. He would have tried to keep your secret, Lynn. He would've asked me to hide my real self from you, and I would have done it. Now he's gone. I raised one of you. One of you is my natural child. But I want all three of you to be mine. My daughters."

Lynn tried to speak. She wiped her face and left the room. Donny followed.

Penny glanced toward the door, then back at Annie. "I should go too if we're going to be sisters. Jesus, Ma, this is heavy stuff."

Annie waited and waited. After an hour or so, she was sure she had made a mistake. She'd torn through thirty-three years of history for three women in five minutes. Maybe they didn't believe her. Maybe they did and didn't want to.

She cursed Andrew in her mind. How could he leave her here to face such a task? How dare he give his life for hers? How dare he leave her alone?

She called the nurse and asked to up her pain medication. Really she just wanted sleep.

The next thing she knew she felt a hand on her face. She was groggy, but she could make out Penny hovering over her. "Lynn wants to know what her name is."

"What?"

"Is she Katlin or Penny?"

"Oh, God," Annie said, panicking herself back to an alert state.

"No, no. She was laughing, Ma."

Penny leaned over and kissed Annie on the forehead.

"And I brought something for you."

Annie felt a slick piece of paper placed into her hand. She held it up to the light. It had a picture printed in the middle. Penny, Lynn, and Donny, arm-in-arm, were standing in front of the nursery, smiling. In bold black letters above the picture, it said, "Get well Mom." Printed below the picture, it said, "Love, your daughters!"

"It ain't the best, but we had to do it up quick," Penny said. "Lynn is pretty beat up. She says she needs a bit of time for all of this to sink in. Donny acts like it's no big deal, but she's not fooling me."

Annie couldn't control the flood of tears.

"They'll come around." Penny was back to looking like her uncomfortable self.

"What about you?" Annie asked, wiping her face.

"Far as I'm concerned, nothing's changed. I got two sisters out of the deal. Besides you got like a jillion dollars. You think I'm skipping out now?"

ACKNOWLEDGMENTS

I want to thank my father-in-law Charles and daughter Patricia for giving this book its first two reviews. And, of course, I could not complete this book without my editor-in-chief, Peggy, my loving spouse for 35 years.

Made in the USA
Middletown, DE
14 June 2022